OXFORD WORLD'S CLASSICS

*For over 100 years Oxford World's Classics have brought
readers closer to the world's great literature. Now with over 700
titles—from the 4,000-year-old myths of Mesopotamia to the
twentieth century's greatest novels—the series makes available
lesser-known as well as celebrated writing.*

*The pocket-sized hardbacks of the early years contained
introductions by Virginia Woolf, T. S. Eliot, Graham Greene,
and other literary figures which enriched the experience of reading.
Today the series is recognized for its fine scholarship and
reliability in texts that span world literature, drama and poetry,
religion, philosophy and politics. Each edition includes perceptive
commentary and essential background information to meet the
changing needs of readers.*

OXFORD WORLD'S CLASSICS

Late Victorian Gothic Tales

Edited with an Introduction and Notes by
ROGER LUCKHURST

OXFORD
UNIVERSITY PRESS

OXFORD

UNIVERSITY PRESS

Great Clarendon Street, Oxford OX2 6DP

Oxford University Press is a department of the University of Oxford.
It furthers the University's objective of excellence in research, scholarship,
and education by publishing worldwide in

Oxford New York

Auckland Cape Town Dar es Salaam Hong Kong Karachi
Kuala Lumpur Madrid Melbourne Mexico City Nairobi
New Delhi Shanghai Taipei Toronto

With offices in

Argentina Austria Brazil Chile Czech Republic France Greece
Guatemala Hungary Italy Japan South Korea Poland Portugal
Singapore Switzerland Thailand Turkey Ukraine Vietnam

Oxford is a registered trade mark of Oxford University Press
in the UK and in certain other countries

Published in the United States
by Oxford University Press Inc., New York

First published as an Oxford World's Classics paperback 2005
Reissued 2009

British Library Cataloguing in Publication Data

Data available

Library of Congress Cataloging in Publication Data

Late Victorian Gothic tales / edited with an introduction and notes by Roger Luckhurst.
p. cm.—(Oxford world's classics)
Includes bibliographical references.
1. Horror tales, English. 2. English fiction—19th century. 3. Gothic revival (Literature)—Great Britain.
I. Luckhurst, Roger. II. Oxford world's classics (Oxford University Press)
PR1309.H6L38 2005   823'.087290808—dc22   2004027976

ISBN 978-0-19-953887-4

1

Typeset by RefineCatch Ltd, Bungay, Suffolk
Printed in Great Britain
on acid-free paper by
Clays Ltd, St Ives plc

ACKNOWLEDGEMENTS

I AM grateful to the British Academy for providing a small research grant to assist in the completion of this edition. This allowed me to employ the expert skills of Dr Anne Witchard, who tracked down and photocopied the original magazine and book editions of these stories. I thank the School of English and Humanities at Birkbeck College for a generous period of leave in which part of this work was completed. For help with particular references, I would like to thank Hilary Fraser, Sally Ledger, Catherine Maxwell, Andy Sawyer, Sally Shuttleworth, Michael Slater, and Brian Stableford. Judith Luna has been a particularly supportive, and extremely patient, editor. As always, this is for Julie.

The editor and publisher gratefully acknowledge permission to include the following copyright stories:

Rudyard Kipling, 'The Mark of the Beast', reprinted by permission of A. P. Watt Ltd on behalf of The National Trust for Places of Historical Interest or Natural Beauty.

Jean Lorrain, 'Magic Lantern' and 'Spectral Hand', translated by Brian Stableford, reprinted by permission of the translator.

Arthur Machen, 'The Great God Pan', copyright © Arthur Machen, reprinted by permission of A. M. Heath & Co. Ltd.

M. P. Shiel, 'Vaila', © Javier Marias (The Estate of M. P. Shiel), 2000. Reprinted by permission.

CONTENTS

INTRODUCTION

MOST histories of Gothic literature suggest a pattern of ebb and flow. Horace Walpole's *The Castle of Otranto: A Gothic Story*, published anonymously in 1764 and the first work of the genre, remained an isolated curiosity before Clara Reeve, Ann Radcliffe, Matthew Lewis, and others turned the Gothic into one of the most popular and controversial types of fiction in the 1790s. After Mary Shelley's *Frankenstein* (1818) and Charles Maturin's *Melmoth the Wanderer* (1820) ended this first wave, the furniture of the Gothic was then dispersed, placed here and there in the nooks and crannies of the Victorian house of fiction. Yet just as Count Dracula can resolve himself back into bodily form from an elusive spectral fog, so the Gothic rematerialized in the late-Victorian period as a distinct form again, producing enduring Gothic icons in a few short years: Robert Louis Stevenson's *Strange Case of Dr Jekyll and Mr Hyde* (1886), Oscar Wilde's *The Picture of Dorian Gray* (1891), H. G. Wells's *The Island of Dr Moreau* (1896), and Bram Stoker's *Dracula* (1897). This wave of the Gothic extended some way into the twentieth century before dispersing again. Many date a third wave from the 'horror' boom of the 1970s, with Stephen King, James Herbert, and a rash of Hollywood B-movies reinventing the genre once more. For about 250 years this lowly, hybrid, barely controlled, vaguely embarrassing literature has not just survived but insisted on coming back repeatedly. It suggests the Gothic works over material for its readers in important ways.

This anthology brings together twelve Gothic stories from the second wave, offering a concentrated body of tales from the 1890s. There are a number of reasons for wanting to do this. The first is to make available Gothic tales by some of the most celebrated writers of the late Victorian period in one volume, and to mix these with lesser-known yet still creepily effective stories by their contemporaries who filled the new journals, weekly and monthly magazines of the *fin de siècle* with a torrent of Gothic imaginings. It can be argued that it is the intense, suggestive form of the tale that best ratchets up Gothic effects: it was certainly more familiar than the novel to readers of the time. The stories also aim to catch the diverse range of the

possibilities of the genre, from the comic and mannerist to the Decadent, from the self-consciously literary to the torrid pulp, from the
subtleties of psychological suggestion to the out-and-out physical
assault on the nerves. This diversity can also tell an important story
about how genre is less a set of fixed narratives and images and more
a constantly modulating mode—almost a way of thinking. In the
1890s the Gothic careers off in numerous, sometimes contradictory
directions, and it is important to have a generous rather than narrow
definition of the genre at a time when it is undergoing rapid transition. Crucially, also, this anthology can act as a laboratory for asking
questions about what it is about the Gothic that makes it emerge and
re-emerge at particular historical moments. The Marquis de Sade
had no doubt that the Gothic in the 1790s responded to the revolutionary fervour of the time, as the leaders of the French Revolution
enforced the new order with the guillotine. What was it in the 1890s
that provoked a resurgence of the Gothic? Ultimately, these tales will
have to answer this for themselves, but this introduction makes some
suggestions about the specificity of the Gothic mode, about the con-
texts that inform the late-Victorian variety, and will briefly introduce
each author and tale.

Gothic Fiction

What is the Gothic? The term came into common use in the
eighteenth century to denote the opposite of Western Europe, of
civilization, of reason and order. The Goths figured for all barbar-
ians, the northern tribes that swept south in the twilight of the
Roman Empire and inaugurated the Dark Ages. The Goths destroyed civilizations, knowledge and language (barbarian derives from
barbar—to stutter, to be only on the verge of speech). In a Protestant
England, self-consciously forging itself as the centre of the modern
world, Gothic also came to mean the dark medieval past, the tyranny
of feudal lords, serfdom, and superstitious Catholic priestcraft that
held the masses in ignorant idolatry. In both of these senses, the
Gothic is not a positive term, but stands for everything *not*: not
modern, not enlightened, not free, not Protestant, not English.
When it came to be used for a certain kind of fiction concerned with
the ghastly and the supernatural, the negative sense was retained.
Gothic fiction was everything that offended neoclassical taste. The

Gothic was disordered, dark, and labyrinthine. The proportionate taste of the beautiful was wrenched out of shape by the excesses of the sublime. It mixed up categories of life and death, past and present, reason and fancy, wakefulness and dream. When Horace Walpole acknowledged his authorship of *The Castle of Otranto* and defended his Gothic story in the preface to the 1765 second edition, he confessed the book 'was an attempt to blend the two kinds of romance, the ancient and the modern. In the former all was imagination and improbability: in the latter, nature is always intended to be, and sometimes has been, copied with success. Invention has not been wanting; but the great resources of fancy have been dammed up, by a strict adherence to common life.'[1] This is what the hybrid, bastard form of the Gothic records: the undamming of dark forces that rush into and insidiously undermine the order of everyday life.

This prospect is a terror but also of course a delightful promise. The genre appears to inflict exorbitant punishments on those who step outside the norm, but at the same time it is in the business of lasciviously imagining these transgressions. It invokes the law by breaking it; it insists on sexual continence by dreaming up all manner of ingenious perversity. It is difficult sometimes to decide if a Gothic text is conservative or subversive for it is often both, simultaneously. This sense that values can suddenly be inverted applies to the very epithet 'Gothic' too. In the nineteenth century, as the Enlightenment project became the Mechanical Age, Thomas Carlyle warned in 'The Signs of the Times' in 1829 that 'Not the external and the physical alone is now managed by machinery, but the internal and spiritual also.'[2] As the world was regulated and disenchanted by the routines of industrial life, the Gothic could take on a positive valence of everything that was being lost: passion, belief, spirit, individual eccentricity, craft. John Ruskin praised medieval architecture in his chapter in 'On the Nature of the Gothic' (in *The Stones of Venice*, 1853) with a list of attributes that included rudeness, love of change, love of nature, disturbed imagination, obstinacy, and generosity. The term can therefore range from monstrous

---

[1] Horace Walpole, 'Preface' to Second Edition of *The Castle of Otranto* (1765), in E. J. Clery and Robert Miles (eds.), *Gothic Documents: A Sourcebook 1700–1820* (Manchester, 2000), 123.
[2] Thomas Carlyle, 'The Signs of the Times', in *A Carlyle Reader: Selections from the Writings of Thomas Carlyle*, ed. G. B. Tennyson (Cambridge, 1984), 35.

monks doing unspeakable things with young virgins to the beauties of Venice. Always remember the dream-like logic of the Gothic is likely to disarm any easy definition.

Readers of the Gothic also need to be aware that the genre appeared to split between relatively distinct strands early in its existence. Ann Radcliffe's posthumously published dialogue, 'On the Supernatural in Poetry' (1826), contained the following distinction: 'Terror and horror are so far opposite, that the first expands the soul, and awakens the faculties to a high degree of life; the other contracts, freezes, and nearly annihilates them.'[3] To some, this suggests the importing of a distinction between high and low art into the genre, a 'respectable' tradition that defines itself against everything lurid and sensational. To others, this distinction produces separate modes of the female and male Gothic that can be traced across the history of the genre. For readings in the 1890s, it is helpful to think of this distinction as producing a continuum from the subtle terrors of the *psychological* Gothic to the body horrors of the *physiological* Gothic. Writers in the psychological mode, like Vernon Lee or Henry James, tended to define themselves against the lowly, vulgar sensations of the physical mode. Yet if we keep the sense that this is a spectrum, with many different shadings and patterns of emphasis, it becomes easier to read what might appear to be flatly contradictory Gothic styles in the late-Victorian era.

Whilst meanings of the Gothic invert or split, we can nevertheless identify some persistent concerns that recur across the history of the genre. The Gothic repeatedly stages moments of transgression because it is obsessed with establishing and policing borders, with delineating strict categories of being. The enduring icons of the Gothic are entities that breach the absolute distinctions between life and death (ghosts, vampires, mummies, zombies, Frankenstein's creature) or between human and beast (werewolves and other animalistic regressions, the creatures spliced together by Dr Moreau), or which threaten the integrity of the individual ego and the exercise of will by merging with another (Jekyll and Hyde, the persecuting double, the Mesmerist who holds victims in his or her power). Ostensibly, conclusions reinstate fixed borders, re-secure autonomy, and destroy any intolerable occupants of these twilight zones. The

[3] Ann Radcliffe, 'On the Supernatural in Poetry' (1826), in Clery and Miles (eds.), *Gothic Documents*, 168.

most successful monsters overdetermine these transgressions to become, in Judith Halberstam's evocative phrase, 'technologies of monstrosity' that condense and process different and even contradictory anxieties about category and border. Some critics hold that the genre speaks to universal, primitive taboos about the very foundational elements of what it means to be human, yet the ebb and flow of the Gothic across the modern period invites more historical readings. Indeed, one of the principal border breaches in the Gothic is history itself—the insidious leakage of the pre-modern past into the sceptical, allegedly enlightened present. The Gothic, Robert Mighall suggests, can be thought of as a way of relating to the past and its legacies.

We can think about this in fairly abstract ways: the ghost, for instance, is structurally a stubborn trace of the past that persists into the present and demands a historical understanding if it is to be laid to rest. Similarly, Sigmund Freud defined the feeling of the uncanny as the shiver of realizing that modern reason has merely repressed rather than replaced primitive superstition. 'All supposedly educated people have ceased to believe officially that the dead can become visible as spirits', yet Freud suspected that at times 'almost all of us think as savages do on this topic'.[4] This return to pre-modern beliefs was itself the product of thinking of human subjectivity as a history of developmental layers that could be stripped away in an instant of dread, returning us to a 'savage' state.

Yet it is also possible to think quite specifically about what histories are subject to horrifying return. I have already indicated that the Gothic in England was full of figures that denoted the recently superseded past of Church and feudal power. Whilst often displaced in time (*Otranto* was passed off as a medieval manuscript) or space (Matthew Lewis's *The Monk* was set in Spain; Radcliffe used Italy), the first wave of the Gothic was the product of an emergent democratic and capitalist nation state sensitive to its own fragility and fearful of political reversion. Violence to the moral and physical fabric of things came from dissolute aristocrats and their perverted priests. One hundred years later, there were still accursed aristocratic houses, as in Sherlock Holmes's investigation in *The Hound of the Baskervilles* (1902), for example. Count Dracula or the vengeful

---

[4] Sigmund Freud, 'The Uncanny' (1919), *Penguin Freud Library*, 14 (Harmondsworth, 1985), 365.

pharaoh's mummy reinvented the aristocratic threat. Fears also came from below: the French Revolution destroyed the *ancien régime,* yet was seemingly overtaken by the uncontrollable vengeance of the mob. Too much democracy risked demagoguery and the arbitrary exercise of Terror. Throughout the Victorian era, a period of democratic reform and franchise extension, fears of the mob were transposed into Gothic images: think of the feral, working-class Hyde slowly but surely displacing the respectable Dr Jekyll. This fear survives into the third wave: the zombies that totter blankly around the shopping mall in the film *Dawn of the Dead* (1978 and remade in 2003) are the mindless mass consumers that we might ourselves become were we not such sharp, discerning spectators. The Gothic, as Jerrold Hogle suggests, is centrally about 'how the middle class dissociates from itself, and then fears, the extremes of what surrounds it: the very high or the decadently aristocratic and the very low or the animalistic, working-class, underfinanced, sexually deviant, childish, or carnivalesque'.[5]

This process of abjecting and demonizing the Other in the Gothic also concerns nationality. England's self-definition as a nation of Protestant individualists defines itself against the decadent southern blood of Spain or Italy, but the Gothic is generated as much from the paranoia that attends the fraught internal boundaries of the United Kingdom. A significant array of Gothic writers emerged from Ireland (from Charles Maturin, Sheridan LeFanu, Bram Stoker, and Oscar Wilde to the contemporary writer Patrick McGrath), in a colonial situation where a Protestant minority was the colonial occupier. The Scottish situation generated its own peculiar sense of psychic splitting in James Hogg's *Confessions of a Justified Sinner* (1824) and Robert Louis Stevenson's various tales of the double sixty years later. Arthur Machen, meanwhile, invoked the ancient Roman and Celtic past of Wales as sites that predated the English occupation. The Gothic was named for the tribes that destroyed the Roman Empire, and the genre pulses in sympathy with the rhythms of expansion and crisis in the British Empire. With its typical ability to invert meaning, it is often unclear whether the Gothic imagination is working in the service of the Empire—heroically defeating threats to the imperial centre like the Aryan 'band of brothers' in *Dracula*—or

---

[5] Jerrold Hogle, 'The Gothic in Western Culture', in Jerrold Hogle (ed.), *The Cambridge Companion to Gothic Fiction* (Cambridge, 2002), 9.

whether it is sapping imperial confidence by conjuring elaborate fantasies of what Stephen Arata has called 'reverse colonisation'. It is this ambiguity that undoubtedly makes the Gothic thrive on colonial margins.

Another way of thinking about the historical reversions of the Gothic is to suggest that the genre repeatedly turns on the question of inheritance. There are family inheritances, the haunted house or castle that embodies the passage of generations, and entrapment within the sins of a lineage. Paternal or familial secrets bear down on the oppressed inheritors, often making them the last of the line (Edgar Allan Poe's 'The Fall of the House of Usher' (1839) has been a hugely influential Gothic narrative in this regard). There are constant anxieties about maternity and birth, about what is inherited from the mother. The Gothic dreams constantly about escaping the mother, yet trying to circumvent reproduction unleashes Frankenstein's creature and Moreau's terrifying menagerie of beast-men. There is the inheritance of political power from the days of the arbitrary and violent exercise of feudal birthright. Does power inherently corrupt? Can the unbounded pleasures of absolute power be resisted? There is also inheritance in the more strictly biological sense: what residues of the primitive or the animalistic lurk in the modern body and mind? How can civilization bolster itself against these legacies of aeons of development? Inheritance works not only in time, down the generations, but also in space. The house, castle, labyrinth, or tomb entrap inheritors. The inheritance from the land, particularly if it has been occupied or violently seized from others, is to experience vengeful attacks from the fugitive traces of the dispossessed. In the twentieth-century work of Algernon Blackwood, William Hope Hodgson, and H. P. Lovecraft supernatural oppressors seem to be the ancient and august forces of nature or the cosmos itself, as if to suggest that humanity has reneged on its inheritance of the planet.

All of these elements are captured by Chris Baldick in one of the most economical definitions of the genre: 'For the Gothic effect to be attained, a tale should combine a fearful sense of inheritance in time with a claustrophobic sense of enclosure in space, these two dimensions reinforcing one another to produce an impression of sickening descent into disintegration.' As Baldick immediately confesses, this is 'too abstract a formula to capture the real accumulation of physical and historical associations'.[6] To do that, let's turn to the late Victorian period and put some flesh on these bones.

The Late-Victorian Revival

The late-Victorian Gothic revival is the result of a complex matrix of factors. There is no single, clinching explanation for this re-emergence: each text nestled in this historical context resonates in different ways, exploiting the multiple possibilities opened up by the Gothic form. The revival is partly a product of the changes in literary production. Victorian Realism was delivered (after serialization) in three hardback volumes and was rarely bought but borrowed from circulating libraries like W. H. Smith. Changing technologies of print, the progressive extension of readerships, and the explosion of new daily, weekly, and monthly magazines in the 1880s exerted pressure on the library control of the literary market. Economics as much as aesthetic taste was the factor that killed off the three-volume novel in 1893. By 1897, only four three-volume novels were printed in England, a remarkably sudden transformation. In its place, publishers sold one-volume novels direct to the public, creating the idea of the 'bestseller' and the celebrity author. There was a Rider Haggard 'boom' in 1888, a Rudyard Kipling one in 1889, and both men were associated with the return of the 'romance', advocated by some critics as a virile and energetic older literature to fight off the effete and morbid turn that had overtaken the modern novel. The magazine market also demanded new forms: the term 'short story' began to be used for the first time in the 1880s. These magazines had to brand themselves in a viciously competitive market. They pitched to certain classes of readers and began to be identified with certain types of story. Popular genres in their recognizable modern shapes began to emerge in this publishing context: detective fiction (Sherlock Holmes appeared in interlinked short stories in the *Strand Magazine* from 1891), the spy thriller (Erskine Childers's *The Riddle of the Sands*, 1893), and science fiction (H. G. Wells's *The Time Machine*, 1895). The Gothic tale resurfaced, its intrinsically hybrid form perfect for this new literary environment. Anxious late-Victorian literary commentators felt that this mass market

[6] Chris Baldick, 'Introduction', *The Oxford Book of Gothic Tales* (Oxford, 1992), p. xix.

encouraged only the lurid, the sensational, and the horrifying: the Gothic was a kind of monstrous embodiment of new popular culture. Yet the Gothic was encouraged to return not just because of this vibrant mass market. One of the defining Gothic themes matched the most notorious high cultural movement of the day: Decadence.

Late-Victorian Decadence was associated with ostentatious but pointless display. The Decadent refused bland, middle-class commerce and became absorbed in an obscure, private, and perverse world. The Decadent style is encrusted with ornament, weighed down with abstruse learning and Latinate constructions. It revels in artifice; it despises the natural and virile. Its colours were the livid, sulphurous yellows of forbidden French novels, or the bilious greens of the ruinous drink absinthe. In 1893, Arthur Symons defined Decadence as 'a new and beautiful and interesting disease' marked by 'an intense self-consciousness, a restless curiosity in research, an over-subtilising refinement upon refinement, a spiritual and moral perversity'.[7] The Decadent luxuriated in transgression, but also in the Catholicism that best delineated the boundaries of sin. Sexual pleasures were sought in the lowly music hall or the brothel, where dalliance with drugs, absinthe, or syphilis seemed more delicious. Although commonly identified as a French disorder, the era's most famous Decadent was of course Oscar Wilde, whose perversities of style and wit finally also extended to include that nameless desire for other men.

Decadence derives from the Latin *cadere*, to fall away, decay, or rot. In what became the encyclopedia and blueprint for the Decadent life, Joris-Karl Huysman's novel *A Rebours* (*Against Nature*, 1884), the peculiar hero, Duc Jean des Esseintes, is marked from the opening page as the last of his aristocratic line. He is frail, sickly, effeminate, and highly strung; he throws away his wealth on increasingly bizarre attempts to stave off crushing boredom by collecting jewels, rare manuscripts, and sexual peculiarities. The positive embrace of the image of the exhausted aristocratic line by the Decadent Movement is a sign of a doomed attempt to mark themselves off from the banalities of bourgeois and mass culture. It also meant that the

---

[7] Arthur Symons, 'The Decadement Movement in Literature', in Sally Ledger and Roger Luckhurst (eds.), *The Fin de Siècle: A Reader in Cultural History c.1880–1900* (Oxford, 2000), 105.

Gothic was one of the privileged modes for exploring this perverse embrace of disease, decay, and aristocratic dwindling.

The writer Théophile Gautier once described the poetry of Charles Baudelaire as invoking 'the morbidly rich tints of decomposition . . . all that gamut of intensified colours, correspondent to autumn, and the setting of the sun, to overripe fruit, and the last hours of civilization'.[8] Decadent writing was modelled on late Latin and Greek authors on the brink of extinction of the classical world. The Victorian *fin de siècle* worried that it repeated this sense of being in the last hours of civilization, the 'sunset of mankind' as Wells put it in *The Time Machine*. And these Decadent last thoughts were also imperial ones, for the late-Victorian era was one of the most expansive phases of empire. Britain annexed some thirty-nine separate areas around the world between 1870 and 1900, in competition with newly aggressive America in the Pacific or the European powers in the so-called 'Scramble for Africa' after the continent was divided up at the Berlin conference of 1885. This is one of the great paradoxes of the late-Victorian era: how could such confident jingoists also harbour intense anxieties about decline and fall? How could the era of the great colonial heroes—Gordon of Khartoum, Lord Kitchener, Robert Baden-Powell, Cecil Rhodes—also envisage repeated invasion of the imperial centre by dastardly Germans, merciless Martians, or supernatural vampires and mummies?

The Gothic, as a signal of its modernity, has always exploited emergent and marginal sciences whose findings potentially naturalize the supernatural. Victor Frankenstein harnesses electricity to give his creature life. Since electricity was a mysterious, occult thing, Anton Mesmer in the same era claimed he could capture and manipulate a parallel substance he called 'animal magnetism', passing it between bodies and throwing others into rapport with his powers. Discredited by many official commissions, belief in Mesmeric power subsisted in the nineteenth century because it seemed to scientize ancient beliefs in occult influence. One of the defining elements of the late-Victorian period was a new authority given to scientific knowledge, a feverish rate of findings in physics and chemistry producing a revolution in electronic technologies, the emergence of an array of human sciences such as anthropology, sociology,

---

[8] Théophile Gautier's 1868 preface to Baudelaire's *Les Fleurs du Mal*, cited by Richard Gilman, *Decadence: The Strange Life of an Epithet* (New York, 1979), 89–90.

or psychology in distinct disciplinary formations, and the con-
sequent pervasion of science across a culture previously organized
on largely religious and classical authorities. In this fervour, all kinds
of cross-fertilizations developed, resulting in unstable and temporary forms of knowledge. Spiritualists and Theosophists borrowed
the language of advanced science, because they held that the findings
of atomic and electrical physics proved the existence of the afterlife
or reincarnation. In 1882, the Society for Psychical Research was
founded to replace Spiritualist belief with the alleged scientific facts
behind occult transmissions (which they called 'telepathy'), ghosts
('veridical hallucinations'), and haunted houses ('phantasmogenetic
centres'). Throughout the 1880s and 1890s, psychical researchers
poured out research findings on dodgy Neapolitan Spiritualist
mediums, haunted Scottish houses, and whether it was possible to
hypnotize at distance, even across the English Channel.

The late-Victorian Gothic is unthinkable without this psychical
context—but not necessarily in the expected ways. Whilst some
exploited the language of the psychical case history, many creative
writers worried that this scientizing mania would destroy the ambiguities on which the supernatural depended. In 1894, Andrew Lang,
writer, critic, and amateur psychical researcher, was depressed at the
thought that the tradition of the ghost story was being displaced by
treatises on the 'dextro-cerebral hemisphere of the brain'.[9] Implicit
in many Gothic tales of the 1890s is an argument with the positivism
of psychical research. Nevertheless, many serious scientists included
psychical research in their range of interests, and the work on subjective states of trance, dream, and psychic splitting were serious
contributions to the new psychology. Robert Louis Stevenson
recorded his own subjective states during fevers for the key theorists
of the society; Henry James's brother was president of the society in
1894. The role of psychical research in the Gothic revival is therefore suitably ambiguous: a source of inspiration, but also potentially
destructive to any creative supernaturalism.

Whilst psychical research was a marginal science even at the
height of its popularity in the 1890s, the extension of the biological
and physiological explanations into nearly every aspect of cultural
activity was an integral element of the late-Victorian era, and

[9] Andrew Lang, 'Ghosts up to Date' (1894), in Ledger and Luckhurst (eds.), *The Fin
de Siècle*, 286.

another critical reason for the return of the Gothic romance. Charles Darwin's theory of evolutionary development expounded in *The Origin of Species* in 1859 had disturbed an earlier generation by challenging the time of the biblical creation and the boundary between human and animal. Nevertheless, Darwin soothed readers that evolution was progressive, and directed towards human perfectibility. The next generation of biologists were less confident or consoling. Using Darwin's theory, and the many rival biological accounts of development then in circulation, scientists suspected that it was just as possible to *devolve*, to slip back down the evolutionary scale to prior states of development. The animal now lurked very close to the human; indeed, it was encoded in the human body and mind as our evolutionary inheritance, and animalistic instincts were never far from swamping the fragile late additions of civilized morals and behaviour. This theory of degeneration started with precise observation of regressions in the life cycle of sea squirts (the focus of Edwin Ray Lankester's book, *Degeneration: A Chapter in Darwinism* in 1880). Relatively rapidly, it was extended to explain the animalism of the criminal classes, female hysterics and the insane, the hereditary taint that caused sons or daughters to regress, or even the decline of races, nations, and empires. In Max Nordau's rant *Degeneration*, a brief sensation when translated into English in 1895, this biologism stretched to explain any of the arts that offended middle-class taste. Decadence, Impressionism, Symbolism, and Naturalism were signs of Western degeneration. The works of Henrik Ibsen, Friedrich Nietzsche, or Émile Zola were symptoms of devolution affecting European intellectuals. Fortunately, the middle classes seemed robust, yet the influence of degenerates could still risk dragging Europe into what Nordau called 'the dusk of nations'.

Degeneracy was the scientized fear of historical reversion, of polluting inheritance, which had driven the Gothic romance from the start. The enduring images of the late-Victorian Gothic are saturated with dramatizations of the process of degeneration. Hyde is not only a working-class figure usurping Jekyll's respectability but also repeatedly described as a monkey or ape, and the transformations are a descent down the evolutionary ladder. The picture that Dorian Gray hides in his house is not only a metaphor of moral corruption, but is a precise record of physical degenerative decay. In this collection of tales, there are many versions of this effect.

Recent critics writing on the Gothic, such as Daniel Pick, Fred Botting, Kelly Hurley, and Robert Mighall, have identified the pseudo-science of degeneration as the defining aspect of the late-Victorian Gothic. It is certainly central to reviving the genre, offering a scientific account that reiterates narratives of decadence and familial inheritance. Yet it is important not to rely on a single motivation for writing that threads together contradictory strands and thrives on ambiguity. Works survive precisely because they are not reducible to a singular explanation, and historical readings need to account for the kind of shifting matrix of influences that I have tried to sketch out briefly here.

The Stories

There is a vast archive of late-Victorian tales from which to choose (the Select Bibliography gives some routes into exploring this area more extensively). This anthology has picked out twelve stories from this archive, ordered in a loosely chronological way between the years 1890 and 1896, but also clustered thematically to emphasize thematic and stylistic links. Although I do not intend to ruin any shocks or shudders, some readers might want to skip this section for now, and treat it is an afterword.

The collection starts with Vernon Lee, the pen-name of Violet Paget (1856–1935). 'Dionea' is set in Italy, invoking the traditional setting of Gothic romances. It also concerns an uncanny, prehistorical return—and in a nunnery no less. Yet Lee was in fact fairly contemptuous of the vulgar pleasures of Gothic and supernatural fiction. Lee had been educated in Germany and Italy, and had published her first work of scholarship, *Studies of the Eighteenth Century in Italy*, in 1880 at the age of 24. It marked her as a literary and cultural historian of high culture, and she was a major figure in the Aesthetic Movement. Unsurprisingly, the preface to *Hauntings*, her collection of tales that opens with 'Dionea', marks out her distance from contemporary Gothic enthusiasms. She dismissed psychical research as ruinous to supernatural mystery, and instead stated: 'That is the thing—the Past, the more or less remote past, of which the prose is clean obliterated by distance—that is the place to get our ghosts from.'[10] Lee's stories all concern a very material past

---

[10] Vernon Lee, preface, *Hauntings: Fantastic Stories* (London, 1890), p. x.

coming to possess the present, forcing victims into compulsive repetitions and very strange trans-historical and trans-gendered identifications. These are decidedly unusual forces: as Angela Leighton has suggested, Lee imagines 'the ghosts of a historicism largely untroubled by supernatural design'. Nevertheless, the structure and furniture of the tale is quintessentially Gothic: 'Dionea' represents Lee's Aestheticist appropriation of the genre, and is indicative of the kind of cross-fertilizations that began to happen in the 1890s.

Oscar Wilde (1854–1900), England's most notorious Decadent, first published the story 'Lord Arthur Savile's Crime' in 1887. It took on a different resonance when he republished it in book form in 1891. This was the year of Wilde's triumph as the most fashionable and controversial writer in London society: he published four books, including his Gothic novel *The Picture of Dorian Gray*, and then travelled to Paris in the autumn, where he was again lionized as the writer of the age. Many Englishmen hoped he would stay in the Parisian den of iniquity and not return: some reviews of *Dorian Gray* were outraged at the strong hints that the central characters in the book were men who desired other men. For some, Wilde was pushing his challenge to middle-class respectability too far and too explicitly. His downfall, arrested for acts of gross indecency with other men in April 1895, inevitably recast these books as evidence for the prosecution. 'Lord Arthur Savile's Crime' might appear to be a piece of light, comic entertainment—a sort of parody of the Gothic, where a terrible destiny, read in a man's physiognomy, is fulfilled without disaster and to comic effect. Yet whilst it reads as a comic defiance of biological degeneracy, it might be read in dialogue with *The Picture of Dorian Gray*, where the consequences of such delightful perversion of ethics results in the horrifying death of the protagonist rather than marriage and social sanction. Lord Savile and Dorian Gray are the inverse of each other, as if Wilde were imagining very different outcomes for the embrace of criminal identity.

We do not always immediately associate Henry James (1843–1916) with the Gothic; he is the principal theorist, after all, of the novel as serious art form, composing the essay, 'The Art of the Novel' in 1884. As if to confirm this, he wrote to Vernon Lee in April 1890 that 'the supernatural story is not the class of fiction I myself most cherish'.[11] Yet James soon took a remarkable turn towards the use of Gothic narratives and tropes. James had given up on the ghost story in 1876: 'The Ghostly Rental' is often read as James's exorcism of the American tradition of tales by the likes of Edgar Allan Poe and Nathaniel Hawthorne. 'Sir Edmund Orme' (1891) marked his return to the ghost story, and he continued to write these tales—including of course *The Turn of the Screw* in 1898—until his death. The so-called 'late phase' in James's work, even the novels that eschew the supernatural, is saturated with metaphors of the ghostly or spectral and with intense reflections on death and the kinds of living on after death possible in memory. Like Vernon Lee, James is interested in renovating the Gothic tradition by transforming the supernatural into a kind of refined aesthetic or nervous experience. Indeed, Martha Banta has hinted at the difficulty of reading the supernatural in James because 'his artistic manipulation so transforms the basic notions that he no longer seems to be writing about the occult'.[12] 'Sir Edmund Orme' was the first trial of this new, intensely subjectivized Gothic tale. It concerns inheritance, a buried wrong, and a familial doom, but it does so through an apparently everyday social setting. That there is a weirdly solid and even polite ghost at the heart of this tale is easier to assert than for some of James's other teasing tales, yet 'Sir Edmund Orme' introduces us to James's interest in the ghost as a crisis of interpretation. As he put it in the Preface he later wrote for the story: 'We want it clear, goodness knows, but we also want it thick, and we get the thickness in the human consciousness that entertains and records, that amplifies and interprets it.' In 'Sir Edmund Orme' this 'thickness' induces in the reader a flurry of competing interpretations as to the significance of the culminating events.

Lee, Wilde, and James renovate or lightly parody the Gothic tradition, and do so from a close engagement with the Aesthetic Movement. Rudyard Kipling (1865–1936), in contrast, grew up in India and published his early writings in the newspaper columns of the *Pioneer*, sandwiched between news stories and advertisements. These were fictions written in the Anglo-Indian vernacular, next printed as

[11] Henry James to Vernon Lee, 27 Apr. 1890, *Henry James Letters*, iii (1883–95), ed. Leon Edel, (London, 1980), 277.

[12] Martha Banta, *Henry James and the Occult: The Great Extension* (Minneapolis, 1972), 5–6.

pamphlets for sale on the Indian railways as ephemeral popular literature. When *Plain Tales from the Hills* was published in England in 1889, Kipling was instantly successful. Returning to London that year, he became the great white hope of English literature and the unofficial laureate of the British Empire. Often considered a literary embarrassment since his death, a record of the imperial mindset at the turn of the century, his early work is actually a subtle account of the ambiguities and anxieties of the colonial frontier. His first books of fiction brought news from an utterly unknown and alien place, the very edges of the Indian empire where handfuls of Englishmen improvised forms of engagement with the native population. Well beyond the centres of imperial administration or the standing armies of occupation, the magical or supernatural were frequently the means by which colonizer and colonized (mis)understood each other. This Gothic thread runs through many of Kipling's early short story collections. 'The Mark of the Beast', included here, was in fact the first piece of fiction Kipling tried to place for English publication. It was read by the critic Andrew Lang, who declared that it was 'poisonous'—although Lang shortly after became one of Kipling's loudest advocates. Lang was presumably disturbed less by the animalistic regression at the heart of the tale than by its profound moral confusions and the thought that men of Empire could be so resolutely unmanned in the colonial encounter. At the frontier, it proves impossible to distinguish knowledge and superstition, or even East and West. 'The Mark of the Beast' is a superb instance of the queasy paranoia that saturates the colonial Gothic.

Bithia Mary Croker (1849–1920) was another Anglo-Indian writer, the Irish-born wife of Lieutenant Colonel Croker of the Royal Scots and Munster Fusiliers who served in India and Burma for fourteen years. She was an extremely popular novelist in her lifetime, recording life in the stations and compounds of the Indian empire and also of rural Ireland. In some ways, she can be seen as a female Kipling, and she encouraged this linkage with titles that echoed Kipling (*Her Own People* redressed Kipling's *Life's Handicap: Stories of Mine Own People*, for example). Although a minor writer, Croker is typical of the work encouraged by the new mass market of journals and cheap fiction. She began to write for this market in the 1880s and developed her skill in the supernatural and Gothic tale because it was a marketable form. These early tales were collected in *To Let, etc.* (1893) from which 'The Dâk Bungalow at Dakor' has been selected. Although sitting safely within the conventions of the haunted house story, the setting does invest the narrative with considerable disquiet about the consequences of colonial possession. The locale, a hostel on the elaborate travel network that existed across the Indian empire, is significant. The systems of road, railway, postal, and telegraphic communications were often held to be the means by which enlightenment would be brought to ignorant and superstitious natives. The Indian railway was a prime symbol of how Empire was advanced and progressive; in the 1890s, the campaign for a Cairo to Cape Town railway through Africa was the rallying cry for many defenders of imperial expansion. All such communication systems developed ghostly doubles, however, and were often sites of uncanny experiences. The so-called native 'bush telegraph' seemed to outrun the colonial machinery wherever the English went. The Mutineers who rebelled against Indian occupation by the British in 1857 were alleged to communicate through hidden message systems. Croker's traditional tale is an emanation of this colonial history and its fragile, rarely recorded pattern of superstitions.

The career of Grant Allen (1848–99) tells us much about the transformations typical of the *fin de siècle*. Allen had hoped to be a man of science, but had little prospect of finding a post. After failing as a colonial educator in Jamaica, he returned to England and set about becoming a journalist and author on topics related broadly to natural history. He wrote prodigious amounts of journalism on botany, biology, anthropology, folklore, philology, and comparative religion. Allen discovered, however, that he could earn more money as a writer of fiction. He initially used a pseudonym in the early 1880s to protect his scientific credentials. This was because the supernatural or Gothic tale proved to be the most lucrative form of writing, even though this was a literature premised on the superstitious beliefs that he was dedicated to eradicating through his scientific writings. There is a consistent tension in Allen's work not only between literature and science, but also between high and low art. He wrote despairingly to his friend Edward Clodd (who later published a fascinating memoir of Allen) that 'I am trying with each new novel to go a step lower to catch the market.'[13] He achieved some financial

---

[13] Allen cited Edward Clodd, *Grant Allen: A Memoir* (London, 1900), 125.

security with *The Woman Who Did* in 1894, a novel about the New Woman that was considered extremely risqué at the time but reads rather conservatively now. He continued to pour out journalism and reviews, but also wrote what he called 'Hill Top' novels, their high moral and aesthetic ambitions figured literally as standing above the lowly valley of contemporary fiction.

'Pallinghurst Barrow' exists at the crossroads of these tensions. It is one of Allen's most effective Gothic tales, because it does not debunk or satirize superstition but evokes dreamy, uncanny states to great effect and leaves the significance of the tale open to the reader to decide. At the same time, the tale is a tissue of quotations from contemporary scientific speculations about the meaning of the ancient burial sites that pepper the English landscape. Allen marshals resources from anthropology, archaeology, and folklore studies for a tale about psychic regression to horrifying primitive states. It is this effective conjunction of interests that means Allen pushes the form of the Gothic in a new direction. Allen has some claim to be among the first to be writing 'science fiction'; indeed, H. G. Wells wrote to Allen shortly after the publication of *The Time Machine* in 1895 that 'I believe that this field of scientific romance with a philosophical element which I am trying to cultivate belongs properly to you.'[14]

Arthur Conan Doyle (1859–1930) was another literary figure of the late Victorian era who suffered torments about the status of his work. The success of the Sherlock Holmes stories from 1891 made Doyle one the highest paid writers of the new journal market and George Newnes, owner of the *Strand Magazine*, simply raised his rate of pay every time Doyle threatened to end the serial. Yet Doyle felt Holmes eclipsed his serious work in the historical novel and that he had been excluded from the literary establishment because of his financial success. Certainly, his most interesting work was his popular fiction, partly because his writing technique sometimes approached 'automatic writing' and it is as if the unconscious of his era speaks through his work. This is particularly so in his supernatural and Gothic tales, one of his favoured modes (by the 1920s Doyle was the world's most famous defender of Spiritualism, that allegedly naturalized form of supernatural belief).

[14] H. G. Wells, *The Correspondence of H. G. Wells*, 4 vols. (London, 1998), i, 245–6

Both tales selected here derive from *Round the Red Lamp: Being Facts and Fancies of the Medical Life* (1894), recalling Doyle's first unsuccessful career as a general practitioner in the 1880s. 'The Case of Lady Sannox' is a hallucinatory tale of sexual mutilation that still has the power to shock for its exorbitant punishment of Lady Sannox. 'Lot No. 249' is one of many mummy tales that began to emerge in the late-Victorian era. England's relation to Egypt had been transformed in 1882, when decades of politicking and intrigue for influence over the government of Egypt were ended by the British military occupation of the country. It was the very beginning of an ideological commitment to imperial expansion, with Egypt a strategic seizure because it ensured control of the Suez Canal and thus routes to India. Just before this occupation came one of the most sensational archaeological discoveries in the nascent science of Egyptology: a cache of thirteen mummies of pharaohs, hidden long before by priests to protect the bodies from grave-robbers. The find included the body of Rameses II, widely held to be the pharaoh at the time of the Exodus led by Moses. This potent mix produced a fascination with the Egyptian undead—Rider Haggard popularized the form in 1889 with his novel *Cleopatra* and it was continued by Bram Stoker in *Jewel of the Seven Stars* in 1903. The mummy in Doyle's 'Lot No. 249' is undifferentiated—nameless and reduced to an ignominious lot number sold in an auction. Perhaps little more than a Gothic icon of transgression in this tale, the mummy nevertheless suggests another area where the Gothic tropes of revenge, inheritance, and the consequences of possession were reanimated by the particular imperial context of the late Victorian era.

Any anthology of this era needs to include some tales from France. For all the Decadent sins hinted at in English fiction, censorship made the English scene positively demur compared to France. The conservative commentator William Barry, writing in the Tory *Quarterly Review* in 1892 about Guy de Maupassant, Gustave Flaubert, and Théophile Gautier pronounced that such writers revealed 'a process of death, moral, intellectual and even physical, has set in among the French'. Someone, Barry hoped, would 'sweep these abominations from the earth'—or at least stop them before they reached England.[15] The publisher of the English translations of

---

[15] [W. F. Barry], 'The French Decadence', *Quarterly Review* (Apr. 1892), 504.

Émile Zola's Naturalist novels had already been prosecuted and his books withdrawn. In 1892, Wilde's play *Salomé* was refused a licence for performance, so he staged it in Paris. There, Decadence flowered in its most elaborate form, in the wake of the dissolute genius of Baudelaire and Gautier. At the heart of the *fin-de-siècle* scene in Paris was Jean Lorrain (1855–1906). Lorrain was a dandy, an exhibitionist, a self-advertisement for a scandalous life of absinthe, ether, and perverse sexuality. He wrote opinionated newspaper columns between 1890 and 1905 that mixed fiction, aesthetic discussion, gossip, and reviews. The reviews were often so vitriolic that his victims demanded recompense: he fought duels with the poet Paul Verlaine and a young first-time novelist called Marcel Proust. He was also introduced to Oscar Wilde in 1891, in the weeks that Wilde experienced the Decadent and homosexual worlds of Paris. On Wilde's arrest in 1895, Lorrain forced a French newspaper to retract a statement that Wilde and Lorrain were 'intimates'. Lorrain's later book, *Monsieur de Phocas* (1902), a confession of a dissolute Decadent and probably his best work, is clearly based on Wilde's *Picture of Dorian Gray*, but also contains a detailed portrait of a corrupting English aesthete whose 'voice gives birth to abominable suggestions within me'.[16] Some suggest this is the story of Wilde's influence on Lorrain.

The two short tales included here reflect the conjunction of Decadence and the Gothic once more, but also show a different national development. The French tradition had incorporated the influence of the English Gothic, the stories of the German Romantic E. T. A. Hoffmann, and particularly (after Baudelaire's translations) the American Edgar Allan Poe. This heady brew produced the *conte frénétique*, which were macabre tales tinged with slightly hysterical humour. A new form, the *contes cruels*, emerged late in the century after Villiers de L'Isle Adam published his *Cruel Tales* in 1883. Lorrain's 'Magic Lantern' and 'The Spectral Hand' sit knowingly— almost wearily—at the end of these literary traditions. The first is a short reflection on the place of the fantastic in the modern world; the second a brief access into the occultism made fashionable by Joris-Karl Huysmans's novel of the Black Magic world in *La Bas* (1891).

Possibly the closest English fiction got to the explicitness of Parisian

---

[16] Jean Lorrain, *Monsieur de Phocas*, trans. Francis Amery (Sawtry, 1994), 85.

Decadence was *The Great God Pan* by Arthur Machen (1863–1947). It was famously denounced by the overexcited *Westminster Review* as 'a nightmare incoherence of sex and the supposed horrible mysteries behind it, such as might conceivably possess a man who was given to a morbid brooding over these matters, but which would soon lead to insanity if unrestrained'.[17] In fact, the fragmentary manuscripts that make up this text only hint: they are full of occlusions and silences because the various male narrators continually break down, unable to say what they have seen or experienced. Some survive by hoarding salacious secret documents. Many appear to die of unbearable terror, or possibly pleasure, or possibly both. Machen's Gothic tales of the 1890s are full of doors shut firmly in our face, with only the barest suggestion of the unimaginable horrors that take place behind them. As a serious scholar of the occult, a close friend of the mystic and occultist A. E. Waite, Machen knew how to suggest, but never show.

Arthur Machen seemed to embrace obscurity. Although published in the Keynotes series by The Bodley Head, the defining Decadent series, he largely avoided the literary scene and he very soon strongly disassociated himself from the literature of the 1890s. He brilliantly evoked the strangeness of London, yet his work was saturated with longing for the Welsh landscape of his childhood, best conjured up in the tortured, Decadent prose of his novel, *The Hill of Dreams* (1907). He had a brief moment of fame again in 1916, when his newspaper fiction appeared to generate the famous modern myths about spectral appearances seen by soldiers in the trenches, before sliding into obscurity once more. Yet Machen's writing has since been rescued, and *The Great God Pan* has become the quintessential text of the late Victorian Gothic for many contemporary critics. The intensity of the tale comes from the way in which central Gothic themes converge on the figure of one elusive yet monstrous woman. The pagan gods are not dead, but can return to topple science with superstition and modern man with bestial pleasures that predate civilization. Many kinds of reversion permeate the story. The tale also neatly plays out the geographical drift of the Gothic from its first inception. Starting on the wild fringes or margins—in this case the ancient woodland of Gwent—the horror moves steadily towards the imperial metropolis and the centre of fashionable society. Like

---

[17] Review cited by Machen in 1916 Introduction to *The Great God Pan*, reprinted by Creation Classics (London, 1993), 26.

Count Dracula's move from the Carpathian mountains via Whitby and Purfleet to Piccadilly, the Gothic relentlessly advances on the centres of urban civilization. London becomes a psychic topography, the grid of streets the map of disordered fantasy and forbidden desire.

The anthology ends with the genuinely unhinged tale, 'Vaila', by Matthew Phipps Shiel (1865–1947). Like Machen's *The Great God Pan*, Shiel's *Shapes in the Fire* was published in the Keynotes series by The Bodley Head, but the extremity of the writing derives from the clash of high and low styles. In many ways, Shiel exemplifies the Decadent style: his work is ornate, with elaborate constructions and a delight in obscure terminology, borrowings from other languages, and obsolete words. It is, as Arthur Symons defined Decadence, a 'learned corruption' of language. Shiel once claimed that 'The English language is like a vast collection of various coloured stones for mosaicking, and can express pretty well any idea or mental sensation.'[18] Shiel's Gothic fiction, in that case, is something akin to crazy paving. This is because Shiel's Decadent ambitions clash with a lowly enthusiasm for the apparatus of the Gothic. It produced a style Shiel memorably described as 'beserk Poe with all genius spent'.[19] Indeed, this early work predicts Shiel's trajectory towards pulp writing—he is perhaps now remembered for *Yellow Danger* in 1898, a virulently racist fantasy about the Asian threat to the European races that he retold in *The Yellow Wave* and again in *The Yellow Peril*. Some speculate that these texts derive from a mixed-race secret in Shiel's family (he was born in the British colony of Montserrat to an Irish preacher, and possibly mixed-race mother). Biography need not explain the insistently racial focus of the Gothic in the 1890s, however, as this Introduction has shown. 'Vaila', with its Northern settings, its dramatization of the last days of a noble, Northern aristocratic family, and its doomed castle and mouldering corpses, is full of the obsession with the destiny of the white race and the fears of degeneration and decline typical of the era.

The Gothic in the 1890s was marked by this fusion of styles, at a time when the distinctions of high and low literature, in their

[18] Shiel, cited A. Reynolds Morse, *The Works of M. P. Shiel: A Study in Bibliography* (Los Angeles, 1948), p. xvi.

[19] Shiel, cited Sam Moskowitz, *Explorers of the Infinite: Shapers of Science Fiction* (Cleveland, Oh., 1963), 144.

modern conception, were just in the process of being formed. In this moment of transition there were some amazing cross-fertilizations, and the Gothic responded so well to this because it has always been a product of hybridity. Soon, the Gothic would become a pulp genre: M. P. Shiel, for instance, became the presiding influence on the American pulp magazine *Weird Tales* which began in 1923 and which fostered the talents of H. P. Lovecraft. Shiel's bibliographer confessed in 1948 that he could not trace a single copy of some editions of his books—books that Shiel had himself now forgotten he had written. This anthology attempts to recover from these losses, to expand the readership, and deepen the understanding of this fascinating phase of the history of the Gothic genre.

NOTE ON SOURCES

Vernon Lee, 'Dionea', from *Hauntings: Fantastic Stories* (London: William Heinemann, 1890), 61–103.

Oscar Wilde, 'Lord Arthur Savile's Crime: A Study of Duty', from *Lord Arthur Savile's Crime and Other Stories* (London: James R. Osgood and McIlvaine, 1891), 1–74.

Henry James, 'Sir Edmund Orme', from *The Lesson of the Master* (London: Macmillan, 1892), 262–302.

Rudyard Kipling, 'The Mark of the Beast', from *Life's Handicap: Being Stories of Mine Own People* (London: Macmillan, 1891), 208–24.

B. M. Croker, 'The Dâk Bungalow at Dakor', from *To Let, Etc.* (London: Chatto and Windus, 1893), 114–44.

Arthur Conan Doyle, 'The Case of Lady Sannox' and 'Lot No. 249', from *Round the Red Lamp, Being Facts and Fancies of Medical Life* (London: Methuen, 1894), 156–73 and 220–80 respectively.

Grant Allen, 'Pallinghurst Barrow', from *Ivan Greet's Masterpiece* (London: Chatto and Windus, 1893), 67–89.

Jean Lorrain, 'Magic Lantern' (1891) and 'The Spectral Hand' (1895), translated by Brian Stableford in Jean Lorrain, *Nightmares of an Ether-Drinker* (Leyburn: Tartarus Press, 2002), 26–33 and 179–86 respectively.

Arthur Machen, 'The Great God Pan', from *The Great God Pan and The Inmost Light* (London: John Lane, 1894), 1–109.

M. P. Shiel, 'Vaila', from *Shapes in the Fire, Being a Mid-Winter-Night's Entertainment in Two Parts* (London: John Lane, 1896), 68–122.

NOTE ON ILLUSTRATIONS

IN their original magazine publications a number of these tales were heavily illustrated. Although unable to reproduce most of these images, this edition conveys a little of the role of illustration in the late-Victorian Gothic at the following points:

p. 82, from the original publication of Henry James's 'Sir Edmund Orme' in *Black and White*, Christmas number, 1891.

pp. 164 and 168, from the original publication of Grant Allen's 'Pallinghurst Barrow' in *Illustrated London News*, Christmas number, November 1892.

p. 246, from the original publication of M. P. Shiel's 'Vaila' in *Shapes in the Fire* (London: John Lane, 1896); reproduced by permission of the British Library.

SELECT BIBLIOGRAPHY

Primary Works

Single Author

Doyle, Arthur Conan, *Best Supernatural Tales of Sir Arthur Conan Doyle*, ed. E. F. Bleiler (New York, 1979).

Gilman, Charlotte Perkins, *The Yellow Wallpaper and Other Stories*, ed. Robert Shulman (Oxford, 1995).

James, Henry, *The Turn of the Screw and Other Stories*, ed. T. J. Lustig (Oxford, 1992).

James, M. R., *Ghost Stories of an Antiquary* (New York, 1971).

—— *Casting the Runes and Other Ghost Stories*, ed. Michael Cox (Oxford, 1987).

Kipling, Rudyard, *Life's Handicap: Being Stories of Mine Own People*, ed. A. O. J. Cockshut (Oxford, 1987).

Lee, Vernon, *Hauntings: Fantastic Stories*, ed. I. Cooper Willis (London, 2004).

Lorrain, Jean, *Monsieur de Phocas*, trans. Francis Amery (Sawtry, 1994).

Machen, Arthur, *The Three Impostors*, ed. Rita Tait, introd. David Trotter (London, 1995).

Stoker, Bram, *Dracula*, ed. Maurice Hindle (London, 1993).

Wilde, Oscar, *The Picture of Dorian Gray*, ed. Isabel Murray (Oxford, 1981).

—— *Complete Short Fiction*, ed. Ian Small (London, 1994).

Anthologies

Baldick, Chris (ed.), *The Oxford Book of Gothic Tales* (Oxford, 1992).

Dalby, Richard (ed.), *The Mammoth Book of Victorian and Edwardian Ghost Stories* (London, 1995).

Hale, Terry (ed.), *The Dedalus Book of French Horror: The 19th Century* (Sawtry, 1998).

Joshi, S. T. (ed.), *Great Tales of Terror* (New York, 2002).

Stableford, Brian (ed.), *Moral Ruins: The Dedalus Book of Decadence* (Sawtry, 1990).

1890s Contextual Material

Ledger, Sally, and Luckhurst, Roger (eds.), *The Fin de Siècle: A Reader in Cultural History c.1880–1900* (Oxford, 2000). Extracts from documents on a wide range of sources on the city, 'outcast' London, imperialism, socialism, psychology, sexology, anthropology, and so on.

Secondary Works

General Criticism on the 1890s

Beckson, Karl, *London in the 1890s* (New York, 1992).

Daly, Nicholas, *Modernism, Romance and the Fin de Siècle* (Cambridge, 1999).

Dowling, Linda, *Language and Decadence in the Victorian Fin de Siècle* (Princeton, 1986).

Greenslade, William, *Degeneration, Culture and the Novel 1880–1940* (Cambridge, 1994).

Hobsbawm, Eric, *The Age of Empire 1875–1914* (London, 1987).

Jackson, Holbrook, *The 1890s* (London, 1913).

Keating, Peter, *The Haunted Study: A Social History of the English Novel 1875–1914* (London, 1991).

Luckhurst, Roger, *The Invention of Telepathy* (Oxford, 2002).

Pick, Daniel, *Faces of Degeneration: A European Disorder c.1848–c.1918* (Cambridge, 1989).

Pittock, Murray, *The Decadent Spectrum: The Literature of the 1890s* (Cambridge, 1990).

Pykett, Lyn (ed.), *Reading Fin-de-Siècle Fictions* (London, 1996).

Showalter, Elaine, *Sexual Anarchy: Gender and Culture at the Fin de Siècle* (London, 1991).

Stokes, John, *In the Nineties* (Hemel Hempstead, 1989).

—— (ed.), *Fin de Siècle / Fin du Globe: Fears and Fantasies of the Late Nineteenth Century* (Basingstoke, 1992).

Thurschwell, Pamela, *Literature, Technology and Magical Thinking 1880–1920* (Cambridge, 2001).

Trotter, David, *The English Novel in History, 1895–1920* (London, 1993).

Walkowitz, Judith, *City of Dreadful Delight: Narratives of Sexual Danger in Late-Victorian London* (London, 1992).

West, Shearer, *The Fin de Siècle* (London, 1993).

Gothic Criticism

Arata, Stephen D., 'The Occidental Tourist: *Dracula* and the Anxiety of Reverse Colonisation', *Victorian Studies*, 33: 4 (1990), 621–45.

Baldick, Chris, 'Introduction', *The Oxford Book of Gothic Tales* (Oxford, 1992), pp. xi–xxiii.

Botting, Fred, *Gothic* (London, 1996).

Bown, Nicola, Burdett, Carolyn, and Thurschwell, Pamela (eds.), *The Victorian Supernatural* (Cambridge, 2004).

Brantlinger, Patrick, 'Imperial Gothic: Atavism and the Occult in the British Adventure Novel 1880–1914', in *Rule of Darkness: British Literature and Imperialism 1830–1914* (New York, 1988).

Clery, E. J., and Miles, Robert (eds.), *Gothic Documents: A Sourcebook 1700–1820* (Manchester, 2000).

Dryden, Linda, *The Modern Gothic and Literary Doubles: Stevenson, Wilde and Wells* (Basingstoke, 2003).

Ellis, Markman, *The History of Gothic Fiction* (Edinburgh, 2000).

Freud, Sigmund, 'The Uncanny' (1919), *Penguin Freud Library*, 14 (Harmondsworth: 1985), 335–76.

Haggerty, George E., *Gothic Fiction / Gothic Form* (Pennsylvania, 1989).

Halberstam, Judith, *Skin Shows: Gothic Horror and the Technology of Monsters* (Durham, NC, 1995).

Hogle, Jerrold E. (ed.), *The Cambridge Companion to Gothic Fiction* (Cambridge, 2002).

Hurley, Kelly, *The Gothic Body: Sexuality, Materialism, and Degeneration at the Fin de Siècle* (Cambridge, 1996).

Malchow, H. L., *Gothic Images of Race in Nineteenth-Century Britain* (Berkeley, 1996).

Mighall, Robert, *A Geography of Victorian Gothic Fiction: Mapping History's Nightmares* (Oxford, 1999).

Miles, Robert, *Gothic Writing: A Genealogy 1750–1820* (London, 1993).

Mulvey-Roberts, Marie, *The Handbook to Gothic Literature* (New York, 1998).

Punter, David, *The Literature of Terror: A History of Gothic Fictions from 1765 to the Present Day* (London, 1980).

—— (ed.), *A Companion to the Gothic* (Oxford, 2000).

Robbins, Ruth, and Wolfreys, Julian (eds.), *Victorian Gothic: Literary and Cultural Manifestations in the Nineteenth Century* (Basingstoke, 2000).

Ruskin, John, 'On the Nature of the Gothic' (1853), *Unto This Last and Other Writings*, ed. Clive Wilmer (London, 1997), 73–109.

Individual Author Criticism

GRANT ALLEN

Clodd, Edward, *Grant Allen: A Memoir* (London, 1900).

Morton, Peter, 'Grant Allen: A Centenary Reassessment', *English Literature in Transition*, 44: 4 (2001), 405–40.

Ruddick, Nicholas, 'Grant Allen', in *Dictionary of Literary Biography*, 178. *British Fantasy and Science Fiction Writers Before World War One*, ed. Darren Harris-Fain (Detroit, 1989), 7–16.

ARTHUR CONAN DOYLE

Barsham, Diana, *Arthur Conan Doyle and the Meaning of Masculinity* (Aldershot, 2000).

Krasner, James, 'Arthur Conan Doyle as Doctor and Writer', *Mosaic*, 33: 4 (2000), 19–34.

Wynne, Catherine, *The Colonial Conan Doyle: British Imperialism, Irish Nationalism and the Gothic* (Greenwood, Conn., 2002).

B. M. CROKER

Black, Helen C., 'Mrs Croker', *Pen, Pencil, Baton and Mask* (London, 1896), 83–92.

Dalby, Richard, 'Introduction' to B. M. Croker, *'Number Ninety' and Other Ghost Stories* (Mountain Ash, 2000), pp. ix–xvi.

HENRY JAMES

Banta, Martha, *Henry James and the Occult: The Great Extension* (Minneapolis, 1972).

Beidler, Peter G., *Ghosts, Demons and Henry James: The Turn of the Screw at the Turn of the Century* (Columbia, Mo., 1989).

Brown, Arthur A., 'Ghosts and the Nature of Death in Literature: Henry James' "Sir Edmund Orme" ', *American Literary Realism 1870–1910*, 31: 1 (1998), 60–74.

Lustig, T. J., *Henry James and the Ghostly* (Cambridge, 1994).

Woolf, Virginia, 'Henry James's Ghost Stories', *Collected Essays*, i (London, 1966), 286–92.

RUDYARD KIPLING

Arata, Stephen, 'A Universal Foreignness: Kipling in the Fin de Siècle', *English Literature in Transition*, 36: 1 (1993), 7–38.

Kemp, Sandra, *Kipling's Hidden Narratives* (Oxford, 1988).

Low, Gail Ching-Liang, *White Skin Black Masks: Representation and Colonialism* (London, 1996).

VERNON LEE

Leighton, Angela, 'Ghosts, Aestheticism and "Vernon Lee" ', *Victorian Literature and Culture* (2000), 1–14.

Maxwell, Catherine, 'Vernon Lee and the Ghosts of Italy', in Alison Chapman and Jane Stabler (eds.), *Unfolding the South: Nineteenth-Century British Women Writers and Artists in Italy* (Manchester, 2003), 201–21.

Robbins, Ruth, 'Apparitions Can Be Deceptive: Vernon Lee's Androgynous Spectres', in Ruth Robbins and Julian Wolfreys (eds.), *Victorian Gothic* (Basingstoke, 2000), 182–200.

JEAN LORRAIN

Amery, Francis, 'Introduction: The Life and Career of Jean Lorrain', in Jean Lorrain, *Monsieur de Phocas*, trans. Francis Amery (Sawtry, 1994), 5–20.

Birkett, Jennifer, *The Sins of the Fathers: Decadence in France 1870–1914* (London, 1986).

Hale, Terry, 'Introduction', *The Dedalus Book of French Horror: The 19th Century* (Sawtry, 1998), 11–35.

Ziegler, Robert, 'Spectacles of the Self: Decadent Aesthetics in Jean Lorrain', *Nineteenth Century French Studies*, 14: 3–4 (1986), 312–23.

ARTHUR MACHEN

Eckersley, Adrian, 'A Theme in the Early Work of Arthur Machen: "Degeneration" ', *English Literature in Transition*, 35: 3 (1992), 277–85.

Merivale, Patricia, *Pan the Goat-God: His Myth in Modern Times* (Cambridge, Mass., 1969).

Owens, Jill, 'Arthur Machen's Supernaturalism: The Decadent Variety', *University of Mississippi Studies in English*, 8 (1990), 117–26.

Sweetser, Wesley D., *Arthur Machen* (New York, 1964).

M. P. SHIEL

Bleiler, E. F., 'M. P. Shiel 1865–1947', *Science Fiction Writers* (New York, 1982), 31–7.

Morse, A. Reynolds, *The Works of M. P. Shiel: A Study in Bibliography* (Los Angeles, 1948).

Moskowitz, Sam, 'M. P. Shiel', *Explorers of the Infinite: Shapers of Science Fiction* (Cleveland, 1963), 142–56.

Svitavsky, William L., 'From Decadence to Racial Antagonism: M. P. Shiel at the Turn of the Century', *Science Fiction Studies*, 31: 1 (2004), 1–24.

OSCAR WILDE

Ellmann, Richard, *Oscar Wilde* (London, 1988).

Gagnier, Regenia, *Idylls of the Marketplace: Oscar Wilde and the Victorian Public* (Aldershot, 1987).

Raby, Peter, *Oscar Wilde* (Cambridge, 1988).

Stokes, John, *Oscar Wilde: Myths, Miracles, and Imitations* (Cambridge, 1996).

Further Reading in Oxford World's Classics

Doyle, Arthur Conan, *The Hound of the Baskervilles*, ed. W. W. Robson.

Gilman, Charlotte Perkins, *The Yellow Wallpaper and Other Stories*, ed. Robert Shulman.

Hogg, James, *The Private Memoirs and Confessions of a Justified Sinner*, ed. John Carey.

Huysmans, Joris-Karl, *Against Nature (A Rebours)*, trans. Margaret Mauldon, ed. Nicholas White.

James, Henry, *The Turn of the Screw and Other Stories*, ed. T. J. Lustig.

Le Fanu, J. Sheridan, *In a Glass Darkly*, ed. Robert Tracy.

Lewis, Matthew, *The Monk*, ed. Emma McEvoy.

Maturin, Charles, *Melmoth the Wanderer*, ed. Douglas Grant and Chris Baldick.

Poe, Edgar Allan, *Selected Tales*, ed. David Van Leer.

Radcliffe, Ann, *The Mysteries of Udolpho*, ed. Bonamy Dobrée and Terry Castle.

Stevenson, Robert Louis, *The Strange Case of Dr Jekyll and Mr Hyde, and Weir of Hermiston*, ed. Emma Letley.

Walpole, Horace, *The Castle of Otranto*, ed. W. S. Lewis and E. J. Clery.

A CHRONOLOGY OF THE 1890s

1890   Explorer Henry Stanley publishes *In Darkest Africa*. William Booth, founder of the Salvation Army, *In Darkest England and the Way Out*. J. G. Frazer, anthropologist, first volumes of *The Golden Bough*. Journalist W. T. Stead launches monthly summation of journalism, *The Review of Reviews*. Henrik Ibsen's *Hedda Gabler* causes storm of protest when performed in London.

    Henry James, *The Tragic Muse*

    William James, *The Principles of Psychology*

    William Morris, *News From Nowhere*

    James Whistler, *The Gentle Art of Making Enemies*

    Émile Zola, *La Bête humaine*

1891   Reverend Jay, *Life in Darkest London,* an exposé of physical and moral decline in London's East End. Cesare Lombroso, in *The Man of Genius*, argues that artistic genius is a result of mental aberration and disease. Death of Madame Blavatsky, founder of the Theosophy Society. A production of Ibsen's *Ghosts* in March causes much dispute; George Bernard Shaw issues his defence, *The Quintessence of Ibsenism*. William Morris, *The Story of the Glittering Plain,* the first imprint of his Kelmscott Press. Launch of *Strand Magazine* by George Newnes (success after serialization of Sherlock Holmes stories begin). Death of former Decadent poet and gun-runner Arthur Rimbaud, in Africa.

    Oscar Wilde, *Intentions* in May, *Lord Arthur Savile's Crime* in July, *The Picture of Dorian Gray* in October, and *A House of Pomegranates* in November

    Thomas Hardy, *Tess of the D'Urbervilles*

    George Gissing, *New Grub Street*

    John Davidson, *In a Music Hall and other poems*

    Margaret Harkness (as 'John Law'), *In Darkest London*

    Charlotte Perkins Gilman's classic Gothic tale, 'The Yellow Wallpaper'

    Joris-Karl Huysmans, *La-Bas,* his novel of Black Magic circles in Paris

1892   Max Nordau, *Degeneration,* an attack on moral and aesthetic decline, published in German. Sidney Webb, *The London Programme,* the manifesto for the Progressive government in the newly formed London County Council. J. A. Symonds privately circulates *A Problem of Modern Ethics,* a defence of homosexual desire. Henry Ford builds his first motor-car. The Rhymer's Club founded, *The Book of the Rhymer's Club* (Yeats later called them 'The Tragic Generation': Ernest Dowson, Lionel Johnson, and Davidson all die young). Yeats's play, *The Countess Cathleen*, performed in Dublin. Death of Alfred Lord Tennyson.

Arthur Conan Doyle, *The Adventures of Sherlock Holmes*

Israel Zangwill, *Children of the Ghetto*, a portrait of the Jewish immigrants of the East End of London

Wilde's play *Salomé* is banned in England

1893 The end of the three-volume novel, as the monopoly of 'circulating' libraries is broken. Cesare Lombroso, *The Degenerate Female* (theory of prostitution as a biologically inherited tendency). Sigmund Freud and Josef Breuer, *Studies in Hysteria*. Campaigning journalist W. T. Stead opens *Borderland*, a quarterly review of the occult sciences. Chicago World Fair. French Decadent poet Paul Verlaine gives readings in London. Grafton Gallery shows Dégas's painting, *L'Absinthe*, to loud objections.

W. B. Yeats, *The Celtic Twilight*

Arthur Symons's essay, 'The Decadent Movement in Literature'

Olive Schreiner, *Dream Life and Real Life*

Stéphane Mallarmé, *Vers et Prose*

Sarah Grand, *The Heavenly Twins*

Erskine Childers, *The Riddle of the Sands*, widely regarded as the first spy thriller

1894 England's year of Decadence. Founding of *The Yellow Book* by Henry Harland and Aubrey Beardsley. Novels by the New Woman cause sensation. Andrew Lang's essay, 'Ghosts up to Date', mourns the 'scientific' attitude to the supernatural. T. H. Huxley, *Evolution and Ethics*. Edward Carpenter circulates essay, 'The Intermediate Sex', on men who desire other men. Havelock Ellis, *Man and Woman: A Study of Human Secondary Sexual Characters*. Death of Robert Louis Stevenson in Samoa—widely mourned in England. Beginning of the 'Dreyfus affair' in France—a Jewish officer is wrongly imprisoned by anti-Semitic, Catholic-dominated military court. Martial Bourdin blows himself up in Anarchist attack on Greenwich Observatory.

George Egerton, *Keynotes* and *Discords*

Ella Hepworth Dixon, *The Story of a Modern Woman*

Iota, *A Yellow Aster*

Arthur Machen, *The Great God Pan* and *The Inmost Light*

Rudyard Kipling, *The Jungle Book*

Arthur Conan Doyle, *The Memoirs of Sherlock Holmes*

George du Maurier, *Trilby*—a best-seller that unleashes
'Trilbymania' in England and America

Anthony Hope, *The Prisoner of Zenda*

Eric Stenbock, *Studies in Death*

1895   Wilde's *The Importance of Being Earnest* opens in February; he is
on trial by April for 'acts of gross indecency between men'. He is
sentenced to two years hard labour. This is the end of English
Decadent movement. *The Yellow Book* closes, the offices of The
Bodley Head stoned. London National Vigilance Association
succeed in temporarily shutting down *The Empire* music hall as a
den of public vice. Nordau's *Degeneration* in English translation
becomes bestseller: replies include George Bernard Shaw, *The
Sanity of Art: An Exposure of the Current Nonsense about Artists
being Degenerate*. Gustave Le Bon, *The Crowd: A Study of the
Popular Mind*, examines the dangerous primitivism of the city
mob. Henry Maudsley, *The Pathology of Mind*, another in a long
line of studies of mental degeneracy by this leading psychologist.
Death of leading Darwinian theorist, T. H. Huxley.

H. G. Wells, *The Time Machine*

Grant Allen, *The Woman Who Did*, a conservative portrait of the
consequences of 'free love'

Thomas Hardy, *Jude the Obscure*

Marie Corelli, *The Sorrows of Satan*

Menie Muriel Dowie, *Gallia*, another central New Woman novel

Arthur Symons, *London Nights*

Arthur Machen, *The Three Impostors*

1896   Arthur Symons edits *The Savoy*, a new magazine that picks up the
mantle of *The Yellow Book*, yet refuses the epithet 'Decadent'.
Alfred Jarry's avant-garde play, *Ubu Roi*, first performed in Paris.
Freud coins the term 'psychoanalysis'. First display of the cine-
matograph in Leicester Square. First medical use of X-ray in
England. *Daily Mail* founded by Arthur Harmsworth: the beginning of the modern tabloid. Death of William Morris.

Max Beerbohm, *The Works of Max Beerbohm*

Ernest Dowson, *Verses*

Joseph Conrad, *An Outcast of the Islands*

H. G. Wells, *The Island of Dr Moreau*

Arthur Morrison, *A Child of the Jago*, 'naturalist' text based on
East End slum life

1897   Rudyard Kipling's poem 'Recessional', written for Victoria's
Jubilee Day. Stéphane Mallarmé's radical Modernist poem, 'Un

coup de dés jamais n'abolira le hasard'. Aubrey Beardsley, *Fifty Drawings*. Émile Durkheim, *Suicide: A Sociological Study.*
Bram Stoker, *Dracula*
Richard Marsh, *The Beetle*
H. G. Wells, *War of the Worlds* and *The Invisible Man*
Olive Schreiner, *Trooper Peter Halket of Mashonaland*

1898   Havelock Ellis, *Sexual Inversion* (prosecuted as a 'wicked, bawdy, scandalous libel'). Janet E. Hogarth's essay, 'The Monstrous Regiment of Women', in *Fortnightly Review*. Wilde released from prison, and travels to France under the name Sebastian Melmoth, derived from Charles Maturin's Gothic novel, *Melmoth the Wanderer*. Henry Kitchener's military campaign in Sudan crushes the Islamic revolution. G. W. Steevens's *With Kitchener to Khartum* becomes a best-seller. Aleister Crowley, soon to be the self-proclaimed Anti-Christ, joins the magical society The Hermetic Order of the Golden Dawn. Death of Aubrey Beardsley from consumption.
        Henry James, *The Turn of the Screw*
        Joseph Conrad, 'Heart of Darkness' in *Blackwood's Magazine*

1899   Start of the Boer War—in the early months, the British army is consistently beaten by ragged groups of Boer farmers, causing national anxiety. After the conclusion of the war in 1902, a commission of investigation blames lack of able-bodied recruits from working-class areas, prompting concern about racial decline. First English translation of Krafft-Ebing's *Psychopathia Sexualis*, the classic 'sexological' study of perversion. Guglielmo Marconi makes the first successful 'telegraphy without wires' communication across the Atlantic. Death of Grant Allen.
        Arthur Symons, *The Symbolist Movement in Literature,* the title changed from *Decadent Movement* after Wilde's trial
        Dick Donovan, *Tales of Terror*

1900   Karl Pearson's *National Life from the Standpoint of Science* addresses fears of national decline by advocating eugenics (good, selective breeding). Founding of the Labour Party. Sigmund Freud's *The Interpretation of Dreams*. Freud also undertakes unsuccessful analysis of Ida Bauer (published as 'Dora' case history in 1904). Death of Oscar Wilde in France.
        Joseph Conrad, *Lord Jim*

1901   Death of Queen Victoria. Death of Ernest Dowson.
        Rudyard Kipling, *Kim*

1902   J. A. Hobson, *Imperialism: A Study,* an early socialist critique of empire. Arnold White, *Efficiency and Empire*. William James, *The Varieties of Religious Experience*. Death of 'Tragic Generation' poet Lionel Johnson. Death of Cecil Rhodes, principal architect of imperial expansion in Southern Africa.

LATE VICTORIAN
GOTHIC TALES

VERNON LEE

Dionea

From the Letters of Doctor Alessandro De Rosis to the
Lady Evelyn Savelli, Princess of Sabina

MONTEMIRTO LIGURE, *June 29*, 1873

I TAKE immediate advantage of the generous offer of your Excellency
(allow an old Republican who has held you on his knees to address
you by that title sometimes, 'tis so appropriate) to help our poor
people. I never expected to come a-begging so soon. For the olive
crop has been unusually plenteous. We semi-Genoese don't pick the
olives unripe, like our Tuscan neighbours, but let them grow big and
black, when the young fellows go into the trees with long reeds and
shake them down on the grass for the women to collect—a pretty
sight which your Excellency must see some day: the grey trees with
the brown, barefoot lads craning, balanced in the branches, and the
turquoise sea as background just beneath. . . . That sea of ours—it is
all along of it that I wish to ask for money. Looking up from my desk,
I see the sea through the window, deep below and beyond the olive
woods, bluish-green in the sunshine and veined with violet under the
cloud-bars, like one of your Ravenna mosaics spread out as pavement
for the world: a wicked sea, wicked in its loveliness, wickeder than
your grey northern ones, and from which must have arisen in times
gone by (when Phœnicians or Greeks built the temples at Lerici and
Porto Venere) a baleful goddess of beauty, a Venus Verticordia, but in
the bad sense of the word, overwhelming men's lives in sudden
darkness like that squall of last week.

To come to the point. I want you, dear Lady Evelyn, to promise
me some money, a great deal of money, as much as would buy you a
little mannish cloth frock—for the complete bringing-up, until years
of discretion, of a young stranger whom the sea has laid upon our
shore. Our people, kind as they are, are very poor, and over-burdened
with children; besides, they have got a certain repugnance for this
poor little waif, cast up by that dreadful storm, and who is doubtless

a heathen, for she had no little crosses or scapulars on, like proper Christian children. So, being unable to get any of our women to adopt the child, and having an old bachelor's terror of my house-keeper, I have bethought me of certain nuns, holy women, who teach little girls to say their prayers and make lace close by here; and of your dear Excellency to pay for the whole business.

Poor little brown mite! She was picked up after the storm (such a set-out of ship-models and votive candles as that storm must have brought the Madonna at Porto Venere!) on a strip of sand between the rocks of our castle: the thing was really miraculous, for this coast is like a shark's jaw, and the bits of sand are tiny and far between. She was lashed to a plank, swaddled up close in outlandish garments; and when they brought her to me they thought she must certainly be dead: a little girl of four or five, decidedly pretty, and as brown as a berry, who, when she came to, shook her head to show she under-stood no kind of Italian, and jabbered some half-intelligible Eastern jabber, a few Greek words embedded in I know not what; the Superior of the College De Propaganda Fidē would be puzzled to know. The child appears to be the only survivor from a ship which must have gone down in the great squall, and whose timbers have been strewing the bay for some days past; no one at Spezia or in any of our ports knows anything about her, but she was seen, apparently making for Porto Venere, by some of our sardine-fishers: a big, lumbering craft, with eyes painted on each side of the prow, which, as you know, is a peculiarity of Greek boats. She was sighted for the last time off the island of Palmaria, entering, with all sails spread, right into the thick of the storm-darkness. No bodies, strangely enough, have been washed ashore.

July 10

I have received the money, dear Donna Evelina. There was tremen-dous excitement down at San Massimo when the carrier came in with a registered letter, and I was sent for, in presence of all the village authorities, to sign my name on the postal register.

The child has already been settled some days with the nuns; such dear little nuns (nuns always go straight to the heart of an old priest-hater and conspirator against the Pope, you know), dressed in brown robes and close, white caps, with an immense round straw-hat flapping behind their heads like a nimbus: they are called Sisters of the Stigmata, and have a convent and school at San Massimo, a little way inland, with an untidy garden full of lavender and cherry-trees. Your *protégée* has already half set the convent, the village, the Episcopal See, the Order of St Francis, by the ears. First, because nobody could make out whether or not she had been christened. The question was a grave one, for it appears (as your uncle-in-law, the Cardinal, will tell you) that it is almost equally undesirable to be christened twice over as not to be christened at all. The first danger was finally decided upon as the less terrible; but the child, they say, had evidently been baptized before, and knew that the operation ought not to be repeated, for she kicked and plunged and yelled like twenty little devils, and positively would not let the holy water touch her. The Mother Superior, who always took for granted that the baptism had taken place before, says that the child was quite right, and that Heaven was trying to prevent a sacrilege; but the priest and the barber's wife, who had to hold her, think the occurrence fearful, and suspect the little girl of being a Protestant. Then the question of the name. Pinned to her clothes—striped Eastern things, and that kind of crinkled silk stuff they weave in Crete and Cyprus—was a piece of parchment, a scapular we thought at first, but which was found to contain only the name *Διονεα*—Dionea,* as they pronounce it here. The question was, Could such a name be fitly borne by a young lady at the Convent of the Stigmata? Half the population here have names as unchristian quite—Norma, Odoacer, Archimedes—my housemaid is called Themis—but Dionea seemed to scandalise every one, perhaps because these good folk had a mysterious instinct that the name is derived from Dione, one of the loves of Father Zeus, and mother of no less a lady than the goddess Venus. The child was very near being called Maria, although there are already twenty-three other Marias, Mariettas, Mariuccias, and so forth at the convent. But the sister-bookkeeper, who apparently detests monotony, bethought her to look out Dionea first in the Calendar, which proved useless; and then in a big vellum-bound book, printed at Venice in 1625, called 'Flos Sanctorum, or Lives of the Saints, by Father Ribadeneira, S.J., with the addition of such Saints as have no assigned place in the Almanack, otherwise called the Movable or Extravagant Saints.' The zeal of Sister Anna Maddalena has been rewarded, for there, among the Extravagant Saints, sure enough, with a border of palm-branches and hour-glasses, stands the name of Saint Dionea, Virgin and Martyr, a lady of Antioch, put to death by the Emperor Decius. I know your Excellency's taste for historical information, so I forward this item. But I fear, dear Lady Evelyn, I fear that the heavenly patroness of your little sea-waif was a much more extravagant saint than that.

December 21, 1879

Many thanks, dear Donna Evelina, for the money for Dionea's schooling. Indeed, it was not wanted yet: the accomplishments of young ladies are taught at a very moderate rate at Montemirto: and as to clothes, which you mention, a pair of wooden clogs, with pretty red tips, costs sixty-five centimes, and ought to last three years, if the owner is careful to carry them on her head in a neat parcel when out walking, and to put them on again only on entering the village. The Mother Superior is greatly overcome by your Excellency's munificence towards the convent, and much perturbed at being unable to send you a specimen of your *protégée's* skill, exemplified in an embroidered pocket-handkerchief or a pair of mittens; but the fact is that poor Dionea *has* no skill. 'We will pray to the Madonna and St Francis to make her more worthy,' remarked the Superior. Perhaps, however, your Excellency, who is, I fear but a Pagan woman (for all the Savelli Popes and St Andrew Savelli's miracles), and insufficiently appreciative of embroidered pocket-handkerchiefs, will be quite as satisfied to hear that Dionea, instead of skill, has got the prettiest face of any little girl in Montemirto. She is tall, for her age (she is eleven) quite wonderfully well proportioned and extremely strong: of all the convent-full, she is the only one for whom I have never been called in. The features are very regular, the hair black, and despite all the good Sisters' efforts to keep it smooth like a Chinaman's, beautifully curly. I am glad she should be pretty, for she will more easily find a husband; and also because it seems fitting that your *protégée* should be beautiful. Unfortunately her character is not so satisfactory: she hates learning, sewing, washing up the dishes, all equally. I am sorry to say she shows no natural piety. Her companions detest her, and the nuns, although they admit that she is not exactly naughty, seem to feel her as a dreadful thorn in the flesh. She spends hours and hours on the terrace overlooking the sea (her great desire, she confided to me, is to get to the sea—to get *back to the sea*, as she expressed it), and lying in the garden, under the big myrtle-bushes, and, in spring and summer, under the rose-hedge. The nuns say that rose-hedge and that myrtle-bush* are growing a great deal too big, one would think from Dionea's lying under them; the fact, I suppose, has drawn attention to them. 'That child makes all the useless weeds grow,' remarked Sister Reparata. Another of Dionea's amusements is playing with pigeons. The number of pigeons she collects about her is quite amazing; you would never have thought that San Massimo or the neighbouring hills contained as many. They flutter down like snowflakes, and strut and swell themselves out, and furl and unfurl their tails, and peek with little sharp movements of their silly, sensual heads and a little throb and gurgle in their throats, while Dionea lies stretched out full length in the sun, putting out her lips, which they come to kiss, and uttering strange, cooing sounds; or hopping about, flapping her arms slowly like wings, and raising her little head with much the same odd gesture as they;—'tis a lovely sight, a thing fit for one of your painters, Burne Jones or Tadema,* with the myrtle-bushes all round, the bright, white-washed convent walls behind, the white marble chapel steps (all steps are marble in this Carrara country), and the enamel blue sea through the ilex-branches beyond. But the good Sisters abominate these pigeons, who, it appears, are messy little creatures, and they complain that, were it not that the Reverend Director likes a pigeon in his pot on a holiday, they could not stand the bother of perpetually sweeping the chapel steps and the kitchen threshold all along of those dirty birds. . . .

August 6, 1882

Do not tempt me, dearest Excellency, with your invitations to Rome. I should not be happy there, and do but little honour to your friendship. My many years of exile, of wanderings in northern countries, have made me a little bit into a northern man: I cannot quite get on with my own fellow-countrymen, except with the good peasants and fishermen all round. Besides—forgive the vanity of an old man, who has learned to make triple acrostic sonnets to cheat the days and months at Theresienstadt and Spielberg—I have suffered too much for Italy to endure patiently the sight of little parliamentary cabals and municipal wranglings, although they also are necessary in this day as conspiracies and battles were in mine. I am not fit for your roomful of ministers and learned men and pretty women: the former would think me an ignoramus, and the latter—what would afflict me much more—a pedant. . . . Rather, if your Excellency really wants to show yourself and your children to your father's old *protégé* of Mazzinian times,* find a few days to come here next spring. You shall have some very bare rooms with brick floors and white curtains opening out on my terrace; and a dinner of all manner of fish and milk (the white garlic flowers shall be mown away from under the olives lest my cow should eat it) and eggs cooked in herbs plucked in the hedges. Your boys can go and see the big ironclads at Spezia; and you shall come with me up our lanes fringed with delicate ferns and overhung by big olives, and into the fields where the cherry-trees shed their blossoms on to the budding vines, the fig-trees stretching out their little green gloves, where the goats nibble perched on their hind legs, and the cows low in the huts of reeds; and there rise from the ravines, with the gurgle of the brooks, from the cliffs with the boom of the surf, the voices of unseen boys and girls, singing about love and flowers and death, just as in the days of Theocritus,* whom your learned Excellency does well to read. Has your Excellency ever read Longus,* a Greek pastoral novelist? He is a trifle free, a trifle nude for us readers of Zola,* but the old French of Amyot has a wonderful charm, and he gives one an idea, as no one else does, how folk lived in such valleys, by such sea-boards, as these in the days when daisy-chains and garlands of roses were still hung on the olive-trees for the nymphs of the grove; when across the bay, at the end of the narrow neck of blue sea, there clung to the marble rocks not a church of Saint Laurence, with the sculptured martyr on his gridiron, but the temple of Venus, protecting her harbour. . . . Yes, dear Lady Evelyn, you have guessed aright. Your old friend has returned to his sins, and is scribbling once more. But no longer at verses or political pamphlets. I am enthralled by a tragic history, the history of the fall of the Pagan Gods. . . . Have you ever read of their wanderings and disguises, in my friend Heine's little book?*

And if you come to Montemirto, you shall see also your *protégée*, of whom you ask for news. It has just missed being disastrous. Poor Dionea! I fear that early voyage tied to the spar did no good to her wits, poor little waif! There has been a fearful row; and it has required all my influence, and all the awfulness of your Excellency's name, and the Papacy, and the Holy Roman Empire, to prevent her expulsion by the Sisters of the Stigmata. It appears that this mad creature very nearly committed a sacrilege: she was discovered handling in a suspicious manner the Madonna's gala frock and her best veil of *pizzo di Cantù*, a gift of the late Marchioness Violante Vigalena of Fornovo. One of the orphans, Zaira Barsanti, whom they call the Rossaccia, even pretends to have surprised Dionea as she was about to adorn her wicked little person with these sacred garments; and, on another occasion, when Dionea had been sent to pass some oil and sawdust over the chapel floor (it was the eve of Easter of the Roses), to have discovered her seated on the edge of the altar, in the very place of the Most Holy Sacrament. I was sent for in hot haste, and had to assist at an ecclesiastical council in the convent parlour, where Dionea appeared, rather out of place, an amazing little beauty, dark, lithe, with an odd, ferocious gleam in her eyes, and a still odder smile, tortuous, serpentine, like that of Leonardo da Vinci's women, among the plaster images of St Francis, and the glazed and framed samplers before the little statue of the Virgin, which wears in summer a kind of mosquito-curtain to guard it from the flies, who, as you know, are creatures of Satan.

Speaking of Satan, does your Excellency know that on the inside of our little convent door, just above the little perforated plate of metal (like the rose of a watering-pot) through which the Sister-portress peeps and talks, is pasted a printed form, an arrangement of holy names and texts in triangles, and the stigmatised hands of St Francis, and a variety of other devices, for the purpose, as is explained in a special notice, of baffling the Evil One, and preventing his entrance into that building? Had you seen Dionea, and the stolid, contemptuous way in which she took, without attempting to refute, the various shocking allegations against her, your Excellency would have reflected, as I did, that the door in question must have been accidentally absent from the premises, perhaps at the joiner's for repair, the day that your *protégée* first penetrated into the convent. The ecclesiastical tribunal, consisting of the Mother Superior, three Sisters, the Capuchin Director, and your humble servant (who vainly attempted to be Devil's advocate), sentenced Dionea, among other things, to make the sign of the cross twenty-six times on the bare floor with her tongue. Poor little child! One might almost expect that, as happened when Dame Venus scratched her hand on the

thorn-bush, red roses should sprout up between the fissures of the
dirty old bricks.

October 14, 1883

You ask whether, now that the Sisters let Dionea go and do half a
day's service now and then in the village, and that Dionea is a
grown-up creature, she does not set the place by the ears with her
beauty. The people here are quite aware of its existence. She is
already dubbed *La bella Dionea*; but that does not bring her any
nearer getting a husband, although your Excellency's generous offer
of a wedding-portion is well known throughout the district of San
Massimo and Montemirto. None of our boys, peasants or fishermen,
seem to hang on her steps; and if they turn round to stare and
whisper as she goes by straight and dainty in her wooden clogs, with
the pitcher of water or the basket of linen on her beautiful crisp dark
head, it is, I remark, with an expression rather of fear than of love.
The women, on their side, make horns with their fingers as she
passes, and as they sit by her side in the convent chapel; but that
seems natural. My housekeeper tells me that down in the village she
is regarded as possessing the evil eye and bringing love misery. 'You
mean,' I said, 'that a glance from her is too much for our lads' peace
of mind.' Veneranda shook her head, and explained, with the defer-
ence and contempt with which she always mentions any of her coun-
tryfolk's superstitions to me, that the matter is different: it's not with
her they are in love (they would be afraid of her eye), but where-ever
she goes the young people must needs fall in love with each other,
and usually where it is far from desirable. 'You know Sora Luisa, the
blacksmith's widow? Well, Dionea did a *half-service* for her last
month, to prepare for the wedding of Luisa's daughter. Well, now,
the girl must say, forsooth! that she won't have Pieriho of Lerici any
longer, but will have that raggamuffin Wooden Pipe from Solaro, or
go into a convent. And the girl changed her mind the very day that
Dionea had come into the house. Then there is the wife of Pippo, the
coffee-house keeper; they say she is carrying on with one of the
coastguards, and Dionea helped her to do her washing six weeks ago.
The son of Sor Temistocle has just cut off a finger to avoid the
conscription, because he is mad about his cousin and afraid of being
taken for a soldier; and it is a fact that some of the shirts which were
made for him at the Stigmata had been sewn by Dionea;' . . . and

thus a perfect string of love misfortunes, enough to make a little 'Decameron,'* I assure you, and all laid to Dionea's account. Certain it is that the people of San Massimo are terribly afraid of Dionea. . . .

July 17, 1884

Dionea's strange influence seems to be extending in a terrible way. I am almost beginning to think that our folk are correct in their fear of the young witch. I used to think, as physician to a convent, that nothing was more erroneous than all the romancings of Diderot and Schubert* (your Excellency sang me his 'Young Nun' once: do you recollect, just before your marriage?), and that no more humdrum creature existed than one of our little nuns, with their pink baby faces under their tight white caps. It appeared the romancing was more correct than the prose. Unknown things have sprung up in these good Sisters' hearts, as unknown flowers have sprung up among the myrtle-bushes and the rose-hedge which Dionea lies under. Did I ever mention to you a certain little Sister Giuliana, who professed only two years ago?—a funny rose and white little creature presiding over the infirmary, as prosaic a little saint as ever kissed a crucifix or scoured a saucepan. Well, Sister Giuliana has disappeared, and the same day has disappeared also a sailor-boy from the port.

August 20, 1884

The case of Sister Giuliana seems to have been but the beginning of an extraordinary love epidemic at the Convent of the Stigmata: the elder schoolgirls have to be kept under lock and key lest they should talk over the wall in the moonlight, or steal out to the little hunch-back who writes love-letters at a penny a-piece, beautiful flourishes and all, under the portico by the Fish-market. I wonder does that wicked little Dionea, whom no one pays court to, smile (her lips like a Cupid's bow or a tiny snake's curves) as she calls the pigeons down around her, or lies fondling the cats under the myrtle-bush, when she sees the pupils going about with swollen, red eyes; the poor little nuns taking fresh penances on the cold chapel flags; and hears the long-drawn guttural vowels, *amore* and *morte* and *mio bene*, which rise up of an evening, with the boom of the surf and the scent of the lemon-flowers, as the young men wander up and down, arm-in-arm, twanging their guitars along the moonlit lanes under the olives?

A terrible, terrible thing has happened! I write to your Excellency
with hands all a-tremble; and yet I *must* write, I must speak, or else I
shall cry out. Did I ever mention to you Father Domenico of Casoria,
the confessor of our Convent of the Stigmata? A young man, tall,
emaciated with fasts and vigils, but handsome like the monk playing
the virginal in Giorgione's 'Concert,' and under his brown serge still
the most stalwart fellow of the country all round? One has heard of
men struggling with the tempter. Well, well, Father Domenico had
struggled as hard as any of the Anchorites recorded by St Jerome,
and he had conquered. I never knew anything comparable to the
angelic serenity of gentleness of this victorious soul. I don't like
monks, but I loved Father Domenico. I might have been his father,
easily, yet I always felt a certain shyness and awe of him; and yet men
have accounted me a clean-lived man in my generation; but I felt,
whenever I approached him, a poor worldly creature, debased by the
knowledge of so many mean and ugly things. Of late Father
Domenico had seemed to me less calm than usual: his eyes had
grown strangely bright, and red spots had formed on his salient
cheekbones. One day last week, taking his hand, I felt his pulse
flutter, and all his strength as it were, liquefy under my touch. 'You
are ill,' I said. 'You have fever, Father Domenico. You have been
overdoing yourself—some new privation, some new penance. Take
care and do not tempt Heaven; remember the flesh is weak.' Father
Domenico withdrew his hand quickly. 'Do not say that,' he cried;
'the flesh is strong!' and turned away his face. His eyes were glistening
and he shook all over. 'Some quinine,' I ordered. But I felt it was no
case for quinine. Prayers might be more useful, and could I have
given them he should not have wanted. Last night I was suddenly
sent for to Father Domenico's monastery above Montemirto: they
told me he was ill. I ran up through the dim twilight of moonbeams
and olives with a sinking heart. Something told me my monk
was dead. He was lying in a little low whitewashed room; they had
carried him there from his own cell in hopes he might still be alive.
The windows were wide open; they framed some olive-branches,
glistening in the moonlight, and far below, a strip of moonlit sea.
When I told them that he was really dead, they brought some tapers
and lit them at his head and feet, and placed a crucifix between his
hands. 'The Lord has been pleased to call our poor brother to Him,'

said the Superior. 'A case of apoplexy, my dear Doctor—a case of apoplexy. You will make out the certificate for the authorities.' I made out the certificate. It was weak of me. But, after all, why make a scandal? He certainly had no wish to injure the poor monks.

Next day I found the little nuns all in tears. They were gathering flowers to send as a last gift to their confessor. In the convent garden I found Dionea, standing by the side of a big basket of roses, one of the white pigeons perched on her shoulder.

'So,' she said, 'he has killed himself with charcoal, poor Padre Domenico!'

Something in her tone, her eyes, shocked me.

'God has called to Himself one of His most faithful servants,' I said gravely.

Standing opposite this girl, magnificent, radiant in her beauty, before the rose-hedge, with the white pigeons furling and unfurling, strutting and pecking all round, I seemed to see suddenly the white-washed room of last night, the big crucifix, that poor thin face under the yellow waxlight. I felt glad for Father Domenico; his battle was over.

'Take this to Father Domenico from me,' said Dionea, breaking off a twig of myrtle starred over with white blossom; and raising her head with that smile like the twist of a young snake, she sang out in a high guttural voice a strange chaunt, consisting of the word *Amor—amor—amor*. I took the branch of myrtle and threw it in her face.

January 3, 1886

It will be difficult to find a place for Dionea, and in this neighbourhood well-nigh impossible. The people associate her somehow with the death of Father Domenico, which has confirmed her reputation of having the evil eye. She left the convent (being now seventeen) some two months back, and is at present gaining her bread working with the masons at our notary's new house at Lerici: the work is hard, but our women often do it, and it is magnificent to see Dionea, in her short white skirt and tight white bodice, mixing the smoking lime with her beautiful strong arms; or, an empty sack drawn over her head and shoulders, walking majestically up the cliff, up the scaffold-ings with her load of bricks. . . . I am, however, very anxious to get Dionea out of the neighbourhood, because I cannot help dreading the annoyances to which her reputation for the evil eye exposes her, and even some explosion of rage if ever she should lose the indifferent contempt with which she treats them. I hear that one of the rich men of our part of the world, a certain Sor Agostino of Sarzana, who owns a whole flank of marble mountain, is looking out for a maid for his daughter, who is about to be married; kind people and patriarchal in their riches, the old man still sitting down to table with all his servants; and his nephew, who is going to be his son-in-law, a splendid young fellow, who has worked like Jacob, in the quarry and at the saw-mill, for love of his pretty cousin. That whole house is so good, simple, and peaceful, that I hope it may tame down even Dionea. If I do not succeed in getting Dionea this place (and all your Excellency's illustriousness and all my poor eloquence will be needed to counteract the sinister reports attaching to our poor little waif), it will be best to accept your suggestion of taking the girl into your household at Rome, since you are curious to see what you call our baleful beauty. I am amused, and a little indignant at what you say about your footmen being handsome: Don Juan himself, my dear Lady Evelyn, would be cowed by Dionea. . . .

May 29, 1886

Here is Dionea back upon our hands once more! but I cannot send her to your Excellency. Is it from living among these peasants and fishing-folk, or is it because, as people pretend, a sceptic is always superstitious? I could not muster courage to send you Dionea, although your boys are still in sailor-clothes and your uncle, the Cardinal, is eighty-four; and as to the Prince, why, he bears the most potent amulet against Dionea's terrible powers in your own dear capricious person. Seriously, there is something eerie in this coincidence. Poor Dionea! I feel sorry for her, exposed to the passion of a once patriarchally respectable old man. I feel even more abashed at the incredible audacity, I should almost say sacrilegious madness, of the vile old creature. But still the coincidence is strange and uncomfortable. Last week the lightning struck a huge olive in the orchard of Sor Agostino's house above Sarzana. Under the olive was Sor Agostino himself, who was killed on the spot; and opposite, not twenty paces off, drawing water from the well, unhurt and calm, was Dionea. It was the end of a sultry afternoon: I was on a terrace in one of those villages of ours, jammed, like some hardy bush, in the gash of a hill-side. I saw the storm rush down the valley, a sudden blackness, and then, like a curse, a flash, a tremendous crash, re-echoed by a dozen hills. 'I told him,' Dionea said very quietly, when she came to stay with me the next day (for Sor Agostino's family would not have her for another half-minute), 'that if he did not leave me alone Heaven would send him an accident.'

July 15, 1886

My book?* Oh, dear Donna Evelina, do not make me blush by talking of my book! Do not make an old man, respectable, a Government functionary (communal physician of the district of San Massimo and Montemirto Ligure), confess that he is but a lazy unprofitable dreamer, collecting materials as a child picks hips out of a hedge, only to throw them away, liking them merely for the little occupation of scratching his hands and standing on tiptoe, for their pretty redness. . . . You remember what Balzac says about projecting any piece of work?—'*C'est fumer des cigarettes enchantées.*'* . . . Well, well! The data obtainable about the ancient gods in their days of adversity are few and far between: a quotation here and there from the Fathers; two or three legends; Venus reappearing; the persecutions of Apollo in Styria; Proserpina going, in Chaucer, to reign over the fairies; a few obscure religious persecutions in the Middle Ages on the score of Paganism; some strange rites practised till lately in the depths of a Breton forest near Lannion. . . . As to Tannhäuser, he was a real knight, and a sorry one, and a real Minnesinger not of the best. Your Excellency will find some of his poems in Von der Hagen's four immense volumes, but, I recommend you to take your notions of Ritter Tannhäuser's poetry rather from Wagner.* Certain it is that the Pagan divinities lasted much longer than we suspect, sometimes in their own nakedness, sometimes in the stolen garb of the Madonna or the saints. Who knows whether they do not exist to this day? And, indeed, is it possible they should not? For the awfulness of the deep woods, with their filtered green light, the creak of the swaying, solitary reeds, exists, and is Pan; and the blue, starry May night exists, the sough of the waves, the warm wind carrying the sweetness of the lemon-blossoms, the bitterness of the myrtle on our rocks, the distant chaunt of the boys cleaning out their nets, of the girls sickling the grass under the olives, *Amor—amor—amor*, and all this is the great goddess Venus. And opposite to me, as I write, between the branches of the ilexes, across the blue sea, streaked like a

Ravenna mosaic with purple and green, shimmer the white houses and walls, the steeple and towers, an enchanted Fata Morgana city,* of dim Porto Venere; . . . and I mumble to myself the verse of Catullus, but addressing a greater and more terrible goddess than he did:—

'Procul a mea sit furor omnis, Hera, domo; alios; age incitatos, alios age rabidos.'*

March 25, 1887

Yes; I will do everything in my power for your friends. Are you well-bred folk as well bred as we, Republican *bourgeois*, with the coarse hands (though you once told me mine were psychic hands when the mania of palmistry had not yet been succeeded by that of the Reconciliation between Church and State), I wonder, that you should apologise, you whose father fed me and housed me and clothed me in my exile, for giving me the horrid trouble of hunting for lodgings? It is like you, dear Donna Evelina, to have sent me photographs of my future friend Waldemar's statue. . . . I have no love for modern sculpture, for all the hours I have spent in Gibson's and Dupré's studio:* 'tis a dead art we should do better to bury. But your Waldemar has something of the old spirit: he seems to feel the divineness of the mere body, the spirituality of a limpid stream of mere physical life. But why among these statues only men and boys, athletes and fauns? Why only the bust of that thin, delicate-lipped little Madonna wife of his? Why no wide-shouldered Amazon or broad-flanked Aphrodite?

April 10, 1887

You ask me how poor Dionea is getting on. Not as your Excellency and I ought to have expected when we placed her with the good Sisters of the Stigmata: although I wager that, fantastic and capricious as you are, you would be better pleased (hiding it carefully from that grave side of you which bestows devout little books and carbolic acid upon the indigent) that your *protégée* should be a witch than a serving-maid, a maker of philters rather than a knitter of stockings and sewer of shirts.

A maker of philters. Roughly speaking, that is Dionea's profession. She lives upon the money which I dole out to her (with many useless objurgations) on behalf of your Excellency; and her ostensible employment is mending nets, collecting olives, carrying bricks, and other miscellaneous jobs; but her real status is that of village sorceress.

You think our peasants are sceptical? Perhaps they do not believe in thought-reading, mesmerism, and ghosts, like you, dear Lady Evelyn. But they believe very firmly in the evil eye, in magic, and in love-potions. Every one has his little story of this or that which happened to his brother or cousin or neighbour. My stable-boy and male factotum's brother-in-law, living some years ago in Corsica, was seized with a longing for a dance with his beloved at one of those balls which our peasants give in the winter, when the snow makes leisure in the mountains. A wizard anointed him for money, and straightway he turned into a black cat, and in three bounds was over the seas, at the door of his uncle's cottage, and among the dancers. He caught his beloved by the skirt to draw her attention; but she replied with a kick which sent him squealing back to Corsica. When he returned in summer he refused to marry the lady, and carried his left arm in a sling. 'You broke it when I came to the Veglia!' he said, and all seemed explained. Another lad, returning from working in the vine-yards near Marseilles, was walking up to his native village, high in our hills, one moonlight night. He heard sounds of fiddle and fife from a roadside barn, and saw yellow light from its chinks; and then entering, he found many women dancing, old and young, and among them his affianced. He tried to snatch her round the waist for a waltz (they play *Mme Angot* at our rustic balls), but the girl was unclutch-able, and whispered, 'Go; for these are witches, who will kill thee; and I am a witch also. Alas! I shall go to hell when I die.'

I could tell your Excellency dozens of such stories. But love-philters are among the commonest things to sell and buy. Do you remember the sad little story of Cervantes' Licentiate,* who, instead of a love-potion, drank a philter which made him think he was made of glass, fit emblem of a poor mad poet? . . . It is love-philters that Dionea prepares. No; do not misunderstand; they do not give love of her, still less her love. Your seller of love-charms is as cold as ice, as pure as snow. The priest has crusaded against her, and stones have flown at her as she went by from dissatisfied lovers; and the very children, paddling in the sea and making mud-pies in the sand, have put out forefinger and little finger and screamed, 'Witch, witch! ugly witch!' as she passed with basket or brick load; but Dionea has only smiled, that snake-like, amused smile, but more ominous than of yore. The other day I determined to seek her and argue with her on the subject of her evil trade. Dionea has a certain regard for me; not,

I fancy, a result of gratitude, but rather the recognition of a certain admiration and awe which she inspires in your Excellency's foolish old servant. She has taken up her abode in a deserted hut, built of dried reeds and thatch, such as they keep cows in, among the olives on the cliffs. She was not there, but about the hut pecked some white pigeons, and from it, startling me foolishly with its unexpected sound, came the eerie bleat of her pet goat. . . . Among the olives it was twilight already, with streakings of faded rose in the sky, and faded rose, like long trails of petals, on the distant sea. I clambered down among the myrtle-bushes and came to a little semicircle of yellow sand, between two high and jagged rocks, the place where the sea had deposited Dionea after the wreck. She was seated there on the sand, her bare foot dabbling in the waves; she had twisted a wreath of myrtle and wild roses on her black, crisp hair. Near her was one of our prettiest girls, the Lena of Sor Tullio the blacksmith, with ashy, terrified face under her flowered kerchief. I determined to speak to the child, but without startling her now, for she is a nervous, hysteric little thing. So I sat on the rocks, screened by the myrtle-bushes, waiting till the girl had gone. Dionea, seated listless on the sands, leaned over the sea and took some of its water in the hollow of her hand. 'Here,' she said to the Lena of Sor Tullio, 'fill your bottle with this and give it to drink to Tommasino the Rosebud.' Then she set to singing:—

'Love is salt, like sea-water—I drink and I die of thirst. . . . Water! water! Yet the more I drink, the more I burn. Love! thou art bitter as the seaweed.'

April 20, 1887

Your friends are settled here, dear Lady Evelyn. The house is built in what was once a Genoese fort, growing like a grey spiked aloes out of the marble rocks of our bay; rock and wall (the walls existed long before Genoa was ever heard of) grown almost into a homogeneous mass, delicate grey, stained with black and yellow lichen, and dotted here and there with myrtle-shoots and crimson snapdragon. In what was once the highest enclosure of the fort, where your friend Gertrude watches the maids hanging out the fine white sheets and pillow-cases to dry (a bit of the North, of Hermann and Dorothea* transferred to the South), a great twisted fig-tree juts out like an eccentric gurgoyle over the sea, and drops its ripe fruit into the deep blue pools. There is but scant furniture in the house, but a great oleander overhangs it, presently to burst into pink splendour; and on all the window-sills, even that of the kitchen (such a background of shining brass saucepans Waldemar's wife has made of it!) are pipkins and tubs full of trailing carnations, and tufts of sweet basil and thyme and mignonette. She pleases me most, your Gertrude, although you foretold I should prefer the husband; with her thin white face, a Memling Madonna finished by some Tuscan sculptor, and her long, delicate white hands ever busy, like those of a mediæval lady, with some delicate piece of work; and the strange blue, more limpid than the sky and deeper than the sea, of her rarely lifted glance.

It is in her company that I like Waldemar best; I prefer to the genius that infinitely tender and respectful, I would not say *lover*— yet I have no other word—of his pale wife. He seems to me, when with her, like some fierce, generous, wild thing from the woods, like the lion of Una, tame and submissive to this saint. . . . This tenderness is really very beautiful on the part of that big lion Waldemar, with his odd eyes, as of some wild animal—odd, and, your Excellency remarks, not without a gleam of latent ferocity. I think that hereby hangs the explanation of his never doing any but male figures: the female figure, he says (and your Excellency must hold him responsible, not me, for such profanity), is almost inevitably inferior in strength and beauty; woman is not form, but expression, and therefore suits painting, but not sculpture. The point of a woman is not her body, but (and here his eyes rested very tenderly upon the thin white profile of his wife) her soul. 'Still,' I answered, 'the ancients, who understood such matters, did manufacture some tolerable female statues: the Fates of the Parthenon, the Phidian Pallas, the Venus of Milo.' . . .

'Ah! yes,' exclaimed Waldemar, smiling, with that savage gleam of his eyes; 'but those are not women, and the people who made them have left us the tales of Endymion, Adonis, Anchises: a goddess might sit for them.' . . .

May 5, 1887

Has it ever struck your Excellency in one of your La Rochefoucauld* fits (in Lent say, after too many balls) that not merely maternal but conjugal unselfishness may be a very selfish thing? There! you toss your little head at my words; yet I wager I have heard you say that *other* women may think it right to humour their husbands, but as to you, the Prince must learn that a wife's duty is as much to chasten her husband's whims as to satisfy them. I really do feel indignant that such a snow-white saint should wish another woman to part with all instincts of modesty merely because that other woman would be a good model for her husband; really it is intolerable. 'Leave the girl alone,' Waldemar said, laughing. 'What do I want with the unæsthetic sex, as Schopenhauer* calls it?' But Gertrude has set her heart on his doing a female figure; it seems that folk have twitted him with never having produced one. She has long been on the look-out for a model for him. It is odd to see this pale, demure, diaphanous creature, not the more earthly for approaching motherhood, scanning the girls of our village with the eyes of a slave-dealer.

'If you insist on speaking to Dionea,' I said, 'I shall insist on speaking to her at the same time, to urge her to refuse your proposal.' But Waldemar's pale wife was indifferent to all my speeches about modesty being a poor girl's only dowry. 'She will do for a Venus,' she merely answered.

We went up to the cliffs together, after some sharp words, Waldemar's wife hanging on my arm as we slowly clambered up the stony path among the olives. We found Dionea at the door of her hut, making faggots of myrtle-branches. She listened sullenly to Gertrude's offer and explanations; indifferently to my admonitions not to accept. The thought of stripping for the view of a man, which would send a shudder through our most brazen village girls, seemed not to startle her, immaculate and savage as she is accounted. She did not answer, but sat under the olives, looking vaguely across the sea. At that moment Waldemar came up to us; he had followed with the intention of putting an end to these wranglings.

'Gertrude,' he said, 'do leave her alone. I have found a model—a fisher-boy, whom I much prefer to any woman.'

Dionea raised her head with that serpentine smile. 'I will come,' she said.

Waldemar stood silent; his eyes were fixed on her, where she stood under the olives, her white shift loose about her splendid throat, her shining feet bare in the grass. Vaguely, as if not knowing what he said, he asked her name. She answered that her name was Dionea; for the rest, she was an Innocentina, that is to say, a foundling; then she began to sing:—

'Flower of the myrtle!
My father is the starry sky:
The mother that made me is the sea.'*

June 22, 1887

I confess I was an old fool to have grudged Waldemar his model. As I watch him gradually building up his statue, watch the goddess gradually emerging from the clay heap, I ask myself—and the case might trouble a more subtle moralist than me—whether a village girl, an obscure, useless life within the bounds of what we choose to call right and wrong, can be weighed against the possession by mankind of a great work of art, a Venus immortally beautiful? Still, I am glad that the two alternatives need not be weighed against each other. Nothing can equal the kindness of Gertrude, now that Dionea has consented to sit to her husband; the girl is ostensibly merely a servant like any other; and, lest any report of her real functions should get abroad and discredit her at San Massimo or Montemirto, she is to be taken to Rome, where no one will be the wiser, and where, by the way, your Excellency will have an opportunity of comparing Waldemar's goddess of love with our little orphan of the Convent of the Stigmata. What reassures me still more is the curious attitude of Waldemar towards the girl. I could never have believed that an artist could regard a woman so utterly as a mere inanimate thing, a form to copy, like a tree or flower. Truly he carries out his theory that sculpture knows only the body, and the body scarcely considered as human. The way in which he speaks to Dionea after hours of the most rapt contemplation of her is almost brutal in its coldness. And yet to hear him exclaim, 'How beautiful she is! Good God, how beautiful!' No love of mere woman was ever so violent as this love of woman's mere shape.

June 27, 1887

You asked me once, dearest Excellency, whether there survived among our people (you had evidently added a volume on folk-lore to that heap of half-cut, dog's-eared books that litter about among the Chineseries and mediæval brocades of your rooms) any trace of Pagan myths. I explained to you then that all our fairy mythology, classic gods, and demons and heroes, teemed with fairies, ogres, and princes. Last night I had a curious proof of this. Going to see the Waldemar, I found Dionea seated under the oleander at the top of the old Genoese fort, telling stories to the two little blonde children who were making the falling pink blossoms into necklaces at her feet; the pigeons, Dionea's white pigeons, which never leave her, strutting and pecking among the basil pots, and the white gulls flying round the rocks overhead. This is what I heard. . . . 'And the three fairies said to the youngest son of the King, to the one who had been brought up as a shepherd, "Take this apple, and give it to her among us who is most beautiful." And the first fairy said, "If thou give it to me thou shalt be Emperor of Rome, and have purple clothes, and have a gold crown and gold armour, and horses and courtiers;" and the second said, "If thou give it to me thou shalt be Pope, and wear a mitre, and have the keys of heaven and hell;" and the third fairy said, "Give the apple to me, for I will give thee the most beautiful lady to wife." And the youngest son of the King sat in the green meadow and thought about it a little, and then said, "What use is there in being Emperor or Pope? Give me the beautiful lady to wife, since I am young myself." And he gave the apple to the third of the three fairies.' . . .

Dionea droned out the story in her half-Genoese dialect, her eyes looking far away across the blue sea, dotted with sails like white sea-gulls, that strange serpentine smile on her lips.

'Who told thee that fable?' I asked.

She took a handful of oleander-blossoms from the ground, and throwing them in the air, answered listlessly, as she watched the little shower of rosy petals descend on her black hair and pale breast—

'Who knows?'

July 6, 1887

How strange is the power of art! Has Waldemar's statue shown me the real Dionea, or has Dionea really grown more strangely beautiful than before? Your Excellency will laugh; but when I meet her I cast down my eyes after the first glimpse of her loveliness; not with the shyness of a ridiculous old pursuer of the Eternal Feminine, but with a sort of religious awe—the feeling with which, as a child kneeling by my mother's side, I looked down on the church flags when the Mass bell told the elevation of the Host. . . . Do you remember the story of Zeuxis and the ladies of Crotona, five of the fairest not being too much for his Juno?* Do you remember—you, who have read everything—all the bosh of our writers about the Ideal in Art? Why, here is a girl who disproves all this nonsense in a minute; she is far, far more beautiful than Waldemar's statue of her. He said so angrily, only yesterday, when his wife took me into his studio (he has made a studio of the long-desecrated chapel of the old Genoese fort, itself, they say, occupying the site of the temple of Venus).

As he spoke that odd spark of ferocity dilated in his eyes, and seizing the largest of his modelling tools, he obliterated at one swoop the whole exquisite face. Poor Gertrude turned ashy white, and a convulsion passed over her face. . . .

July 15

I wish I could make Gertrude understand, and yet I could never, never bring myself to say a word. As a matter of fact, what is there to be said? Surely she knows best that her husband will never love any woman but herself. Yet ill, nervous as she is, I quite understand that she must loathe this unceasing talk of Dionea, of the superiority of the model over the statue. Cursed statue! I wish it were finished, or else that it had never been begun.

July 20

This morning Waldemar came to me. He seemed strangely agitated: I guessed he had something to tell me, and yet I could never ask. Was it cowardice on my part? He sat in my shuttered room, the sunshine making pools on the red bricks and tremulous stars on the ceiling, talking of many things at random, and mechanically turning over the manuscript, the heap of notes of my poor, never-finished book on the Exiled Gods. Then he rose, and walking nervously round my study, talking disconnectedly about his work, his eye suddenly fell upon a little altar, one of my few antiquities, a little block of marble with a carved garland and rams' heads, and a half-effaced inscription dedicating it to Venus, the mother of Love.

'It was found,' I explained, 'in the ruins of the temple, somewhere on the site of your studio: so, at least, the man said from whom I bought it.'

Waldemar looked at it long. 'So,' he said, 'this little cavity was to burn the incense in; or rather, I suppose, since it has two little gutters running into it, for collecting the blood of the victim? Well, well! they were wiser in that day, to wring the neck of a pigeon or burn a pinch of incense than to eat their own hearts out, as we do, all along of Dame Venus;' and he laughed, and left me with that odd ferocious lighting-up of his face. Presently there came a knock at my door. It was Waldemar. 'Doctor,' he said very quietly, 'will you do me a favour? Lend me your little Venus altar—only for a few days, only till the day after to-morrow. I want to copy the design of it for the pedestal of my statue: it is appropriate.' I sent the altar to him: the lad who carried it told me that Waldemar had set it up in the studio, and calling for a flask of wine, poured out two glasses. One he had given to my messenger for his pains; of the other he had drunk a mouthful, and thrown the rest over the altar, saying some unknown words. 'It must be some German habit,' said my servant. What odd fancies this man has!

July 25

You ask me, dearest Excellency, to send you some sheets of my book: you want to know what I have discovered. Alas! dear Donna Evelina, I have discovered, I fear, that there is nothing to discover; that Apollo was never in Styria; that Chaucer, when he called the Queen of the Fairies Proserpine, meant nothing more than an eighteenth century poet when he called Dolly or Betty Cynthia or Amaryllis; that the lady who damned poor Tannhäuser was not Venus, but a mere little Suabian mountain sprite; in fact, that poetry is only the invention of poets, and that that rogue, Heinrich Heine, is entirely responsible for the existence of *Dieux en Exil*.* . . . My poor manuscript can only tell you what St Augustine, Tertullian, and sundry morose old Bishops thought about the loves of Father Zeus and the miracles of the Lady Isis, none of which is much worth your attention. . . . Reality, my dear Lady Evelyn, is always prosaic: at least when investigated into by bald old gentlemen like me.

And yet, it does not look so. The world, at times, seems to be playing at being poetic, mysterious, full of wonder and romance. I am writing, as usual, by my window, the moonlight brighter in its whiteness than my mean little yellow-shining lamp. From the mysterious greyness, the olive groves and lanes beneath my terrace, rises a confused quaver of frogs, and buzz and whirr of insects: something, in sound, like the vague trails of countless stars, the galaxies on galaxies blurred into mere blue shimmer by the moon, which rides slowly across the highest heaven. The olive twigs glisten in the rays: the flowers of the pomegranate and oleander are only veiled as with bluish mist in their scarlet and rose. In the sea is another sea, of molten, rippled silver, or a magic causeway leading to the shining vague offing, the luminous pale sky-line, where the islands of Palmaria and Tino float like unsubstantial, shadowy dolphins. The roofs of Montemirto glimmer among the black, pointing cypresses: farther below, at the end of that half-moon of land, is San Massimo: the Genoese fort inhabited by our friends is profiled black against the sky. All is dark: our fisher-folk go to bed early; Gertrude and the little ones are asleep: they at least are, for I can imagine Gertrude lying awake, the moonbeams on her thin Madonna face, smiling as she thinks of the little ones around her, of the other tiny thing that will soon lie on her breast. . . . There is a light in the old desecrated chapel, the thing that was once the temple of Venus, they say, and is now Waldemar's workshop, its broken roof mended with reeds and thatch. Waldemar has stolen in, no doubt to see his statue again. But he will return, more peaceful for the peacefulness of the night, to his sleeping wife and children. God bless and watch over them! Good-night, dearest Excellency.

July 26

I have your Excellency's telegram in answer to mine. Many thanks for sending the Prince. I await his coming with feverish longing; it is still something to look forward to. All does not seem over. And yet what can he do?

The children are safe: we fetched them out of their bed and brought them up here. They are still a little shaken by the fire, the bustle, and by finding themselves in a strange house; also, they want to know where their mother is; but they have found a tame cat, and I hear them chirping on the stairs.

It was only the roof of the studio, the reeds and thatch, that burned, and a few old pieces of timber. Waldemar must have set fire to it with great care; he had brought armfuls of faggots of dry myrtle and heather from the bakehouse close by, and thrown into the blaze quantities of pine-cones, and of some resin, I know not what, that smelt like incense. When we made our way, early this morning, through the smouldering studio, we were stifled with a hot church-like perfume: my brain swam, and I suddenly remembered going into St Peter's on Easter Day as a child.

It happened last night, while I was writing to you. Gertrude had gone to bed, leaving her husband in the studio. About eleven the maids heard him come out and call to Dionea to get up and come and sit to him. He had had this craze once before, of seeing her and his statue by an artificial light: you remember he had theories about the way in which the ancients lit up the statues in their temples. Gertrude, the servants say, was heard creeping downstairs a little later.

Do you see it? I have seen nothing else these hours, which have seemed weeks and months. He had placed Dionea on the big marble block behind the altar, a great curtain of dull red brocade—you know that Venetian brocade with the gold pomegranate pattern—behind her, like a Madonna of Van Eyck's. He showed her to me once before like this, the whiteness of her neck and breast, the whiteness of the drapery round her flanks, toned to the colour of old marble by the light of the resin burning in pans all round. . . . Before Dionea was the altar—the altar of Venus which he had borrowed from me. He must have collected all the roses about it, and thrown the incense upon the embers when Gertrude suddenly entered. And then, and then . . .

We found her lying across the altar, her pale hair among the ashes of the incense, her blood—she had but little to give, poor white ghost!—trickling among the carved garlands and rams' heads, blackening the heaped-up roses. The body of Waldemar was found at the foot of the castle cliff. Had he hoped, by setting the place on fire, to bury himself among its ruins, or had he not rather wished to complete in this way the sacrifice, to make the whole temple an immense votive pyre? It looked like one, as we hurried down the hills to San Massimo: the whole hillside, dry grass, myrtle, and heather, all burning, the pale short flames waving against the blue moonlit sky, and the old fortress outlined black against the blaze.

August 30

Of Dionea I can tell you nothing certain. We speak of her as little as we can. Some say they have seen her, on stormy nights, wandering among the cliffs: but a sailor-boy assures me, by all the holy things, that the day after the burning of the Castle Chapel—we never call it anything else—he met at dawn, off the island of Palmaria, beyond the Strait of Porto Venere, a Greek boat, with eyes painted on the prow, going full sail to sea, the men singing as she went. And against the mast, a robe of purple and gold about her, and a myrtle-wreath on her head, leaned Dionea, singing words in an unknown tongue, the white pigeons circling around her.

OSCAR WILDE

Lord Arthur Savile's Crime

A STUDY OF DUTY

I

It was Lady Windermere's last reception before Easter, and Bentinck House was even more crowded than usual. Six Cabinet Ministers had come on from the Speaker's Levée in their stars and ribands, all the pretty women wore their smartest dresses, and at the end of the picture-gallery stood the Princess Sophia of Carlsrühe, a heavy Tartar-looking lady, with tiny black eyes and wonderful emeralds, talking bad French at the top of her voice, and laughing immoderately at everything that was said to her. It was certainly a wonderful medley of people. Gorgeous peeresses chatted affably to violent Radicals, popular preachers brushed coat-tails with eminent sceptics, a perfect bevy of bishops kept following a stout prima-donna from room to room, on the staircase stood several Royal Academicians, disguised as artists, and it was said that at one time the supper-room was absolutely crammed with geniuses. In fact, it was one of Lady Windermere's best nights, and the Princess stayed till nearly half-past eleven.

As soon as she had gone, Lady Windermere returned to the picture-gallery, where a celebrated political economist was solemnly explaining the scientific theory of music to an indignant virtuoso from Hungary, and began to talk to the Duchess of Paisley. She looked wonderfully beautiful with her grand ivory throat, her large blue forget-me-not eyes, and her heavy coils of golden hair. *Or pur** they were—not that pale straw colour that nowadays usurps the gracious name of gold, but such gold as is woven into sunbeams or hidden in strange amber; and they gave to her face something of the frame of a saint, with not a little of the fascination of a sinner. She was a curious psychological study. Early in life she had discovered the important truth that nothing looks so like innocence as an indiscretion; and by a series of reckless escapades, half of them quite harmless, she had acquired all the privileges of a personality. She had more than once changed her husband; indeed, Debrett credits her with three marriages; but as she had never changed her lover, the world had long ago ceased to talk scandal about her. She was now forty years of age, childless, and with that inordinate passion for pleasure which is the secret of remaining young.

Suddenly she looked eagerly round the room, and said, in her clear contralto voice, 'Where is my cheiromantist?'

'Your what, Gladys?' exclaimed the Duchess, giving an involuntary start.

'My cheiromantist, Duchess; I can't live without him at present.'

'Dear Gladys! you are always so original,' murmured the Duchess, trying to remember what a cheiromantist really was, and hoping it was not the same as a cheiropodist.

'He comes to see my hand twice a week regularly,' continued Lady Windermere, 'and is most interesting about it.'

'Good heavens!' said the Duchess to herself, 'he is a sort of cheiropodist after all. How very dreadful. I hope he is a foreigner at any rate. It wouldn't be quite so bad then.'

'I must certainly introduce him to you.'

'Introduce him!' cried the Duchess; 'you don't mean to say he is here?' and she began looking about for a small tortoise-shell fan and a very tattered lace shawl, so as to be ready to go at a moment's notice.

'Of course he is here, I would not dream of giving a party without him. He tells me I have a pure psychic hand, and that if my thumb had been the least little bit shorter, I should have been a confirmed pessimist, and gone into a convent.'

'Oh, I see!' said the Duchess, feeling very much relieved; 'he tells fortunes, I suppose?'

'And misfortunes, too,' answered Lady Windermere, 'any amount of them. Next year, for instance, I am in great danger, both by land and sea, so I am going to live in a balloon, and draw up my dinner in a basket every evening. It is all written down on my little finger, or on the palm of my hand, I forget which.'

'But surely that is tempting Providence, Gladys.'

'My dear Duchess, surely Providence can resist temptation by this time. I think every one should have their hands told once a month, so as to know what not to do. Of course, one does it all the same, but it is so pleasant to be warned. Now, if some one doesn't go and fetch Mr Podgers at once, I shall have to go myself.'

'Let me go, Lady Windermere,' said a tall handsome young man, who was standing by, listening to the conversation with an amused smile.

'Thanks so much, Lord Arthur; but I am afraid you wouldn't recognise him.'

'If he is as wonderful as you say, Lady Windermere, I couldn't well miss him. Tell me what he is like, and I'll bring him to you at once.'

'Well, he is not a bit like a cheiromantist. I mean he is not mysterious, or esoteric, or romantic-looking. He is a little, stout man, with a funny, bald head, and great gold-rimmed spectacles; something between a family doctor and a country attorney. I'm really very sorry, but it is not my fault. People are so annoying. All my pianists look exactly like poets, and all my poets look exactly like pianists; and I remember last season asking a most dreadful conspirator to dinner, a man who had blown up ever so many people, and always wore a coat of mail, and carried a dagger up his shirt-sleeve; and do you know that when he came he looked just like a nice old clergyman, and cracked jokes all the evening? Of course, he was very amusing, and all that, but I was awfully disappointed; and when I asked him about the coat of mail, he only laughed, and said it was far too cold to wear in England. Ah, here is Mr Podgers! Now, Mr Podgers, I want you to tell the Duchess of Paisley's hand. Duchess, you must take your glove off. No, not the left hand, the other.'

'Dear Gladys, I really don't think it is quite right,' said the Duchess, feebly unbuttoning a rather soiled kid glove.

'Nothing interesting ever is,' said Lady Windermere: '*on a fait le monde ainsi.** But I must introduce you. Duchess, this is Mr Podgers, my pet cheiromantist. Mr Podgers, this is the Duchess of Paisley, and if you say that she has a larger mountain of the moon than I have, I will never believe in you again.'

'I am sure, Gladys, there is nothing of the kind in my hand,' said the Duchess gravely.

'Your Grace is quite right,' said Mr Podgers, glancing at the little fat hand with its short square fingers, 'the mountain of the moon is not developed. The line of life, however, is excellent. Kindly bend the wrist. Thank you. Three distinct lines on the *rascette*!* You will live to a great age, Duchess, and be extremely happy. Ambition—very moderate, line of intellect not exaggerated, line of heart——'

'Now, do be indiscreet, Mr Podgers,' cried Lady Windermere.

'Nothing would give me greater pleasure,' said Mr Podgers, bowing, 'if the Duchess ever had been, but I am sorry to say that I see great permanence of affection, combined with a strong sense of duty.'

'Pray go on, Mr Podgers,' said the Duchess, looking quite pleased.

'Economy is not the least of your Grace's virtues,' continued Mr Podgers, and Lady Windermere went off into fits of laughter.

'Economy is a very good thing,' remarked the Duchess complacently; 'when I married Paisley he had eleven castles, and not a single house fit to live in.'

'And now he has twelve houses, and not a single castle,' cried Lady Windermere.

'Well, my dear,' said the Duchess, 'I like——'

'Comfort,' said Mr Podgers, 'and modern improvements, and hot water laid on in every bedroom. Your Grace is quite right. Comfort is the only thing our civilisation can give us.'

'You have told the Duchess's character admirably, Mr Podgers, and now you must tell Lady Flora's;' and in answer to a nod from the smiling hostess, a tall girl, with sandy Scotch hair, and high shoulder-blades, stepped awkwardly from behind the sofa, and held out a long, bony hand with spatulate fingers.

'Ah, a pianist! I see,' said Mr Podgers, 'an excellent pianist, but perhaps hardly a musician. Very reserved, very honest, and with a great love of animals.'

'Quite true!' exclaimed the Duchess, turning to Lady Windermere, 'absolutely true! Flora keeps two dozen collie dogs at Macloskie, and would turn our town house into a menagerie if her father would let her.'

'Well, that is just what I do with my house every Thursday evening,' cried Lady Windermere, laughing, 'only I like lions better than collie dogs.'

'Your one mistake, Lady Windermere,' said Mr Podgers, with a pompous bow.

'If a woman can't make her mistakes charming, she is only a female,' was the answer. 'But you must read some more hands for us. Come, Sir Thomas, show Mr Podgers yours;' and a genial-looking old gentleman, in a white waistcoat, came forward, and held out a thick rugged hand, with a very long third finger.

'An adventurous nature; four long voyages in the past, and one to come. Been shipwrecked three times. No, only twice, but in danger of a shipwreck your next journey. A strong Conservative, very punctual, and with a passion for collecting curiosities. Had a severe illness between the ages of sixteen and eighteen. Was left a fortune when about thirty. Great aversion to cats and Radicals.'

'Extraordinary!' exclaimed Sir Thomas; 'you must really tell my wife's hand, too.'

'Your second wife's,' said Mr Podgers quietly, still keeping Sir Thomas's hand in his. 'Your second wife's. I shall be charmed;' but Lady Marvel, a melancholy-looking woman, with brown hair and sentimental eyelashes, entirely declined to have her past or her future exposed; and nothing that Lady Windermere could do would induce Monsieur de Koloff, the Russian Ambassador, even to take his gloves off. In fact, many people seemed afraid to face the odd little man with his stereotyped smile, his gold spectacles, and his bright, beady eyes; and when he told poor Lady Fermor, right out before every one, that she did not care a bit for music, but was extremely fond of musicians, it was generally felt that cheiromancy was a most dangerous science, and one that ought not to be encouraged, except in a *tête-a-tête*.

Lord Arthur Savile, however, who did not know anything about Lady Fermor's unfortunate story, and who had been watching Mr Podgers with a great deal of interest, was filled with an immense curiosity to have his own hand read, and feeling somewhat shy about putting himself forward, crossed over the room to where Lady Windermere was sitting, and, with a charming blush, asked her if she thought Mr Podgers would mind.

'Of course, he won't mind,' said Lady Windermere, 'that is what he is here for. All my lions, Lord Arthur, are performing lions, and jump through hoops whenever I ask them. But I must warn you beforehand that I shall tell Sybil everything. She is coming to lunch with me to-morrow, to talk about bonnets, and if Mr Podgers finds out that you have a bad temper, or a tendency to gout, or a wife living in Bayswater, I shall certainly let her know all about it.'

Lord Arthur smiled, and shook his head. 'I am not afraid,' he answered. 'Sybil knows me as well as I know her.'

'Ah! I am a little sorry to hear you say that. The proper basis for marriage is a mutual misunderstanding. No, I am not at all cynical, I have merely got experience, which, however, is very much the same thing. Mr Podgers, Lord Arthur Savile is dying to have his hand read. Don't tell him that he is engaged to one of the most beautiful girls in London, because that appeared in the *Morning Post* a month ago.'

'Dear Lady Windermere,' cried the Marchioness of Jedburgh, 'do let Mr Podgers stay here a little longer. He has just told me I should go on the stage, and I am so interested.'

'If he has told you that, Lady Jedburgh, I shall certainly take him away. Come over at once, Mr Podgers, and read Lord Arthur's hand.'

'Well,' said Lady Jedburgh, making a little *moue* as she rose from the sofa, 'if I am not to be allowed to go on the stage, I must be allowed to be part of the audience at any rate.'

'Of course; we are all going to be part of the audience,' said Lady Windermere; 'and now, Mr Podgers, be sure and tell us something nice. Lord Arthur is one of my special favourites.'

But when Mr Podgers saw Lord Arthur's hand he grew curiously pale, and said nothing. A shudder seemed to pass through him, and his great bushy eyebrows twitched convulsively, in an odd, irritating way they had when he was puzzled. Then some huge beads of perspiration broke out on his yellow forehead, like a poisonous dew, and his fat fingers grew cold and clammy.

Lord Arthur did not fail to notice these strange signs of agitation, and, for the first time in his life, he himself felt fear. His impulse was to rush from the room, but he restrained himself. It was better to know the worst, whatever it was, than to be left in this hideous uncertainty.

'I am waiting, Mr Podgers,' he said.

'We are all waiting,' cried Lady Windermere, in her quick, impatient manner, but the cheiromantist made no reply.

'I believe Arthur is going on the stage,' said Lady Jedburgh, 'and that, after your scolding, Mr Podgers is afraid to tell him so.'

Suddenly Mr Podgers dropped Lord Arthur's right hand, and seized hold of his left, bending down so low to examine it that the gold rims of his spectacles seemed almost to touch the palm. For a moment his face became a white mask of horror, but he soon recovered his *sang-froid*, and looking up at Lady Windermere, said with a forced smile, 'It is the hand of a charming young man.'

'Of course it is!' answered Lady Windermere, 'but will he be a charming husband? That is what I want to know.'

'All charming young men are,' said Mr Podgers.

'I don't think a husband should be too fascinating,' murmured Lady Jedburgh pensively, 'it is so dangerous.'

'My dear child, they never are too fascinating,' cried Lady Windermere. 'But what I want are details. Details are the only things that interest. What is going to happen to Lord Arthur?'

'Well, within the next few months Lord Arthur will go a voyage——'

'Oh yes, his honeymoon, of course!'

'And lose a relative.'

'Not his sister, I hope?' said Lady Jedburgh, in a piteous tone of voice.

'Certainly not his sister,' answered Mr Podgers, with a deprecating wave of the hand, 'a distant relative merely.'

'Well, I am dreadfully disappointed,' said Lady Windermere. 'I have absolutely nothing to tell Sybil to-morrow. No one cares about distant relatives nowadays. They went out of fashion years ago. However, I suppose she had better have a black silk by her; it always does for church, you know. And now let us go to supper. They are sure to have eaten everything up, but we may find some hot soup. François used to make excellent soup once, but he is so agitated about politics at present, that I never feel quite certain about him. I do wish General Boulanger* would keep quiet. Duchess, I am sure you are tired?'

'Not at all, dear Gladys,' answered the Duchess, waddling towards the door. 'I have enjoyed myself immensely, and the cheiropodist, I mean the cheiromantist, is most interesting. Flora, where can my tortoiseshell fan be? Oh, thank you, Sir Thomas, so much. And my lace shawl, Flora? Oh, thank you, Sir Thomas, very kind, I'm sure;' and the worthy creature finally managed to get downstairs without dropping her scent-bottle more than twice.

All this time Lord Arthur Savile had remained standing by the fireplace, with the same feeling of dread over him, the same sickening sense of coming evil. He smiled sadly at his sister, as she swept past him on Lord Plymdale's arm, looking lovely in her pink brocade and pearls, and he hardly heard Lady Windermere when she called to him to follow her. He thought of Sybil Merton, and the idea that anything could come between them made his eyes dim with tears.

Looking at him, one would have said that Nemesis had stolen the shield of Pallas, and shown him the Gorgon's head.* He seemed turned to stone, and his face was like marble in its melancholy. He had lived the delicate and luxurious life of a young man of birth and fortune, a life exquisite in its freedom from sordid care, its beautiful boyish insouciance; and now for the first time he became conscious of the terrible mystery of Destiny, of the awful meaning of Doom.

How mad and monstrous it all seemed! Could it be that written on his hand, in characters that he could not read himself, but that another could decipher, was some fearful secret of sin, some blood-red sign of crime? Was there no escape possible? Were we no better than chessmen, moved by an unseen power, vessels the potter fashions at his fancy, for honour or for shame? His reason revolted against it, and yet he felt that some tragedy was hanging over him, and that he had been suddenly called upon to bear an intolerable burden. Actors are so fortunate. They can choose whether they will appear in tragedy or in comedy, whether they will suffer or make merry, laugh or shed tears. But in real life it is different. Most men and women are forced to perform parts for which they have no qualifications. Our Guildensterns play Hamlet for us, and our Hamlets have to jest like Prince Hal. The world is a stage, but the play is badly cast.

Suddenly Mr Podgers entered the room. When he saw Lord Arthur he started, and his coarse, fat face became a sort of greenish-yellow colour. The two men's eyes met, and for a moment there was silence.

'The Duchess has left one of her gloves here, Lord Arthur, and has asked me to bring it to her,' said Mr Podgers finally. 'Ah, I see it on the sofa! Good evening.'

'Mr Podgers, I must insist on your giving me a straightforward answer to a question I am going to put to you.'

'Another time, Lord Arthur, but the Duchess is anxious. I am afraid I must go.'

'You shall not go. The Duchess is in no hurry.'

'Ladies should not be kept waiting, Lord Arthur,' said Mr Podgers, with his sickly smile. 'The fair sex is apt to be impatient.'

Lord Arthur's finely-chiselled lips curled in petulant disdain. The poor Duchess seemed to him of very little importance at that moment. He walked across the room to where Mr Podgers was standing, and held his hand out.

'Tell me what you saw there,' he said. 'Tell me the truth. I must know it. I am not a child.'

Mr Podgers's eyes blinked behind his gold-rimmed spectacles, and he moved uneasily from one foot to the other, while his fingers played nervously with a flash watch-chain.

'What makes you think that I saw anything in your hand, Lord Arthur, more than I told you?'

'I know you did, and I insist on your telling me what it was. I will pay you. I will give you a cheque for a hundred pounds.'

The green eyes flashed for a moment, and then became dull again.

'Guineas?' said Mr Podgers at last, in a low voice.

'Certainly. I will send you a cheque tomorrow. What is your club?'

'I have no club. That is to say, not just at present. My address is—, but allow me to give you my card;' and producing a bit of gilt-edged pasteboard from his waistcoat pocket, Mr Podgers handed it, with a low bow, to Lord Arthur, who read on it,

---

MR SEPTIMUS R. PODGERS

Professional Cheiromantist

103*a* WEST MOON STREET

'My hours are from ten to four,' murmured Mr Podgers mechanically, 'and I make a reduction for families.'

'Be quick,' cried Lord Arthur, looking very pale, and holding his hand out.

Mr Podgers glanced nervously round, and drew the heavy *portière** across the door.

'It will take a little time, Lord Arthur, you had better sit down.'

'Be quick, sir,' cried Lord Arthur again, stamping his foot angrily on the polished floor.

Mr Podgers smiled, drew from his breast-pocket a small magnifying glass, and wiped it carefully with his handkerchief.

'I am quite ready,' he said.

II

TEN minutes later, with face blanched by terror, and eyes wild with grief, Lord Arthur Savile rushed from Bentinck House, crushing his way through the crowd of fur-coated footmen that stood round the large striped awning, and seeming not to see or hear anything. The night was bitter cold, and the gas-lamps round the square flared and flickered in the keen wind; but his hands were hot with fever, and his forehead burned like fire. On and on he went, almost with the gait of a drunken man. A policeman looked curiously at him as he passed, and a beggar, who slouched from an archway to ask for alms, grew frightened, seeing misery greater than his own. Once he stopped under a lamp, and looked at his hands. He thought he could detect the stain of blood already upon them, and a faint cry broke from his trembling lips.

Murder! that is what the cheiromantist had seen there. Murder! The very night seemed to know it, and the desolate wind to howl it in his ear. The dark corners of the streets were full of it. It grinned at him from the roofs of the houses.

First he came to the Park, whose sombre woodland seemed to fascinate him. He leaned wearily up against the railings, cooling his brow against the wet metal, and listening to the tremulous silence of the trees. 'Murder! murder!' he kept repeating, as though iteration could dim the horror of the word. The sound of his own voice made him shudder, yet he almost hoped that Echo might hear him, and wake the slumbering city from its dreams. He felt a mad desire to stop the casual passer-by, and tell him everything.

Then he wandered across Oxford Street into narrow, shameful alleys.* Two women with painted faces mocked at him as he went by. From a dark courtyard came a sound of oaths and blows, followed by shrill screams, and, huddled upon a damp doorstep, he saw the crook-backed forms of poverty and eld. A strange pity came over him. Were these children of sin and misery predestined to their end, as he to his? Were they, like him, merely the puppets of a monstrous show?

And yet it was not the mystery, but the comedy of suffering that struck him; its absolute uselessness, its grotesque want of meaning. How incoherent everything seemed! How lacking in all harmony! He was amazed at the discord between the shallow optimism of the day, and the real facts of existence. He was still very young.

After a time he found himself in front of Marylebone Church. The silent roadway looked like a long riband of polished silver, flecked here and there by the dark arabesques of waving shadows. Far into the distance curved the line of flickering gas-lamps, and outside a little walled-in house stood a solitary hansom, the driver asleep inside. He walked hastily in the direction of Portland Place, now and then looking round, as though he feared that he was being followed. At the corner of Rich Street stood two men, reading a small bill upon a hoarding. An odd feeling of curiosity stirred him, and he crossed over. As he came near, the word 'Murder,' printed in black letters, met his eye. He started, and a deep flush came into his cheek. It was an advertisement offering a reward for any information leading to the arrest of a man of medium height, between thirty and forty years of age, wearing a billy-cock hat, a black coat, and check trousers, and with a scar upon his right cheek. He read it over and over again, and wondered if the wretched man would be caught, and how he had been scarred. Perhaps, some day, his own name might be placarded on the walls of London. Some day, perhaps, a price would be set on his head also.

The thought made him sick with horror. He turned on his heel, and hurried on into the night.

Where he went he hardly knew. He had a dim memory of wandering through a labyrinth of sordid houses, of being lost in a giant web of sombre streets, and it was bright dawn when he found himself at last in Piccadilly Circus. As he strolled home towards Belgrave Square, he met the great waggons on their way to Covent Garden. The white-smocked carters, with their pleasant sunburnt faces and coarse curly hair, strode sturdily on, cracking their whips, and calling out now and then to each other; on the back of a huge grey horse, the leader of a jangling team, sat a chubby boy, with a bunch of primroses in his battered hat, keeping tight hold of the mane with his little hands, and laughing; and the great piles of vegetables looked like masses of jade against the morning sky, like masses of green jade against the pink petals of some marvellous rose. Lord Arthur felt curiously affected, he could not tell why. There was something in the dawn's delicate loveliness that seemed to him inexpressibly pathetic, and he thought of all the days that break in beauty, and that set in storm. These rustics, too, with their rough, good-humoured voices, and their nonchalant ways, what a strange London they saw! A

London free from the sin of night and the smoke of day, a pallid, ghost-like city, a desolate town of tombs! He wondered what they thought of it, and whether they knew anything of its splendour and its shame, of its fierce, fiery-coloured joys, and its horrible hunger, of all it makes and mars from morn to eve. Probably it was to them merely a mart where they brought their fruits to sell, and where they tarried for a few hours at most, leaving the streets still silent, the houses still asleep. It gave him pleasure to watch them as they went by. Rude as they were, with their heavy, hobnailed shoes, and their awkward gait, they brought a little of Arcady with them. He felt that they had lived with Nature, and that she had taught them peace. He envied them all that they did not know.

By the time he had reached Belgrave Square the sky was a faint blue, and the birds were beginning to twitter in the gardens.

III

WHEN Lord Arthur woke it was twelve o'clock, and the mid-day sun was streaming through the ivory-silk curtains of his room. He got up and looked out of the window. A dim haze of heat was hanging over the great city, and the roofs of the houses were like dull silver. In the flickering green of the square below some children were flitting about like white butterflies, and the pavement was crowded with people on their way to the Park. Never had life seemed lovelier to him, never had the things of evil seemed more remote.

Then his valet brought him a cup of chocolate on a tray. After he had drunk it, he drew aside a heavy *portière* of peach-coloured plush, and passed into the bathroom. The light stole softly from above, through thin slabs of transparent onyx, and the water in the marble tank glimmered like a moonstone. He plunged hastily in, till the cool ripples touched throat and hair, and then dipped his head right under, as though he would have wiped away the stain of some shameful memory. When he stepped out he felt almost at peace. The exquisite physical conditions of the moment had dominated him, as indeed often happens in the case of very finely-wrought natures, for the senses, like fire, can purify as well as destroy.

After breakfast, he flung himself down on a divan, and lit a cigarette. On the mantelshelf, framed in dainty old brocade, stood a large photograph of Sybil Merton, as he had seen her first at Lady Noel's ball. The small, exquisitely-shaped head drooped slightly to one side, as though the thin, reed-like throat could hardly bear the burden of so much beauty; the lips were slightly parted, and seemed made for sweet music; and all the tender purity of girlhood looked out in wonder from the dreaming eyes. With her soft, clinging dress of *crêpe-de-chine*, and her large leaf-shaped fan, she looked like one of those delicate little figures men find in the olive-woods near Tanagra;* and there was a touch of Greek grace in her pose and attitude. Yet she was not *petite*. She was simply perfectly proportioned—a rare thing in an age when so many women are either over life-size or insignificant.

Now as Lord Arthur looked at her, he was filled with the terrible pity that is born of love. He felt that to marry her, with the doom of murder hanging over his head, would be a betrayal like that of Judas, a sin worse than any the Borgia had ever dreamed of. What happiness could there be for them, when at any moment he might be called upon to carry out the awful prophecy written in his hand? What manner of life would be theirs while Fate still held this fearful fortune in the scales? The marriage must be postponed, at all costs. Of this he was quite resolved. Ardently though he loved the girl, and the mere touch of her fingers, when they sat together, made each nerve of his body thrill with exquisite joy, he recognised none the less clearly where his duty lay, and was fully conscious of the fact that he had no right to marry until he had committed the murder. This done, he could stand before the altar with Sybil Merton, and give his life into her hands without terror of wrongdoing. This done, he could take her to his arms, knowing that she would never have to blush for him, never have to hang her head in shame. But done it must be first; and the sooner the better for both.

Many men in his position would have preferred the primrose path of dalliance to the steep heights of duty; but Lord Arthur was too conscientious to set pleasure above principle. There was more than mere passion in his love; and Sybil was to him a symbol of all that is good and noble. For a moment he had a natural repugnance against what he was asked to do, but it soon passed away. His heart told him that it was not a sin, but a sacrifice; his reason reminded him that there was no other course open. He had to choose between living for himself and living for others, and terrible though the task laid upon him undoubtedly was, yet he knew that he must not suffer selfishness to triumph over love. Sooner or later we are all called upon to decide on the same issue—of us all, the same question is asked. To Lord Arthur it came early in life—before his nature had been spoiled by the calculating cynicism of middle-age, or his heart corroded by the shallow, fashionable egotism of our day, and he felt no hesitation about doing his duty. Fortunately also, for him, he was no mere dreamer, or idle dilettante. Had he been so, he would have hesitated, like Hamlet, and let irresolution mar his purpose. But he was essentially practical. Life to him meant action, rather than thought. He had that rarest of all things, common sense.

The wild, turbid feelings of the previous night had by this time completely passed away, and it was almost with a sense of shame that he looked back upon his mad wanderings from street to street, his fierce emotional agony. The very sincerity of his sufferings made them seem unreal to him now. He wondered how he could have been so foolish as to rant and rave about the inevitable. The only question that seemed to trouble him was, whom to make away with; for he was not blind to the fact that murder, like the religions of the Pagan world, requires a victim as well as a priest. Not being a genius, he had no enemies, and indeed he felt that this was not the time for the gratification of any personal pique or dislike, the mission in which he was engaged being one of great and grave solemnity. He accordingly made out a list of his friends and relatives on a sheet of notepaper, and after careful consideration, decided in favour of Lady Clementina Beauchamp, a dear old lady who lived in Curzon Street, and was his own second cousin by his mother's side. He had always been very fond of Lady Clem, as every one called her, and as he was very wealthy himself, having come into all Lord Rugby's property when he came of age, there was no possibility of his deriving any vulgar monetary advantage by her death. In fact, the more he thought over the matter, the more she seemed to him to be just the right person, and, feeling that any delay would be unfair to Sybil, he determined to make his arrangements at once.

The first thing to be done was, of course, to settle with the cheiromantist; so he sat down at a small Sheraton writing-table that stood near the window, drew a cheque for £105, payable to the order of Mr Septimus Podgers, and, enclosing it in an envelope, told his valet to take it to West Moon Street. He then telephoned to the stables for his hansom, and dressed to go out. As he was leaving the room, he looked back at Sybil Merton's photograph, and swore that, come what may, he would never let her know what he was doing for her sake, but would keep the secret of his self-sacrifice hidden always in his heart.

On his way to the Buckingham, he stopped at a florist's, and sent Sybil a beautiful basket of narcissi, with lovely white petals and staring pheasants' eyes, and on arriving at the club, went straight to the library, rang the bell, and ordered the waiter to bring him a lemon-and-soda, and a book on Toxicology. He had fully decided that poison was the best means to adopt in this troublesome business. Anything like personal violence was extremely distasteful to him, and besides, he was very anxious not to murder Lady Clementina in any way that might attract public attention, as he hated the idea of being lionised at Lady Windermere's, or seeing his name figuring in the paragraphs of vulgar society-newspapers. He had also to think of Sybil's father and mother, who were rather old-fashioned people, and might possibly object to the marriage if there was anything like a scandal, though he felt certain that if he told them the whole facts of the case they would be the very first to appreciate the motives that had actuated him. He had every reason, then, to decide in favour of poison.* It was safe, sure, and quiet, and did away with any necessity for painful scenes, to which, like most Englishmen, he had a rooted objection.

Of the science of poisons, however, he knew absolutely nothing, and as the waiter seemed quite unable to find anything in the library but Ruff's *Guide* and Bailey's *Magazine*,* he examined the book-shelves himself, and finally came across a handsomely-bound edition of the *Pharmacopœia*, and a copy of Erskine's *Toxicology*, edited by Sir Mathew Reid, the President of the Royal College of Physicians, and one of the oldest members of the Buckingham, having been elected in mistake for somebody else; a *contretemps* that so enraged the Committee, that when the real man came up they black-balled him unanimously. Lord Arthur was a good deal puzzled at the technical terms used in both books, and had begun to regret that he had not paid more attention to his classics at Oxford, when in the second volume of Erskine, he found a very interesting and complete account of the properties of aconitine, written in fairly clear English. It seemed to him to be exactly the poison he wanted. It was swift—

indeed, almost immediate, in its effect—perfectly painless, and when taken in the form of a gelatine capsule, the mode recommended by Sir Mathew, not by any means unpalatable. He accordingly made a note, upon his shirt-cuff, of the amount necessary for a fatal dose, put the books back in their places, and strolled up St James's Street, to Pestle and Humbey's, the great chemists. Mr Pestle, who always attended personally on the aristocracy, was a good deal surprised at the order, and in a very deferential manner murmured something about a medical certificate being necessary. However, as soon as Lord Arthur explained to him that it was for a large Norwegian mastiff that he was obliged to get rid of, as it showed signs of incipient rabies, and had already bitten the coachman twice in the calf of the leg, he expressed himself as being perfectly satisfied, complimented Lord Arthur on his wonderful knowledge of Toxicology, and had the prescription made up immediately.

Lord Arthur put the capsule into a pretty little silver *bonbonnière* that he saw in a shop-window in Bond Street, threw away Pestle and Humbey's ugly pill-box, and drove off at once to Lady Clementina's.

'Well, *monsieur le mauvais sujet,**' cried the old lady, as he entered the room, 'why haven't you been to see me all this time?'

'My dear Lady Clem, I never have a moment to myself,' said Lord Arthur, smiling.

'I suppose you mean that you go about all day long with Miss Sybil Merton, buying *chiffons* and talking nonsense? I cannot understand why people make such a fuss about being married. In my day we never dreamed of billing and cooing in public, or in private for that matter.'

'I assure you I have not seen Sybil for twenty-four hours, Lady Clem. As far as I can make out, she belongs entirely to her milliners.'

'Of course; that is the only reason you come to see an ugly old woman like myself. I wonder you men don't take warning. *On a fait des folies pour moi,** and here I am, a poor, rheumatic creature, with a false front and a bad temper. Why, if it were not for dear Lady Jansen, who sends me all the worst French novels she can find, I don't think I could get through the day. Doctors are no use at all, except to get fees out of one. They can't even cure my heartburn.'

'I have brought you a cure for that, Lady Clem,' said Lord Arthur gravely. 'It is a wonderful thing, invented by an American.'

'I don't think I like American inventions, Arthur. I am quite sure I don't. I read some American novels lately, and they were quite nonsensical.'

'Oh, but there is no nonsense at all about this, Lady Clem! I assure you it is a perfect cure. You must promise to try it;' and Lord Arthur brought the little box out of his pocket, and handed it to her.

'Well, the box is charming, Arthur. Is it really a present? That is very sweet of you. And is this the wonderful medicine? It looks like a *bonbon*. I'll take it at once.'

'Good heavens! Lady Clem,' cried Lord Arthur, catching hold of her hand, 'you mustn't do anything of the kind. It is a homœopathic medicine, and if you take it without having heartburn, it might do you no end of harm. Wait till you have an attack, and take it then. You will be astonished at the result.'

'I should like to take it now,' said Lady Clementina, holding up to the light the little transparent capsule, with its floating bubble of liquid aconitine. 'I am sure it is delicious. The fact is that, though I hate doctors, I love medicines. However, I'll keep it till my next attack.'

'And when will that be?' asked Lord Arthur eagerly. 'Will it be soon?'

'I hope not for a week. I had a very bad time yesterday morning with it. But one never knows.'

'You are sure to have one before the end of the month then, Lady Clem?'

'I am afraid so. But how sympathetic you are to-day, Arthur! Really, Sybil has done you a great deal of good. And now you must run away, for I am dining with some very dull people, who won't talk scandal, and I know that if I don't get my sleep now I shall never be able to keep awake during dinner. Good-bye, Arthur, give my love to Sybil, and thank you so much for the American medicine.'

'You won't forget to take it, Lady Clem, will you?' said Lord Arthur, rising from his seat.

'Of course I won't, you silly boy. I think it is most kind of you to think of me, and I shall write and tell you if I want any more.'

Lord Arthur left the house in high spirits, and with a feeling of immense relief.

That night he had an interview with Sybil Merton. He told her how he had been suddenly placed in a position of terrible difficulty, from which neither honour nor duty would allow him to recede. He told her that the marriage must be put off for the present, as until he had got rid of his fearful entanglements, he was not a free man. He implored her to trust him, and not to have any doubts about the future. Everything would come right, but patience was necessary.

The scene took place in the conservatory of Mr Merton's house, in Park Lane, where Lord Arthur had dined as usual. Sybil had never seemed more happy, and for a moment Lord Arthur had been tempted to play the coward's part, to write to Lady Clementina for the pill, and to let the marriage go on as if there was no such person as Mr Podgers in the world. His better nature, however, soon asserted itself, and even when Sybil flung herself weeping into his arms, he did not falter. The beauty that stirred his senses had touched his conscience also. He felt that to wreck so fair a life for the sake of a few months' pleasure would be a wrong thing to do.

He stayed with Sybil till nearly midnight, comforting her and being comforted in turn, and early the next morning he left for Venice, after writing a manly, firm letter to Mr Merton about the necessary postponement of the marriage.

IV

In Venice he met his brother, Lord Surbiton, who happened to have come over from Corfu in his yacht. The two young men spent a delightful fortnight together. In the morning they rode on the Lido, or glided up and down the green canals in their long black gondola; in the afternoon they usually entertained visitors on the yacht; and in the evening they dined at Florian's, and smoked innumerable cigarettes on the Piazza. Yet somehow Lord Arthur was not happy. Every day he studied the obituary column in the *Times*, expecting to see a notice of Lady Clementina's death, but, every day he was disappointed. He began to be afraid that some accident had happened to her, and often regretted that he had prevented her taking the aconitine when she had been so anxious to try its effect. Sybil's letters, too, though full of love, and trust, and tenderness, were often very sad in their tone, and sometimes he used to think that he was parted from her for ever.

After a fortnight Lord Surbiton got bored with Venice, and determined to run down the coast to Ravenna, as he heard that there was some capital cock-shooting in the Pinetum. Lord Arthur, at first, refused absolutely to come, but Surbiton, of whom he was extremely fond, finally persuaded him that if he stayed at Danielli's by himself he would be moped to death, and on the morning of the 15th they started, with a strong nor'-east wind blowing, and a rather sloppy sea. The sport was excellent, and the free, open-air life brought the colour back to Lord Arthur's cheeks, but about the 22nd he became anxious about Lady Clementina, and, in spite of Surbiton's remonstrances, came back to Venice by train.

As he stepped out of his gondola on to the hotel steps, the proprietor came forward to meet him with a sheaf of telegrams. Lord Arthur snatched them out of his hand, and tore them open. Everything had been successful. Lady Clementina had died quite suddenly on the night of the 17th!

His first thought was for Sybil, and he sent her off a telegram announcing his immediate return to London. He then ordered his valet to pack his things for the night mail, sent his gondoliers about five times their proper fare, and ran up to his sitting-room with a light step and a buoyant heart. There he found three letters waiting for him. One was from Sybil herself, full of sympathy and condolence. The others were from his mother, and from Lady Clementina's solicitor. It seemed that the old lady had dined with the Duchess that very night, had delighted every one by her wit and *esprit*, but had gone home somewhat early, complaining of heartburn. In the morning she was found dead in her bed, having apparently suffered no pain. Sir Mathew Reid had been sent for at once, but, of course, there was nothing to be done, and she was to be buried on the 22nd at Beauchamp Chalcote. A few days before she died she had made her will, and left Lord Arthur her little house in Curzon Street, and all her furniture, personal effects, and pictures, with the exception of her collection of miniatures, which was to go to her sister, Lady Margaret Rufford, and her amethyst necklace, which Sybil Merton was to have. The property was not of much value; but Mr Mansfield the solicitor was extremely anxious for Lord Arthur to return at once, if possible, as there were a great many bills to be paid, and Lady Clementina had never kept any regular accounts.

Lord Arthur was very much touched by Lady Clementina's kind remembrance of him, and felt that Mr Podgers had a great deal to answer for. His love of Sybil, however, dominated every other emotion, and the consciousness that he had done his duty gave him peace and comfort. When he arrived at Charing Cross, he felt perfectly happy.

The Mertons received him very kindly, Sybil made him promise that he would never again allow anything to come between them, and the marriage was fixed for the 7th June. Life seemed to him once more bright and beautiful, and all his old gladness came back to him again.

One day, however, as he was going over the house in Curzon Street, in company with Lady Clementina's solicitor and Sybil herself, burning packages of faded letters, and turning out drawers of odd rubbish, the young girl suddenly gave a little cry of delight.

'What have you found, Sybil?' said Lord Arthur, looking up from his work, and smiling.

'This lovely little silver *bonbonnière*, Arthur. Isn't it quaint and Dutch? Do give it to me! I know amethysts won't become me till I am over eighty.'

It was the box that had held the aconitine.

Lord Arthur started, and a faint blush came into his cheek. He had almost entirely forgotten what he had done, and it seemed to him a curious coincidence that Sybil, for whose sake he had gone through all that terrible anxiety, should have been the first to remind him of it.

'Of course you can have it, Sybil. I gave it to poor Lady Clem myself.'

'Oh! thank you, Arthur; and may I have the *bonbon* too? I had no notion that Lady Clementina liked sweets. I thought she was far too intellectual.'

Lord Arthur grew deadly pale, and a horrible idea crossed his mind.

'*Bonbon*, Sybil? What do you mean?' he said, in a slow, hoarse voice.

'There is one in it, that is all. It looks quite old and dusty, and I have not the slightest intention of eating it. What is the matter, Arthur? How white you look!'

Lord Arthur rushed across the room, and seized the box. Inside it was the amber-coloured capsule, with its poison-bubble. Lady Clementina had died a natural death after all!

The shock of the discovery was almost too much for him. He flung the capsule into the fire, and sank on the sofa with a cry of despair.

V

MR MERTON was a good deal distressed at the second postponement of the marriage, and Lady Julia, who had already ordered her dress for the wedding, did all in her power to make Sybil break off the match. Dearly, however, as Sybil loved her mother, she had given her whole life into Lord Arthur's hands, and nothing that Lady Julia could say could make her waver in her faith. As for Lord Arthur himself, it took him days to get over his terrible disappointment, and for a time his nerves were completely unstrung. His excellent common sense, however, soon asserted itself, and his sound, practical mind did not leave him long in doubt about what to do. Poison having proved a complete failure, dynamite, or some other form of explosive, was obviously the proper thing to try.

He accordingly looked again over the list of his friends and relatives, and, after careful consideration, determined to blow up his uncle, the Dean of Chichester. The Dean, who was a man of great culture and learning, was extremely fond of clocks, and had a wonderful collection of timepieces, ranging from the fifteenth century to the present day, and it seemed to Lord Arthur that this hobby of the good Dean's offered him an excellent opportunity for carrying out his scheme. Where to procure an explosive machine was, of course, quite another matter. The London Directory gave him no information on the point, and he felt that there was very little use in going to Scotland Yard about it, as they never seemed to know anything about the movements of the dynamite faction* till after an explosion had taken place, and not much even then.

Suddenly he thought of his friend Rouvaloff, a young Russian of very revolutionary tendencies, whom he had met at Lady Windermere's in the winter. Count Rouvaloff was supposed to be writing a life of Peter the Great, and to have come over to England for the purpose of studying the documents relating to that Tsar's residence in this country as a ship carpenter; but it was generally suspected that he was a Nihilist agent, and there was no doubt that the Russian Embassy did not look with any favour upon his presence in London. Lord Arthur felt that he was just the man for his purpose, and drove down one morning to his lodgings in Bloomsbury, to ask his advice and assistance.

'So you are taking up politics seriously?' said Count Rouvaloff, when Lord Arthur had told him the object of his mission; but Lord Arthur, who hated swagger of any kind, felt bound to admit to him that he had not the slightest interest in social questions, and simply wanted the explosive machine for a purely family matter, in which no one was concerned but himself.

Count Rouvaloff looked at him for some moments in amazement, and then seeing that he was quite serious, wrote an address on a piece of paper, initialled it, and handed it to him across the table.

'Scotland Yard would give a good deal to know this address, my dear fellow.'

'They shan't have it,' cried Lord Arthur, laughing; and after shaking the young Russian warmly by the hand he ran downstairs, examined the paper, and told the coachman to drive to Soho Square.

There he dismissed him, and strolled down Greek Street, till he came to a place called Bayle's Court. He passed under the archway, and found himself in a curious *cul-de-sac*, that was apparently occupied by a French Laundry, as a perfect network of clothes-lines was stretched across from house to house, and there was a flutter of white linen in the morning air. He walked right to the end, and knocked at a little green house. After some delay, during which every window in the court became a blurred mass of peering faces, the door was opened by a rather rough-looking foreigner, who asked him in very bad English what his business was. Lord Arthur handed him the paper Count Rouvaloff had given him. When the man saw it he bowed, and invited Lord Arthur into a very shabby front parlour on the ground-floor, and in a few moments Herr Winckelkopf, as he was called in England, bustled into the room, with a very wine-stained napkin round his neck, and a fork in his left hand.

'Count Rouvaloff has given me an introduction to you,' said Lord Arthur, bowing, 'and I am anxious to have a short interview with you on a matter of business. My name is Smith, Mr Robert Smith, and I want you to supply me with an explosive clock.'

'Charmed to meet you, Lord Arthur,' said the genial little German laughing. 'Don't look so alarmed, it is my duty to know everybody, and I remember seeing you one evening at Lady Windermere's. I hope her ladyship is quite well. Do you mind sitting with me while I finish my breakfast? There is an excellent *pâté*, and my friends are kind enough to say that my Rhine wine is better than any they get at the German Embassy,' and before Lord Arthur had got over his surprise at being recognised, he found himself seated in the back-room, sipping the most delicious Marcobrünner out of a pale yellow hock-glass marked with the Imperial monogram, and chatting in the friendliest manner possible to the famous conspirator.

'Explosive clocks,' said Herr Winckelkopf, 'are not very good things for foreign exportation, as, even if they succeed in passing the Custom House, the train service is so irregular, that they usually go off before they have reached their proper destination. If, however, you want one for home use, I can supply you with an excellent article, and guarantee that you will be satisfied with the result. May I ask for whom it is intended? If it is for the police, or for any one connected with Scotland Yard, I am afraid I cannot do anything for you. The English detectives are really our best friends, and I have always found that by relying on their stupidity, we can do exactly what we like. I could not spare one of them.'

'I assure you,' said Lord Arthur, 'that it has nothing to do with the police at all. In fact, the clock is intended for the Dean of Chichester.'

'Dear me! I had no idea that you felt so strongly about religion, Lord Arthur. Few young men do nowadays.'

'I am afraid you overrate me, Herr Winckelkopf,' said Lord Arthur, blushing. 'The fact is, I really know nothing about theology.'

'It is a purely private matter then?'

'Purely private.'

Herr Winckelkopf shrugged his shoulders, and left the room, returning in a few minutes with a round cake of dynamite about the size of a penny, and a pretty little French clock, surmounted by an ormolu figure of Liberty trampling on the hydra of Despotism.

Lord Arthur's face brightened up when he saw it. 'That is just what I want,' he cried, 'and now tell me how it goes off.'

'Ah! there is my secret,' answered Herr Winckelkopf, contemplating his invention with a justifiable look of pride; 'let me know when you wish it to explode, and I will set the machine to the moment.'

'Well, to-day is Tuesday, and if you could send it off at once——'

'That is impossible; I have a great deal of important work on hand for some friends of mine in Moscow. Still, I might send it off to-morrow.'

'Oh, it will be quite time enough!' said Lord Arthur politely, 'if it is delivered to-morrow night or Thursday morning. For the moment of the explosion, say Friday at noon exactly. The Dean is always at home at that hour.'

'Friday, at noon,' repeated Herr Winckelkopf, and he made a note to that effect in a large ledger that was lying on a bureau near the fireplace.

'And now,' said Lord Arthur, rising from his seat, 'pray let me know how much I am in your debt.'

'It is such a small matter, Lord Arthur, that I do not care to make any charge. The dynamite comes to seven and sixpence, the clock will be three pounds ten, and the carriage about five shillings. I am only too pleased to oblige any friend of Count Rouvaloff's.'

'But your trouble, Herr Winckelkopf?'

'Oh, that is nothing! It is a pleasure to me. I do not work for money; I live entirely for my art.'

Lord Arthur laid down £4. 2s. 6d. on the table, thanked the little German for his kindness, and, having succeeded in declining an invitation to meet some Anarchists at a meat-tea on the following Saturday, left the house and went off to the Park.

For the next two days he was in a state of the greatest excitement, and on Friday at twelve o'clock he drove down to the Buckingham to wait for news. All the afternoon the stolid hall-porter kept posting up telegrams from various parts of the country giving the results of horse-races, the verdicts in divorce suits, the state of the weather, and the like, while the tape ticked out wearisome details about an all-night sitting in the House of Commons, and a small panic on the Stock Exchange. At four o'clock the evening papers came in, and Lord Arthur disappeared into the library with the *Pall Mall*, the *St James's*, the *Globe*, and the *Echo*, to the immense indignation of Colonel Goodchild, who wanted to read the reports of a speech he had delivered that morning at the Mansion House, on the subject of South African Missions, and the advisability of having black Bishops in every province, and for some reason or other had a strong prejudice against the *Evening News*. None of the papers, however, contained even the slightest allusion to Chichester, and Lord Arthur felt that the attempt must have failed. It was a terrible blow to him, and for a time he was quite unnerved. Herr Winckelkopf, whom he went to see the next day, was full of elaborate apologies, and offered to supply him with another clock free of charge, or with a case of nitro-glycerine bombs at cost price. But he had lost all faith in explosives, and Herr Winckelkopf himself acknowledged that everything is so adulterated nowadays, that even dynamite can hardly be got in a pure condition.

The little German, however, while admitting that something must have gone wrong with the machinery, was not without hope that the clock might still go off, and instanced the case of a barometer that he had once sent to the military Governor at Odessa, which, though timed to explode in ten days, had not done so for something like three months. It was quite true that when it did go off, it merely succeeded in blowing a housemaid to atoms, the Governor having gone out of town six weeks before, but at least it showed that dynamite, as a destructive force, was, when under the control of machinery, a powerful, though a somewhat unpunctual agent. Lord Arthur was a little consoled by this reflection, but even here he was destined to disappointment, for two days afterwards, as he was going upstairs, the Duchess called him into her boudoir, and showed him a letter she had just received from the Deanery.

'Jane writes charming letters,' said the Duchess; 'you must really read her last. It is quite as good as the novels Mudie sends us.'

Lord Arthur seized the letter from her hand. It ran as follows:—

'THE DEANERY, CHICHESTER, 27th *May*

'My Dearest Aunt,

'Thank you so much for the flannel for the Dorcas Society,* and also for the gingham. I quite agree with you that it is nonsense their wanting to wear pretty things, but everybody is so Radical and irreligious nowadays, that it is difficult to make them see that they should not try and dress like the upper classes. I am sure I don't know what we are coming to. As papa has often said in his sermons, we live in an age of unbelief.

'We have had great fun over a clock that an unknown admirer sent papa last Thursday. It arrived in a wooden box from London, carriage paid; and papa feels it must have been sent by some one who had read his remarkable sermon, "Is License Liberty?" for on the top of the clock was a figure of a woman, with what papa said was the cap of Liberty on her head. I didn't think it very becoming myself, but papa said it was historical, so I suppose it is all right. Parker unpacked it, and papa put it on the mantelpiece in the library, and we were all sitting there on Friday morning, when just as the clock struck twelve, we heard a whirring noise, a little puff of smoke came from the pedestal of the figure, and the goddess of Liberty fell off, and broke her nose on the fender! Maria was quite alarmed, but it looked so ridiculous, that James and I went off into fits of laughter, and even papa was amused. When we examined it, we found it was a sort of alarum clock, and that, if you set it to a particular hour, and put some gunpowder and a cap under a little hammer, it went off whenever you wanted. Papa said it must not remain in the library, as it made a noise, so Reggie carried it away to the schoolroom, and does nothing but have small explosions all day long. Do you think Arthur would like one for a wedding present? I suppose they are quite fashionable in London. Papa says they should do a great deal of good, as they show that Liberty can't last, but must fall down. Papa says Liberty was invented at the time of the French Revolution. How awful it seems!

'I have now to go to the Dorcas, where I will read them your most instructive letter. How true, dear aunt, your idea is, that in their rank of life they should wear what is unbecoming. I must say it is absurd, their anxiety about dress, when there are so many more important things in this world, and in the next. I am so glad your flowered poplin turned out so well, and that your lace was not torn. I am wearing my yellow satin, that you so kindly gave me, at the Bishop's on Wednesday, and think it will look all right. Would you have bows or not? Jennings says that every one wears bows now, and that the underskirt should be frilled. Reggie has just had another explosion, and papa has ordered the clock to be sent to the stables. I don't think papa likes it so much as he did at first, though he is very flattered at being sent such a pretty and ingenious toy. It shows that people read his sermons, and profit by them.

'Papa sends his love, in which James, and Reggie, and Maria all unite, and, hoping that Uncle Cecil's gout is better, believe me, dear aunt, ever your affectionate niece,

JANE PERCY.

'*P.S.*—Do tell me about the bows. Jennings insists they are the fashion.'

Lord Arthur looked so serious and unhappy over the letter, that the Duchess went into fits of laughter.

'My dear Arthur,' she cried, 'I shall never show you a young lady's letter again! But what shall I say about the clock? I think it is a capital invention, and I should like to have one myself.'

'I don't think much of them,' said Lord Arthur, with a sad smile, and, after kissing his mother, he left the room.

When he got upstairs, he flung himself on a sofa, and his eyes filled with tears. He had done his best to commit this murder, but on both occasions he had failed, and through no fault of his own. He had tried to do his duty, but it seemed as if Destiny herself had turned traitor. He was oppressed with the sense of the barrenness of good intentions, of the futility of trying to be fine. Perhaps, it would be better to break off the marriage altogether. Sybil would suffer, it is true, but suffering could not really mar a nature so noble as hers. As for himself, what did it matter? There is always some war in which a man can die, some cause to which a man can give his life, and as life had no pleasure for him, so death had no terror. Let Destiny work out his doom. He would not stir to help her.

At half-past seven he dressed, and went down to the club. Surbiton was there with a party of young men, and he was obliged to dine with them. Their trivial conversation and idle jests did not interest him, and as soon as coffee was brought he left them, inventing some engagement in order to get away. As he was going out of the club, the hall-porter handed him a letter. It was from Herr Winckelkopf, asking him to call down the next evening, and look at an explosive umbrella, that went off as soon as it was opened. It was the very latest invention, and had just arrived from Geneva. He tore the letter up into fragments. He had made up his mind not to try any more experiments. Then he wandered down to the Thames Embankment, and sat for hours by the river. The moon peered through a mane of tawny clouds, as if it were a lion's eye, and innumerable stars spangled the hollow vault, like gold dust powdered on a purple dome. Now and then a barge swung out into the turbid stream, and floated away with the tide, and the railway signals changed from green to scarlet as the trains ran shrieking across the bridge. After some time, twelve o'clock boomed from the tall tower at Westminster, and at each stroke of the sonorous bell the night seemed to tremble. Then the railway lights went out, one solitary lamp left gleaming like a large ruby on a giant mast, and the roar of the city became fainter.

At two o'clock he got up, and strolled towards Blackfriars. How unreal everything looked! How like a strange dream! The houses on the other side of the river seemed built out of darkness. One would have said that silver and shadow had fashioned the world anew. The huge dome of St Paul's loomed like a bubble through the dusky air.

As he approached Cleopatra's Needle he saw a man leaning over the parapet, and as he came nearer the man looked up, the gas-light falling full upon his face.

It was Mr Podgers, the cheiromantist! No one could mistake the fat, flabby face, the gold-rimmed spectacles, the sickly feeble smile, the sensual mouth.

Lord Arthur stopped. A brilliant idea flashed across him, and he stole softly up behind. In a moment he had seized Mr Podgers by the legs, and flung him into the Thames. There was a coarse oath, a heavy splash, and all was still. Lord Arthur looked anxiously over, but could see nothing of the cheiromantist but a tall hat, pirouetting in an eddy of moonlit water. After a time it also sank, and no trace of Mr Podgers was visible. Once he thought that he caught sight of the bulky misshapen figure striking out for the staircase by the bridge, and a horrible feeling of failure came over him, but it turned out to be merely a reflection, and when the moon shone out from behind a cloud it passed away. At last he seemed to have realised the decree of destiny. He heaved a deep sigh of relief, and Sybil's name came to his lips.

'Have you dropped anything, sir?' said a voice behind him suddenly.

He turned round, and saw a policeman with a bull's-eye lantern.

'Nothing of importance, sergeant,' he answered, smiling, and hailing a passing hansom, he jumped in, and told the man to drive to Belgrave Square.

For the next few days he alternated between hope and fear. There were moments when he almost expected Mr Podgers to walk into the room, and yet at other times he felt that Fate could not be so unjust to him. Twice he went to the cheiromantist's address in West Moon Street, but he could not bring himself to ring the bell. He longed for certainty, and was afraid of it.

Finally it came. He was sitting in the smoking-room of the club having tea, and listening rather wearily to Surbiton's account of the last comic song at the Gaiety, when the waiter came in with the evening papers. He took up the *St James's*, and was listlessly turning over its pages, when this strange heading caught his eye:

SUICIDE OF A CHEIROMANTIST

He turned pale with excitement, and began to read. The paragraph ran as follows:—

Yesterday morning, at seven o'clock, the body of Mr Septimus R. Podgers, the eminent cheiromantist, was washed on shore at Greenwich, just in front of the Ship Hotel. The unfortunate gentleman had been missing for some days, and considerable anxiety for his safety had been felt in cheiromantic circles. It is supposed that he committed suicide under the influence of a temporary mental derangement, caused by overwork, and a verdict to that effect was returned this afternoon by the coroner's jury. Mr Podgers had just completed an elaborate treatise on the subject of the Human Hand, that will shortly be published, when it will no doubt attract much attention. The deceased was sixty-five years of age, and does not seem to have left any relations.

Lord Arthur rushed out of the club with the paper still in his hand, to the immense amazement of the hall-porter, who tried in vain to stop him, and drove at once to Park Lane. Sybil saw him from the window, and something told her that he was the bearer of good news. She ran down to meet him, and, when she saw his face, she knew that all was well.

'My dear Sybil,' cried Lord Arthur, 'let us be married to-morrow!'

'You foolish boy! Why the cake is not even ordered!' said Sybil, laughing through her tears.

VI

WHEN the wedding took place, some three weeks later, St Peter's was crowded with a perfect mob of smart people. The service was read in a most impressive manner by the Dean of Chichester, and everybody agreed that they had never seen a handsomer couple than the bride and bridegroom. They were more than handsome, however—they were happy. Never for a single moment did Lord Arthur regret all that he had suffered for Sybil's sake, while she, on her side, gave him the best things a woman can give to any man— worship, tenderness, and love. For them romance was not killed by reality. They always felt young.

Some years afterwards, when two beautiful children had been born to them, Lady Windermere came down on a visit to Alton Priory, a lovely old place, that had been the Duke's wedding present to his son; and one afternoon as she was sitting with Lady Arthur under a lime-tree in the garden, watching the little boy and girl as they played up and down the rose-walk, like fitful sunbeams, she suddenly took her hostess's hand in hers, and said, 'Are you happy, Sybil?'

'Dear Lady Windermere, of course I am happy. Aren't you?'

'I have no time to be happy, Sybil. I always like the last person who is introduced to me; but, as a rule, as soon as I know people I get tired of them.'

'Don't your lions satisfy you, Lady Windermere?'

'Oh dear, no! lions are only good for one season. As soon as their manes are cut, they are the dullest creatures going. Besides, they behave very badly, if you are really nice to them. Do you remember that horrid Mr Podgers? He was a dreadful impostor. Of course, I didn't mind that at all, and even when he wanted to borrow money I forgave him, but I could not stand his making love to me. He has really made me hate cheiromancy. I go in for telepathy now. It is much more amusing.'

'You mustn't say anything against cheiromancy here, Lady Windermere; it is the only subject that Arthur does not like people to chaff about. I assure you he is quite serious over it.'

'You don't mean to say that he believes in it, Sybil?'

'Ask him, Lady Windermere, here he is;' and Lord Arthur came up the garden with a large bunch of yellow roses in his hand, and his two children dancing round him.

'Lord Arthur?'

'Yes, Lady Windermere.'

'You don't mean to say that you believe in cheiromancy?'

'Of course I do,' said the young man, smiling.

'But why?'

'Because I owe to it all the happiness of my life,' he murmured, throwing himself into a wicker chair.

'My dear Lord Arthur, what do you owe to it?'

'Sybil,' he answered, handing his wife the roses, and looking into her violet eyes.

'What nonsense!' cried Lady Windermere. 'I never heard such nonsense in all my life.'

HENRY JAMES
Sir Edmund Orme

THE statement appears to have been written, though the fragment is undated, long after the death of his wife, whom I take to have been one of the persons referred to. There is, however, nothing in the strange story to establish this point, which is, perhaps, not of importance. When I took possession of his effects I found these pages, in a locked drawer, among papers relating to the unfortunate lady's too brief career (she died in childbirth a year after her marriage), letters, memoranda, accounts, faded photographs, cards of invitation. That is the only connection I can point to, and you may easily and will probably say that the tale is too extravagant to have had a demonstrable origin. I cannot, I admit, vouch for his having intended it as a report of real occurrence—I can only vouch for his general veracity. In any case it was written for himself, not for others. I offer it to others—having full option—precisely because it is so singular. Let them, in respect to the form of the thing, bear in mind that it was written quite for himself. I have altered nothing but the names.*

If there's a story in the matter I recognise the exact moment at which it began. This was on a soft, still Sunday noon in November, just after church, on the sunny Parade. Brighton was full of people; it was the height of the season, and the day was even more respectable than lovely—which helped to account for the multitude of walkers. The blue sea itself was decorous; it seemed to doze, with a gentle snore (if that *be* decorum), as if nature were preaching a sermon. After writing letters all the morning I had come out to take a look at it before luncheon. I was leaning over the rail which separates the King's Road from the beach, and I think I was smoking a cigarette, when I became conscious of an intended joke in the shape of a light walking-stick laid across my shoulders. The idea, I found, had been thrown off by Teddy Bostwick, of the Rifles and was intended as a contribution to talk. Our talk came off as we strolled together—he always took your arm to show you he forgave your obtuseness about his humour—and looked at the people, and bowed to some of them, and wondered who others were, and differed in opinion as to the prettiness of the girls. About Charlotte Marden we agreed, however, as we saw her coming toward us with her mother; and there surely could have been no one who wouldn't have agreed with us. The Brighton air, of old, used to make plain girls pretty and pretty girls prettier still—I don't know whether it works the spell now. The place, at any rate, was rare for complexions, and Miss Marden's was one that made people turn round. It made *us* stop, heaven knows—at least, it was one of the things, for we already knew the ladies.

We turned with them, we joined them, we went where they were going. They were only going to the end and back—they had just come out of church. It was another manifestation of Teddy's humour that he got immediate possession of Charlotte, leaving me to walk with her mother. However, I was not unhappy; the girl was before me and I had her to talk about. We prolonged our walk, Mrs Marden kept me, and presently she said she was tired and must sit down. We found a place on a sheltered bench—we gossiped as the people passed. It had already struck me, in this pair, that the resemblance between the mother and the daughter was wonderful even among such resemblances—the more so that it took so little account of a difference of nature. One often hears mature mothers spoken of as warnings—signposts, more or less discouraging, of the way daughters may go. But there was nothing deterrent in the idea that Charlotte, at fifty-five, should be as beautiful, even though it were conditioned on her being as pale and preoccupied, as Mrs Marden. At twenty-two she had a kind of rosy blankness and she was admirably handsome. Her head had the charming shape of her mother's, and her features the same fine order. Then there were looks and movements and tones (moments when you could scarcely say whether it were aspect or sound), which, between the two personalities, were a reflection, a recall.

These ladies had a small fortune and a cheerful little house at Brighton, full of portraits and tokens and trophies (stuffed animals on the top of bookcases, and sallow, varnished fish under glass), to which Mrs Marden professed herself attached by pious memories. Her husband had been 'ordered' there in ill-health, to spend the last years of his life, and she had already mentioned to me that it was a place in which she felt herself still under the protection of his goodness. His goodness appeared to have been great, and she some- times had the air of defending it against mysterious imputations. Some sense of protection, of an influence invoked and cherished, was evidently necessary to her; she had a dim wistfulness, a longing for security. She wanted friends and she had a good many. She was kind to me on our first meeting and I never suspected her of the vulgar purpose of 'making up' to me—a suspicion, of course, unduly frequent in conceited young men. It never struck me that she wanted me for her daughter, nor yet, like some unnatural mammas, for herself. It was as if they had had a common deep, shy need and had been ready to say: 'Oh, be friendly to us and be trustful! Don't be afraid, you won't be expected to marry us.' 'Of course there's something about mamma; that's really what makes her such a dear!' Charlotte said to me, confidentially, at an early stage of our acquaintance. She worshipped her mother's appearance. It was the only thing she was vain of; she accepted the raised eyebrows as a charming ultimate fact. 'She looks as if she were waiting for the doctor, dear mamma,' she said on another occasion. 'Perhaps *you're* the doctor; do you think you are?' It appeared in the event that I had some healing power. At any rate when I learned, for she once dropped the remark, that Mrs Marden also thought there was something 'awfully strange' about Charlotte, the relation between the two ladies became extremely interesting. It was happy enough, at bottom; each had the other so much on her mind.

On the Parade the stream of strollers held its course, and Charlotte presently went by with Teddy Bostwick. She smiled and nodded and continued, but when she came back she stopped and spoke to us. Captain Bostwick positively declined to go in, he said the occasion was too jolly: might they therefore take another turn? Her mother dropped a 'Do as you like,' and the girl gave me an impertinent smile over her shoulder as they quitted us. Teddy looked at me with his glass in one eye; but I didn't mind that; it was only of Miss Marden I was thinking as I observed to my companion, laughing:

'She's a bit of a coquette, you know.'

'Don't say that—don't say that!' Mrs Marden murmured.

'The nicest girls always are—just a little,' I was magnanimous enough to plead.

'Then why are they always punished?'

The intensity of the question startled me—it had come out in such a vivid flash. Therefore I had to think a moment before I inquired: 'What do you know about it?'

'I was a bad girl myself.'

'And were you punished?'

'I carry it through life,' said Mrs Marden, looking away from me. 'Ah!' she suddenly panted, in the next breath, rising to her feet and staring at her daughter, who had reappeared again with Captain Bostwick. She stood a few seconds, with the queerest expression in her face; then she sank upon the seat again and I saw that she had blushed crimson. Charlotte, who had observed her movement, came straight up to her and, taking her hand with quick tenderness, seated herself on the other side of her. The girl had turned pale—she gave her mother a fixed, frightened look. Mrs Marden, who had had some shock which escaped our detection, recovered herself; that is she sat quiet and inexpressive, gazing at the indifferent crowd, the sunny air, the slumbering sea. My eye happened to fall, however, on the inter-locked hands of the two ladies, and I quickly guessed that the grasp of the elder one was violent. Bostwick stood before them, wondering what was the matter and asking me from his little vacant disk if *I* knew; which led Charlotte to say to him after a moment, with a certain irritation:

'Don't stand there that way, Captain Bostwick; go away—*please* go away.'

I got up at this, hoping that Mrs Marden wasn't ill; but she immediately begged that we would *not* go away, that we would particularly stay and that we would presently come home to lunch. She drew me down beside her and for a moment I felt her hand pressing my arm in a way that might have been an involuntary betrayal of distress and might have been a private signal. What she might have wished to point out to me I couldn't divine: perhaps she had seen somebody or something abnormal in the crowd. She explained to us in a few minutes that she was all right; that she was only liable to palpitations—they came as quickly as they went. It was time to move, and we moved. The incident was felt to be closed. Bostwick and I lunched with our sociable friends, and when I walked away with him he declared that he had never seen such dear kind creatures.

Mrs Marden had made us promise to come back the next day to

tea, and had exhorted us in general to come as often as we could. Yet the next day, when at five o'clock I knocked at the door of the pretty house, it was to learn that the ladies had gone up to town. They had left a message for us with the butler: he was to say that they had suddenly been called—were very sorry. They would be absent a few days. This was all I could extract from the dumb domestic. I went again three days later, but they were still away; and it was not till the end of a week that I got a note from Mrs Marden, saying 'We are back; do come and forgive us.' It was on this occasion, I remember (the occasion of my going just after getting the note), that she told me she had intuitions. I don't know how many people there were in England at that time in that predicament, but there were very few who would have mentioned it; so that the announcement struck me as original, especially as her point was that some of these uncanny promptings were connected with me.* There were other people present—idle Brighton folk, old women with frightened eyes and irrelevant interjections—and I had but a few minutes' talk with Charlotte; but the day after this I met them both at dinner and had the satisfaction of sitting next to Miss Marden. I recall that hour as the hour on which it first completely came over me that she was a beautiful, liberal creature. I had seen her personality in patches and gleams, like a song sung in snatches, but now it was before me in a large rosy glow, as if it had been a full volume of sound—I heard the whole of the air. It was sweet, fresh music—I was often to hum it over.

After dinner I had a few words with Mrs Marden; it was at the moment, late in the evening, when tea was handed about. A servant passed near us with a tray, I asked her if she would have a cup, and, on her assenting, took one and handed it to her. She put out her hand for it and I gave it to her, safely as I supposed; but as she was in the act of receiving it she started and faltered, so that the cup and saucer dropped with a crash of porcelain and without, on the part of my interlocutress, the usual woman's movement to save her dress. I stooped to pick up the fragments and when I raised myself Mrs Marden was looking across the room at her daughter, who looked back at her smiling, but with an anxious light in her eyes. 'Dear mamma, what on earth *is* the matter with you?' the silent question seemed to say. Mrs Marden coloured, just as she had done after her strange movement on the Parade the other week, and I was therefore surprised when she said to me with unexpected assurance: 'You should really have a steadier hand!' I had begun to stammer a defence of my hand when I became aware that she had fixed her eyes upon me with an intense appeal. It was ambiguous at first and only added to my confusion; then suddenly I understood, as plainly as if she had murmured 'Make believe it was you—make believe it was you.' The servant came back to take the morsels of the cup and wipe up the spilt tea, and while I was in the midst of making believe Mrs Marden abruptly brushed away from me and from her daughter's attention and went into another room. I noticed that she gave no heed to the state of her dress.

I saw nothing more of either of them that evening, but the next morning, in the King's Road, I met Miss Marden with a roll of music in her muff. She told me she had been a little way alone, to practice duets with a friend, and I asked her if she would go a little way further in company. She gave me leave to attend her to her door, and as we stood before it I inquired if I might go in. 'No, not to-day—I don't want you,' she said, candidly, though not roughly; while the words caused me to direct a wistful, disconcerted gaze at one of the windows of the house. It fell upon the white face of Mrs Marden, who was looking out at us from the drawing-room. She stood there long enough for me to see that it *was* she and not an apparition, as I had thought for a second, and then she vanished before her daughter had observed her. The girl, during our walk, had said nothing about her. As I had been told they didn't want me I left them alone a little, after which circumstances supervened that kept us still longer apart. I finally went up to London, and while there I received a pressing invitation to come immediately down to Tranton, a pretty old place in Sussex belonging to a couple whose acquaintance I had lately made.

I went to Tranton from town, and on arriving found the Mardens, with a dozen other people in the house. The first thing Mrs Marden said was: 'Will you forgive me?' and when I asked what I had to forgive she answered: 'My throwing my tea over you.' I replied that it had gone over herself; whereupon she said: 'At any rate I was very rude; but some day I think you'll understand, and then you'll make allowances for me.' The first day I was there she dropped two or three of these references (she had already indulged in more than one), to the mystic initiation that was in store for me; so that I began, as the phrase is, to chaff her about it, to say I would rather it were less wonderful and take it out at once. She answered that when it should come to me I would have to take it out—there would be little enough option. That it *would* come was privately clear to her, a deep presentiment, which was the only reason she had ever mentioned the matter. Didn't I remember she had told me she had intuitions? From the first time of her seeing me she had been sure there were things I should not escape knowing. Meanwhile there was nothing to do but wait and keep cool, not to be precipitate. She particularly wished not to be any more nervous than she was. And I was above all not to be nervous myself—one got used to everything. I declared that though I couldn't make out what she was talking about I was terribly frightened; the absence of a clue gave such a range to one's imagination. I exaggerated on purpose; for if Mrs Marden was mystifying I can scarcely say she was alarming. I couldn't imagine what she meant, but I wondered more than I shuddered. I might have said to myself that she was a little wrong in the upper story; but that never occurred to me. She struck me as hopelessly right.

There were other girls in the house, but Charlotte Marden was the most charming; which was so generally felt to be the case that she really interfered with the slaughter of ground game. There were two or three men, and I was of the number, who actually preferred her to the society of the beaters. In short she was recognised as a form of sport superior and exquisite. She was kind to all of us—she made us go out late and come in early. I don't know whether she flirted, but several other members of the party thought *they* did. Indeed, as regards himself, Teddy Bostwick, who had come over from Brighton, was visibly sure.

The third day I was at Tranton was a Sunday, and there was a very pretty walk to morning service over the fields. It was grey, windless weather, and the bell of the little old church that nestled in the hollow of the Sussex down sounded near and domestic. We were a straggling procession, in the mild damp air (which, as always at that season, gave one the feeling that after the trees were bare there was more of it—a larger sky), and I managed to fall a good way behind with Miss Marden. I remember entertaining, as we moved together over the turf, a strong impulse to say something intensely personal, something violent and important—important for *me*, such as that I had never seen her so lovely, or that that particular moment was the sweetest of my life. But always, in youth, such words have been on the lips many times before they are spoken; and I had the sense, not that I didn't know her well enough (I cared little for that), but that she didn't know *me* well enough. In the church, where there were old Tranton tombs and brasses, the big Tranton pew was full. Several of us were scattered, and I found a seat for Miss Marden, and another for myself beside it, at a distance from her mother and from most of our friends. There were two or three decent rustics on the bench, who moved in further to make room for us, and I took my place first, to cut off my companion from our neighbours. After she was seated there was still a space left, which remained empty till service was about half over.

This at least was the moment at which I became aware that another person had entered and had taken the seat. When I noticed him he had apparently been for some minutes in the pew, for he had settled himself and put down his hat beside him, and, with his hands crossed on the nob of his cane, was gazing before him at the altar. He was a pale young man in black, with the air of a gentleman. I was slightly startled on perceiving him, for Miss Marden had not attracted my attention to his entrance by moving to make room for him. After a few minutes, observing that he had no prayer-book, I reached across my neighbour and placed mine before him, on the ledge of the pew; a manœuvre the motive of which was not unconnected with the possibility that, in my own destitution, Miss Marden would give me one side of *her* velvet volume to hold. The pretext, however, was destined to fail, for at the moment I offered him the book the intruder—whose intrusion I had so condoned—rose from his place without thanking me, stepped noiselessly out of the pew (it had no door), and, so discreetly as to attract no attention, passed down the centre of the church. A few minutes had sufficed for his devotions. His behaviour was unbecoming, his early departure even more than his late arrival; but he managed so quietly that we were not incommoded, and I perceived, on turning a little to glance after him, that nobody was disturbed by his withdrawal. I only noticed, and with surprise, that Mrs Marden had been so affected by it as to rise, involuntarily, an instant, in her place. She stared at him as he passed, but he passed very quickly, and she as quickly dropped down again, though not too soon to catch my eye across the church. Five minutes later I asked Miss Marden, in a low voice, if she would kindly pass me back my prayer-book—I had waited to see if she would spontaneously perform the act. She restored this aid to devotion, but had been so far from troubling herself about it that she could say to me as she did so: 'Why on earth did you put it there?' I was on the point of answering her when she dropped on her knees, and I held my tongue. I had only been going to say: 'To be decently civil.'

After the benediction, as we were leaving our places, I was slightly surprised, again, to see that Mrs Marden, instead of going out with her companions, had come up the aisle to join us, having apparently something to say to her daughter. She said it, but in an instant I observed that it was only a pretext—her real business was with me. She pushed Charlotte forward and suddenly murmured to me: 'Did you see him?'

'The gentleman who sat down here? How could I help seeing him?'

'Hush!' she said, with the intensest excitement; 'don't *speak* to her—don't tell her!' She slipped her hand into my arm, to keep me near her, to keep me, it seemed, away from her daughter. The precaution was unnecessary, for Teddy Bostwick had already taken possession of Miss Marden, and as they passed out of church in front of me I saw one of the other men close up on her other hand. It appeared to be considered that I had had my turn. Mrs Marden withdrew her hand from my arm as soon as we got out, but not before I felt that she had really needed the support. 'Don't speak to any one—don't tell any one!' she went on.

'I don't understand. Tell them what?'

'Why, that you saw him.'

'Surely they saw him for themselves.'

'Not one of them, not one of them.' She spoke in a tone of such passionate decision that I glanced at her—she was staring straight before her. But she felt the challenge of my eyes and she stopped short, in the old brown timber porch of the church, with the others well in advance of us, and said, looking at me now and in a quite extraordinary manner: 'You're the only person, the only person in the world.'

'But *you*, dear madam?'

'Oh me—of course. That's my curse!' And with this she moved rapidly away from me to join the body of the party. I hovered on its outskirts on the way home, for I had food for rumination. Whom had I seen and why was the apparition—it rose before my mind's eye very vividly again—invisible to the others? If an exception had been made for Mrs Marden, why did it constitute a curse, and why was I to share so questionable an advantage? This inquiry, carried on in my own locked breast, kept me doubtless silent enough during luncheon. After luncheon I went out on the old terrace to smoke a cigarette, but I had only taken a couple of turns when I perceived Mrs Marden's moulded mask at the window of one of the rooms which opened on the crooked flags. It reminded me of the same flitting presence at the window at Brighton the day I met Charlotte and walked home with her. But this time my ambiguous friend didn't vanish; she tapped on the pane and motioned me to come in. She was in a queer little apartment, one of the many reception-rooms of which the ground-floor at Tranton consisted; it was known as the Indian room* and had a decoration vaguely Oriental—bamboo lounges, lacquered screens, lanterns with long fringes and strange idols in cabinets, objects not held to conduce to sociability. The place was little used, and when I went round to her we had i⁺ to ourselves. As soon as I entered she said to me: 'Please tell me this; are you in love with my daughter?'

I hesitated a moment. 'Before I answer your question will you kindly tell me what gives you the idea? I don't consider that I have been very forward.'

Mrs Marden, contradicting me with her beautiful anxious eyes, gave me no satisfaction on the point I mentioned; she only went on strenuously:

'Did you say nothing to her on the way to church?'

'What makes you think I said anything?'

'The fact that you saw him.'

'Saw whom, dear Mrs Marden?'

'Oh, you know,' she answered, gravely, even a little reproachfully, as if I were trying to humiliate her by making her phrase the unphraseable.

'Do you mean the gentleman who formed the subject of your strange statement in church—the one who came into the pew?'

'You saw him, you saw him!' Mrs Marden panted, with a strange mixture of dismay and relief.

'Of course I saw him; and so did you.'

'It didn't follow. Did you feel it to be inevitable?'

I was puzzled again. 'Inevitable?'

'That you *should* see him?'

'Certainly, since I'm not blind.'

'You might have been; every one else is.' I was wonderfully at sea, and I frankly confessed it to my interlocutress; but the case was not made clearer by her presently exclaiming: 'I knew you would, from the moment you should be really in love with her! I knew it would be the test—what do I mean?—the proof.'

'Are there such strange bewilderments attached to that high state?' I asked, smiling.

'You perceive there are. You see him, you see him!' Mrs Marden announced, with tremendous exaltation. 'You'll see him again.'

'I've no objection; but I shall take more interest in him if you'll kindly tell me who he is.'

She hesitated, looking down a moment; then she said, raising her eyes: 'I'll tell you if you'll tell me first what you said to her on the way to church.'

'Has she told you I said anything?'

'Do I need that?' smiled Mrs Marden.

'Oh yes, I remember—your intuitions! But I'm sorry to see they're at fault this time; because I really said nothing to your daughter that was the least out of the way.'

'Are you very sure?'

'On my honour, Mrs Marden.'

'Then you consider that you're not in love with her?'

'That's another affair!' I laughed.

'You are—you *are!* You wouldn't have seen him if you hadn't been.'

'Who the deuce *is* he, then, madam?' I inquired with some irritation.

She would still only answer me with another question. 'Didn't you at least *want* to say something to her—didn't you come very near it?'

The question was much to the point; it justified the famous intuitions. 'Very near it—it was the turn of a hair. I don't know what kept me quiet.'

'That was quite enough,' said Mrs Marden. 'It isn't what you say that determines it; it's what you feel. *That's* what he goes by.'

I was annoyed, at last, by her reiterated reference to an identity yet to be established, and I clasped my hands with an air of supplication which covered much real impatience, a sharper curiosity and even the first short throbs of a certain sacred dread. 'I entreat you to tell me whom you're talking about.'

She threw up her arms, looking away from me, as if to shake off both reserve and responsibility. 'Sir Edmund Orme.'

'And who is Sir Edmund Orme?'

At the moment I spoke she gave a start. 'Hush, here they come.' Then as, following the direction of her eyes, I saw Charlotte Marden on the terrace, at the window, she added, with an intensity of warning: 'Don't notice him—*never!*'

Charlotte, who had had her hands beside her eyes, peering into the room and smiling, made a sign that she was to be admitted, on which I went and opened the long window. Her mother turned away, and the girl came in with a laughing challenge: 'What plot, in the world are you two hatching here?' Some plan—I forget what—was in prospect for the afternoon, as to which Mrs Marden's participation or consent was solicited—*my* adhesion was taken for granted—and she had been half over the place in her quest. I was flurried, because I saw that Mrs Marden was flurried (when she turned round to meet her daughter she covered it by a kind of extravagance, throwing herself on the girl's neck and embracing her), and to pass it off I said, fancifully, to Charlotte:

'I've been asking your mother for your hand.'

'Oh, indeed, and has she given it?' Miss Marden answered, gayly.

'She was just going to when you appeared there.'

'Well, it's only for a moment—I'll leave you free.'

'Do you like him, Charlotte?' Mrs Marden asked, with a candour I scarcely expected.

'It's difficult to say it *before* him isn't it?' the girl replied, entering into the humour of the thing, but looking at me as if she didn't like me.

She would have had to say it before another person as well, for at that moment there stepped into the room from the terrace (the window had been left open), a gentleman who had come into sight, at least into mine, only within the instant. Mrs Marden had said 'Here *they* come,' but he appeared to have followed her daughter at a certain distance. I immediately recognised him as the personage who had sat beside us in church. This time I saw him better, saw that his face and his whole air were strange. I speak of him as a personage, because one felt, indescribably, as if a reigning prince had come into the room. He held himself with a kind of habitual majesty, as if he were different from us. Yet he looked fixedly and gravely at me, till I wondered what he expected of me. Did he consider that I should bend my knee or kiss his hand? He turned his eyes in the same way on Mrs Marden, but she knew what to do. After the first agitation produced by his approach she took no notice of him whatever; it made me remember her passionate adjuration to me. I had to achieve a great effort to imitate her, for though I knew nothing about him but that he was Sir Edmund Orme I felt his presence as a strong appeal, almost as an oppression. He stood there without speaking—young, pale, handsome, clean-shaven, decorous, with extraordinary light blue eyes and something old-fashioned, like a portrait of years ago, in his head, his manner of wearing his hair. He was in complete mourning (one immediately felt that he was very well dressed), and he carried his hat in his hand. He looked again strangely hard at me, harder than any one in the world had ever looked before; and I remember feeling rather cold and wishing he would say something. No silence had ever seemed to me so soundless. All this was of course an impression intensely rapid; but that it had consumed some instants was proved to me suddenly by the aspect of Charlotte Marden, who stared from her mother to me and back again (he never looked at her, and she had no appearance of looking at him), and then broke out with: 'What on earth is the matter with you? You've such odd faces!' I felt the colour come back to mine, and when she went on in the same tone: 'One would think you had seen a ghost!' I was conscious that I had turned very red. Sir Edmund Orme never blushed, and I could see that he had no capacity for embarrassment. One had met people of that sort, but never any one with such a grand indifference.

'Don't be impertinent; and go and tell them all that I'll join them,' said Mrs Marden with much dignity, but with a quaver in her voice.

'And will you come—*you?*' the girl asked, turning away. I made no answer, taking the question, somehow, as meant for her companion. But he was more silent than I, and when she reached the door (she was going out that way), she stopped, with her hand on the knob, and looked at me, repeating it. I assented, springing forward to open the door for her, and as she passed out she exclaimed to me mockingly: 'You haven't got your wits about you—you shan't have my hand!'

I closed the door and turned round to find that Sir Edmund Orme had during the moment my back was presented to him retired by the window. Mrs Marden stood there and we looked at each other long. It had only then—as the girl flitted away—come home to me that her daughter was unconscious of what had happened. It was *that*, oddly enough, that gave me a sudden, sharp shake, and not my own perception of our visitor, which appeared perfectly natural. It made the fact vivid to me that she had been equally unaware of him in church, and the two facts together—now that they were over—set my heart more sensibly beating. I wiped my forehead, and Mrs Marden broke out with a low distressful wail: 'Now you know my life—now you know my life!'

'In God's name who is he—*what* is he?'

'He's a man I wronged.'

'How did you wrong him?'

'Oh, awfully—years ago.'

'Years ago? Why, he's very young.'

'Young—young?' cried Mrs Marden. 'He was born before *I* was!'

'Then why does he look so?'

She came nearer to me, she laid her hand on my arm, and there was something in her face that made me shrink a little. 'Don't you understand—don't you *feel*?' she murmured, reproachfully.

'I feel very queer!' I laughed; and I was conscious that my laugh betrayed it.

'He's dead!' said Mrs Marden, from her white face.

'Dead?' I panted. 'Then that gentleman was—?' I couldn't even say the word.

'Call him what you like—there are twenty vulgar names. He's a perfect presence.'

'He's a splendid presence!' I cried. 'The place is haunted—*haunted!*' I exulted in the word as if it represented the fulfilment of my dearest dream.

'It isn't the place—more's the pity! That has nothing to do with it!'

'Then it's you, dear lady?' I said, as if this were still better.

'No, nor me either—I wish it were!'

'Perhaps it's me,' I suggested with a sickly smile.

'It's nobody but my child—my innocent, innocent child!' And with this Mrs Marden broke down—she dropped into a chair and burst into tears. I stammered some question—I pressed on her some bewildered appeal, but she waved me off, unexpectedly and passionately. I persisted—couldn't I help her, couldn't I intervene? 'You *have* intervened,' she sobbed; 'you're *in* it, you're *in* it.'

'I'm very glad to be in anything so curious,' I boldly declared.

'Glad or not, you can't get out of it.'

'I don't want to get out of it—it's too interesting.'

'I'm glad you like it. Go away.'

'But I want to know more about it.'

'You'll see all you want—go away!'

'But I want to understand what I see.'

'How can you—when I don't understand myself?'

'We'll do so together—we'll make it out.'

At this she got up, doing what she could to obliterate her tears. 'Yes, it will be better together—that's why I've liked you.'

'Oh, we'll see it through!' I declared.

'Then you must control yourself better.'

'I will, I will—with practice.'

'You'll get used to it,' said Mrs Marden, in a tone I never forgot. 'But go and join them—I'll come in a moment.'

I passed out to the terrace and I felt that I had a part to play. So far from dreading another encounter with the 'perfect presence,' as Mrs Marden called it, I was filled with an excitement that was positively joyous. I desired a renewal of the sensation*—I opened myself wide to the impression, I went round the house as quickly as if I expected to overtake Sir Edmund Orme. I didn't overtake him just then, but the day was not to close without my recognising that, as Mrs Marden had said, I should see all I wanted of him.

We took, or most of us took, the collective sociable walk which, in the English country-house, is the consecrated pastime on Sunday afternoons. We were restricted to such a regulated ramble as the ladies were good for; the afternoons, moreover, were short, and by five o'clock we were restored to the fireside in the hall, with a sense, on my part at least, that we might have done a little more for our tea. Mrs Marden had said she would join us, but she had not appeared; her daughter, who had seen her again before we went out, only explained that she was tired. She remained invisible all the afternoon, but this was a detail to which I gave as little heed as I had given to the circumstance of my not having Miss Marden to myself during all our walk. I was too much taken up with another emotion to care; I felt beneath my feet the threshold of the strange door, in my life, which had suddenly been thrown open and out of which unspeakable vibrations played up through me like a fountain. I had heard all my days of apparitions, but it was a different thing to have seen one and to know that I should in all probability see it familiarly, as it were, again. I was on the look-out for it, as a pilot for the flash of a revolving light, and I was ready to generalise on the sinister subject, to declare that ghosts were much less alarming and much more amusing than was commonly supposed. There is no doubt that I was extremely nervous.* I couldn't get over the distinction conferred upon me—the exception (in the way of mystic enlargement of vision), made in my favour. At the same time I think I did justice to Mrs Marden's absence; it was a commentary on what she had said to me—'Now you know my life.' She had probably been seeing Sir Edmund Orme for years, and, not having my firm fibre, she had broken down under him. Her nerve was gone, though she had also been able to attest that, in a degree, one got used to him. She had got used to breaking down.

Afternoon tea, when the dusk fell early, was a friendly hour at Tranton; the firelight played into the wide, white last-century hall; sympathies almost confessed themselves, lingering together, before dressing, on deep sofas, in muddy boots, for last words, after walks; and even solitary absorption in the third volume of a novel that was wanted by some one else seemed a form of geniality. I watched my moment and went over to Charlotte Marden when I saw she was about to withdraw. The ladies had left the place one by one, and after I had addressed myself particularly to Miss Marden the three men who were near her gradually dispersed. We had a little vague talk— she appeared preoccupied, and heaven knows *I* was—after which she said she must go: she should be late for dinner. I proved to her by book that she had plenty of time, and she objected that she must at any rate go up to see her mother: she was afraid she was unwell.

'On the contrary, she's better than she has been for a long time— I'll guarantee that,' I said. 'She has found out that she can have confidence in me, and that has done her good.' Miss Marden had dropped into her chair again. I was standing before her, and she looked up at me without a smile—with a dim distress in her beautiful eyes; not exactly as if I were hurting her, but as if she were no longer disposed to treat as a joke what had passed (whatever it was, it was at the same time difficult to be serious about it), between her mother and myself. But I could answer her inquiry in all kindness and candour, for I was really conscious that the poor lady had put off a part of her burden on me and was proportionately relieved and eased. 'I'm sure she has slept all the afternoon as she hasn't slept for years,' I went on. 'You have only to ask her.'

Charlotte got up again. 'You make yourself out very useful.'

'You've a good quarter of an hour,' I said. 'Haven't I a right to talk to you a little this way, alone, when your mother has given me your hand?'

'And is it *your* mother who has given me yours? I'm much obliged to her, but I don't want it. I think our hands are not our mothers'— they happen to be our own!' laughed the girl.

'Sit down, sit down and let me tell you!' I pleaded.

I still stood before her, urgently, to see if she wouldn't oblige me. She hesitated a moment, looking vaguely this way and that, as if under a compulsion that was slightly painful. The empty hall was quiet—we heard the loud ticking of the great clock. Then she slowly sank down and I drew a chair close to her. This made me face round to the fire again, and with the movement I perceived, disconcertedly, that we were not alone. The next instant, more strangely than I can say, my discomposure, instead of increasing, dropped, for the person before the fire was Sir Edmund Orme. He stood there as I had seen him in the Indian room, looking at me with the expressionless attention which borrowed its sternness from his sombre distinction. I knew so much more about him now that I had to check a movement of recognition, an acknowledgment of his presence. When once I was aware of it, and that it lasted, the sense that we had company, Charlotte and I, quitted me; it was impressed on me on the contrary that I was more intensely alone with Miss Marden. She evidently saw nothing to look at, and I made a tremendous and very nearly successful effort to conceal from her that my own situation was different. I say 'very nearly,' because she watched me an instant—while my words were arrested—in a way that made me fear she was going to say again, as she had said in the Indian room: 'What on earth is the matter with you?'

What the matter with me was I quickly told her, for the full knowledge of it rolled over me with the touching spectacle of her unconsciousness. It was touching that she became, in the presence of this extraordinary portent. What was portended, danger or sorrow, bliss or bane, was a minor question; all I saw, as she sat there, was that, innocent and charming, she was close to a horror, as she might have thought it, that happened to be veiled from her but that might at any moment be disclosed. I didn't mind it now, as I found, but nothing was more possible than she should, and if it wasn't curious and interesting it might easily be very dreadful. If I didn't mind it for myself, as I afterwards saw, this was largely because I was so taken up with the idea of protecting *her*. My heart beat high with this idea, on the spot; I determined to do everything I could to keep her sense sealed. What I could do might have been very obscure to me if I had not, in all this, become more aware than of anything else that I loved her. The way to save her was to love her, and the way to love her was to tell her, now and here, that I did so. Sir Edmund Orme didn't prevent me, especially as after a moment he turned his back to us and stood looking discreetly at the fire. At the end of another moment he leaned his head on his arm, against the chimneypiece, with an air of gradual dejection, like a spirit still more weary than discreet. Charlotte Marden was startled by what I said to her, and she jumped up to escape it; but she took no offence—my tenderness was too real. She only moved about the room with a deprecating murmur, and I was so busy following up any little advantage that I might have obtained that I didn't notice in what manner Sir Edmund Orme disappeared. I only observed presently that he had gone. This made no difference—he had been so small a hindrance; I only remember being struck, suddenly, with something inexorable in the slow, sweet, sad headshake that Miss Marden gave me.

'I don't ask for an answer now,' I said; 'I only want you to be sure—to know how much depends on it.'

'Oh, I don't want to give it to you, now or ever!' she replied. 'I hate the subject, please—I wish one could be let alone.' And then, as if I might have found something harsh in this irrepressible, artless cry of beauty beset, she added quickly, vaguely, kindly, as she left the room: 'Thank you, thank you—thank you so much!'

At dinner I could be generous enough to be glad, for her, that I was placed on the same side of the table with her, where she couldn't see me. Her mother was nearly opposite to me, and just after we had sat down Mrs Marden gave me one long, deep look, in which all our strange communion was expressed. It meant of course 'She has told me,' but it meant other things beside. At any rate I know what my answering look to her conveyed: 'I've seen him again—I've seen him again!' This didn't prevent Mrs Marden from treating her neighbours with her usual scrupulous blandness. After dinner, when, in the drawing-room, the men joined the ladies and I went straight up to her to tell her how I wished we could have some private conversation, she said immediately, in a low tone, looking down at her fan while she opened and shut it:

'He's here—he's here.'

'Here?' I looked round the room, but I was disappointed.

'Look where *she* is,' said Mrs Marden, with just the faintest asperity. Charlotte was in fact not in the main saloon, but in an apartment into which it opened and which was known as the morning-room. I took a few steps and saw her, through a doorway, upright in the middle of the room, talking with three gentlemen whose backs were practically turned to me. For a moment my quest seemed vain; then I recognised that one of the gentlemen—the middle one—was Sir Edmund Orme. This time it *was* surprising that the others didn't see him. Charlotte seemed to be looking straight at him, addressing her conversation to him. She saw me after an instant, however, and immediately turned her eyes away. I went back to her mother with an annoyed sense that the girl would think I was watching *her*, which would be unjust. Mrs Marden had found a small sofa—a little apart—and I sat down beside her. There were some questions I had so wanted to go into that I wished we were once more in the Indian room. I presently gathered, however, that our privacy was all-sufficient. We communicated so closely and completely now, and with such silent reciprocities, that it would in every circumstance be adequate.

'Oh, yes, he's there,' I said; 'and at about a quarter-past seven he was in the hall.'

'I knew it at the time, and I was so glad!'

'So glad?'

'That it was your affair, this time, and not mine. It's a rest for me.'

'Did you sleep all the afternoon?' I asked.

'As I haven't done for months. But how did you know that?'

'As *you* knew, I take it, that Sir Edmund was in the hall. We shall evidently each of us know things now—where the other is concerned.'

'Where *he* is concerned,' Mrs Marden amended. 'It's a blessing, the way you take it,' she added, with a long, mild sigh.

'I take it as a man who's in love with your daughter.'

'Of course—of course.' Intense as I now felt my desire for the girl to be, I couldn't help laughing a little at the tone of these words; and it led my companion immediately to say: 'Otherwise you wouldn't have seen him.'

'But every one doesn't see him who's in love with her, or there would be dozens.'

'They're not in love with her as you are.'

'I can, of course, only speak for myself; and I found a moment, before dinner, to do so.'

'She told me immediately.'

'And have I any hope—any chance?'

'That's what *I* long for, what I pray for.'

'Ah, how can I thank you enough?' I murmured.

'I believe it will all pass—if she loves you,' Mrs Marden continued. 'It will all pass?'

'We shall never see him again.'

'Oh, if she loves me I don't care how often I see him!'

'Ah, you take it better than I could,' said my companion. 'You have the happiness not to know—not to understand.'

'I don't indeed. What on earth does he want?'

'He wants to make me suffer.' She turned her wan face upon me with this, and I saw now for the first time, fully, how perfectly, if this had been Sir Edmund Orme's purpose, he had succeeded. 'For what I did to him,' Mrs Marden explained.

'And what did you do to him?'

She looked at me a moment. 'I killed him.' As I had seen him fifty yards away only five minutes before the words gave me a start. 'Yes, I make you jump; be careful. He's there still, but he killed himself.* I broke his heart—he thought me awfully bad. We were to have been married, but I broke it off—just at the last. I saw some one I liked better; I had no reason but that. It wasn't for interest, or money, or position, or anything of that sort. All *those* things were his. It was simply that I fell in love with Captain Marden. When I saw him I felt that I couldn't marry any one else. I wasn't in love with Edmund Orme—my mother, my elder sister had brought it about. But he did love me. I told him I didn't care—that I couldn't, that I *wouldn't*. I threw him over, and he took something, some abominable drug or draught that proved fatal. It was dreadful, it was horrible, he was found that way—he died in agony. I married Captain Marden, but not for five years. I was happy, perfectly happy; time obliterates. But when my husband died I began to see him.'

I had listened intently, but I wondered. 'To see your husband?'

'Never, never *that* way, thank God! To see *him*, with Chartie—always with Chartie. The first time it nearly killed me—about seven years ago, when she first came out. Never when I'm by myself—only with her. Sometimes not for months, then every day for a week. I've tried everything to break the spell—doctors and *régimes* and climates; I've prayed to God on my knees. That day at Brighton, on the Parade with you, when you thought I was ill, that was the first for an age. And then, in the evening, when I knocked my tea over you, and the day you were at the door with Charlotte and I saw you from the window—each time he was there.'

'I see, I see.' I was more thrilled than I could say.

'It's an apparition like another.'

'Like another? Have you ever seen another?'

'No, I mean the sort of thing one has heard of. It's tremendously interesting to encounter a case.'

'Do you call me a "case"?' Mrs Marden asked, with exquisite resentment.*

'I mean myself.'

'Oh, you're the right one!' she exclaimed. 'I was right when I trusted you.'

'I'm devoutly grateful you did; but what made you do it?'

'I had thought the whole thing out—I had had time to in those dreadful years, while he was punishing me in my daughter.'

'Hardly that,' I objected, 'if she never knew.'

'That has been my terror, that she *will*, from one occasion to another. I've an unspeakable dread of the effect on her.'

'She shan't, she shan't!' I declared, so loud that several people looked round. Mrs Marden made me get up, and I had no more talk with her that evening. The next day I told her I must take my departure from Tranton—it was neither comfortable nor considerate to remain as a rejected suitor. She was disconcerted, but she accepted my reasons, only saying to me out of her mournful eyes: 'You'll leave me alone then with my burden?' It was of course understood between us that for many weeks to come there would be no discretion in 'worrying poor Charlotte': such were the terms in which, with odd feminine and maternal inconsistency, she alluded to an attitude on my part that she favoured. I was prepared to be heroically considerate, but it seemed to me that even this delicacy permitted me to say a word to Miss Marden before I went. I begged her, after breakfast, to take a turn with me on the terrace, and as she hesitated, looking at me distantly, I informed her that it was only to ask her a question and to say goodbye—I was leaving Tranton for *her*.

She came out with me, and we passed slowly round the house three or four times. Nothing is finer than this great airy platform, from which every look is a sweep of the country, with the sea on the furthest edge. It might have been that as we passed the windows we were conspicuous to our friends in the house, who would divine, sarcastically, why I was so significantly bolting. But I didn't care; I only wondered whether they wouldn't really this time make out Sir Edmund Orme, who joined us on one of our turns and strolled slowly on the other side of my companion. Of what transcendent essence he was composed I knew not; I have no theory about him (leaving that to others), any more than I have one about such or such another of my fellow-mortals whom I have elbowed in life. He was as positive, as individual, as ultimate a fact as any of these. Above all he was as respectable, as sensitive a fact; so that I should no more have thought of taking a liberty, of practicing an experiment with him, of touching him, for instance, or speaking to him, since he set the example of silence, than I should have thought of committing any other social grossness. He had always, as I saw more fully later, the perfect propriety of his position—had always the appearance of being dressed and, in attitude and aspect, of comporting himself, as the occasion demanded. He looked strange, incontestably, but somehow he always looked *right*. I very soon came to attach an idea of beauty to his unmentionable presence, the beauty of an old story of love and pain. What I ended by feeling was that he was on my side, that he was watching over my interest, that he was looking to it that my heart shouldn't be broken. Oh, he had taken it seriously, his own catastrophe—he had certainly proved that in his day. If poor Mrs Marden, as she told me, had thought it out, I also subjected the case to the finest analysis of which my intellect was capable. It was a case of retributive justice.* The mother was to pay, in suffering, for the suffering she had inflicted, and as the disposition to jilt a lover might have been transmitted to the daughter, the daughter was to be watched, so that *she* might be made to suffer should she do an equal wrong. She might reproduce her mother in character as vividly as she did in face. On the day she should transgress, in other words, her eyes would be opened suddenly and unpitiedly to the 'perfect presence,' which she would have to work as she could into her conception of a young lady's universe. I had no great fear for her, because I didn't believe she was, in any cruel degree, a coquette. We should have a good deal of ground to get over before I, at least, should be in a position to be sacrificed by her. She couldn't throw me over before she had made a little more of me.

The question I asked her on the terrace that morning was whether I might continue, during the winter, to come to Mrs Marden's house. I promised not to come too often and not to speak to her for three months of the question I had raised the day before. She replied that I might do as I liked, and on this we parted.

I carried out the vow I had made her; I held my tongue for my three months. Unexpectedly to myself there were moments of this time when she struck me as capable of playing with a man. I wanted so to make her like me that I became subtle and ingenious, wonderfully alert, patiently diplomatic. Sometimes I thought I had earned my reward, brought her to the point of saying: 'Well, well, you're the best of them all—you may speak to me now.' Then there was a greater blankness than ever in her beauty, and on certain days a mocking light in her eyes, of which the meaning seemed to be: 'If you don't take care, I *will* accept you, to have done with you the more effectually.' Mrs Marden was a great help to me simply by believing in me, and I valued her faith all the more that it continued even though there was a sudden intermission of the miracle that had been wrought for me. After our visit to Tranton Sir Edmund Orme gave us a holiday, and I confess it was at first a disappointment to me. I felt less designated, less connected with Charlotte. 'Oh, don't cry till you're out of the wood,' her mother said; 'he has let me off sometimes for six months. He'll break out again when you least expect it—he knows what he's about.' For her these weeks were happy, and she was wise enough not to talk about me to the girl. She was so good as to assure me that I was taking the right way, that I looked as if I felt secure and that in the long run women give way to that. She had

known them do it even when the man was a fool for looking so—or
was a fool on any terms. For herself she felt it to be a good time, a
sort of St Martin's summer of the soul. She was better than she had
been for years, and she had me to thank for it. The sense of visitation
was light upon her—she wasn't in anguish every time she looked
round. Charlotte contradicted me very often, but she contradicted
herself still more. That winter was a wonder of mildness, and we
often sat out in the sun. I walked up and down with Charlotte, and
Mrs Marden, sometimes on a bench, sometimes in a bath-chair,
waited for us and smiled at us as we passed. I always looked out for a
sign in her face—'He's with you, he's with you' (she would see him
before I should), but nothing came; the season had brought us also a
sort of spiritual softness. Toward the end of April the air was so like
June that, meeting my two friends one night at some Brighton
sociability—an evening party with amateur music—I drew Miss
Marden unresistingly out upon a balcony to which a window in one
of the rooms stood open. The night was close and thick, the stars
were dim, and below us, under the cliff, we heard the regular rumble
of the sea. We listened to it a little and we heard mixed with it, from
within the house, the sound of a violin accompanied by a piano—a
performance which had been our pretext for passing out.

'Do you like me a little better?' I asked, abruptly, after a minute.
'Could you listen to me again?'

I had no sooner spoken than she laid her hand quickly, with a
certain force, on my arm. 'Hush!—isn't there some one there?' She
was looking into the gloom of the far end of the balcony. This balcony ran the whole width of the house, a width very great in the best
of the old houses at Brighton. We were lighted a little by the open
window behind us, but the other windows, curtained within, left the
darkness undiminished, so that I made out but dimly the figure of a
gentleman standing there and looking at us. He was in evening dress,
like a guest—I saw the vague shine of his white shirt and the pale
oval of his face—and he might perfectly have been a guest who had
stepped out in advance of us to take the air. Miss Marden took him
for one at first—then evidently, even in a few seconds, she saw that
the intensity of his gaze was unconventional. What else she saw I
couldn't determine; I was too taken up with my own impression to
do more than feel the quick contact of her uneasiness. My own
impression was in fact the strongest of sensations, a sensation of

horror; for what could the thing mean but that the girl at last *saw*?
I heard her give a sudden, gasping 'Ah!' and move quickly into the
house. It was only afterwards that I knew that I myself had had a
totally new emotion—my horror passing into anger, and my anger
into a stride along the balcony with a gesture of reprobation. The
case was simplified to the vision of a frightened girl whom I loved. I
advanced to vindicate her security, but I found nothing there to meet
me. It was either all a mistake or Sir Edmund Orme had vanished.

I followed Miss Marden immediately, but there were symptoms of
confusion in the drawing-room when I passed in. A lady had fainted,
the music had stopped; there was a shuffling of chairs and a pressing
forward. The lady was not Charlotte, as I feared, but Mrs Marden,
who had suddenly been taken ill. I remember the relief with which I
learned this, for to see Charlotte stricken would have been anguish,
and her mother's condition gave a channel to her agitation. It was of
course all a matter for the people of the house and for the ladies, and
I could have no share in attending to my friends or in conducting
them to their carriage. Mrs Marden revived and insisted on going
home, after which I uneasily withdrew.

I called the next morning to ask about her and was informed that
she was better, but when I asked if Miss Marden would see me the
message sent down was that it was impossible. There was nothing for
me to do all day but to roam about with a beating heart. But toward
evening I received a line in pencil, brought by hand—'Please come;
mother wishes you.' Five minutes afterward I was at the door again
and ushered into the drawing-room. Mrs Marden lay upon the sofa,
and as soon as I looked at her I saw the shadow of death in her face.
But the first thing she said was that she was better, ever so much
better; her poor old heart had been behaving queerly again, but now
it was quiet. She gave me her hand and I bent over her with my eyes
in hers, and in this way I was able to read what she didn't speak—
'I'm really very ill, but appear to take what I say exactly as I say it.'
Charlotte stood there beside her, looking not frightened now, but
intensely grave, and not meeting my eyes. 'She has told me—she has
told me!' her mother went on.

'She has told you?' I stared from one of them to the other, wondering if Mrs Marden meant that the girl had spoken to her of the
circumstances on the balcony.

'That you spoke to her again—that you're admirably faithful.'

She had already thrown herself into my arms

I felt a thrill of joy at this; it showed me that that memory had been uppermost, and also that Charlotte had wished to say the thing that would soothe her mother most, not the thing that would alarm her. Yet I now knew, myself, as well as if Mrs Marden had told me, that she knew and had known at the moment what her daughter had seen. 'I spoke—I spoke, but she gave me no answer,' I said.

'She will now, won't you, Chartie? I want it so, I want it!' the poor lady murmured, with ineffable wistfulness.

'You're very good to me,' Charlotte said to me, seriously and sweetly, looking fixedly on the carpet. There was something different in her, different from all the past. She had recognised something, she felt a coercion. I could see that she was trembling.

'Ah, if you would let me show you *how* good I can be!' I exclaimed, holding out my hands to her. As I uttered the words I was touched with the knowledge that something had happened. A form had constituted itself on the other side of the bed, and the form leaned over Mrs Marden. My whole being went forth into a mute prayer that Charlotte shouldn't see it and that I should be able to betray nothing. The impulse to glance toward Mrs Marden was even stronger than the involuntary movement of taking in Sir Edmund Orme; but I could resist even that, and Mrs Marden was perfectly still. Charlotte got up to give me her hand, and with the definite act she saw. She gave, with a shriek, one stare of dismay, and another sound, like a wail of one of the lost, fell at the same instant on my ear. But I had already sprung toward the girl to cover her, to veil her face. She had already thrown herself into my arms. I held her there a moment— bending over her, given up to her, feeling each of her throbs with my own and not knowing which was which; then, all of a sudden, coldly, I gathered that we were alone. She released herself. The figure beside the sofa had vanished; but Mrs Marden lay in her place with closed eyes, with something in her stillness that gave us both another terror. Charlotte expressed it in the cry of 'Mother, mother!' with which she flung herself down. I fell on my knees beside her. Mrs Marden had passed away.

Was the sound I heard when Chartie shrieked—the other and still more tragic sound I mean—the despairing cry of the poor lady's death-shock or the articulate sob (it was like a waft from a great tempest), of the exorcised and pacified spirit? Possibly the latter, for that was, mercifully, the last of Sir Edmund Orme.

RUDYARD KIPLING

The Mark of the Beast

> Your Gods and my Gods—do you or I know which are the
> stronger?
>
> *Native Proverb*

EAST of Suez, some hold, the direct control of Providence ceases;
Man being there handed over to the power of the Gods and Devils of
Asia, and the Church of England Providence only exercising an
occasional and modified supervision in the case of Englishmen.

This theory accounts for some of the more unnecessary horrors of
life in India: it may be stretched to explain my story.

My friend Strickland* of the Police, who knows as much of natives
of India as is good for any man, can bear witness to the facts of the
case. Dumoise,* our doctor, also saw what Strickland and I saw. The
inference which he drew from the evidence was entirely incorrect.
He is dead now; he died in a rather curious manner, which has been
elsewhere described.

When Fleete came to India he owned a little money and some land
in the Himalayas, near a place called Dharmsala. Both properties
had been left him by an uncle, and he came out to finance them. He
was a big, heavy, genial, and inoffensive man. His knowledge of
natives was, of course, limited, and he complained of the difficulties
of the language.

He rode in from his place in the hills to spend New Year in the
station, and he stayed with Strickland. On New Year's Eve there was
a big dinner at the club, and the night was excusably wet. When
men foregather from the uttermost ends of the Empire, they have a
right to be riotous. The Frontier had sent down a contingent o'
Catch'em-Alive-O's* who had not seen twenty white faces for a year,
and were used to ride fifteen miles to dinner at the next Fort at
the risk of a Khyberee bullet where their drinks should lie. They
profited by their new security, for they tried to play pool with a
curled-up hedgehog found in the garden, and one of them carried

the marker round the room in his teeth. Half a dozen planters had come in from the south and were talking 'horse' to the Biggest Liar in Asia, who was trying to cap all their stories at once. Everybody was there, and there was a general closing up of ranks and taking stock of our losses in dead or disabled that had fallen during the past year. It was a very wet night, and I remember that we sang 'Auld Lang Syne' with our feet in the Polo Championship Cup, and our heads among the stars, and swore that we were all dear friends. Then some of us went away and annexed Burma,* and some tried to open up the Soudan and were opened up by Fuzzies in that cruel scrub outside Suakim,* and some found stars and medals, and some were married, which was bad, and some did other things which were worse, and the others of us stayed in our chains and strove to make money on insufficient experiences.

Fleete began the night with sherry and bitters, drank champagne steadily up to dessert, then raw, rasping Capri with all the strength of whisky, took Benedictine with his coffee, four or five whiskies and sodas to improve his pool strokes, beer and bones at half-past two, winding up with old brandy. Consequently, when he came out, at half-past three in the morning, into fourteen degrees of frost, he was very angry with his horse for coughing, and tried to leapfrog into the saddle. The horse broke away and went to his stables; so Strickland and I formed a Guard of Dishonour to take Fleete home.

Our road lay through the bazaar, close to a little temple of Hanuman,* the Monkey-god, who is a leading divinity worthy of respect. All gods have good points, just as have all priests. Personally, I attach much importance to Hanuman, and am kind to his people— the great gray apes of the hills. One never knows when one may want a friend.

There was a light in the temple, and as we passed, we could hear voices of men chanting hymns. In a native temple, the priests rise at all hours of the night to do honour to their god. Before we could stop him, Fleete dashed up the steps, patted two priests on the back, and was gravely grinding the ashes of his cigar-butt in to the forehead of the red, stone image of Hanuman. Strickland tried to drag him out, but he sat down and said solemnly:

'Shee that? 'Mark of the B—beasht!* *I* made it. Ishn't it fine?'

In half a minute the temple was alive and noisy, and Strickland, who knew what came of polluting gods, said that things might occur.

He, by virtue of his official position, long residence in the country, and weakness for going among the natives, was known to the priests and he felt unhappy. Fleete sat on the ground and refused to move. He said that 'good old Hanuman' made a very soft pillow.

Then, without any warning, a Silver Man came out of a recess behind the image of the god. He was perfectly naked in that bitter, bitter cold, and his body shone like frosted silver, for he was what the Bible calls 'a leper as white as snow.'* Also he had no face, because he was a leper of some years' standing, and his disease was heavy upon him. We two stooped to haul Fleete up, and the temple was filling and filling with folk who seemed to spring from the earth, when the Silver Man ran in under our arms, making a noise exactly like the mewing of an otter, caught Fleete round the body and dropped his head on Fleete's breast before we could wrench him away. Then he retired to a corner and sat mewing while the crowd blocked all the doors.

The priests were very angry until the Silver Man touched Fleete. That nuzzling seemed to sober them.

At the end of a few minutes' silence one of the priests came to Strickland and said, in perfect English, 'Take your friend away. He has done with Hanuman but Hanuman has not done with him.' The crowd gave room and we carried Fleete into the road.

Strickland was very angry. He said that we might all three have been knifed, and that Fleete should thank his stars that he had escaped without injury.

Fleete thanked no one. He said that he wanted to go to bed. He was gorgeously drunk.

We moved on, Strickland silent and wrathful, until Fleete was taken with violent shivering fits and sweating. He said that the smells of the bazaar were overpowering, and he wondered why slaughter-houses were permitted so near English residences. 'Can't you smell the blood?' said Fleete.

We put him to bed at last, just as the dawn was breaking, and Strickland invited me to have another whisky and soda. While we were drinking he talked of the trouble in the temple, and admitted that it baffled him completely. Strickland hates being mystified by natives, because his business in life is to overmatch them with their own weapons. He has not yet succeeded in doing this, but in fifteen or twenty years he will have made some small progress.

'They should have mauled us,' he said, 'instead of mewing at us. I wonder what they meant. I don't like it one little bit.'

I said that the Managing Committee of the temple would in all probability bring a criminal action against us for insulting their religion. There was a section of the Indian Penal Code which exactly met Fleete's offence. Strickland said he only hoped and prayed that they would do this. Before I left I looked into Fleete's room, and saw him lying on his right side, scratching his left breast. Then I went to bed cold, depressed, and unhappy, at seven o'clock in the morning.

At one o'clock I rode over to Strickland's house to inquire after Fleete's head. I imagined that it would be a sore one. Fleete was breakfasting and seemed unwell. His temper was gone, for he was abusing the cook for not supplying him with an underdone chop. A man who can eat raw meat after a wet night is a curiosity. I told Fleete this and he laughed.

'You breed queer mosquitoes in these parts,' he said. 'I've been bitten to pieces, but only in one place.'

'Let's have a look at the bite,' said Strickland. 'It may have gone down since this morning.'

While the chops were being cooked, Fleete opened his shirt and showed us, just over his left breast, a mark, the perfect double of the black rosettes—the five or six irregular blotches arranged in a circle—on a leopard's hide. Strickland looked and said, 'It was only pink this morning. It's grown black now.'

Fleete ran to a glass.

'By Jove!' he said, 'this is nasty. What is it?'

We could not answer. Here the chops came in, all red and juicy, and Fleete bolted three in a most offensive manner. He ate on his right grinders only, and threw his head over his right shoulder as he snapped the meat. When he had finished, it struck him that he had been behaving strangely, for he said apologetically, 'I don't think I ever felt so hungry in my life. I've bolted like an ostrich.'

After breakfast Strickland said to me, 'Don't go. Stay here, and stay for the night.'

Seeing that my house was not three miles from Strickland's, this request was absurd. But Strickland insisted, and was going to say something when Fleete interrupted by declaring in a shamefaced way that he felt hungry again. Strickland sent a man to my house to fetch over my bedding and a horse, and we three went down to

Strickland's stables to pass the hours until it was time to go out for a ride. The man who has a weakness for horses never wearies of inspecting them; and when two men are killing time in this way they gather knowledge and lies the one from the other.

There were five horses in the stables, and I shall never forget the scene as we tried to look them over. They seemed to have gone mad. They reared and screamed and nearly tore up their pickets; they sweated and shivered and lathered and were distraught with fear. Strickland's horses used to know him as well as his dogs; which made the matter more curious. We left the stable for fear of the brutes throwing themselves in their panic. Then Strickland turned back and called me. The horses were still frightened, but they let us 'gentle' and make much of them, and put their heads in our bosoms.

'They aren't afraid of *us*,' said Strickland. 'D' you know, I'd give three months' pay if *Outrage* here could talk.'

But *Outrage* was dumb, and could only cuddle up to his master and blow out his nostrils, as is the custom of horses when they wish to explain things but can't. Fleete came up when we were in the stalls, and as soon as the horses saw him, their fright broke out afresh. It was all that we could do to escape from the place unkicked. Strickland said, 'They don't seem to love you, Fleete.'

'Nonsense,' said Fleete; 'my mare will follow me like a dog.' He went to her; she was in a loose-box; but as he slipped the bars she plunged, knocked him down, and broke away into the garden. I laughed, but Strickland was not amused. He took his moustache in both fists and pulled at it till it nearly came out. Fleete, instead of going off to chase his property, yawned, saying that he felt sleepy. He went to the house to lie down, which was a foolish way of spending New Year's Day.

Strickland sat with me in the stables and asked if I had noticed anything peculiar in Fleete's manner. I said that he ate his food like a beast; but that this might have been the result of living alone in the hills out of the reach of society as refined and elevating as ours for instance. Strickland was not amused. I do not think that he listened to me, for his next sentence referred to the mark on Fleete's breast, and I said that it might have been caused by blister-flies, or that it was possibly a birth-mark newly born and now visible for the first time. We both agreed that it was unpleasant to look at, and Strickland found occasion to say that I was a fool.

'I can't tell you what I think now,' said he, 'because you would call me a madman; but you must stay with me for the next few days, if you can. I want you to watch Fleete, but don't tell me what you think till I have made up my mind.'

'But I am dining out to-night,' I said.

'So am I,' said Strickland, 'and so is Fleete. At least if he doesn't change his mind.'

We walked about the garden smoking, but saying nothing—because we were friends, and talking spoils good tobacco—till our pipes were out. Then we went to wake up Fleete. He was wide awake and fidgeting about his room.

'I say, I want some more chops,' he said. 'Can I get them?'

We laughed and said, 'Go and change. The ponies will be round in a minute.'

'All right,' said Fleete. 'I'll go when I get the chops—underdone ones, mind.'

He seemed to be quite in earnest. It was four o'clock, and we had had breakfast at one; still, for a long time, he demanded those underdone chops. Then he changed into riding clothes and went out into the verandah. His pony—the mare had not been caught—would not let him come near. All three horses were unmanageable—mad with fear—and finally Fleete said that he would stay at home and get something to eat. Strickland and I rode out wondering. As we passed the temple of Hanuman, the Silver Man came out and mewed at us.

'He is not one of the regular priests of the temple,' said Strickland. 'I think I should peculiarly like to lay my hands on him.'

There was no spring in our gallop on the racecourse that evening. The horses were stale, and moved as though they had been ridden out.

'The fright after breakfast has been too much for them,' said Strickland.

That was the only remark he made through the remainder of the ride. Once or twice I think he swore to himself; but that did not count.

We came back in the dark at seven o'clock, and saw that there were no lights in the bungalow. 'Careless ruffians my servants are!' said Strickland.

My horse reared at something on the carriage drive, and Fleete stood up under its nose.

'What are you doing, grovelling about the garden?' said Strickland.

But both horses bolted and nearly threw us. We dismounted by the stables and returned to Fleete, who was on his hands and knees under the orange-bushes.

'What the devil's wrong with you?' said Strickland.

'Nothing, nothing in the world,' said Fleete, speaking very quickly and thickly. 'I've been gardening—botanising you know. The smell of the earth is delightful. I think I'm going for a walk—a long walk—all night.'

Then I saw that there was something excessively out of order somewhere, and I said to Strickland, 'I am not dining out.'

'Bless you!' said Strickland. 'Here, Fleete, get up. You'll catch fever there. Come in to dinner and let's have the lamps lit. We'll all dine at home.'

Fleete stood up unwillingly, and said, 'No lamps—no lamps. It's much nicer here. Let's dine outside and have some more chops—lots of 'em and underdone—bloody ones with gristle.'

Now a December evening in Northern India is bitterly cold, and Fleete's suggestion was that of a maniac.

'Come in,' said Strickland sternly. 'Come in at once.'

Fleete came, and when the lamps were brought, we saw that he was literally plastered with dirt from head to foot. He must have been rolling in the garden. He shrank from the light and went to his room. His eyes were horrible to look at. There was a green light behind them, not in them, if you understand, and the man's lower lip hung down.

Strickland said, 'There is going to be trouble—big trouble—to-night. Don't you change your riding-things.'

We waited and waited for Fleete's reappearance, and ordered dinner in the meantime. We could hear him moving about his own room, but there was no light there. Presently from the room came the long-drawn howl of a wolf.

People write and talk lightly of blood running cold and hair standing up and things of that kind. Both sensations are too horrible to be trifled with. My heart stopped as though a knife had been driven through it, and Strickland turned as white as the tablecloth.

The howl was repeated, and was answered by another howl far across the fields.

That set the gilded roof on the horror. Strickland dashed into

Fleete's room. I followed, and we saw Fleete getting out of the window. He made beast-noises in the back of his throat. He could not answer us when we shouted at him. He spat.

I don't quite remember what followed, but I think that Strickland must have stunned him with the long boot-jack or else I should never have been able to sit on his chest. Fleete could not speak, he could only snarl, and his snarls were those of a wolf, not of a man. The human spirit must have been giving way all day and have died out with the twilight. We were dealing with a beast that had once been Fleete.

The affair was beyond any human and rational experience. I tried to say 'Hydrophobia,'* but the word wouldn't come, because I knew that I was lying.

We bound this beast with leather thongs of the punkah-rope, and tied its thumbs and big toes together, and gagged it with a shoe-horn, which makes a very efficient gag if you know how to arrange it. Then we carried it into the dining-room, and sent a man to Dumoise, the doctor, telling him to come over at once. After we had despatched the messenger and were drawing breath, Strickland said, 'It's no good. This isn't any doctor's work.' I, also, knew that he spoke the truth.

The beast's head was free, and it threw it about from side to side. Any one entering the room would have believed that we were curing a wolf's pelt. That was the most loathsome accessory of all.

Strickland sat with his chin in the heel of his fist, watching the beast as it wriggled on the ground, but saying nothing. The shirt had been torn open in the scuffle and showed the black rosette mark on the left breast. It stood out like a blister.

In the silence of the watching we heard something without mewing like a she-otter. We both rose to our feet, and, I answer for myself, not Strickland, felt sick—actually and physically sick. We told each other, as did the men in *Pinafore*, that it was the cat.*

Dumoise arrived, and I never saw a little man so unprofessionally shocked. He said that it was a heartrending case of hydrophobia, and that nothing could be done. At least any palliative measures would only prolong the agony. The beast was foaming at the mouth. Fleete, as we told Dumoise, had been bitten by dogs once or twice. Any man who keeps half a dozen terriers must expect a nip now and again. Dumoise could offer no help. He could only certify that Fleete was dying of hydrophobia. The beast was then howling, for it had managed to spit out the shoe-horn. Dumoise said that he would be

ready to certify to the cause of death, and that the end was certain.
He was a good little man, and he offered to remain with us; but
Strickland refused the kindness. He did not wish to poison Dumoise's
New Year. He would only ask him not to give the real cause of
Fleete's death to the public.

So Dumoise left, deeply agitated; and as soon as the noise of the
cart-wheels had died away, Strickland told me, in a whisper, his
suspicions. They were so wildly improbable that he dared not say
them out aloud; and I, who entertained all Strickland's beliefs, was
so ashamed of owning to them that I pretended to disbelieve.

'Even if the Silver Man had bewitched Fleete for polluting the
image of Hanuman, the punishment could not have fallen so quickly.'

As I was whispering this the cry outside the house rose again, and
the beast fell into a fresh paroxysm of struggling till we were afraid
that the thongs that held it would give way.

'Watch!' said Strickland. 'If this happens six times I shall take the
law into my own hands. I order you to help me.'

He went into his room and came out in a few minutes with the
barrels of an old shot-gun, a piece of fishing-line, some thick cord,
and his heavy wooden bedstead. I reported that the convulsions had
followed the cry by two seconds in each case, and the beast seemed
perceptibly weaker.

Strickland muttered, 'But he can't take away the life! He can't take
away the life!'

I said, though I knew that I was arguing against myself, 'It may be
a cat. It must be a cat. If the Silver Man is responsible, why does he
dare to come here?'

Strickland arranged the wood on the hearth, put the gun-barrels
into the glow of the fire, spread the twine on the table and broke a
walking stick in two. There was one yard of fishing line, gut, lapped
with wire, such as is used for *mahseer*-fishing, and he tied the two
ends together in a loop.

Then he said, 'How can we catch him? He must be taken alive and
unhurt.'

I said that we must trust in Providence, and go out softly with
polo-sticks into the shrubbery at the front of the house. The man or
animal that made the cry was evidently moving round the house as
regularly as a night-watchman. We could wait in the bushes till he
came by and knock him over.

Strickland accepted this suggestion, and we slipped out from a bath-room window into the front verandah and then across the carriage drive into the bushes.

In the moonlight we could see the leper coming round the corner of the house. He was perfectly naked, and from time to time he mewed and stopped to dance with his shadow. It was an unattractive sight, and thinking of poor Fleete, brought to such degradation by so foul a creature, I put away all my doubts and resolved to help Strickland from the heated gun-barrels to the loop of twine—from the loins to the head and back again—with all tortures that might be needful.

The leper halted in the front porch for a moment and we jumped out on him with the sticks. He was wonderfully strong, and we were afraid that he might escape or be fatally injured before we caught him. We had an idea that lepers were frail creatures, but this proved to be incorrect. Strickland knocked his legs from under him and I put my foot on his neck. He mewed hideously, and even through my riding-boots I could feel that his flesh was not the flesh of a clean man.

He struck at us with his hand and feet-stumps. We looped the lash of a dog-whip round him, under the armpits, and dragged him backwards into the hall and so into the dining-room where the beast lay. There we tied him with trunk-straps. He made no attempt to escape, but mewed.

When we confronted him with the beast the scene was beyond description. The beast doubled backwards into a bow as though he had been poisoned with strychnine, and moaned in the most pitiable fashion. Several other things happened also, but they cannot be put down here.

'I think I was right,' said Strickland. 'Now we will ask him to cure this case.'

But the leper only mewed. Strickland wrapped a towel round his hand and took the gun-barrels out of the fire. I put the half of the broken walking stick through the loop of fishing-line and buckled the leper comfortably to Strickland's bedstead. I understood then how men and women and little children can endure to see a witch burnt alive; for the beast was moaning on the floor, and though the Silver Man had no face, you could see horrible feelings passing through the slab that took its place, exactly as waves of heat play across red-hot iron—gun-barrels for instance.

Strickland shaded his eyes with his hands for a moment and we got to work. This part is not to be printed.

*

The dawn was beginning to break when the leper spoke. His mewings had not been satisfactory up to that point. The beast had fainted from exhaustion and the house was very still. We unstrapped the leper and told him to take away the evil spirit. He crawled to the beast and laid his hand upon the left breast. That was all. Then he fell face down and whined, drawing in his breath as he did so.

We watched the face of the beast, and saw the soul of Fleete coming back into the eyes. Then a sweat broke out on the forehead and the eyes—they were human eyes—closed. We waited for an hour but Fleete still slept. We carried him to his room and bade the leper go, giving him the bedstead, and the sheet on the bedstead to cover his nakedness, the gloves and the towels with which we had touched him, and the whip that had been hooked round his body. He put the sheet about him and went out into the early morning without speaking or mewing.

Strickland wiped his face and sat down. A night-gong, far away in the city, made seven o'clock.

'Exactly four-and-twenty hours!' said Strickland. 'And I've done enough to ensure my dismissal from the service, besides permanent quarters in a lunatic asylum. Do you believe that we are awake?'

The red-hot gun-barrel had fallen on the floor and was singeing the carpet. The smell was entirely real.

That morning at eleven we two together went to wake up Fleete. We looked and saw that the black leopard-rosette on his chest had disappeared. He was very drowsy and tired, but as soon as he saw us, he said, 'Oh! Confound you fellows. Happy New Year to you. Never mix your liquors. I'm nearly dead.'

'Thanks for your kindness, but you're over time,' said Strickland. 'To-day is the morning of the second. You've slept the clock round with a vengeance.'

The door opened, and little Dumoise put his head in. He had come on foot, and fancied that we were laying out Fleete.

'I've brought a nurse,' said Dumoise. 'I suppose that she can come in for . . . what is necessary.'

'By all means,' said Fleete cheerily, sitting up in bed. 'Bring on your nurses.'

Dumoise was dumb. Strickland led him out and explained that there must have been a mistake in the diagnosis. Dumoise remained dumb and left the house hastily. He considered that his professional reputation had been injured, and was inclined to make a personal matter of the recovery. Strickland went out too. When he came back, he said that he had been to call on the Temple of Hanuman to offer redress for the pollution of the god, and had been solemnly assured that no white man had ever touched the idol and that he was an incarnation of all the virtues labouring under a delusion. 'What do you think?' said Strickland.

I said, ' "There are more things . . ." '

But Strickland hates that quotation. He says that I have worn it threadbare.

One other curious thing happened which frightened me as much as anything in all the night's work. When Fleete was dressed he came into the dining-room and sniffed. He had a quaint trick of moving his nose when he sniffed. 'Horrid doggy smell, here,' said he. 'You should really keep those terriers of yours in better order. Try sulphur, Strick.'

But Strickland did not answer. He caught hold of the back of a chair, and, without warning, went into an amazing fit of hysterics. It is terrible to see a strong man overtaken with hysteria. Then it struck me that we had fought for Fleete's soul with the Silver Man in that room, and had disgraced ourselves as Englishmen for ever, and I laughed and gasped and gurgled just as shamefully as Strickland, while Fleete thought that we had both gone mad. We never told him what we had done.

Some years later, when Strickland had married and was a church-going member of society for his wife's sake, we reviewed the incident dispassionately, and Strickland suggested that I should put it before the public.

I cannot myself see that this step is likely to clear up the mystery; because, in the first place, no one will believe a rather unpleasant story, and, in the second, it is well known to every right-minded man that the gods of the heathen are stone and brass, and any attempt to deal with them otherwise is justly condemned.

B. M. CROKER

The Dâk Bungalow at Dakor*

When shall these phantoms flicker away,
   Like the smoke of the guns on the wind-swept hill;
Like the sounds and colours of yesterday,
   And the soul have rest, and the air be still?

SIR A. LYALL*

'AND so you two young women are going off on a three days' journey, all by yourselves, in a bullock tonga,* to spend Christmas with your husbands in the jungle?'

The speaker was Mrs Duff, the wife of our deputy commissioner, and the two enterprising young women were Mrs Goodchild, the wife of the police officer of the district, and myself, wife of the forest officer. We were the only ladies in Karwassa, a little up-country station, more than a hundred miles from the line of rail. Karwassa was a pretty place, an oasis of civilization, amid leagues and leagues of surrounding forest and jungle; it boasted a post-office, public gardens (with tennis courts), a tiny church, a few well-kept shady roads, and half a dozen thatched bungalows, surrounded by luxuriant gardens. In the hot weather all the community were at home, under the shelter of their own roof-trees and punkahs, and within reach of ice—for we actually boasted an ice machine! During these hot months we had, so to speak, our 'season.' The deputy commissioner, forest officer, police officer, doctor, and engineer were all 'in,' and our gaieties took the form of tennis at daybreak, moonlight picnics, whist-parties, little dinners, and now and then a beat for tiger, on which occasions we ladies were safely roosted in trustworthy trees.

It is whispered that in small and isolated stations the fair sex are either mortal enemies or bosom-friends! I am proud to be in a position to state that we ladies of Karwassa came under the latter head. Mrs Goodchild and I were especially intimate; we were nearly the same age, we were young, we had been married in the same year and tasted our first experiences of India together. We lent each other books, we read each other our home letters, helped to compose one another's dirzee-made costumes, and poured little confidences into one another's ears. We had made numerous joint excursions in the cold season, had been out in the same camp for a month at a time, and when our husbands were in a malarious or uncivilized district, had journeyed on horseback or in a bullock tonga and joined them at some accessible spot, in the regions of dâk bungalows and bazaar fowl.

Mrs Duff, stout, elderly, and averse to locomotion, contented herself with her comfortable bungalow at Karwassa, her weekly budget of letters from her numerous olive-branches in England, and with adventures and thrilling experiences at secondhand.

'And so you are off to-morrow,' she continued, addressing herself to Mrs Goodchild. 'I suppose you know *where* you are going?'

'Yes,' returned my companion promptly, unfolding a piece of foolscap as she spoke; 'I had a letter from Frank this morning, and he has enclosed a plan copied from the D. P. W. map. We go straight along the trunk road for two days, stopping at Korai bungalow the first night and Kular the second, you see; then we turn off to the left on the Old Jubbulpore Road and make a march of twenty-five miles, halting at a place called Chanda.* Frank and Mr Loyd will meet us there on Christmas Day.'

'Chanda—Chanda,' repeated Mrs Duff, with her hand to her head. 'Isn't there some queer story about a bungalow near there—that is unhealthy—or haunted—or something?'

Julia Goodchild and I glanced at one another significantly. Mrs Duff had set her face against our expedition all along; she wanted us to remain in the station and spend Christmas with her, instead of going this wild-goose chase into a part of the district we had never been in before. She assured us that we would be short of bullocks, and would probably have to walk miles; she had harangued us on the subject of fever and cholera and bad water, had warned us solemnly against dacoits,* and now she was hinting at ghosts.

'Frank says that the travellers' bungalows after we leave the main road are not in very good repair—the road is so little used now that the new railway line comes within twenty miles; but he says that the one at Chanda is very decent, and we will push on there,' returned Julia, firmly. Julia was nothing if not firm; she particularly prided herself on never swerving from any fixed resolution or plan. 'We take my bullock tonga, and Mr Loyd's peon Abdul,* who is a treasure, as you know; he can cook, interpret, forage for provisions, and drive bullocks if the worst comes to the worst.'

'And what about bullocks for three days' journey—a hundred miles if it's a yard?' inquired Mrs Duff, sarcastically.

'Oh, the bazaar master has sent on a chuprassie* and five natives, and we shall find a pair every five miles at the usual stages. As to food, we are taking tea, bread, plenty of tinned stores, and the plum-pudding. We shall have a capital outing, I assure you, and I only wish we could have persuaded you into coming with us.'

'Thank you, my dear,' said Mrs Duff, with a patronizing smile. 'I'm too old, and I *hope* too sensible to take a trip of a hundred miles in a bullock tonga, risking fever and dacoits and dâk bungalows full of bandicoots, just for the sentimental pleasure of eating a pudding with my husband. However, you are both young and hardy and full of spirits, and I wish you a happy Christmas, a speedy journey and safe return. Mind you take plenty of quinine—and a revolver;' and, with this cheerful parting suggestion, she conducted us into the front verandah and dismissed us each with a kiss, that was at once a remonstrance and a valediction.

Behold us the next morning, at sunrise, jogging off, behind a pair of big white bullocks, in the highest spirits. In the front seat of the tonga we had stowed a well-filled tiffin basket, two Gladstone bags, our blankets and pillows, a hamper of provisions, and last, not least, Abdul. Julia and I and Julia's dog 'Boss' occupied the back seat, and as we rumbled past Mrs Duff's bungalow, with its still silent compound and closed venetians, we mutually agreed that she was 'a silly old thing,' that she would have far more enjoyment of life if she was as enterprising as we were.

Our first day's journey went off without a hitch. Fresh and well-behaved cattle punctually awaited us at every stage. The country we passed through was picturesque and well wooded; doves, pea-cocks, and squirrels enlivened the roads; big black-faced monkeys peered at us from amid the crops that they were ravaging within a stone's throw of our route. The haunt of a well-known man-eating tiger was impressively pointed out to us by our cicerone Abdul—this beast resided in some dense jungle, that was unpleasantly close to human traffic. Morning and afternoon wore away speedily, and at sundown we found ourselves in front of the very neat travellers' bungalow at Korai. The interior was scrupulously clean, and contained the usual furniture: two beds, two tables, four chairs, lamps, baths, a motley collection of teacups and plates, and last, not least, the framed rules of the establishment and visitors' book. The khansamah* cooked us an excellent dinner (for a travellers' bungalow), and, tired out, we soon went to bed and slept the sleep of the just. The second day was the same as the first—highly successful in every respect.

On the third morning we left the great highway and turned to the left, on to what was called the Old Jubbulpore Road, and here our troubles commenced! Bullocks were bad, lame, small, or unbroken; one of Mrs Duff's dismal prophecies came to pass, for after enduring bullocks who lay down, who kicked and ran off the road into their owners' houses, or rushed violently down steep places, we arrived at one stage where there were no bullocks *at all!* It was four o'clock, and we were still sixteen miles from Chanda. After a short consultation, Julia and I agreed to walk on to the next stage or village, leaving Abdul to draw the neighbourhood for a pair of cattle and then to overtake us at express speed.

'No one coming much this road now, mem sahib,' he explained apologetically; 'village people never keeping tonga bullocks—only plough bullocks, and plenty bobbery.'*

'Bobbery or not, get them,' said Julia with much decision; 'no matter if you pay four times the usual fare. We shall expect you to overtake us in half an hour.' And having issued this edict we walked on, leaving Abdul, a bullock-man, and two villagers all talking together and yelling at one another at the top of their voices.

Our road was dry and sandy, and lay through a perfectly flat country. It was lined here and there by rows of graceful trees, covered with wreaths of yellow flowers; now and then it was bordered by a rude thorn hedge, inside of which waved a golden field of ripe jawarri; in distant dips in the landscape we beheld noble topes of forest trees and a few red-roofed dwellings—the abodes of the tillers of the soil; but, on the whole, the country was silent and lonely; the few people we encountered driving their primitive little carts stared hard at us in utter stupefaction, as well they might—two mem sahibs trudging along, with no escort except a panting white dog. The insolent crows and lazy blue buffaloes all gazed at us in undisguised amazement as we wended our way through this monotonous and melancholy scene. One milestone was passed and then another, and yet another, and still no sign of Abdul, much less the tonga. At length we came in sight of a large village that stretched in a ragged way at either side of the road. There were the usual little mud hovels, shops displaying, say, two bunches of plantains and a few handfuls of grain, the usual collection of gaunt red pariah dogs, naked children, and unearthly-looking cats and poultry.

Julia and I halted afar off under a tree, preferring to wait for Abdul to chaperon us, ere we ran the gauntlet of the village streets. Time was getting on, the sun was setting; men were returning from the fields, driving bony bullocks before them; women were returning from the well, with water and the last bit of scandal; at last, to our great relief, we beheld Abdul approaching with the tonga, and our spirits rose, for we had begun to ask one another if we were to spend the night sitting on a stone under a tamarind tree without the village.

'No bullocks,' was Abdul's explanation. The same tired pair had come on most reluctantly, and in this village of cats and cocks and hens it was the same story—'no bullocks.' Abdul brought us this heavy and unexpected intelligence after a long and animated interview with the head man of the place.

'What is to be done?' we demanded in a breath.

'Stop here all night; going on to-morrow.'

'Stop where?' we almost screamed.

'Over there,' rejoined Abdul, pointing to a grove of trees at some little distance. 'There is a travellers' bungalow; Chanda is twelve miles off.'

A travellers' bungalow! Sure enough there was a building of some kind beyond the bamboos, and we lost no time in getting into the tonga and having ourselves driven in that direction. As we passed the village street, many came out and stared, and one old woman shook her hand in a warning manner, and called out something in a shrill cracked voice.

An avenue of feathery bamboos led to our destination, which proved to be the usual travellers' rest-house, with white walls, red roof, and roomy verandah; but when we came closer, we discovered that the drive was as grass-grown as a field; jungle grew up to the back of the house, heavy wooden shutters closed all the windows, and the door was locked. There was a forlorn, desolate, dismal appearance about the place; it looked as if it had not been visited for years. In answer to our shouts and calls no one appeared; but, as we were fully resolved to spend the night there, we had the tonga unloaded and our effects placed in the verandah, the bullocks untackled and turned out among the long rank grass. At length an old man in dirty ragged clothes, and with a villainous expression of countenance, appeared from some back cook-house, and seemed anything but pleased to see us. When Abdul told him of our intention of occupying the house, he would not hear of it. 'The bungalow was out of repair; it had not been opened for years; it was full of rats; it was unhealthy; plenty fever coming. We must go on to Chanda.'

Naturally we declined his hospitable suggestion. 'Was he the khansamah—caretaker of the place?' we inquired imperiously.

'Yees,' he admitted with a grunt.

'Drawing government pay, and refusing to open a government travellers' bungalow!' screamed Julia. 'Let us have no more of this nonsense; open the house at once and get it ready for us, or I shall report you to the commissioner sahib.'

The khansamah gave her an evil look, said 'Missus please,' shrugged his shoulders and hobbled away—as we hoped, to get the *key*; but after waiting ten minutes we sent Abdul to search for him, and found that he had departed—his lair was empty. There was nothing for it but to break the padlock on the door, which Abdul effected with a stone, and as soon as the door moved slowly back on its hinges Julia and I hurried in. What a dark, damp place! What a smell of earth, and what numbers of bats; they flew right in our faces as we stood in the doorway and tried to make out the interior. Abdul and the bullock-man quickly removed the shutters and let in the light, and then we beheld the usual dâk sitting-room—a table, chairs, and two charpoys (native beds), and an old pair of candlesticks; the table and chairs were covered with mould; cobwebs hung from the ceiling in dreadful festoons, and the walls were streaked with dreary green stains. I could not restrain an involuntary shudder as I looked about me rather blankly.

'I should think this *was* an unhealthy place!' I remarked to Julia. 'It looks feverish; and see—the jungle comes right up to the back verandah; fever plants, castor-oil plants, young bamboos, all growing up to the very walls.'

'It will do very well for to-night,' she returned. 'Come out and walk down the road whilst Abdul and the bullock-man clean out the rooms and get dinner. Abdul is a wonderful man—and we won't know the place in an hour's time; it's just the same as any other travellers' bungalow, only it has been neglected for years. I shall certainly report that old wretch! The *idea* of a dâk bungalow caretaker refusing admittance and running away with the key! What is the name of this place?' she asked, deliberately taking out her pocket-book; 'did you hear?'

'Yes; I believe it is called Dakor.'

'Ah, well! I shall not forget to tell Frank about the way we were treated at Dakor bungalow.'

The red, red sun had set at last—gone down, as it were, abruptly behind the flat horizon; the air began to feel chilly, and the owl and the jackal were commencing to make themselves heard, so we sauntered back to the bungalow, and found it indeed transformed: swept and garnished, and clean. The table was neatly laid for dinner, and one of our own fine hurricane lamps blazed upon it; our beds had been made up with our rugs and blankets, one at either end of the room; hot water and towels were prepared in a bath-room, and we saw a roaring fire in the cook-house in the jungle. Dinner, consisting of a sudden-death fowl, curry, bread, and *pâté de foie gras*, was, to our unjaded palates, an excellent meal. Our spirits rose to normal, the result of food and light, and we declared to one another that this old bungalow was a capital find, and that it was really both comfortable and cheerful, despite a slight *arrière pensée** of *earth* in the atmosphere!

Before going to bed we explored the next room, a smaller one than that we occupied, and empty save for a rickety camp table, which held some dilapidated crockery and a press. Need you ask if we opened this press? The press smelt strongly of mushrooms, and contained a man's topee,* inch-deep with mould, a tiffin basket, and the bungalow visitors' book. We carried this away with us to read at leisure, for the visitors' book in dâk bungalows occasionally contains some rather amusing observations. There was nothing funny in *this* musty old volume! Merely a statement of who came, and how long they stayed, and what they paid, with a few remarks, not by any means complimentary to the khansamah: 'A dirty, lazy rascal,' said one; 'A murderous-looking ruffian,' said another; 'An insolent, drunken hound,' said a third—the last entry was dated seven years previously.

'Let us write our names,' said Julia, taking out her pencil; ' "Mrs Goodchild and Mrs Loyd, December 23rd. Bungalow deserted, and very dirty khansamah." What shall we say?' she asked, glancing at me interrogatively.

'Why, there he is!' I returned with a little jump; and there he was sure enough, gazing in through the window. It was the face of some malicious animal, more than the face of a man, that glowered out beneath his filthy red turban. His eyes glared and rolled as if they would leave their sockets; his teeth were fangs, like dogs' teeth, and stood out almost perpendicularly from his hideous mouth. He surveyed us for a few seconds in savage silence, and then melted away into the surrounding darkness as suddenly as he appeared.

'He reminds me of the Cheshire cat in "Alice in Wonderland," ' said Julia with would-be facetiousness, but I noticed that she looked rather pale.

'Let us have the shutters up at once,' I replied, 'and have them well barred and the doors bolted. That man looked as if he could cut our throats.'

In a very short time the house was made fast. Abdul and the bullock-man spread their mats in the front verandah, and Julia and I retired for the night. Before going to bed we had a controversy about the lamp. I wished to keep it burning all night (I am a coward at heart), but Julia would not hear of this—impossible for her to sleep with a light in the room—and in the end I was compelled to be content with a candle and matches on a chair beside me. I fell asleep very soon. I fancy I must have slept long and soundly, when I was awoke by a bright light shining in my eyes. So, after the ridiculous fuss she had made, Julia *had* lit the candle after all! This was my first thought, but when I was fully awake I found I was mistaken, or dreaming. No, I was not dreaming, for I pinched my arm and rubbed my eyes. There was a man in the room, apparently another traveller, who appeared to be totally unaware of our vicinity, and to have made himself completely at home. A gun-case, a tiffin basket, a bundle of pillows and rugs—the usual Indian traveller's belongings—lay carelessly scattered about on the chairs and the floor. I leant up on my elbow and gazed at the intruder in profound amazement. He did not notice me, no more than if I had no existence; true, my charpoy was in a corner of the room and rather in the shade, so was Julia's. Julia was sound asleep and (low be it spoken) snoring. The stranger was writing a letter at the table facing me. Both candles were drawn up close to him, and threw a searching light upon his features. He was young and good-looking, but very, very pale; possibly he had just recovered from some long illness. I could not see his eyes, they were bent upon the paper before him; his hands, I noticed, were well shaped, white, and very thin. He wore a signet-ring on the third finger of the left hand, and was dressed with a care and finish not often met with in the jungle. He wore some kind of light Norfolk jacket and a blue bird's-eye tie. In front of him stood an open despatch-box, very shabby and scratched, and I could see that the upper tray contained a stout roundabout bag, presumably full of rupees, a thick roll of notes, and a gold watch. When I had deliberately taken in every item, the unutterable calmness of this stranger, thus establishing himself in our room, came home to me most forcibly, and clearing my throat I coughed—a clear decided cough of expostulation, to draw his attention to the enormity of the situation. It had no effect—he must be stone-deaf! He went on writing as indefatigably as ever. What he was writing was evidently a pleasant theme, possibly a love-letter, for he smiled as he scribbled. All at once I observed that the door was ajar. Two faces were peering in—a strange servant in a yellow turban, with cruel, greedy eyes, and *the khansamah!* Their gaze was riveted on the open despatch-box, the money, the roll of notes, and the watch. Presently the traveller's servant stole up behind his master noiselessly, and seemed to hold his breath; he drew a long knife from his sleeve. At this moment the stranger raised his eyes and looked at me. Oh, what a sad, strange look! a look of appeal. The next instant I saw the flash of the knife—it was buried in his back; he fell forward over his letter with a crash and a groan, and all was darkness. I tried to scream, but I could not. My tongue seemed paralyzed. I covered my head up in the clothes, and oh, how my heart beat! thump, thump, thump—surely *they* must hear it, and discover me? Half suffocated, at length I ventured to peer out for a second. All was still, black darkness. There was nothing to be seen, but much to be heard—the dragging of a heavy body, a *dead* body, across the room; then, after an appreciable pause, the sounds of digging outside the bungalow. Finally, the splashing of water—*some one washing the floor.* When I awoke the next morning, or came to myself—for I believe I had fainted—daylight was demanding admittance at every crevice in the shutters; night, its dark hours and its horrors, was past. The torture, the agony of fear, that had held me captive, had now released me, and, worn out, I fell fast asleep. It was actually nine o'clock when I opened my eyes. Julia was standing over me and shaking me vigorously, and saying, 'Nellie, Nellie, wake; I've been up and out this two hours; I've seen the head man of the village.'

'Have you?' I assented sleepily.

'Yes, and he says there are no bullocks to be had until to-morrow; we must pass another night here.'

'Never!' I almost shrieked. 'Never! Oh, Julia, I've had such a night. I've seen a murder!' And straightway I commenced, and told her of my awful experiences. 'That khansamah murdered him. He is buried just outside the front step,' I concluded tearfully. 'Sooner than stay here another night I'll *walk* to Chanda.'

'Ghosts! murders! walk to Chanda!' she echoed scornfully. 'Why, you silly girl, did *I* not sleep here in this very room, and sleep as sound as a top? It was all the *pâté de foie gras*. You *know* it never agrees with you.'

'I know nothing about *pâté de foie gras*,' I answered angrily; 'but I know what I saw. Sooner than sleep another night in this room I'd *die*. I might as well—for such another night would kill me!'

Bath, breakfast, and Julia brought me round to a certain extent. I thought better of tearing off to Chanda alone and on foot, especially as we heard (per coolie) that our respective husbands would be with us the next morning—Christmas Day. We spent the day cooking, exploring the country, and writing for the English mail. As night fell, I became more and more nervous, and less amenable to Julia and Julia's jokes. I would sleep in the verandah; either there, or in the compound. In the bungalow again—*never*. An old witch of a native woman, who was helping Abdul to cook, agreed to place her mat in the same locality as my mattress, and Julia Goodchild valiantly occupied the big room within, alone. In the middle of the night I and my protector were awoke by the most piercing, frightful shrieks. We lit a candle and ran into the bungalow, and found Julia lying on the floor in a dead faint. She did not come round for more than an hour, and when she opened her eyes she gazed about her with a shudder and displayed symptoms of going off again, so I instantly hunted up our flask and administered some raw brandy, and presently she found her tongue and attacked the old native woman quite viciously.

'Tell the truth about this place!' she said fiercely. 'What is it that is here, in this room?'

'Devils,' was the prompt and laconic reply.

'Nonsense! Murder has been done here; tell the truth.'

'How I knowing?' she whined. 'I only poor native woman.'

'An English sahib was murdered here seven years ago; stabbed and dragged out, and buried under the steps.'

'Ah, bah! ah, bah! How I telling? this not my country,' she wailed most piteously.

'Tell all you know,' persisted Julia. 'You *do* know! My husband is coming to-day; he is a police officer. You had better tell *me* than him.'

After much whimpering and hand-wringing, we extracted the following information in jerks and quavers:—

The bungalow had a bad name, no one ever entered it, and in spite of the wooden shutters there were *lights* in the windows every night up to twelve o'clock. One day (so the villagers said), many years ago, a young sahib came to this bungalow and stayed three days. He was alone. He was in the Forest Department. The last evening he sent his horses and servants on to Chanda, and said he would follow in the morning after having some shooting, he and his 'boy;' but though his people waited two weeks, he never appeared—was never seen again. The khansamah declared that he and his servant had left in the early morning, but no one met them. The khansamah became suddenly very rich; said he had found a treasure; also, he sold a fine gold watch in Jubbulpore, and took to drink. He had a bad name, and the bungalow had a bad name. No one would stay there more than one night, and no one had stayed there for many years till *we* came. The khansamah lived in the cook-house; he was *always* drunk. People said there were devils in the house, and no one would go near it after sundown. This was all she knew.

'Poor fellow, he was so good-looking!' sighed Julia when we were alone. 'Poor fellow, and he was murdered and buried here!'

'So I told you,' I replied, 'and you would not believe me, but insisted on staying to see for yourself.'

'I wish I had not—oh, I wish I had not! I shall never, never forget last night as long as I live.'

'That must have been *his* topee and tiffin basket that we saw in the press,' I exclaimed. 'As soon as your husband comes, we will tell him everything, and set him on the track of the murderers.'

Breakfast on Christmas morning was a very doleful meal; our nerves were completely shattered by our recent experiences, and we could only rouse ourselves up to offer a very melancholy sort of welcome to our two husbands, when they cantered briskly into the compound. In reply to their eager questions as to the cause of our lugubrious appearance, pale faces, and general air of mourning, we favoured them with a vivid description of our two nights in the bungalow. Of course, they were loudly, rudely incredulous, and, of course, *we* were very angry; vainly we re-stated our case, and displayed the old topee and tiffin basket; they merely laughed still more heartily and talked of 'nightmare,' and gave themselves such airs of offensive superiority, that Julia's soul flew to arms.

'Look here,' she cried passionately, '*I* laughed at Nellie as you laugh at *us*. We will go out of this compound, whilst you two dig, or get people to dig, below the front verandah and in front of the steps, and if you don't find the skeleton of a murdered man, then you may laugh at us for ever.'

With Julia impulse meant action, and before I could say three words I was out of the compound, with my arm wedged under hers; we went and sat on a little stone bridge within a stone's throw of the bungalow, glum and silent enough. What a Christmas Day! Half an hour's delay was as much as Julia's patience could brook. We then retraced our steps and discovered what seemed to be the whole village in the dâk bungalow compound. Frank came hurrying towards us, waving us frantically away. No need for questions; his face was enough. They had found it.

*

Frank Goodchild had known him—he was in his own department, a promising and most popular young fellow; his name was Gordon Forbes; he had been missed but never traced, and there was a report that he had been gored and killed in the jungle by a wild buffalo. In the same grave was found the battered despatch-box, by which the skeleton was identified. Mr Goodchild and my husband re-interred the body under a tree, and read the Burial Service over it, Nellie and I and all the village patriarchs attending as mourners. The khansamah was eagerly searched for—alas! in vain. He disappeared from that part of the country, and was said to have been devoured by a tiger in the Jhanas jungles; but this is too good to be true. We left the hateful bungalow with all speed that same afternoon, and spent the remainder of the Christmas Day at Chanda; it was the least merry

Christmas we ever remembered. The Goodehilds and ourselves have
subscribed and placed a granite cross, with his name and the date of
his death, over Gordon Forbes's lonely grave, and the news of the
discovery of the skeleton was duly forwarded to the proper authorities, and also to the unfortunate young man's relations, and to these
were sent the despatch-box, letters, and ring.

Mrs Duff was full of curiosity concerning our trip. We informed
her that we spent Christmas at Chanda, as we had originally intended,
with our husbands, that they had provided an excellent dinner of
black buck and jungle fowl, that the plum-pudding surpassed all
expectations; but we never told her a word about our two nights' halt
at Dakor bungalow.

ARTHUR CONAN DOYLE

Lot No. 249

OF the dealings of Edward Bellingham with William Monkhouse
Lee, and of the cause of the great terror of Abercrombie Smith, it
may be that no absolute and final judgment will ever be delivered. It
is true that we have the full and clear narrative of Smith himself, and
such corroboration as he could look for from Thomas Styles the
servant, from the Reverend Plumptree Peterson, Fellow of Old's,
and from such other people as chanced to gain some passing glance
at this or that incident in a singular chain of events. Yet, in the main,
the story must rest upon Smith alone, and the most will think that it
is more likely that one brain, however outwardly sane, has some
subtle warp in its texture, some strange flaw in its workings, than
that the path of nature has been overstepped in open day in so famed
a centre of learning and light as the University of Oxford. Yet when
we think how narrow and how devious this path of Nature is, how
dimly we can trace it, for all our lamps of science, and how from the
darkness which girds it round great and terrible possibilities loom
ever shadowly upwards, it is a bold and confident man who will put a
limit to the strange by-paths into which the human spirit may
wander.

In a certain wing of what we will call Old College in Oxford there
is a corner turret of an exceeding great age. The heavy arch which
spans the open door has bent downwards in the centre under the
weight of its years, and the grey, lichen-blotched blocks of stone are
bound and knitted together with withes and strands of ivy, as though
the old mother had set herself to brace them up against wind and
weather. From the door a stone stair curves upward spirally, passing
two landings, and terminating in a third one, its steps all shapeless
and hollowed by the tread of so many generations of the seekers after
knowledge. Life has flowed like water down this winding stair, and,
waterlike, has left these smooth-worn grooves behind it. From the
long-gowned, pedantic scholars of Plantagenet days down to the
young bloods of a later age, how full and strong had been that tide of

young English life. And what was left now of all those hopes, those strivings, those fiery energies, save here and there in some old-world churchyard a few scratches upon a stone, and perchance a handful of dust in a mouldering coffin? Yet here were the silent stair and the grey old wall, with bend and saltire and many another heraldic device still to be read upon its surface, like grotesque shadows thrown back from the days that had passed.

In the month of May, in the year 1884, three young men occupied the sets of rooms which opened on to the separate landings of the old stair. Each set consisted simply of a sitting-room and of a bedroom, while the two corresponding rooms upon the ground-floor were used, the one as a coal-cellar, and the other as the living-room of the servant, or scout, Thomas Styles, whose duty it was to wait upon the three men above him. To right and to left was a line of lecture-rooms and of offices, so that the dwellers in the old turret enjoyed a certain seclusion, which made the chambers popular among the more studious undergraduates. Such were the three who occupied them now—Abercrombie Smith above, Edward Bellingham beneath him, and William Monkhouse Lee upon the lowest storey.

It was ten o'clock on a bright spring night, and Abercrombie Smith lay back in his armchair, his feet upon the fender, and his briar-root pipe between his lips. In a similar chair, and equally at his ease, there lounged on the other side of the fireplace his old school friend Jephro Hastie. Both men were in flannels, for they had spent their evening upon the river, but apart from their dress no one could look at their hard-cut, alert faces without seeing that they were open-air men—men whose minds and tastes turned naturally to all that was manly and robust. Hastie, indeed, was stroke of his college boat, and Smith was an even better oar, but a coming examination had already cast its shadow over him and held him to his work, save for the few hours a week which health demanded. A litter of medical books upon the table, with scattered bones, models and anatomical plates, pointed to the extent as well as the nature of his studies, while a couple of single-sticks and a set of boxing-gloves above the mantel-piece hinted at the means by which, with Hastie's help, he might take his exercise in its most compressed and least distant form. They knew each other very well—so well that they could sit now in that soothing silence which is the very highest development of companionship.

'Have some whisky,' said Abercrombie Smith at last between two cloudbursts. 'Scotch in the jug and Irish in the bottle.'

'No, thanks. I'm in for the skulls. I don't liquor when I'm training. How about you?'

'I'm reading hard. I think it best to leave it alone.'

Hastie nodded, and they relapsed into a contented silence.

'By the way, Smith,' asked Hastie, presently, 'have you made the acquaintance of either of the fellows on your stair yet?'

'Just a nod when we pass. Nothing more.'

'Hum! I should be inclined to let it stand at that. I know something of them both. Not much, but as much as I want. I don't think I should take them to my bosom if I were you. Not that there's much amiss with Monkhouse Lee.'

'Meaning the thin one?'

'Precisely. He is a gentlemanly little fellow. I don't think there is any vice in him. But then you can't know him without knowing Bellingham.'

'Meaning the fat one?'

'Yes, the fat one. And he's a man whom I, for one, would rather not know.'

Abercrombie Smith raised his eyebrows and glanced across at his companion.

'What's up, then?' he asked. 'Drink? Cards? Cad? You used not to be censorious.'

'Ah! you evidently don't know the man, or you wouldn't ask. There's something damnable about him—something reptilian. My gorge always rises at him. I should put him down as a man with secret vices—an evil liver. He's no fool, though. They say that he is one of the best men in his line that they have ever had in the college.'

'Medicine or classics?'

'Eastern languages. He's a demon at them. Chillingworth met him somewhere above the second cataract* last long, and he told me that he just prattled to the Arabs as if he had been born and nursed and weaned among them. He talked Coptic to the Copts, and Hebrew to the Jews, and Arabic to the Bedouins, and they were all ready to kiss the hem of his frock-coat. There are some old hermit Johnnies up in those parts who sit on rocks and scowl and spit at the casual stranger. Well, when they saw this chap Bellingham, before he had said five words they just lay down on their bellies and wriggled. Chillingworth said that he never saw anything like it. Bellingham seemed to take it as his right, too, and strutted about among them and talked down to them like a Dutch uncle. Pretty good for an undergrad of Old's, wasn't it?'

'Why do you say you can't know Lee without knowing Bellingham?'

'Because Bellingham is engaged to his sister Eveline. Such a bright little girl, Smith! I know the whole family well. It's disgusting to see that brute with her. A toad and a dove, that's what they always remind me of.'

Abercrombie Smith grinned and knocked his ashes out against the side of the grate.

'You show every card in your hand, old chap,' said he. 'What a prejudiced, green-eyed, evil-thinking old man it is! You have really nothing against the fellow except that.'

'Well, I've known her ever since she was as long as that cherry-wood pipe, and I don't like to see her taking risks. And it is a risk. He looks beastly. And he has a beastly temper, a venomous temper. You remember his row with Long Norton?'

'No; you always forget that I am a freshman.'

'Ah, it was last winter. Of course. Well, you know the towpath along by the river. There were several fellows going along it, Bellingham in front, when they came on an old market-woman coming the other way. It had been raining—you know what those fields are like when it has rained—and the path ran between the river and a great puddle that was nearly as broad. Well, what does this swine do but keep the path, and push the old girl into the mud, where she and her marketings came to terrible grief. It was a blackguard thing to do, and Long Norton, who is as gentle a fellow as ever stepped, told him what he thought of it. One word led to another, and it ended in Norton laying his stick across the fellow's shoulders. There was the deuce of a fuss about it, and it's a treat to see the way in which Bellingham looks at Norton when they meet now. By Jove, Smith, it's nearly eleven o'clock!'

'No hurry. Light your pipe again.'

'Not I. I'm supposed to be in training. Here I've been sitting gossiping when I ought to have been safely tucked up. I'll borrow your skull, if you can share it. Williams has had mine for a month. I'll take the little bones of your ear, too, if you are sure you won't need them. Thanks very much. Never mind a bag, I can carry them very well under my arm. Good-night, my son, and take my tip as to your neighbour.'

When Hastie, bearing his anatomical plunder, had clattered off down the winding stair, Abercrombie Smith hurled his pipe into the waste-paper basket, and drawing his chair nearer to the lamp, plunged into a formidable green-covered volume, adorned with great coloured maps of that strange internal kingdom of which we are the hapless and helpless monarchs. Though a freshman at Oxford, the student was not so in medicine, for he had worked for four years at Glasgow and at Berlin, and this coming examination would place him finally as a member of his profession. With his firm mouth, broad forehead, and clear-cut, somewhat hard-featured face, he was a man who, if he had no brilliant talent, was yet so dogged, so patient, and so strong that he might in the end overtop a more showy genius. A man who can hold his own among Scotchmen and North Germans is not a man to be easily set back. Smith had left a name at Glasgow and at Berlin, and he was bent now upon doing as much at Oxford, if hard work and devotion could accomplish it.

He had sat reading for about an hour, and the hands of the noisy carriage clock upon the side table were rapidly closing together upon the twelve, when a sudden sound fell upon the student's ear—a sharp, rather shrill sound, like the hissing intake of a man's breath who gasps under some strong emotion. Smith laid down his book and slanted his ear to listen. There was no one on either side or above him, so that the interruption came certainly from the neighbour beneath—the same neighbour of whom Hastie had given so unsavoury an account. Smith knew him only as a flabby, pale-faced man of silent and studious habits, a man, whose lamp threw a golden bar from the old turret even after he had extinguished his own. This community in lateness had formed a certain silent bond between them. It was soothing to Smith when the hours stole on towards dawning to feel that there was another so close who set as small a value upon his sleep as he did. Even now, as his thoughts turned towards him, Smith's feelings were kindly. Hastie was a good fellow, but he was rough, strong-fibred, with no imagination or sympathy. He could not tolerate departures from what he looked upon as the model type of manliness. If a man could not be measured by a public-school standard, then he was beyond the pale with Hastie. Like so

many who are themselves robust, he was apt to confuse the constitu-
tion with the character, to ascribe to want of principle what was
really a want of circulation. Smith, with his stronger mind, knew his
friend's habit, and made allowance for it now as his thoughts turned
towards the man beneath him.

There was no return of the singular sound, and Smith was about
to turn to his work once more, when suddenly there broke out in the
silence of the night a hoarse cry, a positive scream—the call of a man
who is moved and shaken beyond all control. Smith sprang out of his
chair and dropped his book. He was a man of fairly firm fibre, but
there was something in this sudden, uncontrollable shriek of horror
which chilled his blood and pringled in his skin. Coming in such a
place and at such an hour, it brought a thousand fantastic possibilities into his head. Should he rush down, or was it better to wait?
He had all the national hatred of making a scene, and he knew so
little of his neighbour that he would not lightly intrude upon his
affairs. For a moment he stood in doubt and even as he balanced the
matter there was a quick rattle of footsteps upon the stairs, and
young Monkhouse Lee, half dressed and as white as ashes, burst into
his room.

'Come down!' he gasped. 'Bellingham's ill.'

Abercrombie Smith followed him closely down stairs into the
sitting-room which was beneath his own, and intent as he was upon
the matter in hand, he could not but take an amazed glance around
him as he crossed the threshold. It was such a chamber as he had
never seen before—a museum rather than a study. Walls and ceiling
were thickly covered with a thousand strange relics from Egypt and
the East. Tall, angular figures bearing burdens or weapons stalked in
an uncouth frieze round the apartments. Above were bull-headed,
stork-headed, cat-headed, owl-headed statues, with viper-crowned,
almond-eyed monarchs, and strange, beetle-like deities cut out of
the blue Egyptian lapis lazuli. Horus and Isis and Osiris* peeped
down from every niche and shelf, while across the ceiling a true son
of Old Nile, a great, hanging-jawed crocodile, was slung in a double
noose.

In the centre of this singular chamber was a large, square table,
littered with papers, bottles, and the dried leaves of some graceful,
palm-like plant. These varied objects had all been heaped together in
order to make room for a mummy case, which had been conveyed

from the wall, as was evident from the gap there, and laid across the front of the table. The mummy itself, a horrid, black, withered thing, like a charred head on a gnarled bush, was lying half out of the case, with its clawlike hand and bony forearm resting upon the table. Propped up against the sarcophagus was an old yellow scroll of papyrus, and in front of it, in a wooden arm-chair, sat the owner of the room, his head thrown back, his widely-opened eyes directed in a horrified stare to the crocodile above him, and his blue, thick lips puffing loudly with every expiration.

'My God! he's dying!' cried Monkhouse Lee distractedly.

He was a slim, handsome young fellow, olive-skinned and dark-eyed, of a Spanish rather than of an English type, with a Celtic intensity of manner which contrasted with the Saxon phlegm of Abercrombie Smith.

'Only a faint, I think,' said the medical student. 'Just give me a hand with him. You take his feet. Now on to the sofa. Can you kick all those little wooden devils off? What a litter it is! Now he will be all right if we undo his collar and give him some water. What has he been up to at all?'

'I don't know. I heard him cry out. I ran up. I know him pretty well, you know. It is very good of you to come down.'

'His heart is going like a pair of castanets,' said Smith, laying his hand on the breast of the unconscious man. 'He seems to me to be frightened all to pieces. Chuck the water over him! What a face he has got on him!'

It was indeed a strange and most repellent face, for colour and outline were equally unnatural. It was white, not with the ordinary pallor of fear, but with an absolutely bloodless white, like the under side of a sole. He was very fat, but gave the impression of having at some time been considerably fatter, for his skin hung loosely in creases and folds, and was shot with a meshwork of wrinkles. Short, stubbly brown hair bristled up from his scalp, with a pair of thick, wrinkled ears protruding on either side. His light grey eyes were still open, the pupils dilated and the balls projecting in a fixed and horrid stare. It seemed to Smith as he looked down upon him that he had never seen nature's danger signals flying so plainly upon a man's countenance, and his thoughts turned more seriously to the warning which Hastie had given him an hour before.

'What the deuce can have frightened him so?' he asked.

'It's the mummy.'

'The mummy? How, then?'

'I don't know. It's beastly and morbid. I wish he would drop it. It's the second fright he has given me. It was the same last winter. I found him just like this, with that horrid thing in front of him.'

'What does he want with the mummy, then?'

'Oh, he's a crank, you know. It's his hobby. He knows more about these things than any man in England. But I wish he wouldn't! Ah, he's beginning to come to.'

A faint tinge of colour had begun to steal back into Bellingham's ghastly cheeks, and his eyelids shivered like a sail after a calm. He clasped and unclasped his hands, drew a long, thin breath between his teeth, and suddenly jerking up his head, threw a glance of recognition around him. As his eyes fell upon the mummy, he sprang off the sofa, seized the roll of papyrus, thrust it into a drawer, turned the key, and then staggered back on to the sofa.

'What's up?' he asked. 'What do you chaps want?'

'You've been shrieking out and making no end of a fuss,' said Monkhouse Lee. 'If our neighbour here from above hadn't come down, I'm sure I don't know what I should have done with you.'

'Ah, it's Abercrombie Smith,' said Bellingham, glancing up at him. 'How very good of you to come in! What a fool I am! Oh, my God, what a fool I am!'

He sunk his head on to his hands, and burst into peal after peal of hysterical laughter.

'Look here! Drop it!' cried Smith, shaking him roughly by the shoulder.

'Your nerves are all in a jangle. You must drop these little midnight games with mummies, or you'll be going off your chump. You're all on wires now.'

'I wonder,' said Bellingham, 'whether you would be as cool as I am if you had seen—'

'What then?'

'Oh, nothing. I meant that I wonder if you could sit up at night with a mummy without trying your nerves. I have no doubt that you are quite right. I dare say that I have been taking it out of myself too much lately. But I am all right now. Please don't go, though. Just wait for a few minutes until I am quite myself.'

'The room is very close,' remarked Lee, throwing open the window and letting in the cool night air.

'It's balsamic resin,' said Bellingham. He lifted up one of the dried palmate leaves from the table and frizzled it over the chimney of the lamp. It broke away into heavy smoke wreaths, and a pungent, biting odour filled the chamber. 'It's the sacred plant—the plant of the priests,' he remarked. 'Do you know anything of Eastern languages, Smith?'

'Nothing at all. Not a word.'

The answer seemed to lift a weight from the Egyptologist's mind.

'By the way,' he continued, 'how long was it from the time that you ran down, until I came to my senses?'

'Not long. Some four or five minutes.'

'I thought it could not be very long,' said he, drawing a long breath. 'But what a strange thing unconsciousness is! There is no measurement to it. I could not tell from my own sensations if it were seconds or weeks. Now that gentleman on the table was packed up in the days of the eleventh dynasty, some forty centuries ago, and yet if he could find his tongue, he would tell us that this lapse of time has been but a closing of the eyes and a reopening of them. He is a singularly fine mummy, Smith.'

Smith stepped over to the table and looked down with a professional eye at the black and twisted form in front of him. The features, though horribly discoloured, were perfect, and two little nut-like eyes still lurked in the depths of the black, hollow sockets. The blotched skin was drawn tightly from bone to bone, and a tangled wrap of black coarse hair fell over the ears. Two thin teeth, like those of a rat, overlay the shrivelled lower lip. In its crouching position, with bent joints and craned head, there was a suggestion of energy about the horrid thing which made Smith's gorge rise. The gaunt ribs, with their parchment-like covering, were exposed, and the sunken, leaden-hued abdomen, with the long slit where the embalmer had left his mark; but the lower limbs were wrapt round with coarse yellow bandages. A number of little clove-like pieces of myrrh and of cassia were sprinkled over the body, and lay scattered on the inside of the case.

'I don't know his name,' said Bellingham, passing his hand over the shrivelled head. 'You see the outer sarcophagus with the inscriptions is missing. Lot 249 is all the title he has now. You see it printed on his case. That was his number in the auction at which I picked him up.'

'He has been a very pretty sort of fellow in his day,' remarked Abercrombie Smith.

'He has been a giant. His mummy is six feet seven in length, and that would be a giant over there, for they were never a very robust race. Feel these great knotted bones, too. He would be a nasty fellow to tackle.'

'Perhaps these very hands helped to build the stones into the pyramids,' suggested Monkhouse Lee, looking down with disgust in his eyes at the crooked, unclean talons.

'No fear. This fellow has been pickled in natron, and looked after in the most approved style. They did not serve hodsmen in that fashion. Salt or bitumen was enough for them. It has been calculated that this sort of thing cost about seven hundred and thirty pounds in our money. Our friend was a noble at the least. What do you make of that small inscription near his feet, Smith?'

'I told you that I know no Eastern tongue.'

'Ah, so you did. It is the name of the embalmer, I take it. A very conscientious worker he must have been. I wonder how many modern works will survive four thousand years?'

He kept on speaking lightly and rapidly, but it was evident to Abercrombie Smith that he was still palpitating with fear. His hands shook, his lower lip trembled, and look where he would, his eye always came sliding round to his gruesome companion. Through all his fear, however, there was a suspicion of triumph in his tone and manner. His eyes shone, and his footstep, as he paced the room, was brisk and jaunty. He gave the impression of a man who has gone through an ordeal, the marks of which he still bears upon him, but which has helped him to his end.

'You're not going yet?' he cried, as Smith rose from the sofa.

At the prospect of solitude, his fears seemed to crowd back upon him, and he stretched out a hand to detain him.

'Yes, I must go. I have my work to do. You are all right now. I think that with your nervous system you should take up some less morbid study.'

'Oh, I am not nervous as a rule; and I have unwrapped mummies before.'

'You fainted last time,' observed Monkhouse Lee.

'Ah, yes, so I did. Well, I must have a nerve tonic or a course of electricity.* You are not going, Lee?'

'I'll do whatever you wish, Ned.'

'Then I'll come down with you and have a shake-down on your sofa. Good-night, Smith. I am so sorry to have disturbed you with my foolishness.'

They shook hands, and as the medical student stumbled up the spiral and irregular stair he heard a key turn in a door, and the steps of his two new acquaintances as they descended to the lower floor.

In this strange way began the acquaintance between Edward Bellingham and Abercrombie Smith, an acquaintance which the latter, at least, had no desire to push further. Bellingham, however, appeared to have taken a fancy to his rough-spoken neighbour, and made his advances in such a way that he could hardly be repulsed without absolute brutality. Twice he called to thank Smith for his assistance, and many times afterwards he looked in with books, papers and such other civilities as two bachelor neighbours can offer each other. He was, as Smith soon found, a man of wide reading, with catholic tastes and an extraordinary memory. His manner, too, was so pleasing and suave that one came, after a time, to overlook his repellent appearance. For a jaded and wearied man he was no unpleasant companion, and Smith found himself, after a time, looking forward to his visits, and even returning them.

Clever as he undoubtedly was, however, the medical student seemed to detect a dash of insanity in the man. He broke out at times into a high, inflated style of talk which was in contrast with the simplicity of his life.

'It is a wonderful thing,' he cried, 'to feel that one can command powers of good and of evil—a ministering angel or a demon of vengeance.' And again, of Monkhouse Lee, he said,—'Lee is a good fellow, an honest fellow, but he is without strength or ambition. He would not make a fit partner for a man with a great enterprise. He would not make a fit partner for me.'

At such hints and innuendoes stolid Smith, puffing solemnly at his pipe, would simply raise his eyebrows and shake his head, with little interjections of medical wisdom as to earlier hours and fresher air.

One habit Bellingham had developed of late which Smith knew to be a frequent herald of a weakening mind. He appeared to be forever talking to himself. At late hours of the night, when there could be no visitor with him, Smith could still hear his voice beneath him in a low, muffled monologue, sunk almost to a whisper, and yet very audible in the silence. This solitary babbling annoyed and distracted the student, so that he spoke more than once to his neighbour about it. Bellingham, however, flushed up at the charge, and denied curtly that he had uttered a sound; indeed, he showed more annoyance over the matter than the occasion seemed to demand.

Had Abercrombie Smith had any doubt as to his own ears he had not to go far to find corroboration. Tom Styles, the little wrinkled man-servant who had attended to the wants of the lodgers in the turret for a longer time than any man's memory could carry him, was sorely put to it over the same matter.

'If you please, sir,' said he, as he tidied down the top chamber one morning, 'do you think Mr Bellingham is all right, sir?'

'All right, Styles?'

'Yes sir. Right in his head, sir.'

'Why should he not be, then?'

'Well, I don't know, sir. His habits has changed of late. He's not the same man he used to be, though I make free to say that he was never quite one of my gentlemen, like Mr Hastie or yourself, sir. He's took to talkin' to himself something awful. I wonder it don't disturb you. I don't know what to make of him, sir.'

'I don't know what business it is of yours, Styles.'

'Well, I takes an interest, Mr Smith. It may be forward of me, but I can't help it. I feel sometimes as if I was mother and father to my young gentlemen. It all falls on me when things go wrong and the relations come. But Mr Bellingham, sir. I want to know what it is that walks about his room sometimes when he's out and when the door's locked on the outside.'

'Eh? you're talking nonsense, Styles.'

'Maybe so, sir; but I heard it more'n once with my own ears.'

'Rubbish, Styles.'

'Very good, sir. You'll ring the bell if you want me.'

Abercrombie Smith gave little heed to the gossip of the old man-servant, but a small incident occurred a few days later which left an unpleasant effect upon his mind, and brought the words of Styles forcibly to his memory.

Bellingham had come up to see him late one night, and was

entertaining him with an interesting account of the rock tombs of Beni Hassan in Upper Egypt, when Smith, whose hearing was remarkably acute, distinctly heard the sound of a door opening on the landing below.

'There's some fellow gone in or out of your room,' he remarked.

Bellingham sprang up and stood helpless for a moment, with the expression of a man who is half incredulous and half afraid.

'I surely locked it. I am almost positive that I locked it,' he stammered. 'No one could have opened it.'

'Why, I hear someone coming up the steps now,' said Smith.

Bellingham rushed out through the door, slammed it loudly behind him, and hurried down the stairs. About half-way down Smith heard him stop, and thought he caught the sound of whispering. A moment later the door beneath him shut, a key creaked in a lock, and Bellingham, with beads of moisture upon his pale face, ascended the stairs once more, and re-entered the room.

'It's all right,' he said, throwing himself down in a chair. 'It was that fool of a dog. He had pushed the door open. I don't know how I came to forget to lock it.'

'I didn't know you kept a dog,' said Smith, looking very thoughtfully at the disturbed face of his companion.

'Yes, I haven't had him long. I must get rid of him. He's a great nuisance.'

'He must be, if you find it so hard to shut him up. I should have thought that shutting the door would have been enough, without locking it.'

'I want to prevent old Styles from letting him out. He's of some value, you know, and it would be awkward to lose him.'

'I am a bit of a dog-fancier myself,' said Smith, still gazing hard at his companion from the corner of his eyes. 'Perhaps you'll let me have a look at it.'

'Certainly. But I am afraid it cannot be tonight; I have an appointment. Is that clock right? Then I am a quarter of an hour late already. You'll excuse me, I am sure.'

He picked up his cap and hurried from the room. In spite of his appointment, Smith heard him re-enter his own chamber and lock his door upon the inside.

This interview left a disagreeable impression upon the medical student's mind. Bellingham had lied to him, and lied so clumsily that it looked as if he had desperate reasons for concealing the truth. Smith knew that his neighbour had no dog. He knew, also, that the step which he had heard upon the stairs was not the step of an animal. But if it were not, then what could it be? There was old Styles's statement about the something which used to pace the room at times when the owner was absent. Could it be a woman? Smith rather inclined to the view. If so, it would mean disgrace and expulsion to Bellingham if it were discovered by the authorities, so that his anxiety and falsehoods might be accounted for. And yet it was inconceivable that an undergraduate could keep a woman in his rooms without being instantly detected. Be the explanation what it might, there was something ugly about it, and Smith determined, as he turned to his books, to discourage all further attempts at intimacy on the part of his soft-spoken and ill-favoured neighbour.

But his work was destined to interruption that night. He had hardly caught up the broken threads when a firm, heavy footfall came three steps at a time from below, and Hastie, in blazer and flannels, burst into the room.

'Still at it!' said he, plumping down into his wonted arm-chair. 'What a chap you are to stew! I believe an earthquake might come and knock Oxford into a cocked hat, and you would sit perfectly placid with your books among the ruins. However, I won't bore you long. Three whiffs of baccy, and I am off.'

'What's the news, then?' asked Smith, cramming a plug of bird's-eye into his briar with his forefinger.

'Nothing very much. Wilson made 70 for the freshmen against the eleven. They say that they will play him instead of Buddicomb, for Buddicomb is clean off colour. He used to be able to bowl a little, but it's nothing but half-volleys and long hops now.'

'Medium right,' suggested Smith, with the intense gravity which comes upon a 'varsity man when he speaks of athletics.

'Inclining to fast, with a work from leg. Comes with the arm about three inches or so. He used to be nasty on a wet wicket. Oh, by-the-way, have you heard about Long Norton?'

'What's that?'

'He's been attacked.'

'Attacked?'

'Yes, just as he was turning out of the High Street, and within a hundred yards of the gate of Old's.'

'But who—'

'Ah, that's the rub! If you said "what," you would be more gram-matical. Norton swears that it was not human, and, indeed, from the scratches on his throat, I should be inclined to agree with him.'

'What, then? Have we come down to spooks?'

Abercrombie Smith puffed his scientific contempt.

'Well, no; I don't think that is quite the idea, either. I am inclined to think that if any showman has lost a great ape lately, and the brute is in these parts, a jury would find a true bill against it. Norton passes that way every night, you know, about the same hour. There's a tree that hangs low over the path—the big elm from Rainy's garden. Norton thinks the thing dropped on him out of the tree. Anyhow, he was nearly strangled by two arms, which, he says, were as strong and as thin as steel bands. He saw nothing; only those beastly arms that tightened and tightened on him. He yelled his head nearly off, and a couple of chaps came running, and the thing went over the wall like a cat. He never got a fair sight of it the whole time. It gave Norton a shake up, I can tell you. I tell him it has been as good as a change at the sea-side for him.'

'A garrotter, most likely,' said Smith.

'Very possibly. Norton says not; but we don't mind what he says. The garrotter had long nails, and was pretty smart at swinging him-self over walls. By-the-way, your beautiful neighbour would be pleased if he heard about it. He had a grudge against Norton, and he's not a man, from what I know of him, to forget his little debts. But hallo, old chap, what have you got in your noddle?'

'Nothing,' Smith answered curtly.

He had started in his chair, and the look had flashed over his face which comes upon a man who is struck suddenly by some unpleasant idea.

'You looked as if something I had said had taken you on the raw. By-the-way, you have made the acquaintance of Master B. since I looked in last, have you not? Young Monkhouse Lee told me something to that effect.'

'Yes; I know him slightly. He has been up here once or twice.'

'Well, you're big enough and ugly enough to take care of yourself. He's not what I should call exactly a healthy sort of Johnny, though, no doubt, he's very clever, and all that. But you'll soon find out for yourself. Lee is all right; he's a very decent little fellow. Well, so long, old chap! I row Mullins for the Vice-Chancellor's pot on Wednesday week, so mind you come down, in case I don't see you before.'

Bovine Smith laid down his pipe and turned stolidly to his books once more. But with all the will in the world, he found it very hard to keep his mind upon his work. It would slip away to brood upon the man beneath him, and upon the little mystery which hung round his chambers. Then his thoughts turned to this singular attack of which Hastie had spoken, and to the grudge which Bellingham was said to owe the object of it. The two ideas would persist in rising together in his mind, as though there were some close and intimate connection between them. And yet the suspicion was so dim and vague that it could not be put down in words.

'Confound the chap!' cried Smith, as he shied his book on pathology across the room. 'He has spoiled my night's reading, and that's reason enough, if there were no other, why I should steer clear of him in the future.'

For ten days the medical student confined himself so closely to his studies that he neither saw nor heard anything of either of the men beneath him. At the hours when Bellingham had been accustomed to visit him, he took care to sport his oak, and though he more than once heard a knocking at his outer door, he resolutely refused to answer it. One afternoon, however, he was descending the stairs when, just as he was passing it, Bellingham's door flew open, and young Monkhouse Lee came out with his eyes sparkling and a dark flush of anger upon his olive cheeks. Close at his heels followed Bellingham, his fat, unhealthy face all quivering with malignant passion.

'You fool!' he hissed. 'You'll be sorry.'

'Very likely,' cried the other. 'Mind what I say. It's off! I won't hear of it!'

'You've promised, anyhow.'

'Oh, I'll keep that! I won't speak. But I'd rather little Eva was in her grave. Once for all, it's off. She'll do what I say. We don't want to see you again.'

So much Smith could not avoid hearing, but he hurried on, for he had no wish to be involved in their dispute. There had been a serious breach between them, that was clear enough, and Lee was going to cause the engagement with his sister to be broken off. Smith thought of Hastie's comparison of the toad and the dove, and was glad to think that the matter was at an end. Bellingham's face when he was in a passion was not pleasant to look upon. He was not a man to whom an innocent girl could be trusted for life. As he walked, Smith wondered languidly what could have caused the quarrel, and what the promise might be which Bellingham had been so anxious that Monkhouse Lee should keep.

It was the day of the sculling match between Hastie and Mullins, and a stream of men were making their way down to the banks of the Isis. A May sun was shining brightly, and the yellow path was barred with the black shadows of the tall elm-trees. On either side the grey colleges lay back from the road, the hoary old mothers of minds looking out from their high, mullioned windows at the tide of young life which swept so merrily past them. Black-clad tutors, prim officials, pale reading men, brown-faced, straw-hatted young athletes in white sweaters or many-coloured blazers, all were hurrying towards the blue winding river which curves through the Oxford meadows.

Abercrombie Smith, with the intuition of an old oarsman, chose his position at the point where he knew that the struggle, if there were a struggle, would come. Far off he heard the hum which announced the start, the gathering roar of the approach, the thunder of running feet, and the shouts of the men in the boats beneath him. A spray of half-clad, deep-breathing runners shot past him, and craning over their shoulders, he saw Hastie pulling a steady thirty-six, while his opponent, with a jerky forty, was a good boat's length behind him. Smith gave a cheer for his friend, and pulling out his watch, was starting off again for his chambers, when he felt a touch upon his shoulder, and found that young Monkhouse Lee was beside him.

'I saw you there,' he said, in a timid, deprecating way. 'I wanted to speak to you, if you could spare me a half-hour. This cottage is mine. I share it with Harrington of King's. Come in and have a cup of tea.'

'I must be back presently,' said Smith. 'I am hard on the grind at present. But I'll come in for a few minutes with pleasure. I wouldn't have come out only Hastie is a friend of mine.'

'So he is of mine. Hasn't he a beautiful style? Mullins wasn't in it. But come into the cottage. It's a little den of a place, but it is pleasant to work in during the summer months.'

It was a small, square, white building, with green doors and shutters, and a rustic trellis-work porch, standing back some fifty yards from the river's bank. Inside, the main room was roughly fitted up as a study—deal table, unpainted shelves with books, and a few cheap oleographs upon the wall. A kettle sang upon a spirit-stove, and there were tea things upon a tray on the table.

'Try that chair and have a cigarette,' said Lee. 'Let me pour you out a cup of tea. It's so good of you to come in, for I know that your time is a good deal taken up. I wanted to say to you that, if I were you, I should change my rooms at once.'

'Eh?'

Smith sat staring with a lighted match in one hand and his unlit cigarette in the other.

'Yes; it must seem very extraordinary, and the worst of it is that I cannot give my reasons, for I am under a solemn promise—a very solemn promise. But I may go so far as to say that I don't think Bellingham is a very safe man to live near. I intend to camp out here as much as I can for a time.'

'Not safe! What do you mean?'

'Ah, that's what I mustn't say. But do take my advice, and move your rooms. We had a grand row to-day. You must have heard us, for you came down the stairs.'

'I saw that you had fallen out.'

'He's a horrible chap, Smith. That is the only word for him. I have had doubts about him ever since that night when he fainted—you remember, when you came down. I taxed him to-day, and he told me things that made my hair rise, and wanted me to stand in with him. I'm not strait-laced, but I am a clergyman's son, you know, and I think there are some things which are quite beyond the pale. I only thank God that I found him out before it was too late, for he was to have married into my family.'

'This is all very fine, Lee,' said Abercrombie Smith curtly. 'But either you are saying a great deal too much or a great deal too little.'

'I give you a warning.'

'If there is real reason for warning, no promise can bind you. If I see a rascal about to blow a place up with dynamite no pledge will stand in my way of preventing him.'

'Ah, but I cannot prevent him, and I can do nothing but warn you.'

'Without saying what you warn me against.'

'Against Bellingham.'

'But that is childish. Why should I fear him, or any man?'

'I can't tell you. I can only entreat you to change your rooms. You are in danger where you are. I don't even say that Bellingham would wish to injure you. But it might happen, for he is a dangerous neighbour just now.'

'Perhaps I know more than you think,' said Smith, looking keenly at the young man's boyish, earnest face. 'Suppose I tell you that some one else shares Bellingham's rooms.'

Monkhouse Lee sprang from his chair in uncontrollable excitement.

'You know, then?' he gasped.

'A woman.'

Lee dropped back again with a groan.

'My lips are sealed,' he said. 'I must not speak.'

'Well, anyhow,' said Smith, rising, 'it is not likely that I should allow myself to be frightened out of rooms which suit me very nicely. It would be a little too feeble for me to move out all my goods and chattels because you say that Bellingham might in some unexplained way do me an injury. I think that I'll just take my chance, and stay where I am, and as I see that it's nearly five o'clock, I must ask you to excuse me.'

He bade the young student adieu in a few curt words, and made his way homeward through the sweet spring evening, feeling half-ruffled, half-amused, as any other strong, unimaginative man might who has been menaced by a vague and shadowy danger.

There was one little indulgence which Abercrombie Smith always allowed himself, however closely his work might press upon him. Twice a week, on the Tuesday and the Friday, it was his invariable custom to walk over to Farlingford, the residence of Doctor Plumptree Peterson, situated about a mile and a half out of Oxford. Peterson had been a close friend of Smith's elder brother Francis, and as he was a bachelor, fairly well-to-do, with a good cellar and a better library, his house was a pleasant goal for a man who was in need of a brisk walk. Twice a week, then, the medical student would swing out there along the dark country roads, and spend a pleasant hour in Peterson's comfortable study, discussing, over a glass of old port, the gossip of the 'varsity or the latest developments of medicine or of surgery.

On the day which followed his interview with Monkhouse Lee,

Smith shut up his books at a quarter past eight, the hour when he usually started for his friend's house. As he was leaving his room, however, his eyes chanced to fall upon one of the books which Bellingham had lent him, and his conscience pricked him for not having returned it. However repellent the man might be, he should not be treated with discourtesy. Taking the book, he walked downstairs and knocked at his neighbour's door. There was no answer; but on turning the handle he found that it was unlocked. Pleased at the thought of avoiding an interview, he stepped inside, and placed the book with his card upon the table.

The lamp was turned half down, but Smith could see the details of the room plainly enough. It was all much as he had seen it before—the frieze, the animal-headed gods, the hanging crocodile, and the table littered over with papers and dried leaves. The mummy case stood upright against the wall, but the mummy itself was missing. There was no sign of any second occupant of the room, and he felt as he withdrew that he had probably done Bellingham an injustice. Had he a guilty secret to preserve, he would hardly leave his door open so that all the world might enter.

The spiral stair was as black as pitch, and Smith was slowly making his way down its irregular steps, when he was suddenly conscious that something had passed him in the darkness. There was a faint sound, a whiff of air, a light brushing past his elbow, but so slight that he could scarcely be certain of it. He stopped and listened, but the wind was rustling among the ivy outside, and he could hear nothing else.

'Is that you, Styles?' he shouted.

There was no answer, and all was still behind him. It must have been a sudden gust of air, for there were crannies and cracks in the old turret. And yet he could almost have sworn that he heard a footfall by his very side. He had emerged into the quadrangle, still turning the matter over in his head, when a man came running swiftly across the smooth-cropped lawn.

'Is that you, Smith?'

'Hullo, Hastie!'

'For God's sake come at once! Young Lee is drowned! Here's Harrington of King's with the news. The doctor is out. You'll do, but come along at once. There may be life in him.'

'Have you brandy?'

'No.'

'I'll bring some. There's a flask on my table.'

Smith bounded up the stairs, taking three at a time, seized the flask, and was rushing down with it, when, as he passed Bellingham's room, his eyes fell upon something which left him gasping and staring upon the landing.

The door, which he had closed behind him, was now open, and right in front of him, with the lamp-light shining upon it, was the mummy case. Three minutes ago it had been empty. He could swear to that. Now it framed the lank body of its horrible occupant, who stood, grim and stark, with his black shrivelled face towards the door. The form was lifeless and inert, but it seemed to Smith as he gazed that there still lingered a lurid spark of vitality, some faint sign of consciousness in the little eyes which lurked in the depths of the hollow sockets. So astounded and shaken was he that he had forgotten his errand, and was still staring at the lean, sunken figure when the voice of his friend below recalled him to himself.

'Come on, Smith!' he shouted. 'It's life and death, you know. Hurry up! Now, then,' he added, as the medical student reappeared, 'let us do a sprint. It is well under a mile, and we should do it in five minutes. A human life is better worth running for than a pot.'

Neck and neck they dashed through the darkness, and did not pull up until panting and spent, they had reached the little cottage by the river. Young Lee, limp and dripping like a broken water-plant, was stretched upon the sofa, the green scum of the river upon his black hair, and a fringe of white foam upon his leaden-hued lips. Beside him knelt his fellow-student Harrington, endeavouring to chafe some warmth back into his rigid limbs.

'I think there's life in him,' said Smith, with his hand to the lad's side. 'Put your watch glass to his lips. Yes, there's dimming on it. You take one arm, Hastie. Now work it as I do, and we'll soon pull him round.'

For ten minutes they worked in silence, inflating and depressing the chest of the unconscious man. At the end of that time a shiver ran through his body, his lips trembled, and he opened his eyes. The three students burst out into an irrepressible cheer.

'Wake up, old chap. You've frightened us quite enough.'

'Have some brandy. Take a sip from the flask.'

'He's all right now,' said his companion Harrington. 'Heavens, what a fright I got! I was reading here, and he had gone out for a stroll as far as the river, when I heard a scream and a splash. Out I ran, and by the time I could find him and fish him out, all life seemed to have gone. Then Simpson couldn't get a doctor, for he has a game-leg, and I had to run, and I don't know what I'd have done without you fellows. That's right, old chap. Sit up.'

Monkhouse Lee had raised himself on his hands, and looked wildly about him.

'What's up?' he asked. 'I've been in the water. Ah, yes; I remember.'

A look of fear came into his eyes, and he sank his face into his hands.

'How did you fall in?'

'I didn't fall in.'

'How, then?'

'I was thrown in. I was standing by the bank, and something from behind picked me up like a feather and hurled me in. I heard nothing, and I saw nothing. But I know what it was, for all that.'

'And so do I,' whispered Smith.

Lee looked up with a quick glance of surprise.

'You've learned, then?' he said. 'You remember the advice I gave you?'

'Yes, and I begin to think that I shall take it.'

'I don't know what the deuce you fellows are talking about,' said Hastie, 'but I think, if I were you, Harrington, I should get Lee to bed at once. It will be time enough to discuss the why and the wherefore when he is a little stronger. I think, Smith, you and I can leave him alone now. I am walking back to college; if you are coming in that direction, we can have a chat.'

But it was little chat that they had upon their homeward path. Smith's mind was too full of the incidents of the evening, the absence of the mummy from his neighbour's rooms, the step that passed him on the stair, the reappearance—the extraordinary, inexplicable reappearance of the grisly thing—and then this attack upon Lee, corresponding so closely to the previous outrage upon another man against whom Bellingham bore a grudge. All this settled in his thoughts, together with the many little incidents which had previously turned him against his neighbour, and the singular circumstances under which he was first called in to him. What had been a dim suspicion, a vague, fantastic conjecture, had suddenly taken form, and stood out in his mind as a grim fact, a thing not to be denied. And yet, how monstrous it was! how unheard of! how entirely beyond all bounds of human experience. An impartial judge, or even the friend who walked by his side, would simply tell him that his eyes had deceived him, that the mummy had been there all the time, that young Lee had tumbled into the river as any other man tumbles into a river, and that a blue pill was the best thing for a disordered liver. He felt that he would have said as much if the positions had been reversed. And yet he could swear that Bellingham was a murderer at heart, and that he wielded a weapon such as no man had ever used in all the grim history of crime.

Hastie had branched off to his rooms with a few crisp and emphatic comments upon his friend's unsociability, and Abercrombie Smith crossed the quadrangle to his corner turret with a strong feeling of repulsion for his chambers and their associations. He would take Lee's advice, and move his quarters as soon as possible, for how could a man study when his ear was ever straining for every murmur or footstep in the room below? He observed, as he crossed over the lawn, that the light was still shining in Bellingham's window, and as he passed up the staircase the door opened, and the man himself looked out at him. With his fat, evil face he was like some bloated spider fresh from the weaving of his poisonous web.

'Good-evening,' said he. 'Won't you come in?'

'No,' cried Smith, fiercely.

'No? You are busy as ever? I wanted to ask you about Lee. I was sorry to hear that there was a rumour that something was amiss with him.'

His features were grave, but there was the gleam of a hidden laugh in his eyes as he spoke. Smith saw it, and he could have knocked him down for it.

'You'll be sorrier still to hear that Monkhouse Lee is doing very well, and is out of all danger,' he answered. 'Your hellish tricks have not come off this time. Oh, you needn't try to brazen it out. I know all about it.'

Bellingham took a step back from the angry student, and half-closed the door as if to protect himself.

'You are mad,' he said. 'What do you mean? Do you assert that I had anything to do with Lee's accident?'

'Yes,' thundered Smith. 'You and that bag of bones behind you; you worked it between you. I tell you what it is, Master B., they have given up burning folk like you, but we still keep a hangman, and, by George! if any man in this college meets his death while you are here, I'll have you up, and if you don't swing for it, it won't be my fault. You'll find that your filthy Egyptian tricks won't answer in England.'

'You're a raving lunatic,' said Bellingham.

'All right. You just remember what I say, for you'll find that I'll be better than my word.'

The door slammed, and Smith went fuming up to his chamber, where he locked the door upon the inside, and spent half the night in smoking his old briar and brooding over the strange events of the evening.

Next morning Abercrombie Smith heard nothing of his neighbour, but Harrington called upon him in the afternoon to say that Lee was almost himself again. All day Smith stuck fast to his work, but in the evening he determined to pay the visit to his friend Doctor Peterson upon which he had started upon the night before. A good walk and a friendly chat would be welcome to his jangled nerves.

Bellingham's door was shut as he passed, but glancing back when he was some distance from the turret, he saw his neighbour's head at the window outlined against the lamp-light, his face pressed apparently against the glass as he gazed out into the darkness. It was a blessing to be away from all contact with him, if but for a few hours, and Smith stepped out briskly, and breathed the soft spring air into his lungs. The half-moon lay in the west between two Gothic pinnacles, and threw upon the silvered street a dark tracery from the stone-work above. There was a brisk breeze, and light, fleecy clouds drifted swiftly across the sky. Old's was on the very border of the town, and in five minutes Smith found himself beyond the houses and between the hedges of a May-scented Oxfordshire lane.

It was a lonely and little frequented road which led to his friend's house. Early as it was, Smith did not meet a single soul upon his way. He walked briskly along until he came to the avenue gate, which opened into the long gravel drive leading up to Farlingford. In front of him he could see the cosy red light of the windows glimmering through the foliage. He stood with his hand upon the iron latch of the swinging gate, and he glanced back at the road along which he had come. Something was coming swiftly down it.

It moved in the shadow of the hedge, silently and furtively, a dark, crouching figure, dimly visible against the black background. Even as he gazed back at it, it had lessened its distance by twenty paces, and was fast closing upon him. Out of the darkness he had a glimpse of a scraggy neck, and of two eyes that will ever haunt him in his dreams. He turned, and with a cry of terror he ran for his life up the avenue. There were the red lights, the signals of safety, almost within a stone's-throw of him. He was a famous runner, but never had he run as he ran that night.

The heavy gate had swung into place behind him, but he heard it dash open again before his pursuer. As he rushed madly and wildly through the night, he could hear a swift, dry patter behind him, and could see, as he threw back a glance, that this horror was bounding like a tiger at his heels, with blazing eyes and one stringy arm out-thrown. Thank God, the door was ajar. He could see the thin bar of light which shot from the lamp in the hall. Nearer yet sounded the clatter from behind. He heard a hoarse gurgling at his very shoulder. With a shriek he flung himself against the door, slammed and bolted it behind him, and sank half-fainting on to the hall chair.

'My goodness, Smith, what's the matter?' asked Peterson, appearing at the door of his study.

'Give me some brandy!'

Peterson disappeared, and came rushing out again with a glass and a decanter.

'You need it,' he said, as his visitor drank off what he poured out for him. 'Why, man, you are as white as a cheese.'

Smith laid down his glass, rose up, and took a deep breath.

'I am my own man again now,' said he. 'I was never so unmanned before. But, with your leave, Peterson, I will sleep here to-night, for I don't think I could face that road again except by daylight. It's weak, I know, but I can't help it.'

Peterson looked at his visitor with a very questioning eye.

'Of course you shall sleep here if you wish. I'll tell Mrs Burney to make up the spare bed. Where are you off to now?'

'Come up with me to the window that overlooks the door. I want you to see what I have seen.'

They went up to the window of the upper hall whence they could look down upon the approach to the house. The drive and the fields on either side lay quiet and still, bathed in the peaceful moonlight.

'Well, really, Smith,' remarked Peterson, 'it is well that I know you to be an abstemious man. What in the world can have frightened you?'

'I'll tell you presently. But where can it have gone? Ah, now look, look! See the curve of the road just beyond your gate.'

'Yes, I see; you needn't pinch my arm off. I saw someone pass. I should say a man, rather thin, apparently, and tall, very tall. But what of him? And what of yourself? You are still shaking like an aspen leaf.'

'I have been within hand-grip of the devil, that's all. But come down to your study, and I shall tell you the whole story.'

He did so. Under the cheery lamp-light, with a glass of wine on the table beside him, and the portly form and florid face of his friend in front, he narrated, in their order, all the events, great and small, which had formed so singular a chain, from the night on which he had found Bellingham fainting in front of the mummy case until his horrid experience of an hour ago.

'There now,' he said as he concluded, 'that's the whole black business. It is monstrous and incredible, but it is true.'

Doctor Plumptree Peterson sat for some time in silence with a very puzzled expression upon his face.

'I never heard of such a thing in my life, never!' he said at last. 'You have told me the facts. Now tell me your inferences.'

'You can draw your own.'

'But I should like to hear yours. You have thought over the matter, and I have not.'

'Well, it must be a little vague in detail, but the main points seem to me to be clear enough. This fellow Bellingham, in his Eastern studies, has got hold of some infernal secret by which a mummy—or possibly only this particular mummy—can be temporarily brought to life. He was trying this disgusting business on the night when he fainted. No doubt the sight of the creature moving had shaken his nerve, even though he had expected it. You remember that almost the first words he said were to call out upon himself as a fool. Well, he got more hardened afterwards, and carried the matter through without fainting. The vitality which he could put into it was evidently only a passing thing, for I have seen it continually in its case as dead as this table. He has some elaborate process, I fancy, by which he brings the thing to pass. Having done it, he naturally bethought

him that he might use the creature as an agent. It has intelligence
and it has strength. For some purpose he took Lee into his confidence; but Lee, like a decent Christian, would have nothing to do
with such a business. Then they had a row, and Lee vowed that he
would tell his sister of Bellingham's true character. Bellingham's
game was to prevent him, and he nearly managed it, by setting this
creature of his on his track. He had already tried its powers upon
another man—Norton—towards whom he had a grudge. It is the
merest chance that he has not two murders upon his soul. Then,
when I taxed him with the matter, he had the strongest reasons for
wishing to get me out of the way before I could convey my knowledge to anyone else. He got his chance when I went out, for he knew
my habits, and where I was bound for. I have had a narrow shave,
Peterson, and it is mere luck you didn't find me on your doorstep in
the morning. I'm not a nervous man as a rule, and I never thought to
have the fear of death put upon me as it was to-night.'

'My dear boy, you take the matter too seriously,' said his companion. 'Your nerves are out of order with your work, and you make
too much of it. How could such a thing as this stride about the
streets of Oxford, even at night, without being seen?'

'It has been seen. There is quite a scare in the town about an
escaped ape, as they imagine the creature to be. It is the talk of the
place.'

'Well, it's a striking chain of events. And yet, my dear fellow, you
must allow that each incident in itself is capable of a more natural
explanation.'

'What! even my adventure of to-night?'

'Certainly. You come out with your nerves all unstrung, and your
head full of this theory of yours. Some gaunt, half-famished tramp
steals after you, and seeing you run, is emboldened to pursue you.
Your fears and imagination do the rest.'

'It won't do, Peterson; it won't do.'

'And again, in the instance of your finding the mummy case
empty, and then a few moments later with an occupant, you know
that it was lamp-light, that the lamp was half turned down, and that
you had no special reason to look hard at the case. It is quite possible
that you may have overlooked the creature in the first instance.'

'No, no; it is out of the question.'

'And then Lee may have fallen into the river, and Norton been

garrotted. It is certainly a formidable indictment that you
have against Bellingham; but if you were to place it before a police
magistrate, he would simply laugh in your face.'

'I know he would. That is why I mean to take the matter into my
own hands.'

'Eh?'

'Yes; I feel that a public duty rests upon me, and, besides, I must
do it for my own safety, unless I choose to allow myself to be hunted
by this beast out of the college, and that would be a little too feeble. I
have quite made up my mind what I shall do. And first of all, may I
use your paper and pens for an hour?'

'Most certainly. You will find all that you want upon that side
table.'

Abercrombie Smith sat down before a sheet of foolscap, and for an
hour, and then for a second hour his pen travelled swiftly over it.
Page after page was finished and tossed aside while his friend leaned
back in his arm-chair, looking across at him with patient curiosity.
At last, with an exclamation of satisfaction, Smith sprang to his
feet, gathered his papers up into order, and laid the last one upon
Peterson's desk.

'Kindly sign this as a witness,' he said.

'A witness? Of what?'

'Of my signature, and of the date. The date is the most important.
Why, Peterson, my life might hang upon it.'

'My dear Smith, you are talking wildly. Let me beg you to go to
bed.'

'On the contrary, I never spoke so deliberately in my life. And I
will promise to go to bed the moment you have signed it.'

'But what is it?'

'It is a statement of all that I have been telling you to-night. I wish
you to witness it.'

'Certainly,' said Peterson, signing his name under that of his
companion. 'There you are! But what is the idea?'

'You will kindly retain it, and produce it in case I am arrested.'

'Arrested? For what?'

'For murder. Is is quite on the cards. I wish to be ready for every
event. There is only one course open to me, and I am determined to
take it.'

'For Heaven's sake, don't do anything rash!'

'Believe me, it would be far more rash to adopt any other course. I hope that we won't need to bother you, but it will ease my mind to know that you have this statement of my motives. And now I am ready to take your advice and to go to roost, for I want to be at my best in the morning.'

Abercrombie Smith was not an entirely pleasant man to have as an enemy. Slow and easy-tempered, he was formidable when driven to action. He brought to every purpose in life the same deliberate resoluteness which had distinguished him as a scientific student. He had laid his studies aside for a day, but he intended that the day should not be wasted. Not a word did he say to his host as to his plans, but by nine o'clock he was well on his way to Oxford.

In the High Street he stopped at Clifford's, the gun-maker's, and bought a heavy revolver, with a box of central-fire cartridges. Six of them he slipped into the chambers, and half-cocking the weapon, placed it in the pocket of his coat. He then made his way to Hastie's rooms, where the big oarsman was lounging over his breakfast, with the *Sporting Times* propped up against the coffee-pot.

'Hullo! What's up?' he asked. 'Have some coffee?'

'No, thank you. I want you to come with me, Hastie, and do what I ask you.'

'Certainly, my boy.'

'And bring a heavy stick with you.'

'Hullo!' Hastie stared. 'Here's a hunting-crop that would fell an ox.'

'One other thing. You have a box of amputating knives. Give me the longest of them.'

'There you are. You seem to be fairly on the war trail. Anything else?'

'No; that will do.' Smith placed the knife inside his coat, and led the way to the quadrangle. 'We are neither of us chickens, Hastie,' said he. 'I think I can do this job alone, but I take you as a precaution. I am going to have a little talk with Bellingham. If I have only him to deal with, I won't, of course, need you. If I shout, however, up you come, and lam out with your whip as hard as you can lick. Do you understand?'

'All right. I'll come if I hear you bellow.'

'Stay here, then. I may be a little time, but don't budge until I come down.'

'I'm a fixture.'

Smith ascended the stairs, opened Bellingham's door and stepped in. Bellingham was seated behind his table, writing. Beside him, among his litter of strange possessions, towered the mummy case, with its sale number 249 still stuck upon its front, and its hideous occupant stiff and stark within it. Smith looked very deliberately round him, closed the door, locked it, took the key from the inside, and then stepping across to the fireplace, struck a match and set the fire alight. Bellingham sat staring, with amazement and rage upon his bloated face.

'Well, really now, you make yourself at home,' he gasped.

Smith sat himself deliberately down, placing his watch upon the table, drew out his pistol, cocked it, and laid it in his lap. Then he took the long amputating knife from his bosom, and threw it down in front of Bellingham.

'Now, then,' said he, 'just get to work and cut up that mummy.'

'Oh, is that it?' said Bellingham with a sneer.

'Yes, that is it. They tell me that the law can't touch you. But I have a law that will set matters straight. If in five minutes you have not set to work, I swear by the God who made me that I will put a bullet through your brain!'

'You would murder me?'

Bellingham had half risen, and his face was the colour of putty.

'Yes.'

'And for what?'

'To stop your mischief. One minute has gone.'

'But what have I done?'

'I know and you know.'

'This is mere bullying.'

'Two minutes are gone.'

'But you must give reasons. You are a madman—a dangerous madman. Why should I destroy my own property? It is a valuable mummy.'

'You must cut it up, and you must burn it.'

'I will do no such thing.'

'Four minutes are gone.'

Smith took up the pistol and he looked towards Bellingham with an inexorable face. As the second-hand stole round, he raised his hand, and the finger twitched upon the trigger.

'There! there! I'll do it!' screamed Bellingham.

In frantic haste he caught up the knife and hacked at the figure of the mummy, ever glancing round to see the eye and the weapon of his terrible visitor bent upon him. The creature crackled and snapped under every stab of the keen blade. A thick yellow dust rose up from it. Spices and dried essences rained down upon the floor. Suddenly, with a rending crack, its backbone snapped asunder, and it fell, a brown heap of sprawling limbs, upon the floor.

'Now into the fire!' said Smith.

The flames leaped and roared as the dried and tinderlike *débris* was piled upon it. The little room was like the stoke-hole of a steamer and the sweat ran down the faces of the two men; but still the one stooped and worked, while the other sat watching him with a set face. A thick, fat smoke oozed out from the fire, and a heavy smell of burned rosin and singed hair filled the air. In a quarter of an hour a few charred and brittle sticks were all that was left of Lot No. 249.

'Perhaps that will satisfy you,' snarled Bellingham, with hate and fear in his little grey eyes as he glanced back at his tormentor.

'No; I must make a clean sweep of all your materials. We must have no more devil's tricks. In with all these leaves! They may have something to do with it.'

'And what now?' asked Bellingham, when the leaves also had been added to the blaze.

'Now the roll of papyrus which you had on the table that night. It is in that drawer, I think.'

'No, no,' shouted Bellingham. 'Don't burn that! Why, man, you don't know what you do. It is unique; it contains wisdom which is nowhere else to be found.'

'Out with it!'

'But look here, Smith, you can't really mean it. I'll share the knowledge with you. I'll teach you all that is in it. Or, stay, let me only copy it before you burn it!'

Smith stepped forward and turned the key in the drawer. Taking out the yellow, curled roll of paper, he threw it into the fire, and pressed it down with his heel. Bellingham screamed, and grabbed at it; but Smith pushed him back, and stood over it until it was reduced to a formless grey ash.

'Now, Master B.,' said he, 'I think I have pretty well drawn your teeth. You'll hear from me again, if you return to your old tricks. And now good-morning, for I must go back to my studies.'

And such is the narrative of Abercrombie Smith as to the singular events which occurred in Old College, Oxford, in the spring of '84. As Bellingham left the university immediately afterwards, and was last heard of in the Soudan, there is no one who can contradict his statement. But the wisdom of men is small, and the ways of nature are strange, and who shall put a bound to the dark things which may be found by those who seek for them?

ARTHUR CONAN DOYLE

The Case of Lady Sannox

THE relations between Douglas Stone and the notorious Lady Sannox were very well known both among the fashionable circles of which she was a brilliant member, and the scientific bodies which numbered him among their most illustrious *confrères*. There was naturally, therefore, a very widespread interest when it was announced one morning that the lady had absolutely and for ever taken the veil, and that the world would see her no more. When, at the very tail of this rumour, there came the assurance that the celebrated operating surgeon, the man of steel nerves, had been found in the morning by his valet, seated on one side of his bed, smiling pleasantly upon the universe, with both legs jammed into one side of his breeches and his great brain about as valuable as a cap full of porridge, the matter was strong enough to give quite a little thrill of interest to folk who had never hoped that their jaded nerves were capable of such a sensation.

Douglas Stone in his prime was one of the most remarkable men in England. Indeed, he could hardly be said to have ever reached his prime, for he was but nine-and-thirty at the time of this little incident. Those who knew him best were aware that famous as he was as a surgeon, he might have succeeded with even greater rapidity in any of a dozen lines of life. He could have cut his way to fame as a soldier, struggled to it as an explorer, bullied for it in the courts, or built it out of stone and iron as an engineer. He was born to be great, for he could plan what another man dare not do, and he could do what another man dare not plan. In surgery none could follow him. His nerve, his judgment, his intuition, were things apart. Again and again his knife cut away death, but grazed the very springs of life in doing it, until his assistants were as white as the patient. His energy, his audacity, his full-blooded self-confidence—does not the memory of them still linger to the south of Marylebone Road and the north of Oxford Street?*

His vices were as magnificent as his virtues, and infinitely more picturesque. Large as was his income, and it was the third largest of all professional men in London, it was far beneath the luxury of his living. Deep in his complex nature lay a rich vein of sensualism, at the sport of which he placed all the prizes of his life. The eye, the ear, the touch, the palate, all were his masters. The bouquet of old vintages, the scent of rare exotics, the curves and tints of the daintiest potteries of Europe, it was to these that the quick-running stream of gold was transformed. And then there came his sudden mad passion for Lady Sannox, when a single interview with two challenging glances and a whispered word set him ablaze. She was the loveliest woman in London, and the only one to him. He was one of the handsomest men in London, but not the only one to her. She had a liking for new experiences, and was gracious to most men who wooed her. It may have been cause or it may have been effect that Lord Sannox looked fifty, though he was but six-and-thirty.

He was a quiet, silent, neutral-tinted man this lord, with thin lips and heavy eyelids, much given to gardening, and full of home-like habits. He had at one time been fond of acting, had even rented a theatre in London, and on its boards had first seen Miss Marion Dawson, to whom he had offered his hand, his title, and the third of a county. Since his marriage this early hobby had become distasteful to him. Even in private theatricals it was no longer possible to persuade him to exercise the talent which he had often shown that he possessed. He was happier with a spud and a watering can among his orchids and chrysanthemums.

It was quite an interesting problem whether he was absolutely devoid of sense, or miserably wanting in spirit. Did he know his lady's ways and condone them, or was he a mere blind, doting fool? It was a point to be discussed over the teacups in snug little drawing-rooms, or with the aid of a cigar in the bow windows of clubs. Bitter and plain were the comments among men upon his conduct. There was but one who had a good word to say for him, and he was the most silent member in the smoking-room. He had seen him break in a horse at the University, and it seemed to have left an impression upon his mind.

But when Douglas Stone became the favourite all doubts as to Lord Sannox's knowledge or ignorance were set for ever at rest. There was no subterfuge about Stone. In his high-handed, impetuous fashion, he set all caution and discretion at defiance. The scandal became notorious. A learned body intimated that his name had been struck from the list of its vice-presidents. Two friends implored him to consider his professional credit. He cursed them all three, and spent forty guineas on a bangle to take with him to the lady. He was at her house every evening, and she drove in his carriage in the afternoons. There was not an attempt on either side to conceal their relations; but there came at last a little incident to interrupt them.

It was a dismal winter's night, very cold and gusty, with the wind whooping in the chimneys and blustering against the window-panes. A thin spatter of rain tinkled on the glass with each fresh sough of the gale, drowning for the instant the dull gurgle and drip from the eaves. Douglas Stone had finished his dinner, and sat by his fire in the study, a glass of rich port upon the malachite table at his elbow. As he raised it to his lips, he held it up against the lamp-light, and watched with the eye of a connoisseur the tiny scales of beeswing which floated in its rich ruby depths. The fire, as it spurted up, threw fitful lights upon his bold, clear-cut face, with its widely-opened grey eyes, its thick and yet firm lips, and the deep, square jaw, which had something Roman in its strength and its animalism. He smiled from time to time as he nestled back in his luxurious chair. Indeed, he had a right to feel well pleased, for, against the advice of six colleagues, he had performed an operation that day of which only two cases were on record, and the result had been brilliant beyond all expectation. No other man in London would have had the daring to plan, or the skill to execute, such a heroic measure.

But he had promised Lady Sannox to see her that evening and it was already half-past eight. His hand was outstretched to the bell to order the carriage when he heard the dull thud of the knocker. An instant later there was the shuffling of feet in the hall, and the sharp closing of a door.

'A patient to see you, sir, in the consulting room,' said the butler.

'About himself?'

'No, sir; I think he wants you to go out.'

'It is too late,' cried Douglas Stone peevishly. 'I won't go.'

'This is his card, sir.'

The butler presented it upon the gold salver which had been given to his master by the wife of a Prime Minister.

' "Hamil Ali, Smyrna." Hum! The fellow is a Turk, I suppose.'

'Yes, sir. He seems as if he came from abroad, sir. And he's in a terrible way.'

'Tut, tut! I have an engagement. I must go somewhere else. But I'll see him. Show him in here, Pim.'

A few moments later the butler swung open the door and ushered in a small and decrepid man, who walked with a bent back and with the forward push of the face and blink of the eyes which goes with extreme short sight. His face was swarthy, and his hair and beard of the deepest black. In one hand he held a turban of white muslin striped with red, in the other a small chamois leather bag.

'Good evening,' said Douglas Stone, when the butler had closed the door. 'You speak English, I presume?'

'Yes, sir. I am from Asia Minor, but I speak English when I speak slow.'

'You wanted me to go out, I understand?'

'Yes, sir. I wanted very much that you should see my wife.'

'I could come in the morning, but I have an engagement which prevents me from seeing your wife to-night.'

The Turk's answer was a singular one. He pulled the string which closed the mouth of the chamois leather bag, and poured a flood of gold on to the table.

'There are one hundred pounds there,' said he, 'and I promise you that it will not take you an hour. I have a cab ready at the door.'

Douglas Stone glanced at his watch. An hour would not make it too late to visit Lady Sannox. He had been there later. And the fee was an extraordinarily high one. He had been pressed by his creditors lately, and he could not afford to let such a chance pass. He would go.

'What is the case?' he asked,

'Oh, it is so sad a one! So sad a one! You have not, perhaps, heard of the daggers of the Almohades?'*

'Never.'

'Ah, they are Eastern daggers of a great age and of a singular shape, with the hilt like what you call a stirrup. I am a curiosity dealer, you understand, and that is why I have come to England from Smyrna, but next week I go back once more. Many things I brought with me, and I have a few things left, but among them, to my sorrow, is one of these daggers.'

'You will remember that I have an appointment, sir,' said the surgeon, with some irritation; 'pray confine yourself to the necessary details.'

'You will see that it is necessary. To-day my wife fell down in a faint in the room in which I keep my wares, and she cut her lower lip upon this cursed dagger of Almohades.'

'I see,' said Douglas Stone, rising. 'And you wish me to dress the wound?'

'No, no, it is worse than that.'

'What then?'

'These daggers are poisoned.'

'Poisoned!'

'Yes, and there is no man, East or West, who can tell now what is the poison or what the cure. But all that is known I know, for my father was in this trade before me, and we have had much to do with these poisoned weapons.'

'What are the symptoms?'

'Deep sleep, and death in thirty hours.'

'And you say there is no cure. Why then should you pay me this considerable fee?'

'No drug can cure, but the knife may.'

'And how?'

'The poison is slow of absorption. It remains for hours in the wound.'

'Washing, then, might cleanse it?'

'No more than in a snake bite. It is too subtle and too deadly.'

'Excision of the wound, then?'

'That is it. If it be on the finger, take the finger off. So said my father always. But think of where this wound is, and that it is my wife. It is dreadful!'

But familiarity with such grim matters may take the finer edge from a man's sympathy. To Douglas Stone this was already an interesting case, and he brushed aside as irrelevant the feeble objections of the husband.

'It appears to be that or nothing,' said he brusquely. 'It is better to lose a lip than a life.'

'Ah, yes, I know that you are right. Well, well, it is kismet, and it must be faced. I have the cab, and you will come with me and do this thing.'

Douglas Stone took his case of bistouries* from a drawer, and placed it with a roll of bandage and a compress of lint in his pocket. He must waste no more time if he were to see Lady Sannox.

'I am ready,' said he, pulling on his overcoat. 'Will you take a glass of wine before you go out into this cold air?'

His visitor shrank away, with a protesting hand upraised.

'You forget that I am a Mussulman, and a true follower of the Prophet,' said he. 'But tell me what is the bottle of green glass which you have placed in your pocket?'

'It is chloroform.'

'Ah, that also is forbidden to us. It is a spirit, and we make no use of such things.'

'What! You would allow your wife to go through an operation without an anæsthetic?'

'Ah! she will feel nothing, poor soul. The deep sleep has already come on, which is the first working of the poison. And then I have given her of our Smyrna opium. Come, sir, for already an hour has passed.'

As they stepped out into the darkness, a sheet of rain was driven in upon their faces, and the hall lamp, which dangled from the arm of a marble Caryatid, went out with a fluff. Pim, the butler, pushed the heavy door to, straining hard with his shoulder against the wind, while the two men groped their way towards the yellow glare which showed where the cab was waiting. An instant later they were rattling upon their journey.

'Is it far?' asked Douglas Stone.

'Oh, no. We have a very little quiet place off the Euston Road.'

The surgeon pressed the spring of his repeater and listened to the little tings which told him the hour. It was a quarter past nine. He calculated the distances, and the short time which it would take him to perform so trivial an operation. He ought to reach Lady Sannox by ten o'clock. Through the fogged windows he saw the blurred gas lamps dancing past, with occasionally the broader glare of a shop front. The rain was pelting and rattling upon the leathern top of the carriage, and the wheels swashed as they rolled through puddle and mud. Opposite to him the white headgear of his companion gleamed faintly through the obscurity. The surgeon felt in his pockets and arranged his needles, his ligatures and his safety-pins, that no time might be wasted when they arrived. He chafed with impatience and drummed his foot upon the floor.

But the cab slowed down at last and pulled up. In an instant Douglas Stone was out, and the Smyrna merchant's toe was at his very heel.

'You can wait,' said he to the driver.

It was a mean-looking house in a narrow and sordid street. The surgeon, who knew his London well, cast a swift glance into the shadows, but there was nothing distinctive,—no shop, no movement, nothing but a double line of dull, flat-faced houses, a double stretch of wet flagstones which gleamed in the lamp-light, and a double rush of water in the gutters which swirled and gurgled towards the sewer gratings. The door which faced them was blotched and discoloured, and a faint light in the fan pane above it served to show the dust and the grime which covered it. Above, in one of the bedroom windows, there was a dull yellow glimmer. The merchant knocked loudly, and, as he turned his dark face towards the light, Douglas Stone could see that it was contracted with anxiety. A bolt was drawn, and an elderly woman with a taper stood in the doorway, shielding the thin flame with her gnarled hand.

'Is all well?' gasped the merchant.

'She is as you left her, sir.'

'She has not spoken?'

'No, she is in a deep sleep.'

The merchant closed the door, and Douglas Stone walked down the narrow passage, glancing about him in some surprise as he did so. There was no oilcloth, no mat, no hat-rack. Deep grey dust and heavy festoons of cobwebs met his eyes everywhere. Following the old woman up the winding stair, his firm footfall echoed harshly through the silent house. There was no carpet.

The bedroom was on the second landing. Douglas Stone followed the old nurse into it, with the merchant at his heels. Here, at least, there was furniture and to spare. The floor was littered and the corners piled with Turkish cabinets, inlaid tables, coats of chain mail, strange pipes, and grotesque weapons. A single small lamp stood upon a bracket on the wall. Douglas Stone took it down, and picking his way among the lumber, walked over to a couch in the corner, on which lay a woman dressed in the Turkish fashion, with yashmak and veil. The lower part of the face was exposed, and the surgeon saw a jagged cut which zigzagged along the border of the under lip.

'You will forgive the yashmak,' said the Turk. 'You know our views about woman in the East.'

But the surgeon was not thinking about the yashmak. This was no longer a woman to him. It was a case. He stooped and examined the wound carefully.

'There are no signs of irritation,' said he. 'We might delay the operation until local symptoms develop.'

The husband wrung his hands in incontrollable agitation.

'Oh! sir, sir,' he cried. 'Do not trifle. You do not know. It is deadly. I know, and I give you my assurance that an operation is absolutely necessary. Only the knife can save her.'

'And yet I am inclined to wait,' said Douglas Stone.

'That is enough,' the Turk cried, angrily. 'Every minute is of importance, and I cannot stand here and see my wife allowed to sink. It only remains for me to give you my thanks for having come, and to call in some other surgeon before it is too late.'

Douglas Stone hesitated. To refund that hundred pounds was no pleasant matter. But of course if he left the case he must return the money. And if the Turk were right and the woman died, his position before a coroner might be an embarrassing one.

'You have had personal experience of this poison?' he asked.

'I have.'

'And you assure me that an operation is needful.'

'I swear it by all that I hold sacred.'

'The disfigurement will be frightful.'

'I can understand that the mouth will not be a pretty one to kiss.'

Douglas Stone turned fiercely upon the man. The speech was a brutal one. But the Turk has his own fashion of talk and of thought, and there was no time for wrangling. Douglas Stone drew a bistoury from his case, opened it and felt the keen straight edge with his forefinger. Then he held the lamp closer to the bed. Two dark eyes were gazing up at him through the slit in the yashmak. They were all iris, and the pupil was hardly to be seen.

'You have given her a very heavy dose of opium.'

'Yes, she has had a good dose.'

He glanced again at the dark eyes which looked straight at his own. They were dull and lustreless, but, even as he gazed, a little shifting sparkle came into them, and the lips quivered.

'She is not absolutely unconscious,' said he.

'Would it not be well to use the knife while it will be painless?'

The same thought had crossed the surgeon's mind. He grasped the wounded lip with his forceps, and with two swift cuts he took out a broad V-shaped piece. The woman sprang up on the couch with a dreadful gurgling scream. Her covering was torn from her face. It was a face that he knew. In spite of that protruding upper lip and that slobber of blood, it was a face that he knew. She kept on putting her hand up to the gap and screaming. Douglas Stone sat down at the foot of the couch with his knife and his forceps. The room was whirling round, and he had felt something go like a ripping seam behind his ear. A bystander would have said that his face was the more ghastly of the two. As in a dream, or as if he had been looking at something at the play, he was conscious that the Turk's hair and beard lay upon the table, and that Lord Sannox was leaning against the wall with his hand to his side, laughing silently. The screams had died away now, and the dreadful head had dropped back again upon the pillow, but Douglas Stone still sat motionless, and Lord Sannox still chuckled quietly to himself.

'It was really very necessary for Marion, this operation,' said he, 'not physically, but morally, you know, morally.'

Douglas Stone stooped forwards and began to play with the fringe of the coverlet. His knife tinkled down upon the ground, but he still held the forceps and something more.

'I had long intended to make a little example,' said Lord Sannox, suavely. 'Your note of Wednesday miscarried, and I have it here in my pocket-book. I took some pains in carrying out my idea. The wound, by the way, was from nothing more dangerous than my signet ring.'

He glanced keenly at his silent companion, and cocked the small revolver which he held in his coat pocket. But Douglas Stone was still picking at the coverlet.

'You see you have kept your appointment after all,' said Lord Sannox.

And at that Douglas Stone began to laugh. He laughed long and loudly. But Lord Sannox did not laugh now. Something like fear sharpened and hardened his features. He walked from the room, and he walked on tiptoe. The old woman was waiting outside.

'Attend to your mistress when she awakes,' said Lord Sannox.

Then he went down to the street. The cab was at the door, and the driver raised his hand to his hat.

'John,' said Lord Sannox, 'you will take the doctor home first. He will want leading downstairs, I think. Tell his butler that he has been taken ill at a case.'

'Very good, sir.'

'Then you can take Lady Sannox home.'

'And how about yourself, sir?'

'Oh, my address for the next few months will be Hotel di Roma, Venice. Just see that the letters are sent on. And tell Stevens to exhibit all the purple chrysanthemums next Monday, and to wire me the result.'

GRANT ALLEN

Pallinghurst Barrow

I

RUDOLPH REEVE sat by himself on the Old Long Barrow on Pallinghurst Common. It was a September evening, and the sun was setting. The west was all aglow with a mysterious red light, very strange and lurid—a light that reflected itself in glowing purple on the dark brown heather and the dying bracken. Rudolph Reeve was a journalist and a man of science; but he had a poet's soul for all that, in spite of his avocations, neither of which is usually thought to tend towards the spontaneous development of a poetic temperament. He sat there long, watching the vivid hues that incarnadined the sky—redder and fiercer than anything he ever remembered to have seen since the famous year of the Krakatoa sunsets*—though he knew it was getting late, and he ought to have gone back long since to the manor-house to dress for dinner. Mrs Bouverie-Barton, his hostess, the famous Woman's Rights woman, was always such a stickler for punctuality and dispatch, and all the other unfeminine virtues! But, in spite of Mrs Bouverie-Barton, Rudolph Reeve sat on. There was something about that sunset and the lights on the bracken—something weird and unearthly—that positively fascinated him.

The view over the common, which stands high and exposed, a veritable waste of heath and gorse, is strikingly wide and expansive. Pallinghurst Ring, or the 'Old Long Barrow,' a well-known landmark, familiar by that name from time immemorial to all the country-side, crowns its actual summit, and commands from its top the surrounding hills far into the shadowy heart of Hampshire. On its terraced slope Rudolph sat and gazed out, with all the artistic pleasure of a poet or a painter (for he was a little of both) in the exquisite flush of the dying reflections from the dying sun upon the dying heather. He sat and wondered to himself why death is always so much more beautiful, so much more poetical, so much calmer than life—and why you invariably enjoy things so very much better when you know you ought to be dressing for dinner.

He was just going to rise, however, dreading the lasting wrath of Mrs Bouverie-Barton, when of a sudden a very weird yet definite feeling caused him for one moment to pause and hesitate. Why he felt it he knew not; but even as he sat there on the grassy tumulus, covered close with short sward of subterranean clover, that curious, cunning plant that buries its own seeds by automatic action, he was aware, through no external sense, but by pure internal consciousness, of something or other living and moving within the barrow. He shut his eyes and listened. No; fancy, pure fancy! Not a sound broke the stillness of early evening, save the drone of insects—those dying insects, now beginning to fail fast before the first chill breath of approaching autumn. Rudolph opened his eyes again and looked down on the ground. In the little boggy hollow by his feet innumerable plants of sundew spread their murderous rosettes of sticky red leaves, all bedewed with viscid gum, to catch and roll round the struggling flies that wrenched their tiny limbs in vain efforts to free themselves. But that was all. Nothing else was astir. In spite of sight and sound, however, he was still deeply thrilled by this strange consciousness as of something living and moving in the barrow underneath; something living and moving—or was it moving and dead? Something crawling and creeping, as the long arms of the sundews crawled and crept around the helpless flies, whose juices they sucked out. A weird and awful feeling, yet strangely fascinating! He hated the vulgar necessity for going back to dinner. Why do people dine at all? So material! so commonplace! And the universe all teeming with strange secrets to unfold! He knew not why, but a fierce desire possessed his soul to stop and give way to this overpowering sense of the mysterious and the marvellous in the dark depths of the barrow.

With an effort he roused himself, and put on his hat, which he had been holding in his hand, for his forehead was burning. The sun had now long set, and Mrs Bouverie-Barton dined at 7.30 punctually. He must rise and go home. Something unknown pulled him down to detain him. Once more he paused and hesitated. He was not a superstitious man, yet it seemed to him as if many strange shapes stood by unseen, and watched with great eagerness to see whether he would rise and go away, or yield to the temptation of stopping and indulging his curious fancy. Strange!—he saw and heard absolutely nobody and nothing; yet he dimly realized that unseen figures were watching him close with bated breath, and anxiously observing his every movement, as if intent to know whether he would rise and move on, or remain to investigate this causeless sensation.

For a minute or two he stood irresolute; and all the time he so stood the unseen bystanders held their breath and looked on in an agony of expectation. He could feel their outstretched necks; he could picture their strained attention. At last he broke away. 'This is nonsense,' he said aloud to himself, and turned slowly homeward. As he did so, a deep sigh, as of suspense relieved, but relieved in the wrong direction, seemed to rise—unheard, impalpable, spiritual— from the invisible crowd that gathered around him immaterial. Clutched hands seemed to stretch after him and try to pull him back. An unreal throng of angry and disappointed creatures seemed to follow him over the moor, uttering speechless imprecations on his head, in some unknown tongue—ineffable, inaudible. This horrid sense of being followed by unearthly foes took absolute possession of Rudolph's mind. It might have been merely the lurid redness of the afterglow, or the loneliness of the moor, or the necessity for being back not one minute late for Mrs Bouverie-Barton's dinner-hour; but, at any rate, he lost all self-control for the moment, and ran—ran wildly, at the very top of his speed, all the way from the barrow to the door of the manor-house garden. There he stopped and looked round with a painful sense of his own stupid cowardice. This was positively childish: he had seen nothing, heard nothing, had nothing definite to frighten him; yet he had run from his own mental shadow, like the veriest schoolgirl, and was trembling still from the profundity of his sense that somebody unseen was pursuing and following him. 'What a precious fool I am,' he said to himself, half angrily, 'to be so terrified at nothing! I'll go round there by-and-by, just to recover my self-respect, and to show, at least, I'm not really frightened.'

And even as he said it he was internally aware that his baffled foes, standing grinning their disappointment with gnashed teeth at the garden gate, gave a chuckle of surprise, delight, and satisfaction at his altered intention.

II

There's nothing like light for dispelling superstitious terrors. Pallinghurst Manor-house was fortunately supplied with electric light; for Mrs Bouverie-Barton was nothing if not intensely modern. Long before Rudolph had finished dressing for dinner, he was smiling once more to himself at his foolish conduct. Never in his life before—at least, since he was twenty—had he done such a thing; and he knew why he'd done it now. It was a nervous breakdown. He had been overworking his brain in town with those elaborate calculations for his *Fortnightly* article on 'The Present State of Chinese Finances'; and Sir Arthur Boyd, the famous specialist on diseases of the nervous system, had earned three honest guineas cheap by recommending him 'a week or two's rest and change in the country.' That was why he had accepted Mrs Bouverie-Barton's invitation to form part of her brilliant autumn party at Pallinghurst Manor; and that was also doubtless why he had been so absurdly frightened at nothing at all just now on the common. Memorandum: Never to overwork his brain in future; it doesn't pay. And yet, in these days, how earn bread and cheese at literature without overworking it?

He went down to dinner, however, in very good spirits. His hostess was kind; she permitted him to take in that pretty American. Conversation with the soup turned at once on the sunset. Conversation with the soup is always on the lowest and most casual plane; it improves with the fish, and reaches its culmination with the sweets and the cheese; after which it declines again to the fruity level. 'You were on the barrow about seven, Mr Reeve,' Mrs Bouverie-Barton observed severely, when he spoke of the after-glow. 'You watched that sunset close. How fast you must have walked home! I was almost half afraid you were going to be late for dinner.'

Rudolph coloured up slightly; 'twas a girlish trick, unworthy of a journalist; but still he had it. 'Oh dear, no, Mrs Bouverie-Barton,' he answered gravely. 'I may be foolish, but not, I hope, criminal. I know better than to do anything so weak and wicked as that at Pallinghurst Manor. I *do* walk rather fast, and the sunset—well, the sunset was just too lovely.'

'Elegant,' the pretty American interposed, in her language.

'It always is, this night every year,' little Joyce said quietly, with the air of one who retails a well-known scientific fact. 'It's the night, you know, when the light burns bright on the Old Long Barrow.'

Joyce was Mrs Bouverie-Barton's only child—a frail and pretty little creature, just twelve years old, very light and fairylike, but with a strange cowed look which, nevertheless, somehow curiously became her.

'What nonsense you talk, my child!' her mother exclaimed, darting a look at Joyce which made her relapse forthwith into instant silence. 'I'm ashamed of her, Mr Reeve; they pick up such nonsense as this from their nurses.' For Mrs Bouverie-Barton was modern, and disbelieved in everything. 'Tis a simple creed; one clause concludes it.

But the child's words, though lightly whispered, had caught the quick ear of Archie Cameron, the distinguished electrician.* He made a spring upon them at once; for the merest suspicion of the super-natural was to Cameron irresistible. 'What's that, Joyce?' he cried, leaning forward across the table. 'No, Mrs Bouverie-Barton, I really *must* hear it. What day is this to-day, and what's that you just said about the sunset and the light on the Old Long Barrow?'

Joyce glanced pleadingly at her mother, and then again at Cameron. A very faint nod gave her grudging leave to proceed with her tale, under maternal disapprobation; for Mrs Bouverie-Barton didn't carry her belief in Woman's Rights quite so far as to apply them to the case of her own daughter. We *must* draw a line some-where. Joyce hesitated and began. 'Well, this is the night, you know,' she said, 'when the sun turns, or stands still, or crosses the tropic, or goes back again, or something.'

Mrs Bouverie-Barton gave a dry little cough. 'The autumnal equinox,' she interposed severely, 'at which, of course, the sun does nothing of the sort you suppose. We shall have to have your astro-nomy looked after, Joyce; such ignorance is exhaustive. But go on with your myth, please, and get it over quickly.'

'The autumnal equinox; that's just it,' Joyce went on, unabashed. 'I remember that's the word, for old Rachel, the gipsy, told me so. Well, on this day every year, a sort of glow comes up on the moor; oh! I know it does, mother, for I've seen it myself; and the rhyme about it goes—

> Every year on Michael's night
> Pallinghurst Barrow burneth bright.

Only the gipsy told me it was Baal's night before it was St Michael's,* and it was somebody else's night, whose name I forget, before it was Baal's. And the somebody was a god to whom you must never sacrifice anything with iron, but always with flint or with a stone hatchet.'

Cameron leaned back in his chair and surveyed the child critically. 'Now, this is interesting.' he said; 'profoundly interesting. For here we get, what is always so much wanted, firsthand evidence. And you're quite sure, Joyce, you've really seen it?'

'Oh! Mr Cameron, how can you?' Mrs Bouverie-Barton cried, quite pettishly; for even advanced ladies are still feminine enough at times to be distinctly pettish. 'I take the greatest trouble to keep all such rubbish out of Joyce's way; and then you men of science come down here and talk like this to her, and undo all the good I've taken months in doing.'

'Well, whether Joyce has ever seen it or not,' Rudolph Reeve said gravely, 'I can answer for it myself that I saw a very curious light on the Long Barrow to-night; and, furthermore, I felt a most peculiar sensation.'

'What was that?' Cameron asked, bending over towards him eagerly. For all the world knows that Cameron, though a disbeliever in most things (except the Brush light), still retains a quaint tinge of Highland Scotch belief in a good ghost story.

'Why, as I was sitting on the barrow,' Rudolph began, 'just after sunset, I was dimly conscious of something stirring inside, not visible or audible, but——'

'Oh, I know, I know!' Joyce put in, leaning forward, with her eyes staring curiously; 'a sort of a feeling that there was somebody somewhere, very faint and dim, though you couldn't see or hear them; they tried to pull you down, clutching at you like this: and when you ran away, frightened, they seemed to follow you and jeer at you. Great gibbering creatures! Oh, I know what all that is! I've been there, and felt it.'

'Joyce!' Mrs Bouverie-Barton put in, with a warning frown, 'what nonsense you talk! You're really too ridiculous. How can you suppose Mr Reeve ran away—a man of science like him—from an imaginary terror?'

'Well, I won't quite say I ran away,' Rudolph answered, somewhat sheepishly. 'We never do admit these things, I suppose, after twenty. But I certainly did hurry home at the very top of my speed—not to be late for dinner, you know, Mrs Bouverie-Barton; and I *will* admit, Joyce, between you and me only, I was conscious by the way of something very much like your grinning followers behind me.'

Mrs Bouverie-Barton darted him another look of intense displeasure. 'I think,' she said, in that chilly voice that has iced whole committees, 'at a table like this, and with such thinkers around, we might surely find something rather better to discuss than such worn-out superstitions. Professor Spence, did you light upon any fresh palæoliths in the gravel-pit this morning?'

III

In the drawing-room, a little later, a small group collected by the corner bay, remotest from Mrs Bouverie-Barton's own presidential chair, to hear Rudolph and Joyce compare experiences on the light above the barrow. When the two dreamers of dreams and seers of visions had finished, Mrs Bruce, the esoteric Buddhist and hostess of Mahatmas* (they often dropped in on her, it was said, quite informally, for afternoon tea), opened the flood-gates of her torrent speech with triumphant vehemence. 'This is just what I should have expected,' she said, looking round for a sceptic, that she might turn and rend him. 'Novalis was right.* Children are early men. They are freshest from the truth. They come straight to us from the Infinite. Little souls just let loose from the free expanse of God's sky see more than we adults do—at least, except a few of us. We ourselves, what are we but accumulated layers of phantasmata? Spirit-light rarely breaks in upon our grimed charnel of flesh. The dust of years overlies us. But the child, bursting new upon the dim world of Karma, trails clouds of glory from the beatific vision. So Wordsworth held; so the Masters of Tibet taught us, long ages before Wordsworth.'

'It's curious,' Professor Spence put in, with a scientific smile, restrained at the corners, 'that all this should have happened to Joyce and to our friend Reeve at a long barrow. For you've seen MacRitchie's last work, I suppose? No? Well, he's shown conclusively that long barrows, which are the graves of the small, squat people who preceded the inroad of Aryan invaders, are the real originals of all the fairy hills and subterranean palaces of popular legend.* You know the old story of how Childe Roland to the dark tower came, of course, Cameron? Well, that dark tower was nothing more or less than a long barrow; perhaps Pallinghurst Barrow itself, perhaps some other; and Childe Roland went into it to rescue his sister, Burd Ellen, who had been stolen by the fairy king, after the fashion of his kind, for a human sacrifice.* The Picts, you recollect, were a deeply religious people, who believed in human sacrifice. They felt they derived from it high spiritual benefit. And the queerest part of it all is that in order to see the fairies you must go round the barrow *widershins*—that is to say, Miss Quackenboss, as Cameron will explain to you, the opposite way from the way of the sun—on this very night of all the year, Michaelmas Eve, which was the accepted old date of the autumnal equinox.'

'All long barrows have a chamber of great stones in the centre, I believe,' Cameron suggested tentatively.

'Yes, all or nearly all; megalithic, you know; unwrought; and that chamber's the subterranean palace, lit up with the fairy light that's so constantly found in old stories of the dead, and which Joyce and you, alone among moderns, have been permitted to see, Reeve.'

'It's a very odd fact,' Dr Porter, the materialist, interposed musingly, 'that the only ghosts people ever see are the ghosts of a generation very, very close to them. One hears of lots of ghosts in eighteenth-century costumes, because everybody has a clear idea of wigs and small-clothes from pictures and fancy dresses. One hears of far fewer in Elizabethan dress, because the class most given to beholding ghosts are seldom acquainted with ruffs and farthingales; and one meets with none at all in Anglo-Saxon or Ancient British or Roman costumes, because those are only known to a comparatively small class of learned people; and ghosts, as a rule, avoid the learned—except you, Mrs Bruce—as they would avoid prussic acid. Millions of ghosts of remote antiquity must swarm about the world, though, after a hundred years or thereabouts, they retire into obscurity and cease to annoy people with their nasty cold shivers. But the queer thing about these long-barrow ghosts is that they must be the spirits of men and women who died thousands and thousands of years ago, which is exceptional longevity for a spiritual being; don't you think so, Cameron?'

'Europe must be chock-full of them!' the pretty American assented, smiling; 'though Amurrica hasn't had time, so far, to collect any considerable population of spirits.'

But Mrs Bruce was up in arms at once against such covert levity, and took the field in full force for her beloved spectres. 'No, no,' she said, 'Dr Porter, there you mistake your subject. You should read what I have written in "The Mirror of Trismegistus."* Man is the focus of the glass of his own senses. There are other landscapes in the fifth and sixth dimensions of space than the one presented to him. As Carlyle said truly, each eye sees in all things just what each eye brings with it the power of seeing. And this is true spiritually as well as physically. To Newton and Newton's dog Diamond what a different universe! One saw the great vision of universal gravitation, the other saw—a little mouse under a chair, as the wise old nursery rhyme so philosophically puts it. Nursery rhymes summarize for us the gain of centuries. Nothing was ever destroyed, nothing was ever changed, and nothing new is ever created. All the spirits of all that is, or was, or ever will be, people the universe everywhere, unseen, around us; and each of us sees of them those only he himself is adapted to seeing. The rustic or the clown meets no ghosts of any sort save the ghosts of the persons he knows about otherwise; if a man like yourself saw a ghost at all—which isn't likely—for you starve your spiritual side by blindly shutting your eyes to one whole aspect of nature—you'd be just as likely to see the ghost of a Stone Age chief as the ghost of a Georgian or Elizabethan exquisite.'

'Did I catch the word "ghost"?' Mrs Bouverie-Barton put in, coming up unexpectedly with her angry glower. 'Joyce, my child, go to bed. This is no talk for you. And don't go chilling yourself by standing at the window in your nightdress, looking out on the common to search for the light on the Old Long Barrow, which is all pure moonshine. You nearly caught your death of cold last year with that nonsense. It's always so. These superstitions never do any good to any one.'

And, indeed, Rudolph felt a faint glow of shame himself at having discussed such themes in the hearing of that nervous and high-strung little creature.

IV

In the course of the evening, Rudolph's head began to ache, as, to say the truth, it often did; for was he not an author? and sufferance is the badge of all our tribe. His head generally ached: the intervals he employed upon magazine articles. He knew that headache well; it was the worst neuralgic kind—the wet-towel variety—the sort that keeps you tossing the whole night long without hope of respite. About eleven o'clock, when the men went into the smoking-room, the pain became unendurable. He called Dr Porter aside. 'Can't you give me anything to relieve it?' he asked piteously, after describing his symptoms.

'Oh, certainly,' the doctor answered, with that brisk medical confidence we all know so well. 'I'll bring you up a draught that will put that all right in less than half an hour. What Mrs Bruce calls Soma— the fine old crusted remedy of our Aryan ancestor; there's nothing like it for cases of nervous inanition.'

Rudolph went up to his room, and the doctor followed him a few minutes later with a very small phial of a very thick green viscid liquid. He poured ten drops carefully into a measured medicine-glass, and filled it up with water. It amalgamated badly. 'Drink that off,' he said, with the magisterial air of the cunning leech. And Rudolph drank it.

'I'll leave you the bottle,' the doctor went on, laying it down on the dressing-table, 'only use it with caution. Ten drops in two hours if the pain continues. Not more than ten, recollect. It's a powerful narcotic—I dare say you know its name: it's Cannabis Indica.'

Rudolph thanked him inarticulately, and flung himself on the bed without undressing. He had brought up a book with him—that delicious volume, Joseph Jacobs's 'English Fairy Tales'—and he tried in some vague way to read the story of Childe Roland, to which Professor Spence had directed his attention. But his head ached so much he could hardly read it; he only gathered with difficulty that Childe Roland had been instructed by witch or warlock to come to a green hill surrounded with terrace-rings—like Pallinghurst Barrow—to walk round it thrice, widershins, saying each time—

'Open door! open door!
And let me come in,'

and when the door opened to enter unabashed the fairy king's palace. And the third time the door did open, and Childe Roland entered a court, all lighted with a fairy light or gloaming; and then he went through a long passage, till he came at last to two wide stone doors;

and beyond them lay a hall—stately, glorious, magnificent—where Burd Ellen sat combing her golden hair with a comb of amber. And the moment she saw her brother, up she stood, and she said—

> 'Woe worth the day, ye luckless fool,
>   Or ever that ye were born;
> For come the King of Elfland in
>   Your fortune is forlorn.'*

When Rudolph had read so far his head ached so much he could read no further; so he laid down the book, and reflected once more in some half-conscious mood on Mrs Bruce's theory that each man could see only the ghosts he expected. That seemed reasonable enough, for according to our faith is it unto us always. If so, then these ancient and savage ghosts of the dim old Stone Age, before bronze or iron, must still haunt the grassy barrows under the waving pines, where legend declared they were long since buried; and the mystic light over Pallinghurst moor must be the local evidence and symbol of their presence.

How long he lay there he hardly quite knew; but the clock struck twice, and his head was aching so fiercely now that he helped himself plentifully to a second dose of the thick green mixture. His hand shook too much to be Puritanical to a drop or two. For a while it relieved him; then the pain grew worse again. Dreamily he moved over to the big north oriel to cool his brow with the fresh night air. The window stood open. As he gazed out a curious sight met his eye. At another oriel in the wing, which ran in an L-shaped bend from the part of the house where he had been put, he saw a child's white face gaze appealingly across to him. It was Joyce, in her white night-dress, peering with all her might, in spite of her mother's pro-hibition, on the mystic common. For a second she started. Her eyes met his. Slowly she raised one pale forefinger and pointed. Her lips opened to frame an inaudible word; but he read it by sight. 'Look!' she said simply. Rudolph looked where she pointed.

A faint blue light hung lambent over the Old Long Barrow. It was ghostly and vague, like matches rubbed on the palm. It seemed to rouse and call him.

He glanced towards Joyce. She waved her hand to the barrow. Her lips said 'Go.' Rudolph was now in that strange semi-mesmeric state of self-induced hypnotism when a command, of whatever sort or by whomsoever given, seems to compel obedience. Trembling he rose, and taking his bedroom candle in his hand, descended the stair noiselessly. Then, walking on tiptoe across the tile-paved hall, he reached his hat from the rack, and opening the front door stole out into the garden.

The Soma had steadied his nerves and supplied him with false courage; but even in spite of it he felt a weird and creepy sense of mystery and the supernatural. Indeed, he would have turned back even now, had he not chanced to look up and see Joyce's pale face still pressed close against the window and Joyce's white hand still motioning him mutely onward. He looked once more in the direction where she pointed. The spectral light now burnt clearer and bluer, and more unearthly than ever, and the illimitable moor seemed haunted from end to end by innumerable invisible and uncanny creatures.

Rudolph groped his way on. His goal was the barrow. As he went, speechless voices seemed to whisper unknown tongues encouragingly in his ear; horrible shapes of elder creeds appeared to crowd round him and tempt him with beckoning fingers to follow them. Alone, erect, across the darkling waste, stumbling now and again over roots of gorse and heather, but steadied, as it seemed, by invisible hands, he staggered slowly forward, till at last, with aching head and trembling feet, he stood beside the immemorial grave of the savage chieftain. Away over in the east the white moon was just rising.

After a moment's pause, he began to walk round the tumulus. But something clogged and impeded him. His feet wouldn't obey his will; they seemed to move of themselves in the opposite direction. Then all at once he remembered he had been trying to go the way of the sun, instead of widershins. Steadying himself, and opening his eyes, he walked in the converse sense. All at once his feet moved easily, and the invisible attendants chuckled to themselves so loud that he could almost hear them. After the third round his lips parted, and he murmured the mystic words: 'Open door! Open door! Let me come in.' Then his head throbbed worse than ever with exertion and giddiness, and for two or three minutes more he was unconscious of anything.

When he opened his eyes again a very different sight displayed itself before him. Instantly he was aware that the age had gone back upon its steps ten thousand years, as the sun went back upon the dial of Ahaz;* he stood face to face with a remote antiquity. Planes of existence faded; new sights floated over him; new worlds were penetrated; new ideas, yet very old, undulated centrically towards him from the universal flat of time and space and matter and motion. He was projected into another sphere and saw by fresh senses. Everything was changed, and he himself changed with it.

The blue light over the barrow now shone clear as day, though infinitely more mysterious. A passage lay open through the grassy slope into a rude stone corridor. Though his curiosity by this time was thoroughly aroused, Rudolph shrank with a terrible shrinking from his own impulse to enter this grim black hole, which led at once, by an oblique descent, into the bowels of the earth. But he couldn't help himself. For, O God! looking round him, he saw, to his infinite terror, alarm, and awe, a ghostly throng of naked and hideous savages. They were spirits, yet savages. Eagerly they jostled and hustled him, and crowded round him in wild groups, exactly as they had done to the spiritual sense a little earlier in the evening, when he couldn't see them. But now he saw them clearly with the outer eye; saw them as grinning and hateful barbarian shadows, neither black nor white, but tawny-skinned and low-browed; their tangled hair falling unkempt in matted locks about their receding foreheads; their jaws large and fierce; their eyebrows shaggy and protruding like a gorilla's; their loins just girt with a few scraps of torn skin; their whole mien inexpressibly repulsive and bloodthirsty.

They were savages, yet they were ghosts. The two most terrible and dreaded foes of civilized experience seemed combined at once in them. Rudolph Reeve crouched powerless in their intangible hands; for they seized him roughly with incorporeal fingers, and pushed him bodily into the presence of their sleeping chieftain. As they did so they raised loud peals of discordant laughter. It was hollow, but it was piercing. In that hateful sound the triumphant whoop of the Red Indian and the weird mockery of the ghost were strangely mingled into some appalling harmony.

Rudolph allowed them to push him in; they were too many to resist; and the Soma had sucked all strength out of his muscles. The women were the worst: ghastly hags of old, witches with pendent breasts and bloodshot eyes, they whirled round him in triumph, and shouted aloud in a tongue he had never before heard, though he understood it instinctively, 'A victim! A victim! We hold him! We have him!'

The grinning skeleton turned its head and regarded Rudolph from its eyeless orbs with a vacant glance of hungry satisfaction

Even in the agonized horror of that awful moment Rudolph knew why he understood those words, unheard till then. They were the first language of our race—the natural and instinctive mother-tongue of humanity.

They haled him forward by main force to the central chamber, with hands and arms and ghostly shreds of buffalo-hide. Their wrists compelled him as the magnet compels the iron bar. He entered the palace. A dim phosphorescent light, like the light of a churchyard or of decaying paganism, seemed to illumine it faintly. Things loomed dark before him; but his eyes almost instantly adapted themselves to the gloom, as the eyes of the dead on the first night in the grave adapt themselves by inner force to the strangeness of their surroundings. The royal hall was built up of cyclopean stones, each as big as the head of some colossal Sesostris.* They were of ice-worn granite and a dusky-grey sandstone, rudely piled on one another, and carved in relief with representations of serpents, concentric lines, interlacing zigzags, and the mystic swastika. But all these things Rudolph only saw vaguely, if he saw them at all; his attention was too much concentrated on devouring fear and the horror of his situation.

In the very centre a skeleton sat crouching on the floor in some loose, huddled fashion. Its legs were doubled up, its hands clasped round its knees, its grinning teeth had long been blackened by time or by the indurated blood of human victims. The ghosts approached it with strange reverence, in impish postures.

'See! We bring you a slave, great king!' they cried in the same barbaric tongue—all clicks and gutturals. 'For this is the holy night of your father, the Sun, when he turns him about on his yearly course through the stars and goes south to leave us. We bring you a slave to renew your youth. Rise! Drink his hot blood! Rise! Kill and eat him!'

The grinning skeleton turned its head and regarded Rudolph from its eyeless orbs with a vacant glance of hungry satisfaction. The sight of human meat seemed to create a soul beneath the ribs of death in some incredible fashion. Even as Rudolph, held fast by the immaterial hands of his ghastly captors, looked and trembled for his fate, too terrified to cry out or even to move and struggle, he beheld the hideous thing rise and assume a shadowy shape, all pallid blue light, like the shapes of his jailers. Bit by bit, as he gazed, the skeleton seemed to disappear, or rather to fade into some unsubstantial form, which was nevertheless more human, more corporeal, more horrible than the dry bones it had come from. Naked and yellow like the rest, it wore round its dim waist just an apron of dry grass, or, what seemed to be such, while over its shoulders hung the ghost of a bearskin mantle. As it rose, the other spectres knocked their foreheads low on the ground before it, and grovelled with their long looks in the ageless dust, and uttered elfin cries of inarticulate homage.

The great chief turned, grinning, to one of his spectral henchmen.

'Give a knife!' he said curtly, for all that these strange shades uttered was snapped out in short, sharp sentences, and in a monosyllabic tongue, like the bark of jackals or the laugh of the striped hyena among the graves at midnight.

The attendant, bowing low once more, handed his liege a flint flake, very keen-edged, but jagged, a rude and horrible instrument of barbaric manufacture. But what terrified Rudolph most was the fact that this flake was no ghostly weapon, no immaterial shred, but a fragment of real stone, capable of inflicting a deadly gash or long torn wound. Hundreds of such fragments, indeed, lay loose on the concreted floor of the chamber, some of them roughly chipped, others ground and polished. Rudolph had seen such things in museums many times before; with a sudden rush of horror, he recognized now for the first time in his life with what object the savages of that far-off day had buried them with their dead in the chambered barrows.

With a violent effort he wetted his parched lips with his tongue, and cried out thrice in his agony the one word 'Mercy!'

At that sound the savage king burst into a loud and fiendish laugh. It was a hideous laugh, halfway between a wild beast's and a murderous maniac's: it echoed through the long hall like the laughter of devils when they succeed in leading a fair woman's soul to eternal perdition. 'What does he say?' the king cried, in the same transparently natural words, whose import Rudolph could understand at once. 'How like birds they talk, these white-faced men, whom we get for our only victims since the years grew foolish! "Mu-mu-mu-moo!" they say; "Mu-mu-mu-moo!" more like frogs than men and women!'

Then it came over Rudolph instinctively, through the maze of his terror, that he could understand the lower tongue of these elfish visions because he and his ancestors had once passed through it; but they could not understand his, because it was too high and too deep for them.

He had little time for thought, however. Fear bounded his horizon. The ghosts crowded round him, gibbering louder than before. With wild cries and heathen screams they began to dance about their victim. Two advanced with measured steps and tied his hands and feet with a ghostly cord. It cut into the flesh like the stab of a great sorrow. They bound him to a stake which Rudolph felt conscious was no earthly and material wood, but a piece of intangible shadow; yet he could no more escape from it than from the iron chain of an earthly prison. On each side the stake two savage hags, long-haired, ill-favoured, inexpressibly cruel-looking, set two small plants of Enchanter's Nightshade. Then a fierce orgiastic shout went up to the low roof from all the assembled people. Rushing forward together, they covered his body with what seemed to be oil and butter; they hung grave-flowers round his neck; they quarrelled among themselves with clamorous cries for hairs and rags torn from his head and clothing. The women, in particular, whirled round him with frantic Bacchanalian gestures, crying aloud as they circled, 'O great chief! O my king! we offer you this victim; we offer you new blood to prolong your life. Give us in return sound sleep, dry graves, sweet dreams, fair seasons!'

They cut themselves with flint knives. Ghostly ichor streamed copious.

The king meanwhile kept close guard over his victim, whom he watched with hungry eyes of hideous cannibal longing. Then, at a given signal, the crowd of ghosts stood suddenly still. There was an awesome pause. The men gathered outside, the women crouched low in a ring close up to him. Dimly at that moment Rudolph noticed almost without noticing it that each of them had a wound on the side of his own skull; and he understood why: they had themselves been sacrificed in the dim long ago to bear their king company to the world of spirits. Even as he thought that thought, the men and women with a loud whoop raised hands aloft in unison. Each grasped a sharp flake, which he brandished savagely. The king gave the signal by rushing at him with a jagged and saw-like knife. It descended on Rudolph's head. At the same moment, the others rushed forward, crying aloud in their own tongue, 'Carve the flesh from his bones! Slay him! hack him to pieces!'

Rudolph bent his head to avoid the blows. He cowered in abject terror. Oh! what fear would any Christian ghost have inspired by the side of these incorporeal pagan savages! Ah! mercy! mercy! They would tear him limb from limb! They would rend him in pieces!

At that instant he raised his eyes, and, as by a miracle of fate, saw another shadowy form floating vague before him. It was the form of a man in sixteenth-century costume, very dim and uncertain. It might have been a ghost—it might have been a vision—but it raised

At that instant he raised his eyes, and, as by a miracle of fate, saw another shadowy form floating vague before him

its shadowy hand and pointed towards the door. Rudolph saw it was unguarded. The savages were now upon him, their ghostly breath blew chill on his cheek. 'Show them iron!' cried the shadow in an English voice. Rudolph struck out with both elbows and made a fierce effort for freedom. It was with difficulty be roused himself, but at last he succeeded. He drew his pocket-knife and opened it. At sight of the cold steel, which no ghost or troll or imp can endure to behold, the savages fell back, muttering. But 'twas only for a moment. Next instant, with a howl of vengeance even louder than before, they crowded round him and tried to intercept him. He shook them off with wild energy, though they jostled and hustled him, and struck him again and again with their sharp flint edges.

Blood was flowing freely now from his hands and arms—red blood of this world; but still he fought his way out by main force with his sharp steel blade towards the door and the moonlight. The nearer he got to the exit, the thicker and closer the ghosts pressed around, as if conscious that their power was bounded by their own threshold. They avoided the knife, meanwhile, with superstitious terror. Rudolph elbowed them fiercely aside, and lunging at them now and again, made his way to the door. With one supreme effort he tore himself madly out, and stood once more on the open heath, shivering like a greyhound. The ghosts gathered grinning by the open vestibule, their fierce teeth, like a wild beast's, confessing their impotent anger. But Rudolph started to run, all wearied as he was, and ran a few hundred yards before he fell and fainted. He dropped on a clump of white heather by a sandy ridge, and lay there unconscious till well on into the morning.

V

When the people from the Manor-house picked him up next day, he was hot and cold, terribly pale from fear, and mumbling incoherently. Dr Porter had him put to bed without a moment's delay. 'Poor fellow!' he said, leaning over him, 'he's had a very narrow escape indeed of a bad brain fever. I oughtn't to have exhibited Cannabis in his excited condition; or, at any rate, if I did, I ought, at least, to have watched its effect more closely. He must be kept very quiet now, and on no account whatever, Nurse, must either Mrs Bruce or Mrs Bouverie-Barton be allowed to come near him.'

But late in the afternoon Rudolph sent for Joyce.

The child came creeping in with an ashen face. 'Well?' she murmured, soft and low, taking her seat by the bedside; 'so the King of the Barrow very nearly had you!'

'Yes,' Rudolph answered, relieved to find there was somebody to whom he could talk freely of his terrible adventure. 'He nearly had me. But how did you come to know it?'

'About two by the clock,' the child replied, with white lips of terror, 'I saw the fires on the moor burn brighter and bluer: and then I remembered the words of a terrible old rhyme the gipsy woman taught me—

Pallinghurst Barrow—Pallinghurst Barrow!
Every year one heart thou'lt harrow!
Pallinghurst Ring—Pallinghurst Ring!
A bloody man is thy ghostly king.
Men's bones he breaks, and sucks their marrow,
In Pallinghurst Ring on Pallinghurst Barrow;

and just as I thought it, I saw the lights burn terribly bright and clear for a second, and I shuddered for horror. Then they died down low at once, and there was moaning on the moor, cries of despair, as from a great crowd cheated, and at that I knew that you were not to be the Ghost-king's victim.'

JEAN LORRAIN

Magic Lantern

THE Orchestra Colonne completed, with muted strings teased by the tips of the bows, the most delightful movements of *The Sleep of Faust: the Choir of Spirits and the Dance of the Sylphs*. Entirely under the spell of that hallucinatory music—and perhaps brought down a little too abruptly from the height of my aesthetic reveries into the prosaic brouhaha of the interlude—I turned to the occupant of the next seat, the physicist Forbster, and took him to task, intending to relieve myself of the burden by means of this facile outburst:

'Admit, Monsieur, that it is as well that Berlioz was born in 1803.* Had he been born yesterday, he would undoubtedly have included an electrophore in his symphony, or the submarine cable, or some other phonographic apparatus. Without that ridiculous and nauseating Romanticism, with which it is manifestly infected and impregnated, we would not be applauding the three hundred and eighty-somethingth performance of his *Damnation* today. Modern science has killed the Fantastic, and with the Fantastic, Poetry—which is also Fantasy. The last Fairy is well and truly buried—or dried, like a rare flower, between two pages of Monsieur Balzac. Michelet* has dissected the Witch and with the assistance of the novels of Monsieur Verne,* not one of our descendants twenty years hence, on hearing the Dance of the Sylphs—not one!—will be capable of the least sensation of that legendary nostalgia which distracts me now.'

'But it is a charming distraction, Monsieur, and a very amicable one.'

'Oh, do you think so? I, Monsieur, am of the old school. I feel the shots fired in *Der Freischutz*.* Yes, assuredly, the one will kill the other. Alas, the one will kill the other. We no longer have a trace of illusion in our heads, my dear Monsieur. We have an abstruse mathematical treatise in place of the heart, the appetites of a piglet in the belly, bridles and racing tips in the imagination, and a clockwork movement in the brain. Look at the man that we have all become, manufactured by the progress of science! If we still have some slight capacity for passion, it is because that old imbecile and simpleton, the Romantic troubadour—the "1830 article" derided by the moderns—clings hard to the saddle within us; but have patience, he is dying. Ten years hence, his whisper will no longer be audible. We shall all be built on the same model: utilitarians, sceptics and engineers. Ah yes, great Pan is dead, and you are numbered among those who have killed him—yes, you, Monsieur Physicist. You, with your horrid mania to explain everything, to put everything to the proof, are one of the Assassins of Fantasy. Compared with you, the savant Coppelius himself—the man with the wax doll*—could almost be reckoned an honest man, at least in my humble opinion.'

'But the aforesaid Coppelius, if I remember rightly, was guilty of conjuring away the reason of the Student Hoffmann. I feel obliged to point out that—so far, at least—I have not the slightest case of mental alienation on my conscience.'

'I believe you! You suppress even Madness, the last citadel in which a man of spirit, at the limit of his patience, might retrench himself!'

'I suppress Madness? I'm glad to hear it—it's a rare and novel privilege . . .'

'Yes and no. You suppress it in the end . . . after you have analysed it, explained it, determined it, localised it, you heal it as required—and by what means! By electricity and therapy! You have killed the Fantastic, Monsieur.'

'Now then,' said André Forbster, suddenly changing his tone as he half-turned towards me, 'are you really serious in what you say? Where have you got hold of the notion that we have killed the Fantastic, and that the dear nobleman has disappeared from our mores? Never—never, in any era, not even the Middle Ages, when the mandrake shrieked in the middle of every night beneath the frightful dew dripping from the gallows—never has the Fantastic flourished, so sinister and so terrifying, as in modern life! We live in a world full of sorcery. The Fantastic surrounds us; worse than that, it invades us, chokes us and obsesses us—and one would have to be blind or very obstinate not to see that.'

'Yes, I know. Hypnotism, magnetism, suggestion and hysteria. The experiments of Charcot at the Salpêtrière,* the wild women who stretch themselves out on their hands and merrily make hoops of themselves under the false pretext that the reflection of a spoon has manifested itself in their eye, the daily reproduction of the phenomena of somnambulism, and the table-turning of Mesdames Donatos. For myself, I prefer the demon-possessed, the nuns of Loudun* and the convulsants of Saint-Médard;* at least the scenery was right.'

'And you're in favour of appropriate scenery?'

'Absolutely. Tombs by moonlight, foggy winter skies, and—far above the writhings and whitenings of the damned—the eternal battle of the clouds, and the black cones of cypresses shaken by the wind . . . that, at least, grips the nerves and meets the expectations of the imagination. And what a *mise en scène* the most trivial exorcism makes! But what do we have in place of that now? A miserable little whitewashed hospital room, very clean and very cold, a window without curtains, and—thrown across a modern table—some unhappy woman of Saint-Lazare, stupefied in advance with morphine, naked to the waist. And clustered around that female meat, the decorated men—professors of the Faculty—and the undecorated men: interns and curiosity-seekers. Utterly lacking in dignity, the modern victims of possession lack any authority.'

'Lacking, above all, the half-light of the church, the ambiguous light of stained-glass windows and the music of the organ. Admit that you miss all that Tony Johannot stuff!'*

'Certainly I miss it.'

'Very picturesque, to be sure, and sometimes moving—but how obstinate you are! If you would only take a little trouble, and set aside for the moment your gallows, undulous plants and cemetery crosses, you could very easily convince yourself that we live, even in the fullness of modernity, in the midst of the damned, surrounded by the spectres of human heads and other horrors; that every day we brush up against vampires and ghouls. I will lay you a bet if you like, that you number at least three or four witches among your acquaintances. I myself am acquainted with two egregores, and I shall easily be able, here in the Châtelet, to point out to you and to name more than fifteen people who are absolutely defunct, but whose cadavers have every appearance of life.'

'You're joking, Monsieur.'

'No more than you are, I think. Just take the trouble to look around you. We are in the full assembly of the Sabbat of Sabbats here, and I put it to you that every evening, every arena of Parisian society—including the Opera and the gatherings of the great and the good of France—is a rendezvous of necromantic mages.'

'Monsieur, this the joke to end all jokes.'

'Then I shall put an end to it. Do me the favour of taking up those opera-glasses, and follow the directions that I will give to you. Look over there, at those three elegant women on the balcony dressed in plush with fashionable hats: three unmarried women, evidently. Look at those chalky complexions, those eyes blackened with kohl and the scarlet stains of their pained lips, like bloody wounds gaping in the flesh of those dead faces. Are they not verit-able ghouls: damnable cadavers spewed from the tomb and escaped from the cemetery into the world of the living; flowers of the charnel-house sent forth to seduce, enchant and ruin young men? What is the magic that emanates from such creatures—for they are not even pretty, these marrow-crushers, but rather frightful, with their mor-tuary tint and their blood-tinged smiles? Well, do you see the thin-nest? One of my friends killed himself for her. She has already devoured three racing stables and their proprietors, and is at this very moment consuming Bompard, the fat banker of the Rue des Petits-Champs. The others are of the same ilk. The Comte de Santiego, husband of a delightful young wife—perhaps the most beautiful in all the Spanish colonies—and, what's more, father of two adorable blonde Murillos, is in the process of ruining himself for Irma, the oldest of the three. By means of what horrible secret lust has that woman got her claws into him? Hold on, she has recognised me, and she is smiling at us: it is the smile of the ghoul, all moist with blood!

'Would you like to read a tale by Hoffmann now? Look down there, to the right of the fore-stage; see the beautiful Madame G——. Take note of those eyes, with their irises of crystal, and that gleaming tint of porcelain! Her hair is silken, her teeth authentically pearly, like those of dolls. She is enamelled, one presumes, to the navel, so that her ballgowns may be cut as low as fashion requires. Thanks to the articulated springs in her bodice she can say "Papa", "Mama", and "Bonjour, Excellency". Produced for export, she is bound for America. She knows how to handle a fan, to curtsey deeply, to flutter her eyelashes and to appear to breathe like a real person. Vaucanson* is surpassed. Is that not the Olympia of Doctor Coppelius? And if a mechanism does not actually animate that mannequin on parade, what sort of vague and intermediary soul could possibly inhabit that breast? To hold between one's arms that rotating Sidonie, to run into those lips, as cold as lips of wax: does the idea not make you shudder?

'Use the opera-glasses to delve into the dim depths of the ground-floor boxes. See those flared nostrils, those linen pallors, those hypnotic eyes, those bloodless arms poking out of red crushed velvet, the nervous and febrile hands clutching bottles of salts or flapping fans. Those are the great melomaniac women of the world . . . the wives of Merchant Bankers and Sugar-Refiners, all of them morphinated, cauterised, dosed, drugged by psychotherapeutic novels and ether: medicated, anaemiated androgynes, hysterics and consumptives. They are the possessed of the new aristocracy.

'Up there, in the second tier, I can see a young woman as honest and fresh as a rose, who never misses an execution. I know her and I recognise her: she was at Marchandon; she was at Gamahut; during the summer of the crime of the Rue Montaigne she was seen going to the Place de la Roquette on eight successive days so as not to miss the execution of Pranzini, a veritable fête. She is an exquisite young woman, but she has adored assassins for twenty years, and shivers with profound sensuality every time she sees the fall of a severed head—eternally young, though, as if kept fresh by the sight of blood! The thirst for new sensations now extends to horrors! The witches of the Middle Ages were likewise excessively fond of the blood of executed criminals.

'Over there, three rows of seats behind us: that great hearty fellow with huge russet moustaches and the torso of a horseman is a specialist; he only loves consumptive women. All his mistresses die within the year. The lover of the condemned deserves a place in the finest comedy of Jules Lemaître,* that kind of bizarre love should be classified under the heading of Demoniality.

'Finally, I see elsewhere a very pretty brunette—I shall not point her out to you because she is my friend—whom the Holy Inquisitions of the fifteen and sixteen hundreds would most certainly have put on the rack, pricked and burnt. In the year of grace 1891, however, she comes and she goes, operating in perfect liberty. That lovely woman is on her fourth experiment; three gallant husbands have already died in harness: a master of wolfhounds and two perfectly healthy captains of the army, one of them a cuirassier. Two years in the household: going, going, gone. Emptied, crushed to the marrow, breasts hollow, legs shaking: broken puppets . . .

'She, meanwhile, is always plump, pink and well-heeled: heir to their fortunes and, I suppose, their health. They melted like wax in the warmth of her bed. The fourth survives, for the moment, but he has already been deeply cut into. Have you read, in Balzac's *Contes drolatiques*,* a fable called "The Succubus"? Under the Valois, nothing more would have been necessary for a wife to be dragged in a shift to the Place de Grève.

'But excuse me, Monsieur, the music is beginning. Much obliged.'

JEAN LORRAIN

The Spectral Hand

WHEN the world was rocked by the scandal of the murder of the Comtesse d'Orthyse, my friend Jacques and I were by no means as astonished as everyone else. We had known for some time what tragic end that adorable woman was destined to meet, for an irrefutable sign had been shown to us—although had we told anyone else what we knew we would probably have been deemed mad. We even knew, by virtue of the revelation vouchsafed to us, whose brutal hand it was that would put a revolver to her heart and destroy her.

*

It all happened two years ago, when the woman in question had not yet become the second Comtesse d'Orthyse. She was the widow of the Marquis de Strada. She was still in the full flower of her enduring beauty, and was famed in Parisian Society for her taste, her flamboyance and her elegance. A portrait by Whistler shown at Champ-de-Mars had made her the most fashionable woman of that season. Her gowns—made up by a theatrical costumier from fabrics obtainable only from *Chez Morice* in London, in accordance with unpublished patterns by Burne-Jones—wrought a revolution among the couturiers of Paris. In all the clubs and boudoirs of the city people discussed reports of her dressing-room, whose lacquered green chairs were each encrusted with a trefoil of diamonds, and whose Dresden china bath-tub, supported by three bronze Japanese frogs, was the epitome of symbolic extravagance.*

The luncheons and dinner-parties which the Marquise held— where artists, poets and painters gathered, and from which other women were virtually excluded—were also a perennial topic of conversation. Her little town-house in the Place des États-Unis, and its antechamber with white enamelled walls and carpets like snowdrifts, was the centre of attention of the entire tribe of society reporters. The Comte de Montesquiou was regularly to be seen there, with his ornamental cane and his blue hydrangeas.* The smart set had quite forgotten the road to Versailles; the fashionable pilgrimage of the day was to the drawing-room of the Mansion Strada, with its drapes of rose-coloured Pékin and its furniture by Riessener.

On the evening with which my story is concerned there had been an intimate dinner at the home of the Marquise. Apart from Jacques and myself the only guests were Henri Tramsel and the poet Pierre de Lisse. The Marquise was deliciously displayed in one of those close-fitting and flexible gowns whose secret only she knew. To surprise her, we had bedecked her dining-table with yellow tulips; there were tulips in clusters about the candelabras, tulips in sheaves in the silver centrepiece, tulips scattered like rushes about the tablecloth.* The conversation—whose principal topics were art and literature—was sparkling; it extended from the new illustrations for Grimm's tales done by Walter Crane* to the recent acquisition by the Louvre of nightmarish paintings by Breughel and Hokusai,* taking in *en passant* Maeterlinck and the Goncourts,* Ibsen and Outamaro.*

Afterwards, we retired to the drawing-room, following in the wake of the rustling train of the marquise's gown. The train was the colour of mauve hydrangeas, a mauve that was almost pink, like the rosy colour of a dewy dawn, but which became blue when it was shadowed. We sat down again, the marquise stretching herself out among the cushions of a narrow couch, delicately nibbling the long stem of a tulip which she had picked up from the table. She told us all about some strange and mysterious event which she recalled from childhood. While she related the story it seemed that she became again the little girl that she had been, rather than the young woman she now was, all a-shiver with the thrilling fear of the supernatural.

Once the subject had been broached, the conversation took up the occult theme, sliding easily into a discussion of magic, spiritualism and all the mysterious sciences which so fascinate our tired and enervated *fin-de-siècle*. Someone mentioned the phenomenon of table-turning, and the marquise immediately came to her feet, rang for a servant and demanded a small round table. She was suddenly animated by a fervent interest which coloured her pale features; the superstitious aspect of her child-like personality had been stirred by the notion of invoking the spirit-world and bringing about some incursion of the marvellous. She paced back and forth, her hands fluttering wildly. Her former indolence had turned into a fever, and she continually glanced about the huge redly-illuminated drawing-room, as if expecting spirits to manifest themselves at any moment.

Unfortunately, the marquise's home was furnished in such a manner that a table of the necessary size could not be found—all the tables she had were in the English style of the previous century. After a few fruitless attempts to persuade the spirits to tilt a little copper stand we were compelled to abandon that particular line of enquiry. In any case, the marquise, with her eternal tulip lodged between her lips, kept interrupting the circle in order to make sure that the flower was still secure. The failure of our enterprise irritated our beautiful but short-tempered hostess, so much so that Henri Tramsel proposed that we should try another method of evocation, which he called 'the spectral hand'.

We asked him what he meant by that, and he assured us that it was one of the most certain means by which the living might enter into communication with the dead. It required, he said, a very particular set of conditions—but the marquise's drawing-room, which was connected to the dining-room by a large curtained bay, was ideal. He warned us solemnly, however, that the experiment was dangerous, and that it would require stern courage and strength of character.

'Dangerous?' responded the marquise. 'Oh, how delicious! What must we do?'

Henri Tramsel extinguished all save one of the shaded lamps which illuminated the huge chamber, and required all five of us to sit down before the soft silk curtains that hung in the bay which separated the drawing-room from the dining-room.

'The first necessity,' he said, in a very solemn voice, 'is to believe. None of us has the least doubt as to the immortality of the soul, isn't that so? We all accept the reality of spirits and other invisible beings which exist all around us, and the possibility that there is a world beyond our own, existing in parallel with it, into whose mysteries we desire to be initiated.'

We all nodded our heads in acquiescence, a little discomfited by the profound silence which had suddenly taken possession of the room. Only a moment before it had been filled with luminous gaiety, but now it had been invaded by a host of shadows which stirred strangely in the flickering light of the one remaining lamp. That lamp had a shade of bluish gauze with a design representing the head of an owl, and it surrounded us with a curiously lunar light. The billowing pleats of the great awning of soft silk which separated us from the pitch-dark dining-room acted strangely upon the imagination. The five of us sat side by side facing the drapes as though they were the curtains of a theatre, and the imperial harp which the marquise had set to stand in an alcove beside the bay confirmed the impression of a dramatic spectacle.

'This is what must be done,' Henri continued. 'I shall attempt to invoke an invisible presence, requesting it to manifest itself by means of a sensation of coldness. Whichever one of us experiences that sensation most keenly is the one who is chosen to be summoned. His duty is to get up, and extend his hand into the gap between the curtains, into the dark void beyond. There he must wait until his hand is gripped by another, at which point he may ask questions of the spirit which has come.'

With a slight shiver, Henri Tramsel addressed his brief prayer to the spirits, invoking the souls of those departed whom we had held most dear. The strangest thing happened! It was as though a sudden current of air blew from the deserted dining room. It brought us briefly to our feet. Was it an illusion born of apprehension? For myself, I distinctly felt a chill in my blood, and a constriction in my heart, but none of us dared make the decision to step forward until Henri accepted the responsibility himself. Approaching the bay, he dared to stretch out his hand and insert it into the gap between the curtains of pale silk.

Several minutes passed, during which interval we scarcely allowed ourselves to breathe, but in the end Henri said: 'My hand feels a little heavy, but nothing more. Let someone else try.'

Pierre de Lisse took his turn to extend his hand into the shadowed room, then the marquise took hers. I replaced her, feeling the hairs stand up on the back of my hand as I did so. The sensation of cold increased; I reported, as the others also had, that my hand became heavy but no obvious contact was made, nothing touched my flesh.

Jacques was the only one who refused to take his turn, which he did with determined obstinacy. We were amused by his fearful reluctance, and had just begun to carry forward the experiment by taking our turns again, in a far lighter mood, when we suddenly saw him grow pale. He lifted himself from his seat and took a few steps forward, his eyes huge and round—and then he fell down at the foot of the harp, whose strings gave out a muted groan.

He had certainly seen something; the invisible had undoubtedly made itself manifest. We immediately crowded around him and lifted him up.

The lamps were relit, filling the room with a roseate glow. We harassed him with questions regarding his experience, but he said that he had seen nothing, that it was an ordinary dizzy spell without any evident cause. Plainly, he did not wish to reveal what he had seen.

*

Some time afterwards, I visited Jacques in his studio.

'You have known the family of the marquise for a long time, have you not?' he asked me, rather brusquely. 'You used to visit her home when you were a child, did you not?'

When I answered in the affirmative, he went on: 'The other evening in the Place des États-Unis, when I had a fit of dizziness during that imprudent spiritualist seance, I did in fact see something—but I dared not say what it was at the time, for fear that I might strike terror, perhaps irremediably, into someone's heart.'

'What was it, then?' I asked. 'What did you see?'

'As soon as Henri Tramsel took up his station for a second time,' he said, 'a female figure—which was at first as faint as smoke—appeared plainly to me, leaning against the frame of that imperial harp. She was dressed in a manner which was fashionable five or six years ago, and she stared fixedly at the marquise.'

'The Marquise de Strada?'

'Exactly. And you know, don't you, what it signifies when a spectre of that kind looks long and hard at one of the living?'

I did not, and said so.

'It is,' he said, 'an infallible indication of approaching death. The figure appeared, moreover, to have an expression of infinite sadness and infinite pity. That face has haunted my dreams ever since, and I have painted it from memory, in order that I might show it to you. You knew the Duchess d'Esparre, who was the mother of the marquise, and you will be sure to recognise her if that is who the spectre was.'

He abruptly turned around a canvas so that I might look at it. It held the image of a young girl, dressed in white—but there was not the slightest resemblance to the Duchess d'Esparre. The name of another woman, whom I had also known quite well, sprang instead to my lips.

'The Comtesse d'Orthyse!'

It was the first wife of the man whom the marquise was later to marry—though we did not know that at the time. We could not understand, then, why that particular spectre should have sought to communicate with the elegant and charming young widow of the Marquis de Strada. But the inexplicable vision acquired a terrible significance six months later, when the marquise announced that she was to marry the handsome Émery de Montenor, whose several titles included that of Comte d'Orthyse.

*

I will never forget the circumstances in which the proposed union was announced to us. It chanced that we had come together again, Jacques and myself, at an afternoon gathering at the home of our beautiful friend. She was dressed in white, as though she were already a bride, and while the hot tea was poured from the samovar she nibbled—as was her habit—a red rose with a long stem, which was on the point of shedding its leaves.

While she told us of her forthcoming marriage, making the announcement with a mischievous insouciance, as though she were announcing a dinner party, three petals detached themselves from the rose and came to rest like three large spots of blood upon her corseted bosom; at precisely that moment she pronounced the name *d'Orthyse*, and Jacques and I each experienced a sudden constriction of the heart. Jacques went eerily pale, and I thought that I would be compelled to prop him up—but the marquise's salon was very crowded that day, and we were able to leave without attracting too much attention.

'He will murder her,' Jacques said to me, as soon as we were outside. 'That etheric phantom, of the first Comtesse d'Orthyse, was behind her again today. He will kill her, with a revolver shot to the heart. Did you see the three drops of blood shed by the rose? They did not fall by chance!'

Subsequent events, alas, showed all too clearly that we were not deceived.

ARTHUR MACHEN

The Great God Pan*

The Experiment

'I AM glad you came, Clarke; very glad indeed. I was not sure you could spare the time.'

'I was able to make arrangements for a few days; things are not very lively just now. But have you no misgivings, Raymond? Is it absolutely safe?'

The two men were slowly pacing the terrace in front of Dr Raymond's house. The sun still hung above the western mountain-line, but it shone with a dull red glow that cast no shadows, and all the air was quiet; a sweet breath came from the great wood on the hillside above, and with it, at intervals, the soft murmuring call of the wild doves. Below, in the long lovely valley, the river wound in and out between the lonely hills, and, as the sun hovered and vanished into the west, a faint mist, pure white, began to rise from the banks. Dr Raymond turned sharply to his friend.

'Safe? Of course it is. In itself the operation is a perfectly simple one; any surgeon could do it.'

'And there is no danger at any other stage?'

'None; absolutely no physical danger whatever, I give you my word. You were always timid, Clarke, always; but you know my history. I have devoted myself to transcendental medicine for the last twenty years. I have heard myself called quack, and charlatan and impostor, but all the while I knew I was on the right path. Five years ago I reached the goal, and since then every day has been a preparation for what we shall do to-night.'

'I should like to believe it is all true.' Clarke knit his brows, and looked doubtfully at Dr Raymond. 'Are you perfectly sure, Raymond, that your theory is not a phantasmagoria—a splendid vision, certainly, but a mere vision after all?'

Dr Raymond stopped in his walk and turned sharply. He was a middle-aged man, gaunt and thin, of a pale yellow complexion, but as he answered Clarke and faced him, there was a flush on his cheek.

'Look about you, Clarke. You see the mountain, and hill following after hill, as wave on wave, you see the woods and orchards, the fields of ripe corn, and the meadows reaching to the reed-beds by the river. You see me standing here beside you, and hear my voice; but I tell you that all these things—yes, from that star that has just shone out in the sky to the solid ground beneath our feet—I say that all these are but dreams and shadows: the shadows that hide the real world from our eyes. There *is* a real world, but it is beyond this glamour and this vision, beyond these "chases in Arras, dreams in a career,"* beyond them all as beyond a veil. I do not know whether any human being has ever lifted that veil; but I do know, Clarke, that you and I shall see it lifted this very night from before another's eyes. You may think all this strange nonsense; it may be strange, but it is true, and the ancients knew what lifting the veil means. They called it seeing the god Pan.'

Clarke shivered; the white mist gathering over the river was chilly.

'It is wonderful indeed,' he said. 'We are standing on the brink of a strange world, Raymond, if what you say is true. I suppose the knife is absolutely necessary?'

'Yes; a slight lesion in the grey matter, that is all; a trifling rearrangement of certain cells, a microscopical alteration that would escape the attention of ninety-nine brain specialists out of a hundred. I don't want to bother you with "shop," Clarke; I might give you a mass of technical detail which would sound very imposing, and would leave you as enlightened as you are now. But I suppose you have read, casually, in out-of-the-way corners of your paper, that immense strides have been made recently in the physiology of the brain. I saw a paragraph the other day about Digby's theory,* and Browne Faber's discoveries.* Theories and discoveries! Where they are standing now, I stood fifteen years ago, and I need not tell you that I have not been standing still for the last fifteen years. It will be enough if I say that five years ago I made the discovery to which I alluded when I said that then I reached the goal. After years of labour, after years of toiling and groping in the dark, after days and nights of disappointment and sometimes of despair, in which I used now and then to tremble and grow cold with the thought that perhaps there were others seeking for what I sought, at last, after so long, a pang of sudden joy thrilled my soul, and I knew the long journey was at an end. By what seemed then and still seems a chance, the suggestion of a moment's idle thought followed up upon familiar lines and paths that I had tracked a hundred times already, the great truth burst upon me, and I saw, mapped out in lines of light a whole world, a sphere unknown; continents and islands, and great oceans in which no ship has sailed (to my belief) since a Man first lifted up his eyes and beheld the sun, and the stars of heaven, and the quiet earth beneath. You will think all this high-flown language, Clarke, but it is hard to be literal. And yet; I do not know whether what I am hinting at cannot be set forth in plain and homely terms. For instance, this world of ours is pretty well girded now with the telegraph wires and cables; thought, with something less than the speed of thought, flashes from sunrise to sunset, from north to south, across the floods and the desert places. Suppose that an electrician of to-day were suddenly to perceive that he and his friends have merely been playing with pebbles and mistaking them for the foundations of the world; suppose that such a man saw uttermost space lie open before the current, and words of men flash forth to the sun and beyond the sun into the systems beyond, and the voices of articulate-speaking men echo in the waste void that bounds our thought. As analogies go, that is a pretty good analogy of what I have done; you can understand now a little of what I felt as I stood here one evening; it was a summer evening, and the valley looked much as it does now; I stood here, and saw before me the unutterable, the unthinkable gulf that yawns profound between two worlds, the world of matter and the world of spirit; I saw the great empty deep stretch dim before me, and in that instant a bridge of light leapt from the earth to the unknown shore, and the abyss was spanned. You may look in Browne Faber's book, if you like, and you will find that to the present day men of science are unable to account for the presence, or to specify the functions of a certain group of nerve-cells in the brain. That group is, as it were, land to let, a mere waste place for fanciful theories. I am not in the position of Browne Faber and the special-ists, I am perfectly instructed as to the possible functions of those nerve-centres in the scheme of things. With a touch I can bring them into play, with a touch, I say, I can set free the current, with a touch I can complete the communication between this world of sense and—we shall be able to finish the sentence later on. Yes, the knife is necessary; but think what that knife will effect. It will level utterly the solid wall of sense, and probably, for the first time since man was made, a spirit will gaze on a spirit-world. Clarke, Mary will see the god Pan!'

'But you remember what you wrote to me? I thought it would be requisite that she——'

He whispered the rest into the doctor's ear.

'Not at all, not at all. That is nonsense, I assure you. Indeed, it is better as it is; I am quite certain of that.'

'Consider the matter well, Raymond. It's a great responsibility. Something might go wrong; you would be a miserable man for the rest of your days.'

'No, I think not, even if the worst happened. As you know, I rescued Mary from the gutter, and from almost certain starvation, when she was a child; I think her life is mine, to use as I see fit. Come, it is getting late; we had better go in.'

Dr Raymond led the way into the house, through the hall, and down a long dark passage. He took a key from his pocket and opened a heavy door, and motioned Clarke into his laboratory. It had once been a billiard-room, and was lighted by a glass dome in the centre of the ceiling, whence there still shone a sad grey light on the figure of the doctor as he lit a lamp with a heavy shade and placed it on a table in the middle of the room.

Clarke looked about him. Scarcely a foot of wall remained bare; there were shelves all around laden with bottles and phials of all shapes and colours, and at one end stood a little Chippendale book-case. Raymond pointed to this.

'You see that parchment Oswald Crollius?* He was one of the first to show me the way, though I don't think he ever found it himself. That is a strange saying of his: "In every grain of wheat there lies hidden the soul of a star." '

There was not much of furniture in the laboratory. The table in the centre, a stone slab with a drain in one corner, the two armchairs on which Raymond and Clarke were sitting; that was all, except an odd-looking chair at the furthest end of the room. Clarke looked at it, and raised his eyebrows.

'Yes, that is the chair,' said Raymond. 'We may as well place it in position.' He got up and wheeled the chair to the light, and began raising and lowering it, letting down the seat, setting the back at various angles, and adjusting the foot-rest. It looked comfortable enough, and Clarke passed his hand over the soft green velvet, as the doctor manipulated the levers.

'Now, Clarke, make yourself quite comfortable. I have a couple of hours' work before me; I was obliged to leave certain matters to the last.'

Raymond went to the stone slab, and Clarke watched him drearily as he bent over a row of phials and lit the flame under the crucible. The doctor had a small hand-lamp, shaded as the larger one, on a ledge above his apparatus, and Clarke, who sat in the shadows, looked down the great dreary room, wondering at the bizarre effects of brilliant light and undefined darkness contrasting with one another. Soon he became conscious of an odd odour, at first the merest suggestion of odour, in the room; and as it grew more decided he felt surprised that he was not reminded of the chemist's shop or the surgery. Clarke found himself idly endeavouring to analyse the sensation, and, half conscious, he began to think of a day, fifteen years ago, that he had spent in roaming through the woods and meadows near his old home. It was a burning day at the beginning of August, the heat had dimmed the outlines of all things and all distances with a faint mist, and people who observed the thermometer spoke of an abnormal register, of a temperature that was almost tropical. Strangely that wonderful hot day of 185- rose up in Clarke's imagination; the sense of dazzling all-pervading sunlight seemed to blot out the shadows and the lights of the laboratory, and he felt again the heated air beating in gusts about his face, saw the shimmer rising from the turf, and heard the myriad murmur of the summer.

'I hope the smell doesn't annoy you, Clarke; there's nothing unwholesome about it. It may make you a bit sleepy, that's all.'

Clarke heard the words quite distinctly, and knew that Raymond was speaking to him, but for the life of him he could not rouse himself from his lethargy. He could only think of the lonely walk he had taken fifteen years ago; it was his last look at the fields and woods he had known since he was a child, and now it all stood out in brilliant light, as a picture, before him. Above all there came to his nostrils the scent of summer, the smell of flowers mingled, and the odour of the woods, of cool shaded places, deep in the green depths, drawn forth by the sun's heat; and the scent of the good earth, lying as it were with arms stretched forth, and smiling lips, overpowered all. His fancies made him wander, as he had wandered long ago, from the fields into the wood, tracking a little path between the shining undergrowth of beech-trees; and the trickle of water dropping from the limestone rock sounded as a clear melody in the dream. Thoughts began to go astray and to mingle with other recollections; the beech-alley was transformed to a path beneath ilex-trees, and here and there a vine climbed from bough to bough, and sent up waving tendrils and drooped with purple grapes, and the sparse grey green leaves of a wild olive-tree stood out against the dark shadows of the ilex. Clarke, in the deep folds of dream, was conscious that the path from his father's house had led him into an undiscovered country, and he was wondering at the strangeness of it all, when suddenly, in place of the hum and murmur of the summer, an infinite silence seemed to fall on all things, and the wood was hushed, and for a moment of time he stood face to face there with a presence, that was neither man nor beast, neither the living nor the dead, but all things mingled, the form of all things but devoid of all form. And in that moment, the sacrament of body and soul was dissolved, and a voice seemed to cry 'let us go hence,' and then the darkness of darkness beyond the stars, the darkness of everlasting.

When Clarke woke up with a start he saw Raymond pouring a few drops of some oily fluid into a green phial, which he stoppered tightly.

'You have been dozing,' he said, 'the journey must have tired you out. It is done now. I am going to fetch Mary; I shall be back in ten minutes.'

Clarke lay back in his chair and wondered. It seemed as if he had but passed from one dream into another. He half expected to see the walls of the laboratory melt and disappear, and to awake in London, shuddering at his own sleeping fancies. But at last the door opened, and the doctor returned, and behind him came a girl of about seventeen, dressed all in white. She was so beautiful that Clarke did not wonder at what the doctor had written to him. She was blushing now over face and neck and arms, but Raymond seemed unmoved.

'Mary,' he said, 'the time has come. You are quite free. Are you willing to trust yourself to me entirely?'

'Yes, dear.'

'You hear that, Clarke? You are my witness. Here is
Mary. It is quite easy. Just sit in it and lean back. Are you read
'Yes, dear, quite ready. Give me a kiss before you begin.'

The doctor stooped and kissed her mouth, kindly enough. 'Now
shut your eyes,' he said. The girl closed her eyelids, as if she were
tired, and longed for sleep, and Raymond held the green phial to her
nostrils. Her face grew white, whiter than her dress; she struggled
faintly, and then with the feeling of submission strong within her,
crossed her arms upon her breast as a little child about to say her
prayers. The bright light of the lamp beat full upon her, and Clarke
watched changes fleeting over that face as the changes of the hills
when the summer clouds float across the sun. And then she lay all
white and still, and the doctor turned up one of her eyelids. She was
quite unconscious. Raymond pressed hard on one of the levers and
the chair instantly sank back. Clarke saw him cutting away a circle,
like a tonsure, from her hair, and the lamp was moved nearer.
Raymond took a small glittering instrument from a little case, and
Clarke turned away shuddering. When he looked again the doctor
was binding up the wound he had made.

'She will awake in five minutes.' Raymond was still perfectly cool.
'There is nothing further to be done; we can only wait.'

The minutes passed slowly; they could hear a slow, heavy ticking.
There was an old clock in the passage. Clarke felt sick and faint; his
knees shook beneath him, he could hardly stand.

Suddenly, as they watched, they heard a long-drawn sigh, and
suddenly did the colour that had vanished return to the girl's cheeks,
and suddenly her eyes opened. Clarke quailed before them. They
shone with an awful light, looking far away, and a great wonder fell
upon her face, and her hands stretched out as if to touch what was
invisible; but in an instant the wonder faded, and gave place to the
most awful terror. The muscles of her face were hideously convulsed, she shook from head to foot; the soul seemed struggling and
shuddering within the house of flesh. It was a horrible sight, and
Clarke rushed forward, as she fell shrieking to the floor.

Three days later Raymond took Clarke to Mary's bedside. She was
lying wide-awake, rolling her head from side to side, and grinning
vacantly.

'Yes,' said the doctor, still quite cool, 'it is a great pity; she is a hopeless idiot. However, it could not be helped; and, after all, she has seen the Great God Pan.'

Mr Clarke's Memoirs

MR CLARKE, the gentleman chosen by Dr Raymond to witness the strange experiment of the god Pan, was a person in whose character caution and curiosity were oddly mingled; in his sober moments he thought of the unusual and the eccentric with undisguised aversion, and yet, deep in his heart, there was a wide-eyed inquisitiveness with respect to all the more recondite and esoteric elements in the nature of men. The latter tendency had prevailed when he accepted Raymond's invitation, for though his considered judgment had always repudiated the doctor's theories as the wildest nonsense, yet he secretly hugged a belief in fantasy, and would have rejoiced to see that belief confirmed. The horrors that he witnessed in the dreary laboratory were to a certain extent salutary, he was conscious of being involved in an affair not altogether reputable, and for many years afterwards he clung bravely to the commonplace, and rejected all occasions of occult investigation. Indeed, on some homœopathic principle, he for some time attended the séances of distinguished mediums, hoping that the clumsy tricks of these gentlemen would make him altogether disgusted with mysticism of every kind, but the remedy, though caustic, was not efficacious. Clarke knew that he still pined for the unseen, and little by little, the old passion began to reassert itself, as the face of Mary, shuddering and convulsed with an unknowable terror, faded slowly from his memory. Occupied all day in pursuits both serious and lucrative, the temptation to relax in the evening was too great, especially in the winter months, when the fire cast a warm glow over his snug bachelor apartment, and a bottle of some choice claret stood ready by his elbow. His dinner digested, he would make a brief pretence of reading the evening paper, but the mere catalogue of news soon palled upon him, and Clarke would find himself casting glances of warm desire in the direction of an old Japanese bureau, which stood at a pleasant distance from the hearth. Like a boy before a jam-closet, for a few minutes he would hover indecisive, but lust always prevailed, and Clarke ended by drawing up his chair, lighting a candle, and sitting down before the bureau.

Its pigeon-holes and drawers teemed with documents on the most morbid subjects, and in the well reposed a large manuscript volume, in which he had painfully entered the gems of his collection. Clarke had a fine contempt for published literature; the most ghostly story ceased to interest him if it happened to be printed; his sole pleasure was in the reading, compiling, arranging, and rearranging what he called his 'Memoirs to prove the Existence of the Devil,' and engaged in this pursuit the evening seemed to fly and the night appeared too short.

On one particular evening, an ugly December night, black with fog, and raw with frost, Clarke hurried over his dinner, and scarcely deigned to observe his customary ritual of taking up the paper and laying it down again. He paced two or three times up and down the room, and opened the bureau, stood still a moment, and sat down. He leant back, absorbed in one of those dreams to which he was subject, and at length drew out his book, and opened it at the last entry. There were three or four pages densely covered with Clarke's round, set penmanship, and at the beginning he had written in a somewhat larger hand:

Singular Narrative told me by my Friend, Dr Phillips. He assures me that all the Facts related therein are strictly and wholly True, but refuses to give either the Surnames of the Persons concerned, or the Place where these Extraordinary Events occurred.

Mr Clarke began to read over the account for the tenth time, glancing now and then at the pencil notes he had made when it was told him by his friend. It was one of his humours to pride himself on a certain literary ability; he thought well of his style, and took pains in arranging the circumstances in dramatic order. He read the following story:

The persons concerned in this statement are Helen V., who, if she is still alive, must now be a woman of twenty-three, Rachel M., since deceased, who was a year younger than the above, and Trevor W., an imbecile, aged eighteen. These persons were at the period of the story inhabitants of a village on the borders of Wales, a place of some importance in the time of the Roman occupation, but now a scattered hamlet, of not more than five hundred souls. It is situated on rising ground, about six miles from the sea, and is sheltered by a large and picturesque forest.

Some eleven years ago, Helen V. came to the village under rather peculiar circumstances. It is understood that she, being an orphan, was adopted in her infancy by a distant relative, who brought her up in his own house till she was twelve years old. Thinking, however, that it would be better for the child to have playmates of her own age, he advertised in several local papers for a good home in a comfortable farm-house for a girl of twelve, and this advertisement was answered by Mr R., a well-to-do farmer in the above-mentioned village. His references proving satisfactory, the gentleman sent his adopted daughter to Mr R., with a letter, in which he stipulated that the girl should have a room to herself, and stated that her guardians need be at no trouble in the matter of education, as she was already sufficiently educated for the position in life which she would occupy. In fact, Mr R. was given to understand that the girl was to be allowed to find her own occupations, and to spend her time almost as she liked. Mr R. duly met her at the nearest station, a town some seven miles away from his house, and seems to have remarked nothing extraordinary about the child, except that she was reticent as to her former life and her adopted father. She was, however, of a very different type from the inhabitants of the village; her skin was a pale, clear olive, and her features were strongly marked, and of a somewhat foreign character. She appears to have settled down, easily enough, into farm-house life, and became a favourite with the children, who sometimes went with her on her rambles in the forest, for this was her amusement. Mr R. states that he has known her go out by herself directly after their early breakfast, and not return till after dusk, and that, feeling uneasy at a young girl being out alone for so many hours, he communicated with her adopted father, who replied in a brief note that Helen must do as she chose. In the winter, when the forest paths are impassable, she spent most of her time in her bed-room, where she slept alone, according to the instructions of her relative. It was on one of these expeditions to the forest, that the first of the singular incidents with which this girl is connected occurred, the date being about a year after her arrival at the village. The preceding winter had been remarkably severe, the snow drifting to a great depth, and the frost continuing for an unexampled period, and the summer following was as noteworthy for its extreme heat. On one of the very hottest days in this summer, Helen V. left the farm-house for one of her long rambles in the forest, taking with her, as usual, some bread and meat for lunch. She was seen by some men in the fields making for the old Roman Road, a green causeway which traverses the highest part of the wood, and they were astonished to observe that the girl had taken off her hat, though the heat of the sun was already almost tropical. As it happened, a labourer, Joseph W. by name, was working in the forest near the Roman Road, and at twelve o'clock, his little son, Trevor, brought the man his dinner of bread and cheese. After the meal, the boy, who was about seven years old at the time, left his father at work, and, as he says, went to look for flowers in the wood, and the man, who could hear him shouting with delight over his discoveries, felt no uneasiness. Suddenly, however, he was horrified at hearing the most dreadful screams, evidently the result of great terror, proceeding from the direction in which his son had gone, and he hastily threw down his tools and ran to see what had happened. Tracing his path by the sound, he met the little boy who was running headlong, and was evidently terribly frightened, and on questioning him the man at last elicited that after picking a posy of flowers he felt tired, and lay down on the grass and fell asleep. He was suddenly awakened, as he stated, by a peculiar noise, a sort of singing he called it, and on peeping through the branches he saw Helen V. playing on the grass with a 'strange naked man,' whom he seemed unable to describe further. He said he felt dreadfully frightened, and ran away crying for his father. Joseph W. proceeded in the direction indicated by his son, and found Helen V. sitting on the grass in the middle of a glade or open space left by charcoal burners. He angrily charged her with frightening his little boy, but she entirely denied the accusation and laughed at the child's story of a 'strange man,' to which he himself did not attach much credence. Joseph W. came to the conclusion that the boy had woke up with a sudden fright, as children sometimes do, but Trevor persisted in his story, and continued in such evident distress that at last his father took him home, hoping that his mother would be able to soothe him. For many weeks, however, the boy gave his parents much anxiety; he became nervous and strange in his manner, refusing to leave the cottage by himself, and constantly alarming the household by waking in the night with cries of 'the man in the wood! father! father!' In course of time, however, the impression seemed to have worn off, and about three months later he accompanied his father to the house of a gentleman in the neighbourhood, for whom Joseph W.

occasionally did work. The man was shown into the study, and the little boy was left sitting in the hall, and a few minutes later, while the gentleman was giving W. his instructions, they were both horrified by a piercing shriek and the sound of a fall, and rushing out they found the child lying senseless on the floor, his face contorted with terror. The doctor was immediately summoned, and after some examination he pronounced the child to be suffering from a kind of fit, apparently produced by a sudden shock. The boy was taken to one of the bed-rooms, and after some time recovered consciousness, but only to pass into a condition described by the medical man as one of violent hysteria. The doctor exhibited a strong sedative, and in the course of two hours pronounced him fit to walk home, but in passing through the hall the paroxysms of fright returned and with additional violence. The father perceived that the child was pointing at some object, and heard the old cry, 'the man in the wood,' and looking in the direction indicated saw a stone head of grotesque appearance, which had been built into the wall above one of the doors. It seems that the owner of the house had recently made alterations in his premises, and on digging the foundations for some offices, the men had found a curious head, evidently of the Roman period, which had been placed in the hall in the manner described. The head is pronounced by the most experienced archæologists of the district to be that of a faun or satyr.[1]

From whatever cause arising, this second shock seemed too severe for the boy Trevor, and at the present date he suffers from a weakness of intellect, which gives but little promise of amending. The matter caused a good deal of sensation at the time, and the girl Helen was closely questioned by Mr R., but to no purpose, she steadfastly denying that she had frightened or in any way molested Trevor.

The second event with which this girl's name is connected took place about six years ago, and is of a still more extraordinary character.

At the beginning of the summer of 188— Helen contracted a friendship of a peculiarly intimate character with Rachel M., the daughter of a prosperous farmer in the neighbourhood. This girl, who was a year younger than Helen, was considered by most people

---

[1] Dr Phillips tells me that he has seen the head in question, and assures me that he has never received such a vivid presentment of intense evil.

to be the prettier of the two, though Helen's features had to a great extent softened as she became older. The two girls, who were together on every available opportunity, presented a singular contrast, the one with her clear olive skin and almost Italian appearance, and the other of the proverbial red and white of our rural districts. It must be stated that the payments made to Mr R. for the maintenance of Helen were known in the village for their excessive liberality, and the impression was general that she would one day inherit a large sum of money from her relative. The parents of Rachel were therefore not averse to their daughter's friendship with the girl, and even encouraged the intimacy, though they now bitterly regret having done so. Helen still retained her extraordinary fondness for the forest, and on several occasions Rachel accompanied her, the two friends setting out early in the morning, and remaining in the wood till dusk. Once or twice after these excursions Mrs M. thought her daughter's manner rather peculiar; she seemed languid and dreamy, and as it has been expressed, 'different from herself,' but these peculiarities seem to have been thought too trifling for remark. One evening, however, after Rachel had come home, her mother heard a noise which sounded like suppressed weeping in the girl's room, and on going in found her lying, half-undressed, upon the bed, evidently in the greatest distress. As soon as she saw her mother, she exclaimed, 'Ah, mother, mother, why did you let me go to the forest with Helen?' Mrs M. was astonished at so strange a question, and proceeded to make inquiries. Rachel told her a wild story. She said——

Clarke closed the book with a snap, and turned his chair towards the fire. When his friend sat one evening in that very ch[ ] and told his story, Clarke had interrupted him at a point a li[ ] 'My God!' he this, had cut short his words in a paroxysm of [ ] it is too incredible, had exclaimed, 'think, think, what you are [ ] us quiet world, where too monstrous; such things can nev[er] and conquer, or maybe men and women live and die, a[n]s, Phillips, grieve and suffer strange fail, and fall down under [ ]ation, some not such things as fortunes for many a y[ ]ere possible, way out of the terror. this. There must [ ]his story our earth would be a Why, man, i[ ] to the end, concluding: nightma[ ]

P[ ]

'Her flight remains a mystery to this day; she vanished in broad sunlight, they saw her walking in a meadow, and a few moments later she was not there.'

Clarke tried to conceive the thing again, as he sat by the fire, and again his mind shuddered and shrank back, appalled before the sight of such awful, unspeakable elements enthroned as it were, and triumphant in human flesh. Before him stretched the long dim vista of the green causeway in the forest, as his friend had described it: he saw the swaying leaves and the quivering shadows on the grass, he saw the sunlight and the flowers, and far away, far in the long distance, the two figures moved towards him. One was Rachel, but the other?

Clarke had tried his best to disbelieve it all, but at the end of the account, as he had written it in his book, he had placed the inscription:

ET DIABOLUS INCARNATUS EST. ET HOMO FACTUS EST.*

The City of Resurrections

HERBERT! Good God! Is it possible?'

'Yes, my name's Herbert. I think I know your face too, but I don't remember your name. My memory is very queer.'

'Don't you recollect Villiers of Wadham?'

'So it is, so it is. I beg your pardon, Villiers, I didn't think I was begging of an old college friend. Good-night.'

'My dear fellow, this haste is unnecessary. My rooms are close by, but we won't go there just yet. Suppose we walk up Shaftesbury Avenue a little way? But how in heaven's name have you come to this pass, Herbert?'

'It's a long story, Villiers, and a strange one too, but you can hear it if you like.'

'Come on, then.'

The ill-assorted take my arm, you don't seem very strong.'

in dirty, evil-looking moved slowly up Rupert Street; the one uniform of a man about and the other attired in the regulation Villiers had emerged from am, glossy, and eminently well-to-do. many courses, assisted by in that frame of mind which ant after an excellent dinner of delayed a moment by the door, little flask of Chianti, and, street in search of those mysterio m almost chronic, had n the dimly-lighted persons with which the streets of London teem in every quarter and at every hour. Villiers prided himself as a practised explorer of such obscure mazes and byways of London life, and in this unprofitable pursuit he displayed an assiduity which was worthy of more serious employment. Thus he stood beside the lamp-post surveying the passers-by with undisguised curiosity, and with that gravity only known to the systematic diner, had just enunciated in his mind the formula: 'London has been called the city of encounters; it is more than that, it is the city of Resurrections,' when these reflections were suddenly interrupted by a piteous whine at his elbow, and a deplorable appeal for alms. He looked round in some irritation, and with a sudden shock found himself confronted with the embodied proof of his somewhat stilted fancies. There, close beside him, his face altered and disfigured by poverty and disgrace, his body barely covered by greasy ill-fitting rags, stood his old friend Charles Herbert, who had matriculated on the same day as himself, and with whom he had been merry and wise for twelve revolving terms. Different occupations and varying interests had interrupted the friendship, and it was six years since Villiers had seen Herbert; and now he looked upon this wreck of a man with grief and dismay, mingled with a certain inquisitiveness as to what dreary chain of circumstance had dragged him down to such a doleful pass. Villiers felt together with compassion all the relish of the amateur in mysteries, and congratulated himself on his leisurely speculations outside the restaurant.

They walked on in silence for some time, and more than one passer-by stared in astonishment at the unaccustomed spectacle of a well-dressed man with an unmistakable beggar hanging on to his arm, and, observing this, Villiers led the way to an obscure street in Soho. Here he repeated his question.

'How on earth has it happened, Herbert? I always understood you would succeed to an excellent position in Dorsetshire. Did your father disinherit you? Surely not?'

'No, Villiers; I came into all the property at my poor father's death; he died a year after I left Oxford. He was a very good father to me, and I mourned his death sincerely enough. But you know what young men are; a few months later I came up to town and went a good deal into society. Of course I had excellent introductions, and I managed to enjoy myself very much in a harmless sort of way. I played a little, certainly, but never for heavy stakes, and the few bets

I made on races brought me in money—only a few pounds, you know, but enough to pay for cigars and such petty pleasures. It was in my second season that the tide turned. Of course you have heard of my marriage?'

'No, I never heard anything about it.'

'Yes, I married, Villiers. I met a girl, a girl of the most wonderful and most strange beauty, at the house of some people whom I knew. I cannot tell you her age; I never knew it, but, so far as I can guess, I should think she must have been about nineteen when I made her acquaintance. My friends had come to know her at Florence; she told them she was an orphan, the child of an English father and an Italian mother, and she charmed them as she charmed me. The first time I saw her was at an evening party; I was standing by the door talking to a friend, when suddenly above the hum and babble of conversation a voice, which seemed to thrill to my heart. She was singing an Italian song, I was introduced to her that evening, and in three months I married Helen. Villiers, that woman, if I can call her woman, corrupted my soul. The night of the wedding I found myself sitting in her bedroom in the hotel, listening to her talk. She was sitting up in bed, and I listened to her as she spoke in her beautiful voice, spoke of things which even now I would not dare whisper in blackest night, though I stood in the midst of a wilderness. You, Villiers, you may think you know life, and London, and what goes on, day and night, in this dreadful city; for all I can say you may have heard the talk of the vilest, but I tell you you can have no conception of what I know, no, not in your most fantastic, hideous dreams can you have imaged forth the faintest shadow of what I have heard—and seen. Yes, seen; I have seen the incredible, such horrors that even I myself sometimes stop in the middle of the street, and ask whether it is possible for a man to behold such things and live. In a year, Villiers, I was a ruined man, in body and soul,—in body and soul.'

'But your property, Herbert? You had land in Dorset.'

'I sold it all; the fields and woods, the dear old house—everything.'

'And the money?'

'She took it all from me.'

'And then left you?'

'Yes; she disappeared one night, I don't know where she went, but I am sure if I saw her again it would kill me. The rest of my story is of no interest; sordid misery, that is all. You may think, Villiers, that

I have exaggerated and talked for effect; but I have not told you half. I could tell you certain things which would convince you, but you would never know a happy day again. You would pass the rest of your life, as I pass mine, a haunted man, a man who has seen hell.'

Villiers took the unfortunate man to his rooms, and gave him a meal. Herbert could eat little, and scarcely touched the glass of wine set before him. He sat moody and silent by the fire, and seemed relieved when Villiers sent him away with a small present of money.

'By the way, Herbert,' said Villiers, as they parted at the door, 'what was your wife's name? You said Helen, I think? Helen what?'

'The name she passed under when I met her was Helen Vaughan, but what her real name was I can't say. I don't think she had a name. No, no, not in that sense. Only human beings have names, Villiers; I can't say any more. Good-bye; yes, I will not fail to call if I see any way in which you can help me. Good-night.'

The man went out into the bitter night, and Villiers returned to his fireside. There was something about Herbert which shocked him inexpressibly; not his poor rags or the marks which poverty had set upon his face, but rather an indefinite terror which hung about him like a mist. He had acknowledged that he himself was not devoid of blame, the woman, he had avowed, had corrupted him body and soul, and Villiers felt that this man, once his friend, had been an actor in scenes evil beyond the power of words. His story needed no confirmation; he himself was the embodied proof of it. Villiers mused curiously over the story he had heard, and wondered whether he had heard both the first and the last of it. 'No,' he thought, 'certainly not the last, probably only the beginning. A case like this is like a nest of Chinese boxes; you open one after another and find a quainter workmanship in every box. Most likely poor Herbert is merely one of the outside boxes; there are stranger ones to follow.'

Villiers could not take his mind away from Herbert and his story, which seemed to grow wilder as the night wore on. The fire began to burn low, and the chilly air of the morning crept into the room; Villiers got up with a glance over his shoulder, and shivering slightly, went to bed.

A few days later he saw at his club a gentleman of his acquaintance, named Austin, who was famous for his intimate knowledge of London life, both in its tenebrous and luminous phases. Villiers, still full of his encounter in Soho and its consequences, thought Austin might possibly be able to shed some light on Herbert's history, and so after some casual talk he suddenly put the question:

'Do you happen to know anything of a man named Herbert— Charles Herbert?'

Austin turned round sharply and stared at Villiers with some astonishment.

'Charles Herbert? Weren't you in town three years ago? No; then you have not heard of the Paul Street case? It caused a good deal of sensation at the time.'

'What was the case?'

'Well, a gentleman, a man of very good position, was found dead, stark dead, in the area of a certain house in Paul Street, off Tottenham Court Road. Of course the police did not make the discovery; if you happen to be sitting up all night and have a light in your window, the constable will ring the bell, but if you happen to be lying dead in somebody's area, you will be left alone. In this instance as in many others the alarm was raised by some kind of vagabond; I don't mean a common tramp, or a public-house loafer, but a gentleman, whose business or pleasure, or both, made him a spectator of the London Streets at five o'clock in the morning. This individual was, as he said, "going home," it did not appear whence or whither, and had occasion to pass through Paul Street between four and five AM. Something or other caught his eye at Number 20; he said, absurdly enough, that the house had the most unpleasant physiognomy he had ever observed, but, at any rate, he glanced down the area, and was a good deal astonished to see a man lying on the stones, his limbs all huddled together, and his face turned up. Our gentleman thought this face looked peculiarly ghastly, and so set off at a run in search of the nearest policeman. The constable was at first inclined to treat the matter lightly, suspecting a mere drunken freak; however, he came, and after looking at the man's face changed his tone, quickly enough. The early bird, who had picked up this fine worm, was sent off for a doctor, and the policeman rang and knocked at the door till a slatternly servant girl came down looking more than half asleep. The constable pointed out the contents of the area to the maid, who screamed loudly enough to wake up the street, but she knew nothing of the man; had never seen him at the house, and so forth. Meanwhile the original discover had come back with a medical man, and the next thing was to get into the area. The gate was open, so the whole quartet stumped down the steps. The doctor hardly needed a moment's examination; he said the poor fellow had been dead for several hours, and he was moved away to the police-station for the time being. It was then the case began to get interesting. The dead man had not been robbed, and in one of his pockets were papers identifying him as—well, as a man of good family and means, a favourite in society, and nobody's enemy, so far as could be known. I don't give his name, Villiers, because it has nothing to do with the story, and because it's no good raking up these affairs about the dead, when there are relations living. The next curious point was that the medical men couldn't agree as to how he met his death. There were some slight bruises on his shoulders, but they were so slight that it looked as if he had been pushed roughly out of the kitchen door, and not thrown over the railings from the street, or even dragged down the steps. But there were positively no other marks of violence about him, certainly none that would account for his death; and when they came to the autopsy there wasn't a trace of poison of any kind. Of course the police wanted to know all about the people at Number 20, and here again, so I have heard from private sources, one or two other very curious points came out. It appears that the occupants of the house were a Mr and Mrs Charles Herbert; he was said to be a landed proprietor, though it struck most people that Paul Street was not exactly the place to look for county gentry. As for Mrs Herbert, nobody seemed to know who or what she was, and, between our-selves, I fancy the divers after her history found themselves in rather strange waters. Of course they both denied knowing anything about the deceased, and in default of any evidence against them they were discharged. But some very odd things came out about them. Though it was between five and six in the morning when the dead man was removed, a large crowd had collected, and several of the neighbours ran to see what was going on. They were pretty free with their comments, by all accounts, and from these it appeared that Number 20 was in very bad odour in Paul Street. The detectives tried to trace down these rumours to some solid foundation of fact, but could not get hold of anything. People shook their heads and raised their eye-brows and thought the Herberts rather "queer," "would rather not be seen going into their house," and so on, but there was nothing tangible. The authorities were morally certain that the man met his death in some way or another in the house and was thrown out by the kitchen door, but they couldn't prove it, and the absence of any indications of violence or poisoning left them helpless. An odd case, wasn't it? But curiously enough, there's something more that I haven't told you. I happened to know one of the doctors who was consulted as to the cause of death, and some time after the inquest I met him, and asked him about it. "Do you really mean to tell me," I said, "that you were baffled by the case, that you actually don't know what the man died of?" "Pardon me," he replied, "I know perfectly well what caused death. Blank died of fright, of sheer, awful terror; I never saw features so hideously contorted in the entire course of my practice, and I have seen the faces of a whole host of dead." The doctor was usually a cool customer enough, and a certain vehemence in his manner struck me, but I couldn't get anything more out of him. I suppose the Treasury didn't see their way to prosecuting the Herberts for frightening a man to death; at any rate, nothing was done, and the case dropped out of men's minds. Do you happen to know anything of Herbert?'

'Well,' replied Villiers, 'he was an old college friend of mine.'

'You don't say so? Have you ever seen his wife?'

'No, I haven't. I have lost sight of Herbert for many years.'

'It's queer, isn't it, parting with a man at the college gate or at Paddington, seeing nothing of him for years, and then finding him pop up his head in such an odd place. But I should like to have seen Mrs Herbert; people said extraordinary things about her.'

'What sort of things?'

'Well, I hardly know how to tell you. Every one who saw her at the police court said she was at once the most beautiful woman and the most repulsive they had ever set eyes on. I have spoken to a man who saw her, and I assure you he positively shuddered as he tried to describe the woman, but he couldn't tell why. She seems to have been a sort of enigma; and I expect if that one dead man could have told tales, he would have told some uncommonly queer ones. And there you are again in another puzzle; what could a respectable country gentleman like Mr Blank (we'll call him that if you don't mind) want in such a very queer house as Number 20? It's altogether a very odd case, isn't it?'

'It is indeed, Austin; an extraordinary case. I didn't think, when I asked you about my old friend, I should strike on such strange metal. Well, I must be off; good-day.'

Villiers went away, thinking of his own conceit of the Chinese boxes; here was quaint workmanship indeed.

The Discovery in Paul Street

A FEW months after Villiers's meeting with Herbert, Mr Clarke was sitting, as usual, by his after-dinner hearth, resolutely guarding his fancies from wandering in the direction of the bureau. For more than a week he had succeeded in keeping away from the 'Memoirs,' and he cherished hopes of a complete self-reformation; but, in spite of his endeavours, he could not hush the wonder and the strange curiosity that that last case he had written down had excited within him. He had put the case, or rather the outline of it, conjecturally to a scientific friend, who shook his head, and thought Clarke getting queer, and on this particular evening Clarke was making an effort to rationalise the story, when a sudden knock at his door roused him from his meditations.

'Mr Villiers to see you, sir.'

'Dear me, Villiers, it is very kind of you to look me up; I have not seen you for many months; I should think nearly a year. Come in, come in. And how are you, Villiers? Want any advice about investments?'

'No, thanks, I fancy everything I have in that way is pretty safe. No, Clarke, I have really come to consult you about a rather curious matter that has been brought under my notice of late. I am afraid you will think it all rather absurd when I tell my tale, I sometimes think so myself, and that's just why I made up my mind to come to you, as I know you're a practical man.'

Mr Villiers was ignorant of the 'Memoirs to prove the Existence of the Devil.'

'Well, Villiers, I shall be happy to give you my advice, to the best of my ability. What is the nature of the case?'

'It's an extraordinary thing altogether. You know my ways; I always keep my eyes open in the streets, and in my time I have chanced upon some queer customers, and queer cases too, but this, I think, beats all. I was coming out of a restaurant one nasty winter night about three months ago; I had had a capital dinner and a good bottle of Chianti, and I stood for a moment on the pavement, thinking what a mystery there is about London streets and the companies that pass along them. A bottle of red wine encourages these fancies, Clarke, and I daresay I should have thought a page of small type, but I was cut short by a beggar who had come behind me, and was making the usual appeals. Of course I looked round, and this beggar turned out to be what was left of an old friend of mine, a man named Herbert. I asked him how he had come to such a wretched pass, and he told me. We walked up and down one of those long dark Soho streets, and there I listened to his story. He said he had married a beautiful girl, some years younger than himself, and, as he put it, she had corrupted him body and soul. He wouldn't go into details; he said he dare not, that what he had seen and heard haunted him by night and day, and when I looked in his face I knew he was speaking the truth. There was something about the man that made me shiver. I don't know why, but it was there. I gave him a little money and sent him away, and I assure you that when he was gone I gasped for breath. His presence seemed to chill one's blood.'

'Isn't all this just a little fanciful, Villiers? I suppose the poor fellow had made an imprudent marriage, and, in plain English, gone to the bad.'

'Well, listen to this.' Villiers told Clarke the story he had heard from Austin.

'You see,' he concluded, 'there can be but little doubt that this Mr Blank, whoever he was, died of sheer terror; he saw something so awful, so terrible, that it cut short his life. And what he saw, he most certainly saw in that house, which, somehow or other, had got a bad name in the neighbourhood. I had the curiosity to go and look at the place for myself. It's a saddening kind of street; the houses are old enough to be mean and dreary, but not old enough to be quaint. As far as I could see most of them are let in lodgings, furnished and unfurnished, and almost every door has three bells to it. Here and there the ground floors have been made into shops of the commonest kind; it's a dismal street in every way. I found Number 20 was to let, and I went to the agent's and got the key. Of course I should have heard nothing of the Herberts in that quarter, but I asked the man, fair and square, how long they have left the house, and whether there had been other tenants in the meanwhile. He looked at me queerly for a minute, and told me the Herberts had left immediately after the unpleasantness, as he called it, and since then the house had been empty.'

Mr Villiers paused for a moment.

'I have always been rather fond of going over empty houses; there's a sort of fascination about the desolate empty rooms, with the nails sticking in the walls, and the dust thick upon the window-sills. But I didn't enjoy going over Number 20 Paul Street. I had hardly put my foot inside the passage before I noticed a queer, heavy feeling about the air of the house. Of course all empty houses are stuffy, and so forth, but this was something quite different; I can't describe it to you, but it seemed to stop the breath. I went into the front room and the back room, and the kitchens downstairs; they were all dirty and dusty enough, as you would expect, but there was something strange about them all. I couldn't define it to you, I only know I felt queer. It was one of the rooms on the first floor, though, that was the worst. It was a largish room, and once on a time the paper must have been cheerful enough, but when I saw it, paint, paper, and everything were most doleful. But the room was full of horror; I felt my teeth grinding as I put my hand on the door, and when I went in, I thought I should have fallen fainting to the floor. However I pulled myself together, and stood against the end wall, wondering what on earth there could be about the room to make my limbs tremble, and my heart beat as if I were at the hour of death. In one corner there was a pile of newspapers littered about on the floor and I began looking at them, they were papers of three or four years ago, some of them half torn, and some crumpled as if they had been used for packing. I turned the whole pile over, and amongst them I found a curious drawing; I will show it you presently. But I couldn't stay in the room; I felt it was overpowering me. I was thankful to come out, safe and sound, into the open air. People stared at me as I walked along the street, and one man said I was drunk. I was staggering about from one side of the pavement to the other, and it was as much as I could do to take the key back to the agent and get home. I was in bed for a week, suffering from what my doctor called nervous shock and exhaustion. One of those days I was reading the evening paper, and happened to notice a paragraph headed: "Starved to Death." It was the usual style of thing; a model lodging-house in Marylebone, a door locked for several days, and a dead man in his chair when they broke in. "The deceased," said the paragraph, "was known as Charles

Herbert, and is believed to have been once a prosperous country gentleman. His name was familiar to the public three years ago in connection with the mysterious death in Paul Street, Tottenham Court Road, the deceased being the tenant of the house Number 20, in the area of which a gentleman of good position was found dead under circumstances not devoid of suspicion." A tragic ending, wasn't it? But after all, if what he told me were true, which I am sure it was, the man's life was all a tragedy, and a tragedy of a stranger sort than they put on the boards.'

'And that is the story, is it?' said Clarke musingly.

'Yes, that is the story.'

'Well, really, Villiers, I scarcely know what to say about it. There are no doubt circumstances in the case which seem peculiar, the finding of the dead man in the area of the Herberts' house, for instance, and the extraordinary opinion of the physician as to the cause of death, but, after all, it is conceivable that the facts may be explained in a straightforward manner. As to your own sensations when you went to see the house, I would suggest that they were due to a vivid imagination; you must have been brooding, in a semi-conscious way, over what you had heard. I don't exactly see what more can be said or done in the matter; you evidently think there is a mystery of some kind, but Herbert is dead; where then do you propose to look?'

'I propose to look for the woman; the woman whom he married. *She* is the mystery.'

The two men sat silent by the fireside; Clarke secretly congratulating himself on having successfully kept up the character of advocate of the commonplace, and Villiers wrapt in his gloomy fancies.

'I think I will have a cigarette,' he said at last, and put his hand in his pocket to feel for the cigarette-case.

'Ah!' he said, starting slightly, 'I forgot I had something to show you. You remember my saying that I had found a rather curious sketch amongst the pile of old newspapers at the house in Paul Street?—here it is.'

Villiers drew out a small thin parcel from his pocket. It was covered with brown paper, and secured with string, and the knots were troublesome. In spite of himself Clarke felt inquisitive; he bent forward on his chair as Villiers painfully undid the string, and unfolded the outer covering. Inside was a second wrapping of tissue, and Villiers took it off and handed the small piece of paper to Clarke without a word.

There was dead silence in the room for five minutes or more; the two men sat so still that they could hear the ticking of the tall old-fashioned clock that stood outside in the hall, and in the mind of one of them the slow monotony of sound woke up a far, far memory. He was looking intently at the small pen-and-ink sketch of a woman's head; it had evidently been drawn with great care, and by a true artist, for the woman's soul looked out of the eyes, and the lips were parted with a strange smile. Clarke gazed still at the face; it brought to his memory one summer evening long ago; he saw again the long lovely valley, the river winding between the hills, the meadows and the cornfields, the dull red sun, and the cold white mist rising from the water. He heard a voice speaking to him across the waves of many years, and saying, 'Clarke, Mary will see the God Pan!' and then he was standing in the grim room beside the doctor, listening to the heavy ticking of the clock, waiting and watching, watching the figure lying on the green chair beneath the lamp-light. Mary rose up, and he looked into her eyes, and his heart grew cold within him.

'Who is this woman?' he said at last. His voice was dry and hoarse.

'That is the woman whom Herbert married.'

Clarke looked again at the sketch; it was not Mary after all. There certainly was Mary's face, but there was something else, something he had not seen on Mary's features when the white-clad girl entered the laboratory with the doctor, nor at her terrible awakening, nor when she lay grinning on the bed. Whatever it was, the glance that came from those eyes, the smile on the full lips, or the expression of the whole face, Clarke shuddered before it in his inmost soul, and thought, unconsciously, of Dr Phillips's words, 'the most vivid presentment of evil I have ever seen.' He turned the paper over mechanically in his hand and glanced at the back.

'Good God! Clarke, what is the matter? You are as white as death.'

Villiers had started wildly from his chair, as Clarke fell back with a groan, and let the paper drop from his hands.

'I don't feel very well, Villiers, I am subject to these attacks. Pour me out a little wine; thanks, that will do. I shall be better in a few minutes.'

Villiers picked up the fallen sketch and turned it over as Clarke had done.

'You saw that?' he said. 'That's how I identified it as being a portrait of Herbert's wife, or I should say his widow. How do you feel now?'

'Better, thanks, it was only a passing faintness. I don't think I quite catch your meaning. What did you say enabled you to identify the picture?'

'This word—Helen—written on the back. Didn't I tell you her name was Helen? Yes; Helen Vaughan.'

Clarke groaned; there could be no shadow of doubt.

'Now, don't you agree with me,' said Villiers, 'that in the story I have told you to-night, and in the part this woman plays in it, there are some very strange points?'

'Yes, Villiers,' Clarke muttered, 'it is a strange story indeed; a strange story indeed. You must give me time to think it over; I may be able to help you or I may not. Must you be going now? Well, good-night, Villiers, good-night. Come and see me in the course of a week.'

The Letter of Advice

'Do you know, Austin,' said Villiers, as the two friends were pacing sedately along Piccadilly one pleasant morning in May, 'do you know I am convinced that what you told me about Paul Street and the Herberts is a mere episode in an extraordinary history. I may as well confess to you that when I asked you about Herbert a few months ago I had just seen him.'

'You had seen him? Where?'

'He begged of me in the street one night. He was in the most pitiable plight, but I recognised the man, and I got him to tell me his history, or at least the outline of it. In brief, it amounted to this—he had been ruined by his wife.'

'In what manner?'

'He would not tell me; he would only say that she had destroyed him body and soul. The man is dead now.'

'And what has become of his wife?'

'Ah, that's what I should like to know, and I mean to find her sooner or later. I know a man named Clarke, a dry fellow, in fact a man of business, but shrewd enough. You understand my meaning;

not shrewd in the mere business sense of the word, but a man who really knows something about men and life. Well, I laid the case before him, and he was evidently impressed. He said it needed consideration, and asked me to come again in the course of a week. A few days later I received this extraordinary letter.'

Austin took the envelope, drew out the letter, and read it curiously. It ran as follows:—

'My dear Villiers,

'I have thought over the matter on which you consulted me the other night, and my advice to you is this. Throw the portrait into the fire, blot out the story from your mind. Never give it another thought, Villiers, or you will be sorry. You will think, no doubt, that I am in possession of some secret information, and to a certain extent that is the case. But I only know a little; I am like a traveller who has peered over an abyss, and has drawn back in terror. What I know is strange enough and horrible enough, but beyond my knowledge there are depths and horrors more frightful still, more incredible than any tale told of winter nights about the fire. I have resolved, and nothing shall shake that resolve, to explore no whit further, and if you value your happiness you will make the same determination.

'Come and see me by all means; but we will talk on more cheerful topics than this.'

Austin folded the letter methodically, and returned it to Villiers.

'It is certainly an extraordinary letter,' he said; 'what does he mean by the portrait?'

'Ah! I forgot to tell you I have been to Paul Street and have made a discovery.'

Villiers told his story as he had told it to Clarke, and Austin listened in silence. He seemed puzzled.

'How very curious that you should experience such an unpleasant sensation in that room!' he said at length. 'I hardly gather that it was a mere matter of the imagination; a feeling of repulsion, in short.'

'No, it was more physical than mental. It was as if I were inhaling at every breath some deadly fume, which seemed to penetrate to every nerve and bone and sinew of my body. I felt racked from head to foot, my eyes began to grow dim; it was like the entrance of death.'

'Yes, yes, very strange, certainly. You see, your friend confesses that there is some very black story connected with this woman. Did you notice any particular emotion in him when you were telling your tale?'

'Yes, I did. He became very faint, but he assured me that it was a mere passing attack to which he was subject.'

'Did you believe him?'

'I did at the time, but I don't now. He heard what I had to say with a good deal of indifference, till I showed him the portrait. It was then he was seized with the attack of which I spoke. He looked ghastly, I assure you.'

'Then he must have seen the woman before. But there might be another explanation; it might have been the name, and not the face, which was familiar to him. What do you think?'

'I couldn't say. To the best of my belief it was after turning the portrait in his hands that he nearly dropped from his chair. The name, you know, was written on the back.'

'Quite so. After all, it is impossible to come to any resolution in a case like this. I hate melodrama, and nothing strikes me as more commonplace and tedious than the ordinary ghost story of commerce; but really, Villiers, it looks as if there were something very queer at the bottom of all this.'

The two men had, without noticing it, turned up Ashley Street, leading northward from Piccadilly. It was a long street, and rather a gloomy one, but here and there a brighter taste had illuminated the dark houses with flowers, and gay curtains, and a cheerful paint on the doors. Villiers glanced up as Austin stopped speaking, and looked at one of these houses; geraniums, red and white, drooped from every sill, and daffodil-coloured curtains were draped back from each window.

'It looks cheerful, doesn't it?' he said.

'Yes, and the inside is still more cheery. One of the pleasantest houses of the season, so I have heard. I haven't been there myself, but I have met several men who have, and they tell me it's uncommonly jovial.'

'Whose house is it?'

'A Mrs Beaumont's.'

'And who is she?'

'I couldn't tell you. I have heard she comes from South America, but, after all, who she is is of little consequence. She is a very wealthy woman, there's no doubt of that, and some of the best people have taken her up. I hear she has some wonderful claret, really marvellous wine, which must have cost a fabulous sum. Lord Argentine was telling me about it; he was there last Sunday evening. He assures me he has never tasted such a wine, and Argentine, as you know, is an expert. By the way, that reminds me, she must be an oddish sort of woman, this Mrs Beaumont. Argentine asked her how old the wine was, and what do you think she said? "About a thousand years, I believe." Lord Argentine thought she was chaffing him, you know, but when he laughed she said she was speaking quite seriously, and offered to show him the jar. Of course, he couldn't say anything more after that; but it seems rather antiquated for a beverage, doesn't it? Why, here we are at my rooms. Come in, won't you?'

'Thanks, I think I will. I haven't seen the curiosity-shop for some time.'

It was a room furnished richly, yet oddly, where every chair and bookcase and table, every rug and jar and ornament seemed to be a thing apart, preserving each its own individuality.

'Anything fresh lately?' said Villiers after a while.

'No; I think not; you saw those queer jugs, didn't you? I thought so. I don't think I have come across anything for the last few weeks.'

Austin glanced round the room from cupboard to cupboard, from shelf to shelf, in search of some new oddity. His eyes fell at last on an old chest, pleasantly and quaintly carved, which stood in a dark corner of the room.

'Ah,' he said, 'I was forgetting, I have got something to show you.' Austin unlocked the chest, drew out a thick quarto volume, laid it on the table, and resumed the cigar he had put down.

'Did you know Arthur Meyrick the painter, Villiers?'

'A little; I met him two or three times at the house of a friend of mine. What has become of him? I haven't heard his name mentioned for some time.'

'He's dead.'

'You don't say so! Quite young, wasn't he?'

'Yes; only thirty when he died.'

'What did he die of?'

'I don't know. He was an intimate friend of mine, and a thoroughly good fellow. He used to come here and talk to me for hours, and he was one of the best talkers I have met. He could even talk about painting, and that's more than can be said of most painters. About eighteen months ago he was feeling rather over-worked, and partly at my suggestion he went off on a sort of roving expedition, with no very definite end or aim about it. I believe New York was to be his first port, but I never heard from him. Three months ago I got this book, with a very civil letter from an English doctor practising at Buenos Ayres, stating that he had attended the late Mr Meyrick during his illness, and that the deceased had expressed an earnest wish that the enclosed packet should be sent to me after his death. That was all.'

'And haven't you written for further particulars?'

'I have been thinking of doing so. You would advise me to write to the doctor?'

'Certainly. And what about the book?'

'It was sealed up when I got it. I don't think the doctor had seen it.'

'It is something very rare? Meyrick was a collector, perhaps?'

'No, I think not, hardly a collector. Now, what do you think of those Ainu jugs?'

'They are peculiar, but I like them. But aren't you going to show me poor Meyrick's legacy?'

'Yes, yes, to be sure. The fact is, it's rather a peculiar sort of thing, and I haven't shown it to any one. I wouldn't say anything about it if I were you. There it is.'

Villiers took the book, and opened it at haphazard. 'It isn't a printed volume then?' he said.

'No. It is a collection of drawings in black and white by my poor friend Meyrick.'

Villiers turned to the first page, it was blank; the second bore a brief inscription, which he read:

Silet per diem universus, nec sine horrore secretus est; lucet nocturnis ignibus, chorus Ægipanum undique personatur: audiuntur et cantus tibiarum, et tinnitus cymbalorum per oram maritimam.*

On the third page was a design which made Villiers start and look up at Austin; he was gazing abstractedly out of the window. Villiers turned page after page, absorbed, in spite of himself, in the frightful Walpurgis Night of evil, strange monstrous evil, that the dead artist had set forth in hard black and white. The figures of Fauns and Satyrs and Ægipans danced before his eyes, the darkness of the thicket, the dance on the mountain-top, the scenes by lonely shores, in green vineyards, by rocks and desert places, passed before him; a world before which the human soul seemed to shrink back and shudder. Villiers whirled over the remaining pages, he had seen enough, but the picture on the last leaf caught his eye, as he almost closed the book.

'Austin!'

'Well, what is it?'

'Do you know who that is?'

It was a woman's face, alone on the white page.

'Know who it is? No, of course not.'

'I do.'

'Who is it?'

'It is Mrs Herbert.'

'Are you sure?'

'I am perfectly certain of it. Poor Meyrick! He is one more chapter in her history.'

'But what do you think of the designs?'

'They are frightful. Lock the book up again, Austin. If I were you I would burn it; it must be a terrible companion, even though it be in a chest.'

'Yes, they are singular drawings. But I wonder what connection there could be between Meyrick and Mrs Herbert, or what link between her and these designs?'

'Ah, who can say? It is possible that the matter may end here, and we shall never know, but in my own opinion this Helen Vaughan, or Mrs Herbert, is only beginning. She will come back to London, Austin, depend upon it, she will come back, and we shall hear more about her then. I don't think it will be very pleasant news.'

The Suicides

LORD ARGENTINE was a great favourite in London society. At twenty he had been a poor man, decked with the surname of an illustrious family, but forced to earn a livelihood as best he could, and the most speculative of money-lenders would not have intrusted him with fifty pounds on the chance of his ever changing his name for a title, and his poverty for a great fortune. His father had been near enough to the fountain of good things to secure one of the family livings, but the son, even if he had taken orders, would scarcely have obtained so much as this, and moreover felt no vocation for the ecclesiastical estate. Thus he fronted the world with no better armour than the bachelor's gown and the wits of a younger son's grandson, with which equipment he contrived in some way to make a very tolerable fight of it. At twenty-five Mr Charles Aubernoun saw himself still a man of struggles and of warfare with the world, but out of the seven who stood between him and the high places of his family three only remained. These three, however, were 'good lives,' but yet not proof against the Zulu assegais and typhoid fever, and so one morning Aubernoun woke up and found himself Lord Argentine, a man of thirty who had faced the difficulties of existence, and had conquered. The situation amused him immensely, and he resolved that riches should be as pleasant to him as poverty had always been. Argentine, after some little consideration, came to the conclusion that dining, regarded as a fine art, was perhaps the most amusing pursuit open to fallen humanity, and thus his dinners became famous in London, and an invitation to his table a thing covetously desired. After ten years of lordship and dinners Argentine still declined to be jaded, still persisted in enjoying life, and by a kind of infection had become recognised as the cause of joy in others, in short as the best of company. His sudden and tragical death therefore caused a wide and deep sensation. People could scarce believe it, even though the newspaper was before their eyes, and the cry of 'Mysterious Death of a Nobleman' came ringing up from the street. But there stood the brief paragraph: 'Lord Argentine was found dead this morning by his valet under distressing circumstances. It is stated that there can be no doubt that his lordship committed suicide, though no motive can be assigned for the act.* The deceased nobleman was widely known in society, and much liked for his genial manner and sumptuous hospitality. He is succeeded by etc. etc.'

By slow degrees the details came to light, but the case still remained a mystery. The chief witness at the inquest was the dead nobleman's valet, who said that the night before his death Lord Argentine had dined with a lady of good position, whose name was suppressed in the newspaper reports. At about eleven o'clock Lord Argentine had returned, and informed his man that he should not require his services till the next morning. A little later the valet had occasion to cross the hall and was somewhat astonished to see his master quietly letting himself out at the front door. He had taken off his evening clothes, and was dressed in a Norfolk coat and knickerbockers, and wore a low brown hat. The valet had no reason to suppose that Lord Argentine had seen him, and though his master rarely kept late hours, thought little of the occurrence till the next morning, when he knocked at the bedroom door at a quarter to nine as usual. He received no answer, and, after knocking two or three times, entered the room, and saw Lord Argentine's body leaning forward at an angle from the bottom of the bed. He found that his master had tied a cord securely to one of the short bed-posts, and, after making a running noose and slipping it round his neck, the unfortunate man must have resolutely fallen forward, to die by slow strangulation. He was dressed in the light suit in which the valet had seen him go out, and the doctor who was summoned pronounced that life had been extinct for more than four hours. All papers, letters, and so forth, seemed in perfect order, and nothing was discovered which pointed in the most remote way to any scandal either great or small. Here the evidence ended; nothing more could be discovered. Several persons had been present at the dinner-party at which Lord Argentine had assisted, and to all these he seemed in his usual genial spirits. The valet, indeed, said he thought his master appeared a little excited when he came home, but he confessed that the alteration in his manner was very slight, hardly noticeable, indeed. It seemed hopeless to seek for any clue, and the suggestion that Lord Argentine had been suddenly attacked by acute suicidal mania was generally accepted.

It was otherwise, however, when within three weeks, three more gentlemen, one of them a nobleman, and the two others men of good position and ample means, perished miserably in almost precisely the same manner. Lord Swanleigh was found one morning in his dressing-room, hanging from a peg affixed to the wall, and Mr Collier-Stuart and Mr Herries had chosen to die as Lord Argentine. There was no explanation in either case; a few bald facts; a living man in the evening, and a dead body with a black swollen face in the morning. The police had been forced to confess themselves powerless to arrest or to explain the sordid murders of Whitechapel; but before the horrible suicides of Piccadilly and Mayfair, they were dumfoundered, for not even the mere ferocity which did duty as an explanation of the crimes of the East End, could be of service in the West.* Each of these men who had resolved to die a tortured shameful death was rich, prosperous, and to all appearance in love with the world, and not the acutest research could ferret out any shadow of a lurking motive in either case. There was a horror in the air, and men looked at one another's faces when they met, each wondering whether the other was to be the victim of a fifth nameless tragedy. Journalists sought in vain in their scrap-books for materials whereof to concoct reminiscent articles; and the morning paper was unfolded in many a house with a feeling of awe; no man knew when or where the blow would next light.

A short while after the last of these terrible events, Austin came to see Mr Villiers. He was curious to know whether Villiers had succeeded in discovering any fresh traces of Mrs Herbert, either through Clarke or by other sources, and he asked the question soon after he had sat down.

'No,' said Villiers, 'I wrote to Clarke, but he remains obdurate, and I have tried other channels, but without any result. I can't find out what became of Helen Vaughan after she left Paul Street, but I think she must have gone abroad. But to tell the truth, Austin, I haven't paid very much attention to the matter for the last few weeks; I knew poor Herries intimately, and his terrible death has been a great shock to me, a great shock.'

'I can well believe it,' answered Austin gravely, 'you know Argentine was a friend of mine. If I remember rightly, we were speaking of him that day you came to my rooms.'

'Yes; it was in connection with that house in Ashley Street, Mrs Beaumont's house. You said something about Argentine's dining there.'

'Quite so. Of course you know it was there Argentine dined the night before—before his death.'

'No, I haven't heard that.'

'Oh yes; the name was kept out of the papers to spare Mrs Beaumont. Argentine was a great favourite of hers, and it is said she was in a terrible state for some time after.'

A curious look came over Villiers's face; he seemed undecided whether to speak or not. Austin began again.

'I never experienced such a feeling of horror as when I read the account of Argentine's death. I didn't understand it at the time, and I don't now. I knew him well, and it completely passes my understanding for what possible cause he—or any of the others for the matter of that—could have resolved in cold blood to die in such an awful manner. You know how men babble away each other's characters in London, you may be sure any buried scandal or hidden skeleton would have been brought to light in such a case as this; but nothing of the sort has taken place. As for the theory of mania, that is very well, of course, for the coroner's jury, but everybody knows that it's all nonsense. Suicidal mania is not smallpox.'

Austin relapsed into gloomy silence. Villiers sat silent also, watching his friend. The expression of indecision still fleeted across his face, he seemed as if weighing his thoughts in the balance, and the considerations he was revolving left him still silent. Austin tried to shake off the remembrance of tragedies as hopeless and perplexed as the labyrinth of Dædalus, and began to talk in an indifferent voice of the more pleasant incidents and adventures of the season.

'That Mrs Beaumont,' he said, 'of whom we were speaking, is a great success; she has taken London almost by storm. I met her the other night at Fulham's; she is really a remarkable woman.'

'You have met Mrs Beaumont?'

'Yes; she had quite a court around her. She would be called very handsome, I suppose, and yet there is something about her face which I didn't like. The features are exquisite, but the expression is strange. And all the time I was looking at her, and afterwards, when I was going home, I had a curious feeling that that very expression was in some way or other familiar to me.'

'You must have seen her in the Row.'*

'No, I am sure I never set eyes on the woman before; it is that which makes it puzzling. And to the best of my belief I have never seen anybody like her; what I felt was a kind of dim far-off memory, vague but persistent. The only sensation I can compare it to, is that odd feeling one sometimes has in a dream, when fantastic cities and wondrous lands and phantom personages appear familiar and accustomed.'

Villiers nodded and glanced aimlessly round the room, possibly in search of something on which to turn the conversation. His eyes fell on an old chest somewhat like that in which the artist's strange legacy lay hid beneath a Gothic scutcheon.

'Have you written to the doctor about poor Meyrick?' he asked.

'Yes; I wrote asking for full particulars as to his illness and death. I don't expect to have an answer for another three weeks or a month. I thought I might as well inquire whether Meyrick knew an Englishwoman named Herbert, and if so, whether the doctor could give me any information about her. But it's very possible that Meyrick fell in with her at New York, or Mexico, or San Francisco; I have no idea as to the extent or direction of his travels.'

'Yes, and it's very possible that the woman may have more than one name.'

'Exactly. I wish I had thought of asking you to lend me the portrait of her which you possess. I might have enclosed it in my letter to Dr Mathews.'

'So you might; that never occurred to me. We might even now do so. Hark! what are those boys calling?'

While the two men had been talking together a confused noise of shouting had been gradually growing louder. The noise rose from the eastward and swelled down Piccadilly, drawing nearer and nearer, a very torrent of sound; surging up streets usually quiet, and making every window a frame for a face, curious or excited. The cries and voices came echoing up the silent street where Villiers lived, growing more distinct as they advanced, and, as Villiers spoke, an answer rang up from the pavement:

'The West End Horrors; Another Awful Suicide; Full Details!'

Austin rushed down the stairs and bought a paper and read out the paragraph to Villiers as the uproar in the street rose and fell. The window was open and the air seemed full of noise and terror.

'Another gentleman has fallen a victim to the terrible epidemic of suicide which for the last month has prevailed in the West End. Mr Sidney Crashaw of Stoke House, Fulham, and King's Pomeroy, Devon, was found, after a prolonged search, hanging from the branch of a tree in his garden at one o'clock to-day. The deceased gentleman dined last night at the Carlton Club and seemed in his usual health and spirits. He left the Club at about ten o'clock, and was seen walking leisurely up St James's Street a little later. Subsequent to this his movements cannot be traced. On the discovery of the body medical aid was at once summoned, but life had evidently been long extinct. So far as is known Mr Crashaw had no trouble or anxiety of any kind. This painful suicide, it will be remembered, is the fifth of the kind in the last month. The authorities at Scotland

Yard are unable to suggest any explanation of these terrible occurrences.'

Austin put down the paper in mute horror.

'I shall leave London to-morrow,' he said, 'it is a city of nightmares. How awful this is, Villiers!'

Mr Villiers was sitting by the window quietly looking out into the street. He had listened to the newspaper report attentively, and the hint of indecision was no longer on his face.

'Wait a moment, Austin,' he replied, 'I have made up my mind to mention a little matter that occurred last night. It is stated, I think, that Crashaw was last seen alive in St James's Street shortly after ten?'

'Yes, I think so. I will look again. Yes, you are quite right.'

'Quite so. Well, I am in a position to contradict that statement at all events. Crashaw was seen after that; considerably later indeed.'

'How do you know?'

'Because I happened to see Crashaw myself at about two o'clock this morning.'

'You saw Crashaw? You, Villiers?'

'Yes, I saw him quite distinctly; indeed there were but a few feet between us.'

'Where, in heaven's name, did you see him?'

'Not far from here. I saw him in Ashley Street. He was just leaving a house.'

'Did you notice what house it was?'

'Yes. It was Mrs Beaumont's.'

'Villiers! Think what you are saying; there must be some mistake. How could Crashaw be in Mrs Beaumont's house at two o'clock in the morning? Surely, surely, you must have been dreaming, Villiers, you were always rather fanciful.'

'No; I was wide awake enough. Even if I had been dreaming as you say, what I saw would have roused me effectually.'

'What you saw? What did you see? Was there anything strange about Crashaw? But I can't believe it; it is impossible.'

'Well, if you like I will tell you what I saw, or if you please, what I think I saw, and you can judge for yourself.'

'Very good, Villiers.'

The noise and clamour of the street had died away, though now and then the sound of shouting still came from the distance, and the dull, leaden silence seemed like the quiet after an earthquake or a storm. Villiers turned from the window and began speaking.

'I was at a house near Regent's Park last night, and when I came away the fancy took me to walk home instead of taking a hansom. It was a clear pleasant night enough, and after a few minutes I had the streets pretty much to myself. It's a curious thing, Austin, to be alone in London at night, the gas-lamps stretching away in perspective, and the dead silence, and then perhaps the rush and clatter of a hansom on the stones, and the fire starting up under the horse's hoofs. I walked along pretty briskly, for I was feeling a little tired of being out in the night, and as the clocks were striking two I turned down Ashley Street, which, you know, is on my way. It was quieter than ever there, and the lamps were fewer, altogether it looked as dark and gloomy as a forest in winter. I had done about half the length of the street when I heard a door closed very softly, and naturally I looked up to see who was abroad like myself at such an hour. As it happens, there is a street lamp close to the house in question, and I saw a man standing on the step. He had just shut the door and his face was towards me, and I recognised Crashaw directly. I never knew him to speak to, but I had often seen him, and I am positive that I was not mistaken in my man. I looked into his face for a moment, and then—I will confess the truth—I set off at a good run, and kept it up till I was within my own door.'

'Why?'

'Why? Because it made my blood run cold to see that man's face. I could never have supposed that such an infernal medley of passions could have glared out of any human eyes; I almost fainted as I looked. I knew I had looked into the eyes of a lost soul, Austin, the man's outward form remained, but all hell was within it. Furious lust, and hate that was like fire, and the loss of all hope and horror that seemed to shriek aloud to the night, though his teeth were shut; and the utter blackness of despair. I am sure he did not see me; he saw nothing that you or I can see, but he saw what I hope we never shall. I do not know when he died; I suppose in an hour, or perhaps two, but when I passed down Ashley Street and heard the closing door, that man no longer belonged to this world; it was a devil's face that I looked upon.'

There was an interval of silence in the room when Villiers ceased speaking. The light was failing, and all the tumult of an hour ago was quite hushed. Austin had bent his head at the close of the story, and his hand covered his eyes.

'What can it mean?' he said at length.

'Who knows, Austin, who knows? It's a black business, but I think we had better keep it to ourselves, for the present at any rate. I will see if I cannot learn anything about that house through private channels of information, and if I do light upon anything I will let you know.'

The Encounter in Soho

THREE weeks later Austin received a note from Villiers, asking him to call either that afternoon or the next. He chose the nearer date and found Villiers sitting as usual by the window, apparently lost in meditation on the drowsy traffic of the street. There was a bamboo table by his side, a fantastic thing, enriched with gilding and queer painted scenes, and on it lay a little pile of papers arranged and docketed as neatly as anything in Mr Clarke's office.

'Well, Villiers, have you made any discoveries in the last three weeks?'

'I think so; I have here one or two memoranda which struck me as singular, and there is a statement to which I shall call your attention.'

'And these documents relate to Mrs Beaumont? it was really Crashaw whom you saw that night standing on the doorstep of the house in Ashley Street?'

'As to that matter my belief remains unchanged, but neither my inquiries nor their results have any special relation to Crashaw. But my investigations have had a strange issue; I have found out who Mrs Beaumont is!'

'Who she is? In what way do you mean?'

'I mean that you and I know her better under another name.'

'What name is that?'

'Herbert.'

'Herbert!' Austin repeated the word, dazed with astonishment.

'Yes, Mrs Herbert of Paul Street, Helen Vaughan of earlier adventures unknown to me. You had reason to recognise the expression of her face; when you go home look at the face in Meyrick's book of horrors, and you will know the sources of your recollection.'

'And you have proof of this?'

'Yes, the best of proof; I have seen Mrs Beaumont, or shall we say Mrs Herbert?'

'Where did you see her?'

'Hardly in a place where you would expect to see a lady who lives in Ashley Street, Piccadilly. I saw her entering a house in one of the meanest and most disreputable streets in Soho.* In fact, I had made an appointment, though not with her, and she was precise both to time and place.'

'All this seems very wonderful, but I cannot call it incredible. You must remember, Villiers, that I have seen this woman, in the ordinary adventure of London society, talking and laughing, and sipping her chocolate in a commonplace drawing-room, with common-place people. But you know what you are saying.'

'I do; I have not allowed myself to be led by surmises or fancies. It was with no thought of finding Helen Vaughan that I searched for Mrs Beaumont in the dark waters of the life of London, but such has been the issue.'

'You must have been in strange places, Villiers.'

'Yes, I have been in very strange places. It would have been useless, you know, to go to Ashley Street, and ask Mrs Beaumont to kindly give me a short sketch of her previous history. No; assuming, as I had to assume, that her record was not of the cleanest, it would be pretty certain that at some previous time she must have moved in circles not quite so refined as her present ones. If you see mud on the top of a stream, you may be sure that it was once at the bottom. I went to the bottom. I have always been fond of diving into Queer Street for my amusement, and I found my knowledge of that locality and its inhabitants very useful. It is perhaps needless to say that my friends had never heard the name of Beaumont, and as I had never seen the lady, and was quite unable to describe her, I had to set to work in an indirect way. The people there know me, I have been able to do some of them a service now and again, so they made no difficulty about giving their information; they were aware I had no communication direct or indirect with Scotland Yard. I had to cast out a good many lines though, before I got what I wanted, and when I landed the fish I did not for a moment suppose it was my fish. But I listened to what I was told out of a constitutional liking for useless information, and I found myself in possession of a very curious story, though, as I imagined, not the story I was looking for. It was to this effect. Some five or six years ago a woman named Raymond suddenly made her appearance in the neighbourhood to which I am referring. She was described to me as being quite young, probably not more than seventeen or eighteen, very handsome, and looking as if she came from the country. I should be wrong in saying that she found her level in going to this particular quarter, or associating with these people, for from what I was told, I should think the worst den in London far too good for her. The person from whom I got my information, as you may suppose, no great Puritan, shuddered and grew sick in telling me of the nameless infamies which were laid to her charge. After living there for a year, or perhaps a little more, she disappeared as suddenly as she came, and they saw nothing of her till about the time of the Paul Street case. At first she came to her old haunts only occasionally, then more frequently, and finally took up her abode there as before, and remained for six or eight months. It's of no use my going into details as to the life that woman led; if you want particulars you can look at Meyrick's legacy. Those designs were not drawn from his imagination. She again disappeared, and the people of the place saw nothing of her till a few months ago. My informant told me that she had taken some rooms in a house which he pointed out, and these rooms she was in the habit of visiting two or three times a week and always at ten in the morning. I was led to expect that one of these visits would be paid on a certain day about a week ago, and I accordingly managed to be on the look-out in company with my cicerone at a quarter to ten, and the hour and the lady came with equal punctuality. My friend and I were standing under an archway, a little way back from the street, but she saw us, and gave me a glance that I shall be long in forgetting. That look was quite enough for me; I knew Miss Raymond to be Mrs Herbert; as for Mrs Beaumont she had quite gone out of my head. She went into the house, and I watched it till four o'clock, when she came out, and then I followed her. It was a long chase, and I had to be very careful to keep a long way in the background, and yet not to lose sight of the woman. She took me down to the Strand, and then to Westminster, and then up St James's Street, and along Piccadilly. I felt queerish when I saw her turn up Ashley Street; the thought that Mrs Herbert was Mrs Beaumont came into my mind, but it seemed too improbable to be true. I waited at the corner, keeping my eye on her all the time, and I took particular care to note the house at which she stopped. It was the house with the gay curtains, the house of flowers, the house out of which Crashaw came the night he hanged himself in his garden. I was just going away with my discovery, when I saw an empty carriage come round and draw up in front of the house, and I came to the conclusion that Mrs Herbert was going out for a drive, and I was right. I took a hansom and followed the carriage into the Park. There, as it happened, I met a man I know, and we stood talking together a little distance from the carriage-way, to which I had my back. We had not been there for ten minutes when my friend took off his hat, and I glanced round and saw the lady I had been following all day. "Who is that?" I said, and his answer was, "Mrs Beaumont; lives in Ashley Street." Of course there could be no doubt after that. I don't know whether she saw me, but I don't think she did. I went home at once, and, on consideration, I thought that I had a sufficiently good case with which to go to Clarke.'

'Why to Clarke?'

'Because I am sure that Clarke is in possession of facts about this woman, facts of which I know nothing.'

'Well, what then?'

Mr Villiers leaned back in his chair and looked reflectively at Austin for a moment before he answered:

'My idea was that Clarke and I should call on Mrs Beaumont.'

'You would never go into such a house as that? No, no, Villiers, you cannot do it. Besides, consider; what result . . .'

'I will tell you soon. But I was going to say that my information does not end here; it has been completed in an extraordinary manner.

'Look at this neat little packet of manuscript; it is paginated, you see, and I have indulged in the civil coquetry of a ribbon of red tape. It has almost a legal air, hasn't it? Run your eye over it, Austin. It is an account of the entertainment Mrs Beaumont provided for her choicer guests. The man who wrote this escaped with his life, but I do not think he will live many years. The doctors tell him he must have sustained some severe shock to the nerves.'

Austin took the manuscript, but never read it. Opening the neat pages at haphazard his eye was caught by a word and a phrase that followed it; and, sick at heart, with white lips and a cold sweat pouring like water from his temples, he flung the paper down.

'Take it away, Villiers, never speak of this again. Are you made of stone, man? Why, the dread and horror of death itself, the thoughts of the man who stands in the keen morning air on the black platform, bound, the bell tolling in his ears, and waits for the harsh rattle of the bolt, are as nothing compared to this. I will not read it; I should never sleep again.'

'Very good. I can fancy what you saw. Yes; it is horrible enough; but after all, it is an old story, an old mystery played in our day, and in dim London streets instead of amidst the vineyards and the olive gardens. We know what happened to those who chanced to meet the Great God Pan, and those who are wise know that all symbols are symbols of something, not of nothing. It was, indeed, an exquisite symbol beneath which men long ago veiled their knowledge of the most awful, most secret forces which lie at the heart of all things; forces before which the souls of men must wither and die and blacken, as their bodies blacken under the electric current. Such forces cannot be named, cannot be spoken, cannot be imagined except under a veil and a symbol, a symbol to the most of us appearing a quaint, poetic fancy, to some a foolish, silly tale. But you and I, at all events, have known something of the terror that may dwell in the secret place of life, manifested under human flesh; that which is without form taking to itself a form. Oh, Austin, how can it be? How is it that the very sunlight does not turn to blackness before this thing, the hard earth melt and boil beneath such a burden?'

Villiers was pacing up and down the room, and the beads of sweat stood out on his forehead. Austin sat silent for a while, but Villiers saw him make a sign upon his breast.

'I say again, Villiers, you will surely never enter such a house as that? You would never pass out alive.'

'Yes, Austin, I shall go out alive—I, and Clarke with me.'

'What do you mean? You cannot, you would not dare . . .'

'Wait a moment. The air was very pleasant and fresh this morning; there was a breeze blowing, even through this dull street, and I thought I would take a walk. Piccadilly stretched before me a clear, bright vista, and the sun flashed on the carriages and on the quivering leaves in the park. It was a joyous morning, and men and women looked at the sky and smiled as they went about their work or their pleasure, and the wind blew as blithely as upon the meadows and the scented gorse. But somehow or other I got out of the bustle and the gaiety, and found myself walking slowly along a quiet, dull street, where there seemed to be no sunshine and no air, and where the few foot-passengers loitered as they walked, and hung indecisively about corners and archways. I walked along, hardly knowing where I was going or what I did there, but feeling impelled, as one sometimes is, to explore still further, with a vague idea of reaching some unknown goal. Thus I forged up the street, noting the small traffic of the milk-shop, and wondering at the incongruous medley of penny pipes, black tobacco, sweets, newspapers, and comic songs which here and there jostled one another in the short compass of a single window. I think it was a cold shudder that suddenly passed through me that first told me I had found what I wanted. I looked up from the pavement and stopped before a dusty shop, above which the lettering had faded, where the red bricks of two hundred years ago had grimed to black; where the windows had gathered to themselves the fog and the dirt of winters innumerable. I saw what I required; but I think it was five minutes before I had steadied myself and could walk in and ask for it in a cool voice and with a calm face. I think there must even then have been a tremor in my words, for the old man who came out from his back parlour, and fumbled slowly amongst his goods, looked oddly at me as he tied the parcel. I paid what he asked, and stood leaning by the counter, with a strange reluctance to take up my goods and go. I asked about the business, and learnt that trade was bad and profits cut down sadly; but then the street was not what it was before traffic had been diverted, but that was done forty years ago, 'just before my father died,' he said. I got away at last, and walked along sharply; it was a dismal street indeed, and I was glad to return to the bustle and the noise. Would you like to see my purchase?'

Austin said nothing, but nodded his head slightly; he still looked white and sick. Villiers pulled out a drawer in the bamboo table, and showed Austin a long coil of cord, hard and new; and at one end was a running noose.

'It is the best hempen cord,' said Villiers, 'just as it used to be made for the old trade, the man told me. Not an inch of jute from end to end.'

Austin set his teeth hard, and stared at Villiers, growing whiter as he looked.

'You would not do it,' he murmured at last. 'You would not have blood on your hands. My God!' he exclaimed, with sudden vehemence, 'you cannot mean this, Villiers, that you will make yourself a hangman?'

'No. I shall offer a choice, and leave the thing alone with this cord in a locked room for fifteen minutes. If when we go in it is not done, I shall call the nearest policeman. That is all.'

'I must go now. I cannot stay here any longer; I cannot bear this. Good-night.'

'Good-night, Austin.'

The door shut, but in a moment it was opened again, and Austin stood, white and ghastly, in the entrance.

'I was forgetting,' he said, 'that I too have something to tell. I have received a letter from Dr Harding of Buenos Ayres. He says that he attended Meyrick for three weeks before his death.'

'And does he say what carried him off in the prime of life? It was not fever?'

'No, it was not fever. According to the doctor, it was an utter collapse of the whole system, probably caused by some severe shock. But he states that the patient would tell him nothing, and that he was consequently at some disadvantage in treating the case.'

'Is there anything more?'

'Yes. Dr Harding ends his letter by saying: "I think this is all the information I can give you about your poor friend. He had not been long in Buenos Ayres, and knew scarcely any one, with the exception of a person who did not bear the best of characters, and has since left—a Mrs Vaughan."'

The Fragments

[Amongst the papers of the well-known physician, Dr Robert Matheson, of Ashley Street, Piccadilly, who died suddenly, of apoplectic seizure, at the beginning of 1892, a leaf of manuscript paper was found, covered with pencil jottings. These notes were in Latin, much abbreviated, and had evidently been made in great haste.* The MS was only deciphered with great difficulty, and some words have up to the present time evaded all the efforts of the expert employed. The date, 'xxv Jul. 1888,' is written on the right-hand corner of the MS. The following is a translation of Dr Matheson's manuscript.]

'WHETHER science would benefit by these brief notes if they could be published, I do not know, but rather doubt. But certainly I shall never take the responsibility of publishing or divulging one word of what is here written, not only on account of my oath freely given to those two persons who were present, but also because the details are too loathsome. It is probable that, upon mature consideration, and after weighing the good and evil, I shall one day destroy this paper, or at least leave it under seal to my friend D., trusting in his discretion, to use it or to burn it, as he may think fit.

'As was befitting I did all that my knowledge suggested to make sure that I was suffering under no delusion. At first astounded, I could hardly think, but in a minute's time I was sure that my pulse was steady and regular and that I was in my real and true senses. I ran over the anatomy of the foot and arm and repeated the formulæ of some of the carbon compounds, and then fixed my eyes quietly on what was before me.

'Though horror and revolting nausea rose up within me, and an odour of corruption choked my breath, I remained firm. I was then privileged or accursed, I dare not say which, to see that which was on the bed, lying there black like ink, transformed before my eyes. The skin, and the flesh, and the muscles, and the bones, and the firm structure of the human body that I had thought to be unchangeable, and permanent as adamant, began to melt and dissolve.

'I knew that the body may be separated into its elements by external agencies, but I should have refused to believe what I saw. For here there was some internal force, of which I knew nothing, that caused dissolution and change.

'Here too was all the work by which man has been made repeated before my eyes. I saw the form waver from sex to sex, dividing itself from itself, and then again reunited. Then I saw the body descend to the beasts whence it ascended, and that which was on the heights go down to the depths, even to the abyss of all being. The principle of life, which makes organism, always remained, while the outward form changed.

'The light within the room had turned to blackness, not the darkness of night, in which objects are seen dimly, for I could see clearly and without difficulty. But it was the negation of light; objects were presented to my eyes, if I may say so, without any medium, in such a manner that if there had been a prism in the room, I should have seen no colours represented in it.

'I watched, and at last I saw nothing but a substance as jelly. Then the ladder was ascended again . . . [*Here the MS is illegible*] . . . for one instant I saw a Form, shaped in dimness before me, which I will not further describe. But the symbol of this form may be seen in ancient sculptures, and in paintings which survived beneath the lava, too foul to be spoken of . . . as a horrible and unspeakable shape, neither man nor beast, was changed into human form, there came finally death.

'I who saw all this, not without great horror and loathing of soul, here write my name, declaring all that I have set on this paper to be true.

'ROBERT MATHESON, Med. Dr.'

*

. . . Such, Raymond, is the story of what I know, and what I have seen. The burden of it was too heavy for me to bear alone, and yet I could tell it to none but you. Villiers, who was with me at the last knows nothing of that awful secret of the wood, of how what we both saw die, lay upon the smooth sweet turf amidst the summer flowers, half in sun and half in shadow, and holding the girl Rachel's hand, called and summoned those companions, and shaped in solid form, upon the earth we tread on, the horror which we can but hint at, which we can only name under a figure. I would not tell Villiers of this, nor of that resemblance, which struck me as with a blow upon my heart, when I saw the portrait, which filled the cup of terror at the end. What this can mean I dare not guess. I know that what I saw perish was not Mary, and yet in the last agony Mary's eyes looked into mine. Whether there be any one who can show the last link in this chain of awful mystery, I do not know, but if there be any one who can do this, you, Raymond, are the man. And if you know the secret, it rests with you to tell it or not, as you please.

I am writing this letter to you immediately on my getting back to town. I have been in the country for the last few days; perhaps you may be able to guess in what part. While the horror and wonder of London was at its height,—for 'Mrs Beaumont,' as I have told you, was well known in society,—I wrote to my friend Dr Phillips, giving some brief outline, or rather hint, of what had happened, and asking him to tell me the name of the village where the events he had related to me occurred. He gave me the name, as he said with the less hesitation, because Rachel's father and mother were dead, and the rest of the family had gone to a relative in the State of Washington six months before. The parents, he said, had undoubtedly died of grief and horror caused by the terrible death of their daughter, and by what had gone before that death. On the evening of the day on which I received Phillips's letter I was at Caermaen, and standing beneath the mouldering Roman walls, white with the winters of seventeen hundred years, I looked over the meadow where once had stood the older temple of the 'God of the Deeps,' and saw a house gleaming in the sunlight. It was the house where Helen had lived. I stayed at Caermaen for several days. The people of the place, I found, knew little and had guessed less. Those whom I spoke to on the matter seemed surprised that an antiquarian (as I professed myself to be) should trouble about a village tragedy, of which they gave a very commonplace version, and, as you may imagine, I told nothing of what I knew. Most of my time was spent in the great wood that rises just above the village and climbs the hillside, and goes down to the river in the valley; such another long lovely valley, Raymond, as that on which we looked one summer night, walking to and fro before your house. For many an hour I strayed through the maze of the forest, turning now to right and now to left, pacing slowly down long alleys of undergrowth, shadowy and chill, even under the mid-day sun, and halting beneath great oaks; lying on the short turf of a clearing where the faint sweet scent of wild roses came to me on the wind and mixed with the heavy perfume of the elder whose mingled odour is like the odour of the room of the dead, a vapour of incense and corruption. I stood by rough banks at the edges of the wood, gazing at all the pomp and procession of the foxgloves towering amidst the bracken and shining red in the broad sunshine, and beyond them into deep thickets of close undergrowth where springs boil up from the rock and nourish the water-weeds, dank and evil. But in all my wanderings I avoided one part of the wood; it was not till yesterday that I climbed to the summit of the hill, and stood upon the ancient Roman road that threads the highest ridge of the wood. Here they had walked, Helen and Rachel, along this quiet causeway, upon the pavement of green turf, shut in on either side by high banks of red earth, and tall hedges of shining beech, and here I followed in their steps, looking out, now and again, through partings in the boughs, and seeing on one side the sweep of the wood stretching far to right and left, and sinking into the broad level, and beyond, the yellow sea, and the land over the sea. On the other side was the valley and the river, and hill following hill as wave on wave, and wood and meadow, and cornfield, and white houses gleaming, and a great wall of mountain, and far blue peaks in the north. And so at last, I came to the place. The track went up a gentle slope, and widened out into an open space with a wall of thick undergrowth around it, and then, narrowing again, passed on into the distance and the faint blue mist of summer heat. And into this pleasant summer glade Rachel passed a girl, and left it, who shall say what? I did not stay long there.

*

In a small town near Caermaen there is a museum, containing for the most part Roman remains which have been found in the neighbourhood at various times. On the day after my arrival at Caermaen I walked over to the town in question, and took the opportunity of inspecting this museum. After I had seen most of the sculptured stones, the coffins, rings, coins, and fragments of tessellated pavement which the place contains, I was shown a small square pillar of white stone, which had been recently discovered in the wood of which I have been speaking, and, as I found on inquiry, in that open space where the Roman road broadens out. On one side of the pillar was an inscription, of which I took a note. Some of the letters have been defaced, but I do not think there can be any doubt as to those which I supply. The inscription is as follows:

DEVOMNODEN*Ti*
FLA*vi*VSSENILISPOSS*Vit*
PROPTERNVP*tias*
*qua*SVIDITSVBVMB*ra*

'To the great god Nodens (the god of the Great Deep or Abyss), Flavius Senilis has erected this pillar on account of the marriage which he saw beneath the shade.'

The custodian of the museum informed me that local antiquaries were much puzzled, not by the inscription, or by any difficulty in translating it, but as to the circumstance or rite to which allusion is made.

*

... And now, my dear Clarke, as to what you tell me about Helen Vaughan, whom you say you saw die under circumstances of the utmost and almost incredible horror. I was interested in your account, but a good deal, nay, all of what you told me, I knew already. I can understand the strange likeness you remarked both in the portrait and in the actual face; you have seen Helen's mother. You remember that still summer night so many years ago, when I talked to you of the world beyond the shadows, and of the god Pan. You remember Mary. She was the mother of Helen Vaughan, who was born nine months after that night.

Mary never recovered her reason. She lay, as you saw her, all the while upon her bed, and a few days after the child was born, she died. I fancy that just at the last she knew me; I was standing by the bed, and the old look came into her eyes for a second, and then she shuddered and groaned and died. It was an ill work I did that night, when you were present; I broke open the door of the house of life, without knowing or caring what might pass forth or enter in. I recollect your telling me at the time, sharply enough, and rightly enough too, in one sense, that I had ruined the reason of a human being by a foolish experiment, based on an absurd theory. You did well to blame me, but my theory was not all absurdity. What I said Mary would see, she saw, but I forgot that no human eyes could look on such a vision with impunity. And I forgot, as I have just said, that when the house of life is thus thrown open, there may enter in that for which we have no name, and human flesh may become the veil of a horror one dare not express. I played with energies which I did not understand and you have seen the ending of it. Helen Vaughan did well to bind the cord about her neck and die, though the death was horrible. The blackened face, the hideous form upon the bed, changing and melting before your eyes from woman to man, from man to beast, and from beast to worse than beast, all the strange horror that you witnessed, surprises me but little. What you say the doctor whom you sent for saw and shuddered at I noticed long ago; I knew what I had done the moment the child was born, and when it was scarcely five years old I surprised it, not once or twice but several times with a playmate, you may guess of what kind. It was for me a constant, an incarnate horror, and after a few years I felt I could bear it no longer, and I sent Helen Vaughan away. You know now what frightened the boy in the wood. The rest of the strange story, and all else that you tell me, as discovered by your friend, I have contrived to learn from time to time, almost to the last chapter. And now Helen is with her companions. . . .

THE END

NOTE.—*Helen Vaughan was born on August 5th, 1865, at the Red House, Breconshire, and died on July 25th, 1888, in her house in a street off Piccadilly, called Ashley Street in the story.*

M. P. SHIEL

Vaila

E caddi come l'uome cui sonno piglia.*

DANTE

A GOOD many years ago, a young man, student in Paris, I was informally associated with the great Corot, and eyewitnessed by his side several of those cases of mind-malady, in the analysis of which he was a past master. I remember one little girl of the Marais, who, till the age of nine, in no way seemed to differ from her playmates. But one night, lying a-bed, she whispered into her mother's ear: 'Maman, can you not hear the *sound of the world*?' It appears that her recently-begun study of geography had taught her that the earth flies, with an enormous velocity, on an orbit about the sun; and that *sound of the world* to which she referred was a faint (quite subjective) musical humming, like a shell-murmur, heard in the silence of night, and attributed by her fancy to the song of this high motion. Within six months the excess of lunacy possessed her.

I mentioned the incident to my friend, Haco Harfager, then occupying with me the solitude of an old place in S. Germain, shut in by a shrubbery and high wall from the street. He listened with singular interest, and for a day seemed wrapped in gloom.

Another case which I detailed produced a profound impression upon my friend. A young man, a toy-maker of S. Antoine, suffering from chronic congenital phthisis,* attained in the ordinary way his twenty-fifth year. He was frugal, industrious, self-involved. On a winter's evening, returning to his lonely garret, he happened to purchase one of those vehemently factious sheets which circulate by night, like things of darkness, over the Boulevards. This simple act was the herald of his doom. He lay a-bed, and perused the *feuille*.* He had never been a reader; knew little of the greater world, and the deep hum of its travail. But the next night he bought another leaf. Gradually he acquired interest in politics, the large movements, the roar of life. And this interest grew absorbing. Till late into the night, and every night, he lay poring over the furious mendacity, the turbulent wind, the printed passion. He would awake tired, spitting blood, but intense in spirit—and straightway purchased a morning leaf. His being lent itself to a retrograde evolution. The more his teeth gnashed, the less they ate. He became sloven, irregular at work, turning on his bed through the day. Rags overtook him. As the greater interest, and the vaster tumult, possessed his frail soul, so every lesser interest, tumult, died to him. There came an early day when he no longer cared for his own life; and another day, when his maniac fingers rent the hairs from his head.

As to this man, the great Corot said to me:

'Really, one does not know whether to laugh or weep over such a business. Observe, for one thing, how diversely men are made! There are minds precisely so sensitive as a cupful of melted silver; *every* breath will roughen and darken them: and what of the simoon, tornado? And that is not a metaphor but a simile. For such, this earth—I had almost said this universe—is clearly no fit habitation, but a Machine of Death, a baleful Vast. *Too* horrible to many is the running shriek of Being—they *cannot* bear the world. Let each look well to his own little whisk of life, say I, and leave the big fiery Automaton alone. Here in this poor toy-maker you have a case of the ear: it is only the neurosis, Oxyecoia.* Splendid was that Greek myth of the Harpies: by *them* was this man snatched—or, say, caught by a limb in the wheels of the universe, and so perished. It is quite a grand exit, you know—translation in a chariot of flame. Only remember that the member first involved was *the pinna:** he bent *ear* to the howl of Europe, and ended by himself howling. Can a straw ride composedly on the primeval whirlwinds? Between chaos and our shoes wobbles, I tell you, the thinnest film! I knew a man who had this peculiarity of aural hyperæsthesia: that every sound brought him minute information of the matter causing the sound; that is to say, he had an ear bearing to the normal ear the relation which the spectroscope bears to the telescope. A rod, for instance, of mixed copper and iron impinging, in his hearing, upon a rod of mixed tin and lead, conveyed to him not merely the proportion of each metal in each rod, but some strange knowledge of the essential meaning and spirit, as it were, of copper, of iron, of tin, and of lead. Of course, he went mad; but, beforehand, told me this singular thing: that precisely such a sense as his was, according to his *certain* intuition, employed by the Supreme Being in his permeation of space to apprehend the nature and movements of mind and matter. And he went on to add that *Sin*—what we call *sin*—is only the movement of matter or mind into such places, or in such a way, as to give offence or pain to this delicate diplacusis (so I must call it) of the Creator; so that the "Law" of Revelation became, in his eyes, edicts promulgated by their Maker merely in self-protection from aural pain; and divine punishment for, say murder, nothing more than retaliation for unease caused to the divine aural consciousness by the matter in a particular dirk or bullet lodged, at a particular moment, in a non-intended place! Him, too, I say, did the Harpies whisk aloft.'

My recital of these cases to my friend, Harfager, I have mentioned. I was surprised, not so much at his acute interest—for he was interested in all knowledge—as at the obvious pains which he took to conceal that interest. He hurriedly turned the leaves of a volume, but could not hide his panting nostrils.

From first days when we happened to attend the same seminary in Stockholm, a tacit intimacy had sprung between us. I loved him greatly; that he so loved me I knew. But it was an intimacy not accompanied by many of the usual interchanges of close friendships. Harfager was the shyest, most isolated, insulated, of beings. Though our joint *ménage* (brought about by a chance meeting at a midnight *séance* in Paris) had now lasted some months, I knew nothing of his plans, motives. Through the day we pursued our intense readings together, he rapt quite back into the past, I equally engrossed upon the present; late at night we reclined on couches within the vast cave of an old fireplace Louis Onze, and smoked to the dying flame in a silence of worm-wood and terebinth.* Occasionally a *soirée* or lecture might draw me from the house; except once, I never understood that Harfager left it. I was, on that occasion, returning home at a point of the Rue St Honoré where a rush of continuous traffic rattled over the old coarse pavements retained there, when I came suddenly upon him. In this tumult he stood abstracted on the trottoir in a listening attitude, and for a moment seemed not to recognise me when I touched him.

Even as a boy I had discerned in my friend the genuine Noble, the inveterate patrician. One saw that in him. Not at all that his personality gave an impression of any species of loftiness, opulence; on the contrary. He did, however, give an impression of incalculable *ancientness.* He suggested the last moment of an æon. No nobleman have I seen who so bore in his wan aspect the assurance of the inevitable aristocrat, the essential prince, whose pale blossom is of yesterday, and will perish to-morrow, but whose root fills the ages. This much I knew of Harfager; also that on one or other of the bleak islands of his patrimony north of Zetland* lived his mother and a paternal aunt; that he was somewhat deaf; but liable to transports of pain or delight at variously-combined musical sounds, the creak of a door, the note of a bird. More I cannot say that I then knew.

He was rather below the middle height, and gave some promise of stoutness. His nose rose highly aquiline from that species of fore-head called by phrenologists 'the musical,' that is to say, flanked by temples which incline *outward* to the cheek-bones, making breadth for the base of the brain;* while the direction of the heavy-lidded, faded-blue eyes, and of the eyebrows, was a downward *droop* from the nose to their outer extremities. He wore a thin chin-beard. But the astonishing feature of his face were the ears: they were nearly circular, very small, and flat, being devoid of that outer volution known as the *helix.* The two tiny discs of cartilage had always the effect of making me think of the little ancient round shields, without rims, called *clipeus* and *peltè.* I came to understand that this was a peculiarity which had subsisted among the members of his race for some centuries. Over the whole white face of my friend was stamped a look of woful inability, utter gravity of sorrow. One said 'Sardanapalus,' frail last of the great line of Nimrod.*

After a year I found it necessary to mention to Harfager my intention of leaving Paris. We reclined by night in our accustomed nooks within the fireplace. To my announcement he answered with a merely polite 'Indeed!' and continued to gloat upon the flame; but after an hour turned upon me, and said:

'Well, it seems to be a hard and selfish world.'

Truisms uttered with just such an air of new discovery I had occasionally heard from him; but the earnest gaze of eyes, and plaint of voice, and despondency of shaken head, with which he now spoke shocked me to surprise.

'*À propos* of what?' I asked.

'My friend, do not leave me!'

He spread his arms. His utterance choked.

I learned that he was the object of a devilish malice; that he was the prey of a hellish temptation. That a lure, a becking hand, a lurking lust, which it was the effort of his life to eschew (and to which he was especially liable in solitude), continually enticed him; and that thus it had been almost from the day when, at the age of five, he had been sent by his father from his desolate home in the sea.

And whose was this malice?

He told me his mother's and aunt's.

And what was this temptation?

He said it was the temptation to return—to fly with the very frenzy of longing—back to that dim home.

I asked with what motives, and in what particulars, the malice of his mother and aunt manifested itself. He replied that there was, he believed, no specific motive, but only a determined malevolence, involuntary and fated; and that the respect in which it manifested itself was to be found in the multiplied prayers and commands with which, for years, they had importuned him to seek again the far hold of his ancestors.

All this I could in no way comprehend, and plainly said as much. In what consisted this horrible magnetism, and equally horrible peril, of his home? To this question Harfager did not reply, but rose from his seat, disappeared behind the drawn curtains of the hearth, and left the room. He presently returned with a quarto tome bound in hide. It proved to be Hugh Gascoigne's *Chronicle of Norse Families*, executed in English black-letter. The passage to which he pointed I read as follows:*

Now of these two brothers the older, Harold, being of seemly personage and prowess, did go a pilgrimage into Danemark, wherefrom he repaired again home to Hjaltland (Zetland), and with him fetched the amiable Thronda for his wife, who was a daughter of the sank (blood) royal of Danemark. And his younger brother, Sweyn, that was sad and debonair, but far surpassed the other in cunning, received him with all good cheer.

But eftsoons (soon after) fell Sweyn sick for all his love that he had of Thronda, his brother's wife. And while the worthy Harold ministered about the bed where Sweyn lay sick, lo, Sweyn fastened on him a violent stroke with a sword, and with no longer tarrying enclosed his hands in bonds, and cast him in the bottom of a deep hold. And because Harold would not deprive himself of the governance of Thronda his wife, Sweyn cut off both his ear[s], and put out one of his eyes, and after divers such torments was ready to slay him. But on a day the valliant Harold, breaking his bonds, and embracing his adversary, did by the sleight of wrestling overthrow him, and escaped. Notwithstanding, he faltered when he came to the Somburg Head, not far from the Castle, and, albeit that he was swift-foot, could no farther run, by reason that he was faint with the long plagues of his brother. And whilst he there lay in a swoon, did Sweyn come upon him, and when he had stricken him with a dart, cast him from Somburg Head into the sea.

Not long hereafterward did the lady Thronda (though she knew not the manner of her lord's death, nor, verily, if he was dead or alive) receive Sweyn into favour, and with great gaudying and blowing of beamous (trumpets) did become his wife. And right soon they two went thence to sojourn in far parts.

Now, it befell that Sweyn was minded by a dream to have built a great mansion in Hjaltland for the home-coming of the lady Thronda; wherefore he called to him a cunning Master-workman, and sent him to England to gather men for the building of this lusty House, while he himself remained with his lady at Rome. Then came this Architect to London, but passing thence to Hjaltland was drowned, he and his feers (mates), all and some.

And after two years, which was the time assigned, Sweyn Harfager sent a letter to Hjaltland to understand how his great House did: for he knew not of the drowning of the Architect: and soon after he received answer that the House *did well*, and was building on the Isle of Rayba. But that was not the Isle where Sweyn had appointed the building to be: and he was afeard, and near fell down dead for dread, because, in the letter, he saw before him the manner of writing of his brother Harold. And he said in this form: 'Surely Harold is alive, else be this letter writ with ghostly hand.' And he was wo many days, seeing that this was a deadly stroke.

Thereafter he took himself back to Hjaltland to know how the matter was, and there the old Castle on Somburg Head was break down to the earth. Then Sweyn was wode-wroth, and cried: 'Jhesu mercy, where is all the great house of my fathers gone? alas! this wicked day of destiny!' And one of the people told him that a host of workmen from far parts had break it down. And he said: 'Who hath bid them?' but that could none answer. Then he said again: 'nis (is not) my brother Harold alive? for I have behold his writing': and that, too, could none answer. So he went to Rayba, and saw there a great House stand, and when he looked on it, he said: 'This, sooth, was y-built by my brother Harold, be he dead or be he on-live.' And there he dwelt, and his lady, and his sons' sons until now: for that the House is ruthless and without pity; wherefore 'tis said that upon all who dwell there falleth a wicked madness and a lecherous anguish; and that by way of the ears do they drinck the cup of the furie of the earless Harold, till the time of the House be ended.

I read the narrative half-aloud, and smiled.

'This, Harfager,' I said, 'is very tolerable romance on the part of the good Gascoigne; but has the look of indifferent history.'

'It is, nevertheless, genuine *history*,' he replied.

'You believe that?'

'The house still stands solidly on Vaila.'

'The brothers Sweyn and Harold were literary for their age, I think?'

'No member of my race,' he replied, with a suspicion of hauteur, 'has been illiterate.'

'But, at least, you do not believe that mediæval ghosts super-intended the building of their family mansions?'

'Gascoigne nowhere says that; for to be stabbed is not necessarily to die; nor, if he did say it, would it be true to assert that I have any knowledge on the subject.'

'And what, Harfager, is the nature of that "wicked madness," that "lecherous agonie," of which Gascoigne speaks?'

'Do you ask me?' He spread his arms. 'What do I know? I know nothing! I was banished from the place at the age of five. Yet the cry of it still reverberates in my soul. And have I not *told* you of agonies—even within myself—of inherited longing and loathing . . .'

But, at any rate, I answered, my journey to Heidelberg was just then indispensable. I would compromise by making absence short, and rejoin him quickly, if he would wait a few weeks for me. His moody silence I took to mean consent, and soon afterward left him.

But I was unavoidably detained; and when I returned to our old quarters, found them empty. Harfager had vanished.

It was only after twelve years that a letter was forwarded me—a rather wild letter, an excessively long one—in the well-remembered hand of my friend. It was dated at Vaila. From the character of the writing I conjectured that it had been penned *with furious haste*, so that I was all the more astonished at the very trivial nature of the voluminous contents. On the first half page he spoke of our old friendship, and asked if, in memory of that, I would see his mother who was dying; the rest of the epistle, sheet upon sheet, consisted of a tedious analysis of his mother's genealogical tree, the apparent aim being to prove that she was a genuine Harfager, and a cousin of his father. He then went on to comment on the extreme prolificness of his race, asserting that since the fourteenth century, over four millions of its members had lived and died in various parts of the world; three only of them, he believed, being now left. That determined, the letter ended.

Influenced by this communication, I travelled northward; reached Caithness; passed the stormy Orkneys; reached Lerwick; and from Unst, the most bleak and northerly of the Zetlands, contrived, by dint of bribes, to pit the weather-worthiness of a lug-sailed 'sixern' (said to be identical with the 'lang-schips' of the Vikings) against a flowing sea and a darkly-brooding heaven. The voyage, I was warned, was, at such a time, of some risk. It was the Cimmerian* December of those interboreal latitudes. The weather here, they said, though never cold, is hardly ever other than tempestuous. A dense and dank sea-born haze now lay, in spite of vapid breezes, high along the water, enclosing the boat in a vague domed cavern of doleful twilight and sullen swell. The region of the considerable islands was past, and there was a spectral something in the unreal aspect of silent sea and sunless dismalness of sky which produced upon my nerves the impression of a voyage *out* of nature, a cruise *beyond* the world. Occasionally, however, we careered past one of those solitary 'skerries,' or sea-stacks, whose craggy sea-walls, cannonaded and disintegrated by the inter-shock of the tidal wave and the torrent currents of the German Ocean, wore, even at some distance, an appearance of frightful ruin and havoc. Three only of these I saw, for before the dim day had well run half its course, sudden blackness of night was upon us, and with it one of those tempests, of which the winter of this semi-polar sea is, throughout, an ever-varying succession. During the haggard and dolorous crepuscule of the next brief day, the rain did not cease; but before darkness had quite supervened, my helmsman, who talked continuously to a mate of seal-maidens, and water-horses, and *grülies*, paused to point to a mound of gloomier grey on the weather-bow, which was, he assured me, Vaila.

Vaila, he added, was the centre of quite a system of those *rösts* (dangerous eddies) and cross-currents, which the action of the tidal wave hurls hurrying with complicated and corroding swirl among the islands; in the neighbourhood of Vaila, said the mariner, they hurtled with more than usual precipitancy, owing to the palisade of lofty sea-crags which barbicaned the place about; approach was, therefore, at all times difficult, and by night fool-hardy. With a

running sea, however, we came sufficiently near to discern the mane
of surf which bristled high along the beetling coast-wall. Its shock,
according to the man's account, had ofttimes more than all the efficiency of a bombing of real artillery, slinging tons of rock to heights
of several hundred feet upon the main island.

When the sun next feebly climbed above the horizon to totter with
marred visage through a wan low segment of funereal murk, we had
closely approached the coast; and it was then for the first time that
the impression of some *spinning* motion in the island (born no doubt
of the circular movement of the water) was produced upon me. We
effected a landing at a small *voe*, or sea-arm, on the western side; the
eastern, though the point of my aim, being, on account of the swell,
out of the question for that purpose. Here I found in two feal-
thatched *skeoes* (or sheds), which crouched beneath the shelter of a
far over-hanging hill, five or six poor peasant-seamen, whose livelihood no doubt consisted in periodically trading for the necessaries of
the great house on the east. Beside these there were no dwellers on
Vaila; but with one of them for guide, I soon began the ascent and
transit of the island. Through the night in the boat I had been
strangely aware of an oppressive booming in the ears, for which
even the roar of the sea round all the coast seemed quite insufficient
to account. This now, as we advanced, became fearfully intensified,
and with it, once more, the unaccountable conviction within me of
spinning motions to which I have referred. Vaila I discovered to be a
land of hill and precipice, made of fine granite and flaggy gneiss; at
about the centre, however, we came upon a high tableland sloping
gradually from west to east, and covered by a series of lochs, which
sullenly and continuously flowed one into the other. To this chain
of sombre, black-gleaming water I could see no terminating shore,
and by dint of shouting to my companion, and bending close ear to
his answering shout, I came to know that there *was* no such shore: I
say *shout*, for nothing less could have prevailed over the steady
bellowing as of ten thousand bisons, which now resounded on every
hand. A certain tremblement, too, of the earth became distinct. In
vain did the eye seek in its dreary purview a single trace of tree or
shrub; for, as a matter of course, no kind of vegetation, save peat,
could brave, even for a day, that perennial agony of the tempest
which makes of this turbid and benighted zone its arena. Darkness,
an hour after noon, commenced to overshadow us; and it was

shortly afterward that my guide, pointing down a precipitous defile near the eastern coast, hurriedly set forth upon the way he had come. I frantically howled a question after him as he went; but at this point the human voice had ceased to be in the faintest degree audible.

Down this defile, with a sinking of the heart, and a most singular feeling of giddiness, I passed. Having reached the end, I emerged upon a wide ledge which shuddered to the immediate onsets of the sea. But all this portion of the island was, in addition, subject to a sharp continuous ague evidently not due to the heavy ordnance of the ocean. Hugging a point of cliff for steadiness from the wind, I looked forth upon a spectacle of weirdly morne, of dismal wildness. The opening lines of *Hecuba*, or some drear district of the *Inferno*, seemed realised before me.* Three black 'skerries,' encompassed by a fantastic series of stacks, crooked as a witch's fore-finger, and giving herbergage to shrill routs of osprey and scart, to seal and walrus, lay at some fathoms' distance; and from its race and rage among them, the sea, in arrogance of white, tumultuous, but in-audible wrath, ramped terrible as an army with banners toward the land. Leaving my place, I staggered some distance to the left: and now, all at once, a vast amphitheatre opened before me, and there burst upon my gaze a panorama of such heart-appalling sublimity, as imagination could never have conceived, nor can now utterly recall.

'A vast amphitheatre' I have said; yet it was rather the shape of a round-Gothic (or Norman) doorway which I beheld. Let the reader picture such a door-frame, nearly a mile in breadth, laid flat upon the ground, the curved portion farthest from the sea; and round it let a perfectly smooth and even wall of rock tower in perpendicular regu-larity to an altitude not unworthy the vulture's eyrie; and now, down the depth of this Gothic shape, and *over all its extent*, let bawling oceans dash themselves triumphing in spendthrift cataclysm of emerald and hoary fury,—and the stupor of awe with which I looked, and then the shrinking *fear*, and then the instinct of instant flight, will find easy comprehension.

This was the thrilling disemboguement of the lochs of Vaila.

And within the arch of this Gothic cataract, volumed in the world of its smoky torment and far-excursive spray, stood a palace of brass . . . circular in shape . . . huge in dimension.

The last gleam of the ineffectual day had now almost passed, but I could yet discern, in spite of the perpetual rain-fall which bleakly nimbused it as in a halo of tears, that the building was low in proportion to the vastness of its circumference; that it was roofed with a shallow dome; and that about it ran two serried rows of shuttered Norman windows, the upper row being of smaller size than the lower. Certain indications led me to assume that the house had been built upon a vast natural bed of rock which lay, circular and detached, within the arch of the cataract; but this did not quite emerge above the flood, for the whole ground-area upon which I looked dashed a deep and incense-reeking river to the beachless sea; so that passage would have been impossible, were it not that, from a point near me, a massive bridge, thick with algæ, rose above the tide, and led to the mansion. Descending from my ledge, I passed along it, now drenched in spray. As I came nearer, I could see that the house, too, was to half its height more thickly bearded than an old hull with barnacles and every variety of brilliant seaweed; and—what was very surprising—that from many points near the top of the brazen wall huge iron chains, slimily barbarous with the trailing tresses of ages, reached out in symmetrical divergent rays to points on the ground hidden by the flood: the fabric had thus the look of a many-anchored ark; but without pausing for minute observation, I pushed forward, and dashing through the smooth circular waterfall which poured all round from the eaves, by one of its many small projecting porches, entered the dwelling.

Darkness now was around me—and sound. I seemed to stand in the very throat of some yelling planet. An infinite sadness descended upon me; I was near to the abandonment of tears. 'Here,' I said, 'is Khoreb,* and the limits of weeping; not elsewhere is the valley of sighing.' The tumult resembled the continuous volleying of many thousands of cannon, mingled with strange crashing and bursting uproars. I passed forward through a succession of halls, and was wondering as to my further course, when a hideous figure, bearing a lamp, stalked rapidly towards me. I shrank aghast. It seemed the skeleton of a tall man, wrapped in a winding-sheet. The glitter of a tiny eye, however, and a sere film of skin over part of the face, quickly reassured me. Of ears, he showed no sign. He was, I afterwards learned, Aith; and the singularity of his appearance was partially explained by his pretence—whether true or false—that he had once suffered *burning*, almost to the cinder-stage, but had miraculously recovered. With an expression of malignity, and strange excited gestures, he led the way to a chamber on the upper stage, where having struck light to a vesta, he pointed to a spread table and left me.

For a long time I sat in solitude. The earthquake of the mansion was intense; but all sense seemed swallowed up and confounded in the one impression of sound. Water, water, was the world— nightmare on my chest, a horror in my ears, an intolerable tingling on my nerves. The feeling of being infinitely drowned and ruined in the all-obliterating deluge—the impulse to gasp for breath— overwhelmed me. I rose and paced; but suddenly stopped, angry, I scarce knew why, with myself. I had, in fact, found myself walking with a certain *hurry*, not usual with me, not natural to me. The feeling of giddiness, too, had abnormally increased. I forced myself to stand and take note of the hall. It was of great size, and damp with mists, so that the tattered, but rich, mediæval furniture seemed lost in its extent; its centre was occupied by a broad low marble tomb bearing the name of a Harfager of the fifteenth century; its walls were old brown panels of oak. Having drearily observed these things, I waited on with an intolerable consciousness of loneliness; but a little after midnight the tapestry parted, and Harfager, with hurried stride, approached me.

In twelve years my friend had grown old. He showed, it is true, a tendency to corpulence; yet, to a knowing eye, he was, in reality, tabid, ill-nourished. And his neck protruded from his body; and his lower back had quite the forward curve of age; and his hair floated about his face and shoulders in a disarray of awful whiteness. A chin-beard hung grey to his chest. His attire was a simple robe of bauge, which, as he went, waved aflaunt from his bare and hirsute shins, and he was shod in those soft slippers called *rivlins*.

To my surprise, he spoke. When I passionately shouted that I could gather no fragment of sound from his moving lips, he clapped both palms to his ears, and thereupon renewed a vehement siege to mine: but again without result. And now, with a seemingly angry fling of the hand, he caught up the taper, and swiftly strode from the chamber.

There was something singularly unnatural in his manner— something which irresistibly reminded me of the skeleton, Aith: an

Rude impression of Harfager

excess of zeal, a fever, a rage, a *loudness*, an eagerness of walk, a wild
extravagance of gesture. His hand constantly dashed the hair-whiffs
from his face. Though his countenance was of the saffron of death,
the eyes were turgid and red with blood—heavy-lidded eyes, fixed in
a downward and sideward intentness of gaze. He presently returned
with a folio of ivory and a stylus of graphite hanging from a cord
about his garment.

He rapidly wrote a petition that I would, if not too tired, take part
with him in the funeral obsequies of his mother. I shouted assent.

Once more he clapped palms to ears; then wrote: 'Do not shout:
no whisper in any part of the building is inaudible to me.'

I remembered that, in early life, he had seemed slightly *deaf*.

We passed together through many apartments, he shading the

taper with his hand. This was necessary; for, as I quickly discovered, in no part of the shivering fabric was the air in a state of rest, but seemed for ever commoved by a curious agitation, a faint windiness, like the echo of a storm, which communicated a gentle universal trouble to the tapestries. Everywhere I was confronted with the same past richness, present raggedness of decay. In many of the chambers were old marble tombs; one was a museum piled with bronzes, urns; but broken, imbedded in fungoids, dripping wide with moisture. It was as if the mansion, in ardour of travail, sweated. An odour of decomposition was heavy on the swaying air. With difficulty I followed Harfager through the labyrinth of his headlong passage. Once only he stopped short, and with face madly wild above the glare of the light, heaved up his hand, and uttered a single word. From the shaping of the lips, I conjectured the word, 'Hark!'

Presently we entered a very long black hall wherein, on chairs beside a bed near the centre, rested a deep coffin, flanked by a row of tall candlesticks of ebony. It had, I noticed, this singularity, that the foot-piece was absent, so that the soles of the corpse were visible as we approached. I beheld, too, three upright rods secured to the coffin-side, each fitted at its summit with a small silver bell of the kind called *morrice* pendent from a flexible steel spring. At the head of the bed, Aith, with an appearance of irascibility, stamped to and fro within a small area. Harfager, having rapidly traversed the apartment to the coffin, deposited the taper upon a stone table near, and stood poring with crazy intentness upon the body. I too, looking, stood. Death so rigorous, Gorgon, I had not seen. The coffin seemed full of tangled grey hair. The lady was, it was clear, of great age, osseous, scimitar-nosed. Her head shook with solemn continuity to the vibration of the house. From each ear trickled a black streamlet; the mouth was ridged with froth. I observed that over the corpse had been set three thin laminæ of polished wood, resembling in position, and shape, the bridge of a violin. Their sides fitted into groves in the coffin-sides, and their top was of a shape to exactly fit the inclination of the two coffin-lids when closed. One of these laminæ passed over the knees of the dead lady; another bridged the abdomen; the third the region of the neck. In each of them was a small circular hole. Across each of the three holes passed vertically a tense cord from the morrice-bell nearest to it; the three holes being thus divided by the three cords into six vertical semicircles. Before I could conjecture the significance of this arrangement, Harfager closed the folding coffin-lid, which in the centre had tiny intervals for the passage of the cords. He then turned the key in the lock, and uttered a word, which I took to be, 'Come.'

At his summons, Aith, approaching, took hold of the handle at the head; and from the dark recesses of the hall a lady, in black, moved forward. She was very tall, pallid, and of noble aspect. From the curvature of the nose, and her circular ears, I conjectured the lady Swertha, aunt of Harfager. Her eyes were red, but if with weeping I could not determine.

Harfager and I, taking each a handle near the coffin-foot, and the lady bearing before us one of the candlesticks, the procession began. As we came to the doorway, I noticed standing in a corner yet two coffins, inscribed with the names of Harfager and his aunt. We passed at length down a wide-curving stairway to the lower stage; and descending thence still lower by narrow brazen steps, came to a portal of metal, at which the lady, depositing the candlestick, left us.

The chamber of death into which we now bore the coffin had for its outer wall the brazen outer wall of the whole house at a point where this approached nearest the cataract, and must have been deep washed by the infuriate caldron without. The earthquake here was, indeed, intense. On every side the vast extent of surface was piled with coffins, rotted or rotting, ranged upon tiers of wooden shelves. The floor, I was surprised to see, was of brass. From the wide scamp-ering that ensued on our entrance, the place was, it was clear, the abode of hordes of water-rats. As it was inconceivable that these could have corroded a way through sixteen brazen feet, I assumed that some fruitful pair must have found in the house, on its building, an ark from the waters; though even this hypothesis seemed wild. Harfager, however, afterwards confided to me his suspicion, that they had, for some purpose, been *placed* there by the original architect.

Upon a stone bench in the middle we deposited our burden, whereupon Aith made haste to depart. Harfager then rapidly and repeatedly walked from end to end of the long sepulchre, examining with many an eager stoop and peer, and upward strain, the shelves and their props. Could he, I was led to wonder, have any doubts as to their security? Damp, indeed, and decay pervaded all. A piece of woodwork which I handled softened into powder between my fingers.

He presently beckoned to me, and with yet one halt and uttered 'Hark!' from him, we traversed the house to my chamber. Here, left alone, I paced long about, fretted with a strange vagueness of anger; then, weary, tumbled to a horror of sleep.

In the far interior of the mansion even the bleared day of this land of heaviness never rose upon our settled gloom. I was able, however, to regulate my *levées* by a clock which stood in my chamber. With Harfager, in a startlingly short time, I renewed more than all our former intimacy. That I should say *more*, is itself startling, considering that an interval of twelve years stretched between us. But so, in fact, it was; and this was proved by the circumstance that we grew to take, and to pardon, freedoms of expression and manner which, as two persons of more than usual reserve, we had once never dreamed of permitting to ourselves in reference to each other. Down corridors that vanished either way in darkness and length of perspective remoteness we linked ourselves in perambulations of purposeless urgency. Once he wrote that my step was excruciatingly deliberate. I replied that it was just such a step as fitted my then mood. He wrote: 'You have developed an aptitude to *fret*.' I was profoundly offended, and replied: 'There are at least more fingers than one in the universe which *that* ring will wed.'

Something of the secret of the unhuman sensitiveness of his hearing I quickly surmised. I, too, to my dismay, began, as time passed, to catch hints of loudly-uttered words. The reason might be found, I suggested, in an increased excitability of the auditory nerve, which, if the cataract were absent, the roar of the ocean, and bombast of the incessant tempest about us, would by themselves be sufficient to cause; in which case, his own aural interior must, I said, be inflamed to an exquisite pitch of hyperpyrexial fever. The affection I named to him as the Paracusis Willisii.* He frowned dissent, but I, undeterred, callously proceeded to recite the case, occurring within my own experience, of a very deaf lady who could hear the fall of a pin in a rapidly-moving railway-train.[1] To this he only replied: 'Of

[1] Such cases are known, or at least easily comprehensible, to every medical man. The concussion on the deaf nerves is said to be the cause of the acquired sensitiveness. Nor is there any *limit* to such sensitiveness when the concussion is abnormally increased.

ignorant persons I am accustomed to consider the mere scientist as
the most profoundly ignorant.'

Yet that he should affect darkness as to the highly morbid condition
of his hearing I regarded as simply far-fetched. Himself, indeed,
confided to me his own, Aith's, and his aunt's proneness to violent
paroxysms of *vertigo*. I was startled; for I had myself shortly before
been twice roused from sleep by sensations of reeling and nausea,
and a conviction that the chamber furiously spun with me in a direction from right to left. The impression passed away, and I attributed
it, perhaps hastily (though on well-known pathological grounds), to
some disturbance in the nerve-endings of the 'labyrinth,' or inner
ear. In Harfager, however, the conviction of wheeling motions in the
house, in the world, attained so horrible a degree of certainty, that its
effects sometimes resembled those of lunacy or energumenal possession. Never, he said, was the sensation of giddiness wholly absent;
seldom the feeling that he stared with stretched-out arms over the
verge of abysmal voids which wildly wooed his half-consenting
foot. Once, as we went, he was hurled, as by unseen powers, to the
ground; and there for an hour sprawled, cold in a flow of sweat, with
distraught bedazzlement and amaze in eyes that watched the racing
house. He was constantly racked, moreover, with the consciousness
of sounds so very peculiar in their nature, that I could account for
them upon no other hypothesis than that of *tinnitus* highly exaggerated. Through the heaped-up roar, there sometimes visited him,
he said, the high lucid warbling of some Orphic bird, from the
pitch of whose impassioned madrigals he had the inner consciousness that it came from a far country, was of the whiteness of
snow, and crested with a comb of mauve. Else he was aware
of accumulated human voices, remotely articulate, contending in
volubility, and finally melting into chaotic musical tones. Or, anon,
he was stunned by an infinite and imminent crashing, like the huge
crackling of a universe of glass about his ears. He said, too, that he
could often see, rather than hear, the parti-coloured whorls of a mazy
sphere-music deep, deep, within the black dark of the cataract's
roar. These impressions, which I ardently protested *must* be purely
entotic, had sometimes upon him a pleasing effect, and long would
he stand and listen with raised hand to their seduction; others
again inflamed him to the verge of angry madness. I guessed that
they were the origin of those irascibly uttered 'Harks!' which at

intervals of about an hour did not fail to break from him. In this I was wrong: and it was with a thrill of dismay that I shortly came to know the truth.

For, as once we passed together by an iron door on the lower stage, he stopped, and for several minutes stood, listening with an expression most keen and cunning. Presently the cry 'Hark!' escaped him; and he then turned to me, and wrote upon the tablet: 'You did not hear?' I had heard nothing but the monotonous roar. He shouted into my ear in accents now audible to me as an echo heard far off in dreams: 'You shall see.'

He lifted the candlestick; produced from the pocket of his garment a key; unlocked the door. We entered a chamber, circular, very loftily domed in proportion to its extent, and apparently empty, save that a pair of ladder-steps leaned against its wall. Its flooring was of marble, and in its centre gloomed a pool, resembling the impluvium of Roman atriums, but round in shape; a pool evidently deep, full of an unctuous miasmal water. I was greatly startled by its present aspect; for as the light burned upon its jet-black surface, I could see that this had been quite recently *disturbed*, in a manner for which the shivering of the house could not account, inasmuch as *ripples* of slimy ink sullenly rounded from the centre toward its marble brink. I glanced at Harfager for explanation. He signed to me to wait, and for about an hour, with arms in their accustomed fold behind his back, perambulated. At the end of that time he stopped, and standing together by the margin, we gazed into the water. Suddenly his clutch tightened upon my arm, and I saw, not without a thrill of horror, a tiny ball, doubtless of lead, but smeared blood-red by some chymical pigment, fall from the direction of the roof and disappear into the centre of the black depths. It hissed, on contact with the water, a thin puff of vapour.

'In the name of all that is sinister!' I cried, 'what thing is this you show me?'

Again he made me a busy and confident sign to wait; snatched then the ladder-steps toward the pool; handed me the taper. I, mounting, held high the flame, and saw hanging from the misty centre of the dome a form—a sphere of tarnished old copper, lengthened out into balloon-shape by a down-looking neck, at the end of which I thought I could discern a tiny orifice. Painted

across the bulge was barely visible in faded red characters the
hieroglyph:

'harfager-hous: 1389–188-.'

Something—I know not what—of *eldritch* in the combined
aspect of spotted globe, and gloomy pool, and contrivance of
hourly hissing ball, gave expedition to my feet as I slipped down
the ladder.

'But the meaning?'

'Did you see the writing?'

'Yes. The meaning?'

He wrote: 'By comparing Gascoigne with Thrunster, I find that
the mansion was *built* about 1389.'

'But the final figures?'

'After the last 8,' he replied, 'there is another figure, nearly, but
not quite, obliterated by a tarnish-spot.'

'What figure?'

'It cannot be read, but may be surmised. The year 1888 is now all
but passed. It can only be the figure 9.'

'You are *horribly* depraved in mind!' I cried, flaring into anger.
'You assume—you dare to *state*—in a manner which no mind trained
to base its conclusions upon fact could hear with patience.'

'And you, on the other hand, are simply absurd,' he wrote. 'You
are not, I presume, ignorant of the common formula of Archimedes
by which, the diameter of a sphere being known, its volume may be
determined. Now, the diameter of the sphere in the dome there I
have ascertained to be four and a half feet; and the diameter of the
leaden balls about the third of an inch. Supposing then that 1389 was
the year in which the sphere was full of balls, you may readily calcu-
late that not many fellows of the four million and odd which have
since dropped at the rate of one an hour are now left within it. It
could not, in fact, have contained many more. The fall of balls *cannot*
persist another year. The figure 9 is therefore forced upon us.'

'But you assume, Harfager,' I cried, 'most wildly you assume!
Believe me, my friend, this is the very wantonness of wickedness! By
what algebra of despair do you know that the last date *must* be such,
was intended to be such, as to correspond with the stoppage of the
horologe? And, even if so, what is the significance of the whole. It

has—it can have—*no significance!* Was the contriver of this dwelling, of all the gnomes, think you, a being pulsing with omniscience?'

'Do you seek to madden me?' he shouted. Then furiously writing: 'I know—I swear that I know—nothing of its significance! But is it not evident to you that the work is a stupendous hour-glass, intended to record the hours not of a day, but of a cycle? and of a cycle of five hundred years?'

'But the whole thing,' I passionately cried, 'is a baleful phantasm of our brains! an evil impossibility! How is the fall of the balls regulated? Ah, my friend, you wander—your mind is debauched in this bacchanal of tumult.'

'I have not ascertained,' he replied, 'by what internal mechanism, or viscous medium, or spiral coil, dependent no doubt for its action upon the vibration of the house, the balls are retarded in their fall; that is a matter well within the cunning of the mediæval artisan, the inventor of the watch; but this at least is clear, that one element of their retardation is the minuteness of the aperture through which they have to pass; that this element, by known, though recondite, statical laws, will cease to operate when no more than three balls remain; and that, consequently, the last three will fall at nearly the same moment.'

'In God's name!' I exclaimed, careless what folly I poured out, 'but your mother is *dead*, Harfager! You dare not deny that there remain but you and the lady Swertha!'

A contemptuous glance was all the reply he then vouchsafed me.

But he confided to me a day or two later that the leaden balls were a constant bane to his ears; that from hour to hour his life was a keen waiting for their fall; that even from his brief slumbers he infallibly startled into wakefulness at each descent; that, in whatever part of the mansion he happened to be, they failed not to find him out with a clamorous and insistent *loudness*; and that every drop wrung him with a twinge of physical anguish in the inner ear. I was therefore appalled at his declaration that these droppings had now become to him as the life of life; had acquired an intimacy so close with the hue of his mind, that their cessation might even mean for him the shattering of reason. Convulsed, he stood then, face wrapped in arms, leaning against a pillar. The paroxysm past, I asked him if it was out of the question that he should once and for all cast off the fascination of the horologe, and fly with me from the place. He wrote in mysterious reply: 'A *three*fold cord is not easily broken.' I started. How threefold? He wrote with bitterest smile: 'To be enamoured of pain—to pine after aching—to dote upon Marah—is not that a wicked madness?' I was overwhelmed. Unconsciously he had quoted Gascoigne: a wicked madness! a lecherous agonie! 'You have seen the face of my aunt,' he proceeded; 'your eyes were dim if you did not there behold an impious calm, the glee of a blasphemous patience, a grin behind her daring smile.' He then spoke of a prospect, at the infinite terror of which his whole nature trembled, yet which sometimes laughed in his heart in the aspect of a maniac *hope*. It was the prospect of any considerable increase in the volume of sound about him. At *that*, he said, the brain must totter. On the night of my arrival the noise of my booted tread, and, since then, my occasionally raised voice, had caused him acute unease. To a sensibility such as this, I understood him further to say, the luxury of torture involved in a large sound-increase in his environment was an allurement from which no human strength could turn; and when I expressed my powerlessness even to conceive such an increase, much less the means by which it could be effected, he produced from the archives of the house some annals, kept by the successive heads of his race. From these it appeared that the tempests which continually harried the lonely latitude of Vaila did not fail to give place, at periodic intervals of some years, to one sovereign *ouragan**—one Sirius among the suns—one *ultimate* lyssa* of elemental atrocity. At such periods the rains descended—and the floods came—even as in the first world-deluge; those *rösts*, or eddies, which at all times encompassed Vaila, spurning then the bands of lateral space, shrieked themselves aloft into a multitudinous death-dance of water-spouts, and like snaky Deinotheria,* or say towering monolithic in a stonehenge of columned and cyclopean awe, thronged about the little land, upon which, with converging *débâcle*, they discharged their momentous waters; and the lochs to which the cataract was due thus redoubled their volume, and fell with redoubled tumult. It was, said Harfager, like a miracle that for twenty years no such great event had transacted itself at Vaila.

And what, I asked, was the third strand of that threefold cord of which he had spoken?

He took me to a circular hall, which, he told me, he had ascertained to be the geometrical centre of the circular mansion. It was a very great hall—so great as I think I never saw—so great that the amount of segment illumined at any one time by the taper seemed nearly flat. And nearly the whole of its space from floor to roof was occupied by a pillar of brass, the space between wall and cylinder being only such as to admit of a stretched-out arm.

'This cylinder, which seems to be solid,' wrote Harfager, 'ascends to the dome and passes beyond it; it descends hence to the floor of the lower stage, and passes through that; it descends thence to the brazen flooring of the vaults, and *passes through that* into the rock of the ground. Under each floor it spreads out laterally into a vast capital, helping to support the floor. What is the precise quality of the impression which I have made upon your mind by this description?'

'I do not know!' I answered, turning from him; 'propound me none of your questions, Harfager. I feel a giddiness . . .'

'Nevertheless you shall answer me,' he proceeded; 'consider the *strangeness* of that brazen lowest floor, which I have discovered to be some ten feet thick, and whose under-surface, I have reason to believe, is somewhat above the level of the ground; remember that the fabric is at no point *fastened* to the cylinder; think of the *chains* that ray out from the outer walls, seeming to anchor the house to the ground. Tell me, what impression have I *now* made?'

'And is it for this you wait?' I cried,—'for *this*? Yet there may have been no malevolent intention! You jump at conclusions! Any human dwelling, if solidly based upon earth, would be at all times liable to overthrow on such a land, in such a situation, as this, by some superlative tempest! What if it were the intention of the architect that in such eventuality the chains should break, and the house, by yielding, be saved?'

'You have no lack of charity at least,' he replied; and we returned to the book we then read together.

He had not wholly lost the old habit of study, but could no longer constrain himself to sit to read. With a volume, often tossed down and resumed, he walked to and fro within the radius of the lamp-light; or I, unconscious of my voice, read to him. By a strange whim of his mood, the few books which now lay within the limits of his patience had all for their motive something of the *picaresque*, or the foppishly speculative: Quevedo's *Tacaño*; or the mundane system of Tycho Brahe; above all, George Hakewill's *Power and Providence of*

God.* One day, however, as I read, he interrupted me with the sentence, seemingly *à propos* of nothing: 'What I *cannot* understand is that you, a scientist, should believe that the physical life ceases with the cessation of the breath'—and from that moment the tone of our reading changed. He led me to the crypts of the library in the lowest part of the building, and hour after hour, with a certain *furore* of triumph, overwhelmed me with volumes evidencing the longevity of man after 'death.' A sentence of Haller had rooted itself in his mind; he repeated, insisted upon it: 'sapientia denique consilia dat quibus longævitas obtineri queat, nitro, opio, purgationibus subinde repetitis . . .'; and as opium was the elixir of long-drawn life, so death itself, he said, was that opium, whose more potent nepenthe lullabied the body to a peace not all-insentient, far within the gates of the gardens of dream.* From the *Dhammapada* of the Buddhist canon, to Zwinger's *Theatrum*, to Bacon's *Historia Vitæ et Mortis*, he ranged to find me heaped-up certainty of his faith.* What, he asked, was my opinion of Baron Verulam's account of the dead man who was heard to utter words of prayer; or of the leaping bowels of the dead *condamné*? On my expressing incredulity, he seemed surprised, and reminded me of the writhings of dead serpents, of the *visible* beating of a frog's heart many hours after 'death.' 'She is not dead,' he quoted, 'but *sleepeth*.'* The whim of Bacon and Paracelsus that the principle of life resides in a subtle spirit or fluid which pervades the organism he coerced into elaborate proof that such a spirit must, from its very nature, be incapable of any *sudden* annihilation, so long as the organs which it permeates remain connected and integral. I asked what limit he then set to the persistence of sensibility in the physical organism. He replied that when slow decay had so far advanced that the nerves could no longer be called nerves, or their cell-origins cell-origins, or the brain a brain—or when by artificial means the brain had for any length of time been disconnected at the cervical region from the body—*then* was the king of terrors king indeed, and the body was as though it had not been. With an indiscretion strange to me before my residence at Vaila, I blurted the question whether all this *Aberglaube* could have any reference, in his mind, to the body of his mother. For a while he stood thoughtful, then wrote: 'Had I not reason to believe that my own and my aunt's life in some way hinged upon the final cessation of hers, I should still have taken precautions to ascertain the progress of the destroyer upon her mortal frame; as it is, I shall not lack even the minutest information.' He then explained that the rodents which swarmed in the sepulchre would, in the course of time, do their full work upon her; but would be unable to penetrate to the region of the throat without first gnawing their way through the three cords stretched across the holes of the laminæ within the coffin, and thus, one by one, liberating the three morrisco bells to a tinkling agitation.

The winter solstice had passed; another year opened. I slept a deep sleep by night when Harfager entered my chamber, and shook me. His face was ghastly in the taper-light. A transformation within a few hours had occurred upon him. He was not the same. He resembled some poor wight into whose unexpecting eyes—at midnight—have glared the sudden eye-balls of Terrour.

He informed me that he was aware of singular intermittent straining and creaking sounds, which gave him the sensation of hanging in aerial spaces by a thread which must shortly snap to his weight. He asked if, for God's sake, I would accompany him to the sepulchre. We passed together through the house, he craven, shivering, his step for the first time laggard. In the chamber of the dead he stole to and fro examining the shelves, furtively intent. His eyes were sunken, his face drawn like death. From the footless coffin of the dowager trembling on its bench of stone, I saw an old water-rat creep. As Harfager passed beneath one of the shortest of the shelves which bore a single coffin, it suddenly fell from a height with its burthen into fragments at his feet. He screamed the cry of a frighted creature, and tottered to my support. I bore him back to the upper house.

He sat with hidden face in the corner of a small room doddering, overcome, as it were, with the extremity of age. He no longer marked with his usual 'Hark!' the fall of the leaden drops. To my remonstrances he answered only with the words, So soon! so soon! Whenever I sought I found him there. His manhood had collapsed in an ague of trepidancy. I do not think that during this time he slept.

On the second night, as I approached him, he sprang suddenly straight with the furious outcry: 'The first bell tinkles!'

And he had hardly larynxed the wild words when, from some great distance, a faint wail, which at its origin must have been a most piercing shriek, reached my now feverishly sensitive ears. Harfager at the sound clapped hands to ears, and dashed insensate from his place, I following in hot pursuit, through the black breadth of the mansion. We ran until we reached a round chamber, containing a candelabrum, and arrased in faded red. In an alcove at the furthest circumference was a bed. On the floor lay in swoon the lady Swertha. Her dark-grey hair in disarray wrapped her like an angry sea, and many tufts of it lay scattered wide, torn from the roots. About her throat were livid prints of strangling fingers. We bore her to the bed, and, having discovered some tincture in a cabinet, I administered it between her fixed teeth. In the rapt and dreaming face I saw that death was not, and, as I found something appalling in her aspect, shortly afterward left her to Harfager.

When I next saw him his manner had assumed a species of change which I can only describe as hideous. It resembled the officious self-importance seen in a person of weak intellect, incapable of affairs, who goads himself with the exhortation, 'to business! the time is short—I must even bestir myself!' His walk sickened me with a suggestion of *ataxie locomotrice.** I asked him as to the lady, as to the meaning of the marks of violence on her body. Bending ear to his deep and unctuous tones, I heard, 'A stealthy attempt has been made upon her life by the skeleton, Aith.'

My unfeigned astonishment at this announcement he seemed not to share. To my questions, repeatedly pressed upon him, as to the reason for retaining such a domestic in the house, as to the origin of his service, he could give no lucid answer. Aith, he informed me, had been admitted into the mansion during the period of his own long absence in youth. He knew little of him beyond the fact that he was of extraordinary physical strength. *Whence* he had come, or how, no living being except the lady Swertha had knowledge; and she, it seems, feared, or at least persistently declined, to admit him into the mystery. He added that, as a matter of fact, the lady, from the day of his return to Vaila, had for some reason imposed upon herself a silence upon all subjects, which he had never once known her to break except by an occasional note.

With a curious, irrelevant *impressement*, with an intensely voluntary, ataxic strenuousness, always with the air of a drunken man constraining himself to ordered action, Harfager now set himself to the osten-tatious adjustment of a host of insignificant matters. He collected chronicles and arranged them in order of date. He tied and ticketed bundles of documents. He insisted upon my help in turning the faces of portraits to the wall. He was, however, now constantly interrupted by paroxysms of vertigo; six times in a single day he was hurled to the ground. Blood occasionally gushed from his ears. He complained to me in a voice of piteous wail of the clear luting of a silver *piccolo*, which did not cease to invite him. As he bent sweating upon his momentous futilities, his hands fluttered like shaken reeds. I noted the movements of his muttering and whimpering lips, the rheum of his far-sunken eyes. The decrepitude of dotage had overtaken his youth.

On a day he cast it utterly off, and was young again. He entered my chamber, roused me from sleep; I saw the mad *gaudium* in his eyes, heard the wild hiss of his cry in my ear:

'Up! It is sublime. The *storm!*'

Ah! I had known it—in the spinning nightmare of my sleep. I felt it in the tormented air of the chamber. It had come, then. I saw it lurid by the lamplight on the hell of Harfager's distorted visage.

I glanced at the face of the clock. It was nine—in the morning. A sardonic glee burst at once into being within me. I sprang from the couch. Harfager, with the naked stalk of some maniac old prophet, had already rapt himself away. I set out in pursuit. A clear deepening was manifest in the quivering of the edifice; sometimes for a second it paused still, as if, breathlessly, to listen. Occasionally there visited me, as it were, the faint dirge of some far-off lamentation and voice in Ramah;* but if this was subjective, or the screaming of the storm, I could not say. Else I heard the distinct note of an organ's peal. The air of the mansion was agitated by a vaguely puffy unease. About noon I sighted Harfager, lamp in hand, running along a corridor. His feet were bare. As we met he looked at me, but hardly with recognition, and passed by; stopped, however, returned, and howled into my ear the question: 'Would you *see?*' He beckoned before me. I followed to a very small window in the outer wall closed with a slab of iron. As he lifted a latch the metal flew inward with instant impetuosity and swung him far, while a blast of the storm, braying and booming through the aperture with buccal and reboant bravura, caught and pinned me against an angle of the wall. Down the corridor a long crashing *bouleversement** of pictures and furniture ensued. I nevertheless contrived to push my way, crawling on the belly, to the opening. Hence the sea should have been visible. My senses, however, were met by nothing but a reeling vision of tumbled blackness, and a general impression of the letter O. The sun of Vaila had gone out. In a moment of opportunity our united efforts prevailed to close the slab.

'Come'—he had obtained fresh light, and beckoned before me— 'let us see how the dead fare in the midst of the great desolation and *dies iræ!* * Running, we had hardly reached the middle of the stairway, when I was thrilled by the consciousness of a momentous shock, the bass of a dull and far-reverberating thud, which nothing conceivable save the huge simultaneous thumping to the ground of the whole piled mass of the coffins of the sepulchre could have occasioned. I turned to Harfager, and for an instant beheld him, panic flying in his scuttling feet, headlong on the way he had come, with stopped ears and wide mouth. Then, indeed, fear overtook me—a tremor in the midst of the exultant daring of my heart—a thought that *now* at least I must desert him in his extremity, now work out my own salvation. Yet it was with a most strange hesitancy that I turned to seek him for the last time—a hesitancy which I fully felt to be selfish and diseased. I wandered through the midnight house in search of light, and having happened upon a lamp, proceeded to hunt for Harfager. Several hours passed in this way. It became clear from the state of the atmosphere that the violence about me was being abnormally intensified. Sounds as of distant screams—unreal, like the screamings of spirits—broke now upon my ear. As the time of evening drew on, I began to detect in the vastly augmented baritone of the cataract something new—a shrillness—the whistle of an ecstasy—a malice— the menace of a rabies blind and deaf. It must have been at about the hour of six that I found Harfager. He sat in an obscure apartment with bowed head, hands on knees. His face was covered with hair, and blood from the ears. The right sleeve of his garment had been rent away in some renewed attempt, as I imagined, to manipulate a window; the slightly-bruised arm hung lank from the shoulder. For some time I stood and watched the mouthing of his mumblings. Now that I had found him I said nothing of departure. Presently he looked sharply up with the cry 'Hark!'—then with imperious impatience, 'Hark! Hark!'—then with rapturous shout, 'The second bell!' And *again*, in instant sequence upon his cry, there sounded a wail, vague but unmistakably real, through the house. Harfager at the moment dropped reeling with vertigo; but I, snatching a lamp, hasted forth, trembling, but eager. For some time the high wailing continued, either actually, or by reflex action of my ear. As I ran toward the lady's apartment, I saw, separated from it by the breadth of a corridor, the open door of an armoury, into which I passed, and seized a battle-axe; and, thus armed, was about to enter to her aid, when Aith, with blazing eye, rushed from her chamber by a further door. I raised my weapon, and, shouting, flew forward to fell him; but by some chance the lamp dropped from me, and before I knew aught, the axe leapt from my grasp, myself hurled far backward. There was, however, sufficiency of light from the chamber to show that the skeleton had dashed into a door of the armoury: that near me, by which I had procured the axe, I instantly slammed and locked; and hasting to the other, similarly secured it. Aith was thus a prisoner. I then entered the lady's room. She lay half-way across the bed in the alcove, and to my bent ear loudly croaked the *râles* of death.* A glance at the mangled throat convinced me that her last hours were surely come. I placed her supine upon the bed; curtained her utterly from sight within the loosened festoons of the hangings of black, and inhumanly turned from the fearfulness of her sight. On an *escritoire* near I saw a note, intended apparently for Harfager: 'I mean to defy, and fly. Think not from fear—but for the glow of the Defiance itself. *Can* you come?' Taking a flame from the candelabrum, I hastily left her to solitude, and the ultimate throes of her agony.

I had passed some distance backward when I was startled by a singular sound—a clash—resembling in *timbre* the clash of a tambourine. I heard it rather loudly, and that I should *now* hear it at all, proceeding as it did from a distance, implied the employment of some prodigious energy. I waited, and in two minutes it again broke, and thenceforth at like regular intervals. It had somehow an effect of pain upon me. The conviction grew gradually that Aith had unhung two of the old brazen shields from their pegs; and that, holding them by their handles, and smiting them viciously together, he thus expressed the frenzy which had now overtaken him. I found my way back to Harfager, in whom the very nerve of anguish now seemed to stamp and stalk about the chamber. He bent his head; shook it like a hail-tormented horse; with his deprecating hand brushed and barred from his hearing each recurrent clash of the brazen shields. 'Ah, when—when—when—' he hoarsely groaned into my ear, 'will that rattle of hell choke in her throat? I will myself, I tell you—*with my own hand!*—oh God . . .' Since the morning his auditory inflammation (as, indeed, my own also) seemed to have heightened in steady proportion with the roaring and screaming chaos round; and the *râles* of the lady hideously filled for him the measured intervals of the grisly cymbaling of Aith. He presently hurled twinkling fingers into the air, and with wide arms rushed swiftly into the darkness.

And again I sought him, and long again in vain. As the hours passed, and the slow Tartarean day deepened toward its baleful midnight, the cry of the now redoubled cataract, mixed with the throng and majesty of the now climactic tempest, assumed too definite and intentional a *shriek* to be longer tolerable to any mortal reason. My own mind escaped my governance, and went its way. Here, in the hot-bed of fever, I was fevered; among the children of wrath, was strong with the strength, and weak with the feebleness of delirium. I wandered from chamber to chamber, precipitate, bemused, giddy on the up-buoyance of a joy. 'As a man upon whom sleep seizes,' so had I fallen. Even yet, as I approached the region of the armoury, the noisy ecstasies of Aith did not fail to clash faintly upon my ear. Harfager I did not see, for he too, doubtless, roamed a headlong Ahasuerus* in the round world of the house. At about midnight, however, observing light shine from a door on the lower stage, I entered and found him there. It was the chamber of the dropping horologe. He half-sat, swaying self-hugged, on the ladder-steps, and stared at the blackness of the pool. The last flicker of the riot of the day seemed dying in his eyes. He cast no glance as I approached. His hands, his bare right arm, were red with new-shed blood; but of this, too, he appeared unconscious. His mouth gaped wide to his pantings. As I looked, he leapt suddenly high, smiting hands, with the yell, 'The last bell tinkles!' and galloped forth, a-rave. He therefore did not see (though he may have understood by hearing) the spectacle which, with cowering awe, I immediately thereupon beheld: for from the horologe there slipped with hiss of vapour a ball into the torpid pool: and while the clock once ticked, another; and while the clock yet ticked, another! and the vapour of the first had not *utterly* passed, when the vapour of the third, intermingling, floated with it into grey tenuity aloft. Understanding that the sands of the house were run, I, too, flinging maniac arms, rushed from the spot. I was, however, suddenly stopped in my career by the instinct of some stupendous doom emptying its vials upon the mansion; and was quickly made aware, by the musketry of a shrill crackling from aloft, and the imminent downpour of a world of waters, that a water-spout had, wholly or partly, hurled the catastrophe of its broken floods upon us, and crashed ruining through the dome of the building. At that moment I beheld Harfager running toward me, hands buried in hair. As he flew past, I seized him. 'Harfager! save yourself!' I cried—'the very fountains, man,—by the living God, Harfager'—I hissed it into his inmost ear—'*the very fountains of the Great Deep . . .!*' Stupid, he glared at me, and passed on his way. I, whisking myself into a room, slammed the door. Here for some time, with smiting knees, I waited; but the impatience of my frenzy urged me, and I again stepped forth. The corridors were everywhere thigh-deep with water. Rags of the storm, irrageous by way of the orifice in the shattered dome, now blustered with hoiden wantonness through the house. My light was at once extinguished; and immediately I was startled by the presence of *another* light—most ghostly, gloomy, bluish—most soft, yet wild, phosphorescent—which now perfused the whole building. For this I could in no way account. But as I stood in wonder, a gust of greater vehemence romped through the house, and I was instantly conscious of the harsh *snap* of something near me. There was a minute's breathless pause—and then—quick, quick—ever quicker—came the throb, and the snap, and the pop, in vastly wide circular succession, of the anchoring chains of the mansion before the urgent shoulder of the hurricane. And *again* a second of eternal calm—and then—deliberately—its hour came—the ponderous palace *moved*. My flesh writhed like the glutinous flesh of a serpent. Slowly moved, and stopped:—then was a sweep—and a swirl—and a pause! then a swirl—and a sweep—and a pause!—then steady industry of labour on the monstrous brazen axis, as the husbandman plods by the plough; then increase of zest, assuetude of a fledgeling to the wing— then intensity—then the last light ecstasy of flight. And now, once again, as staggering and plunging I spun, the thought of escape for a moment visited me: but this time I shook an impious fist. 'No, but God, no, no,' I cried, 'I will no more wander hence, my God! I will even perish with Harfager! Here let me waltzing pass, in this Ball of the Vortices, Anarchie of the Thunders! Did not the great Corot call it translation in a chariot of flame? But this is gaudier than that! redder than that! This is jaunting on the scoriac tempests and reeling bullions of hell! It is baptism in a sun!' Recollection gropes in a dimmer gloaming as to all that followed. I struggled up the stairway now flowing a steep river, and for a long time ran staggering and plunging, full of wild words, about, amid the downfall of ceilings and the wide ruin of tumbling walls. The air was thick with splashes, the whole roof now, save three rafters, snatched by the wind away. In that blue sepulchral moonlight, the tapestries flapped and trailed wildly out after the flying house like the streaming hair of some ranting fakeer stung gyratory by the gadflies and tarantulas of distraction. The flooring gradually assumed a slant like the deck of a sailing ship, its covering waters flowing all to accumulation in one direction. At one point, where the largest of the porticoes projected, the mansion began at every revolution to bump with horrid shiverings against some obstruction. It bumped, and while the lips said one-two-three, it three times bumped again. It was the levity of hugeness! it was the mænadism of mass! Swift—ever swifter, swifter, swifter—in ague of urgency, it reeled and raced, every portico a sail to the storm, vexing and wracking its tremendous frame to fragments. I, chancing by the door of a room littered with the *débris* of a fallen wall, saw through that wan and livid light Harfager sitting on a tomb. A large drum was beside him, upon which, club grasped in bloody hand, he feebly and persistently beat. The velocity of the leaning house had now attained the *sleeping* stage, that ultimate energy of the spinning-top. Harfager sat, head sunk to chest; suddenly he dashed the hairy wrappings from his face; sprang; stretched horizontal arms; and began to spin—dizzily!—in the same direction as the mansion!—nor less sleep-embathed!—with floating hair, and quivering cheeks, and the starting eye-balls of horror, and tongue that lolled like a panting wolf's from his bawling degenerate mouth. From such a sight I turned with the retching of loathing, and taking to my heels, staggering and plunging, presently found myself on the lower stage opposite a porch. An outer door crashed to my feet, and the breath of the storm smote freshly upon me. An *élan*, part of madness, more of heavenly sanity, spurred in my brain. I rushed through the doorway, and was tossed far into the limbo without.

The river at once swept me deep-drowned toward the sea. Even here, a momentary shrill din like the splitting asunder of a world reached my ears. It had hardly passed, when my body collided in its course upon one of the basalt piers, thick-cushioned by sea-weed, of the not all-demolished bridge. Nor had I utterly lost consciousness.

A clutch freed my head from the surge, and I finally drew and heaved myself to the level of a timber. Hence to the ledge of rock by which I had come, the bridge was intact. I rowed myself feebly on the belly beneath the poundings of the wind. The rain was a steep rushing, like a shimmering of silk, through the air. Observing the same wild glow about me which had blushed through the broken dome into the mansion, I glanced backward—and saw that the dwelling of the Harfagers was a memory of the past; then upward—and lo, the whole northern sky, to the zenith, burned one tumbled and fickly-undulating ocean of gaudy flames. It was the *aurora borealis** which, throeing at every aspen instant into rays and columns, cones and obelisks, of vivid vermil and violet and rose, was fairly whiffed and flustered by the storm into a vast silken oriflamme of tresses and swathes and breezes of glamour; whilst, low-bridging the horizon, the flushed beams of the polar light assembled into a changeless boreal corona of bedazzling candor. At the augustness of this great phenomenon I was affected to blessed tears. And with them, the dream broke!—the infatuation passed!— a hand skimmed back from my brain the blind films and media of delusion; and sobbing on my knees, I jerked to heaven the arms of grateful oblation for my surpassing Rephidim,* and marvel of deliverance from all the temptation—and the tribulation—and the tragedy—of Vaila.

EXPLANATORY NOTES

VERNON LEE *Dionea*

First printed in *Hauntings: Fantastic Stories* (London, 1890). In the preface to *Hauntings*, Lee suggested that the supernatural was a peculiar kind of history: 'we live ourselves, we educated folk of modern times, on the borderland of the Past, in houses looking down on its troubadours' orchards and Greek folks' pillared courtyards; and a legion of ghosts, very vague and changeful, are perpetually to and fro, fetching and carrying for us between it and the Present' (pp. x–xi). A consequence is that her writing is a dense network of references and allusions to literary, mythological, classical, and European history.

5 *Dionea*: the Greek translates as 'divine queen'. In myth, Dione bore Zeus a daughter, Aphrodite. Associations are to mother earth, to female sexuality, to the feminine powers of seduction and reproduction. There are also consistent associations with Venus throughout the story. To the Greeks, Dione and Aphrodite were considered to have foreign, Oriental origins: they were dangerous, impure figures in the pantheon of gods.

7 *that myrtle-bush*: Dionea is consistently associated with the myrtle-bush. Lizzie Deas, in *Flower Favourites: Their Legends, Symbolism and Significance* (London, 1898), records: 'the myrtle for the Romans, as for the Greeks, was before all an erotic plant, dedicated to Venus and to Hymen, god of marriage, and it is emblematic of *pure love* and of *fertility*' (p. 200).

Burne Jones or Tadema: Edward Burne-Jones (1833–98) and Sir Lawrence Alma-Tadema (1836–1912), Victorian painters popular in England. Burne-Jones co-founded the Pre-Raphaelite Brotherhood of painters, poets, and artisans in the 1850s, and was central to the Aesthetic Movement in the *fin de siècle*. Alma-Tadema was famous for his female nudes in classical mythological settings.

8 *Mazzinian times*: Giuseppe Mazzini (1805–72) was one of the central architects of the unification of Italy and its foundation as a modern nation state. He founded the Young Italy political movement in exile in the 1830s in Paris and agitated for Italian nationalism from London throughout the 1850s. Lee's narrator shares this context of exile in the north.

Theocritus: Greek poet of the third century BC, known for poetic idylls.

Longus: author of the pastoral story of *Daphnis and Chloe* in the second century AD. The narrative is an erotic text on developing sexual awareness.

Zola: the French 'Naturalist', Émile Zola (1840–1902), was the epitome of the modern novelist, hugely controversial for his frank depictions of lower-class working conditions and sexuality.

my friend Heine's little book: Heinrich Heine, German poet (1797–1856). The book is named later in the tale as *Gods in Exile* (1853), and is a key reference point for 'Dionea'. Heine argues that the Greek gods have been displaced by an ascetic and dour Christian tradition, and in one passage writes: 'All this joy and gay laughter has long been silent, and in the ruins of the ancient temples the old Greek deities still dwell; but they have lost their majesty by the victory of Christ, and now they are sheer devils who hide by day in gloomy wreck and rubbish, but by night arise in charming loveliness to bewilder and allure some heedless wanderer or daring youth' (from *The Sword and the Flame: Selections from Heinrich Heine's Prose*, ed. Alfred Werner (New York, 1960), 547).

11 *Decameron*: text published by Giovanni Bocaccio in 1350, a compendium of 100 tales told by ten people over ten days.

Diderot and Schubert: Denis Diderot's *The Nun*, about a young girl forced to become a nun against her will, was written in 1760, but published in 1796 at the height of the French Revolution. Franz Schubert's song 'The Young Nun' was first performed in 1825.

15 *My book?*: this letter shows the doctor is toying with a project to update Heine's idea of 'gods in exile' by tracking the fugitive signs of returning gods through folklore, literature, and myth. He goes on to list numerous sources over the next two pages.

C'est fumer des cigarettes enchantées: a well-known aphorism of the French novelist, Honoré de Balzac: 'To conceive is to enjoy; it is to smoke enchanted cigarettes; but, without the execution, everything goes up in smoke.'

Tannhäuser ... Wagner: the Tannhäuser story is a medieval German folktale, told in numerous songs and lyrics. Friedrich von der Hagen (1780–1866) collected and published medieval Minnesinger in 1838. The narrator recommends Richard Wagner's opera *Tannhäuser* (1845), which accentuates the contrast between female carnality in the court of Venus against northern asceticism. Lee's fascination with opera permeates many of the stories in *Hauntings*.

16 *Fata Morgana city*: also known as Morgan Le Fay, Fata Morgana was a fairy enchantress in Arthurian legend. Complex mirages of castles and cityscapes are named after her.

Procul a mea ... rabidos: citation from Roman poet Catullus (*c*.84–54 BC). It is from 'Attis', a poem that describes the fate of a young man devoted to the goddess of fertility, Cybele: 'far from my house be all your fury, O my Queen / Others drive you to frenzy, others drive you to madness.'

Gibson's and Dupré's studio: John Gibson (1790–1866), a prominent English sculptor, known for his work on mythological figures like Aphrodite; Giovanni Dupré (1817–82), an Italian sculptor, mainly of Catholic religious works, but also of classical female subjects.

17 *Cervantes' Licentiate*: Miguel de Cervantes (1547–1616), Spanish prose

writer. This is a reference to 'The Glass Graduate', one of his *Exemplary Stories*, published in 1613.

18 *Hermann and Dorothea*: the title of a novel in verse by Johann Wolfgang von Goethe, published in 1798.

19 *La Rochefoucauld*: François La Rochefoucauld (1613–80) was noted for his maxims on living the moral life.

20 *Schopenhauer*: Arthur Schopenhauer (1788–1860), philosopher. Waldemar is quoting from Schopenhauer's notorious essay 'On Women' in which he derides the term 'fair sex', claiming that 'The female sex could be more aptly called the *unaesthetic*.'

21 *'Flower of the myrtle . . . the sea'*: this is a stornello, an Italian folk verse of three lines, originating in seventeenth-century Tuscany, often sung in praise of a flower. Robert Browning imitated the form. By singing this, Dionea once again appears to be an emanation of the folkloric.

22 *Zeuxis . . . Juno*: as told by the Roman writer Cicero, Zeuxis was commissioned to paint Helen of Troy and tried to synthesize the ideal Helen from the most beautiful women in Crotona. This scene had just been painted by Edwin Long as *The Chosen Five (Zeuxis at Crotona)*, displayed in London in 1885.

24 *Dieux en Exil*: see note to p. 8 above on Heinrich Heine's *Gods in Exile*.

OSCAR WILDE *Lord Arthur Savile's Crime: A Study of Duty*

First serialized in *Court and Society* on 11, 18, and 25 May 1887, where it was subtitled 'A Study of Cheiromancy'. Very slightly revised for *Lord Arthur Savile's Crime and Other Stories* (1891). The cheiromancy, or palmistry, at the centre of this story was one of a number of fashionable 'occult sciences' at the *fin de siècle*. Fortune-telling for money was disreputable and illegal, with prosecutions still occasionally taking place at the time. Oscar Wilde's wife, Constance, had a number of occult interests including astrology and she later joined the secret magical society, The Hermetic Order of the Golden Dawn. The Wildes asked their friend Edward Heron-Allen to cast the horoscope of their first child, Cyril, in 1885. Heron-Allen also sent Wilde his translation of C. S. d'Arpentigny's *The Science of the Hand* in 1886 and his essay 'The Cheiromancy of Today' immediately followed a serialized part of Wilde's *The Picture of Dorian Gray* in *Lippincott's Monthly Magazine* in 1890. Later, the famous palmist, Cheiro, recalled reading Wilde's palm at a dinner in April 1893. Wilde was told: 'The left hand is the hand of a king, but the right hand that of a king who will send himself into exile.' Wilde allegedly left the party distraught (see Cheiro, *Cheiro's Memoirs: The Reminiscences of the Society Palmist* (London, 1912).

27 *Or pur*: pure gold.

29 *on a fait le monde ainsi*: it is the way of the world.

   rascette: in palmistry, the lines that join the wrist and hand.

33 *General Boulanger*: populist politician, who founded the League of Patriots and stirred up the Parisian voters with a by-election victory in 1888.

34 *Nemesis had stolen the shield of Pallas . . . Gorgon's head*: in Greek mythology, the Gorgon's head was cut off by Perseus and fixed to the shield of Pallas, the goddess of wisdom. Nemesis was the goddess of retribution.

35 *portière*: door-curtain.

36 *narrow shameful alleys*: these same streets appear in both Conan Doyle's 'The Case of Lady Sannox' and Arthur Machen's *The Great God Pan*, see below. They had a low reputation as places of crime and vice; in 1889, the Cleveland Street scandal exposed a male brothel. This nightmare walk through a hallucinatory London is reworked in chapter 7 of *The Picture of Dorian Gray*.

39 *Tanagra*: funerary statues found in the tombs of this ancient Greek city.

41 *to decide in favour of poison*: Wilde evidently had a fascination with poison. In 1889, Wilde published the essay 'Pen, Pencil and Poison', his 'celebration' of Thomas Griffiths Wainewright—the poet, painter, forger, and subtle poisoner.

Ruff's Guide and Bailey's Magazine: these are references to the contemporary journals, *Ruff's Guide to the Turf* and *Baily's Magazine of Sports and Pastimes*.

42 *monsieur le mauvais sujet*: you rascal.

On a fait des folies pour moi: many lost their heads over me.

47 *dynamite faction*: the European refugee population that crowded into London in the latter half of the nineteenth century included revolutionaries like Karl Marx and numerous Anarchist and Nihilist factions who were committed to the violent overthrow of the state. Although treated as inept and comic by Wilde (following Robert Louis Stevenson's portrait in *The Dynamiters* in 1885), there was a real terror of foreign agents plotting overthrow in London. Bombings targeted the Palace of Westminster and in 1894 Martial Bourdin of the Autonomie Club in Tottenham Court Road blew himself up carrying a bomb to the Greenwich Observatory. This was the basis for Joseph Conrad's *The Secret Agent* (1907).

51 *Dorcas Society*: the Dorcas Society was a church ladies' association that provided clothes for the poor.

HENRY JAMES *Sir Edmund Orme*

First published in *Black and White* Christmas number, 1891. Collected the following year in *The Lesson of the Master*, James then revised the story for volume xvii of the New York edition of his work in 1909. I have used the 1892 text, but will note significant changes or additions in the later version. 'Sir Edmund Orme' marked James's first return to the ghost story since 1876, and it initiated a whole sequence of supernatural and Gothic stories. In the preface for the volume containing the tale in the New York edition, James spoke of the supernatural as being best filtered through 'the human consciousness that entertains and records, that amplifies and interprets', 'looming through some other history—the indispensable history of somebody's normal relation to something'. The reader is to be an interpreter of subtle ambiguities: in this, and in many other ways, 'Sir Edmund Orme' anticipates James's most celebrated ghost story, *The Turn of the Screw* (1898).

57 *I . . . but the names*: framing devices like this are common in Gothic and supernatural tales; the very first modern Gothic novel, Horace Walpole's *The Castle of Otranto*, had a 'fake' preface that tried to pass the text off as a medieval manuscript. James uses the framing device to instil ambiguity about the status of the text we are about to read: is it a factual report or not? What is the relation of the anonymous couple in the frame to the events of the story? Rereading this opening paragraph after finishing the story is also instructive.

61 *intuitions. . . . connected with me*: Mrs Marden, in other words, reveals that she has psychic sensitivity. This language emerged with the foundation of the Society for Psychical Research in 1882. The society collected evidence of hauntings, apparitions, 'second sight', and moments of 'telepathic' connection. All cases were anonymized in the society's *Proceedings*, which might explain the coyness of Mrs Marden's confession and the narrator's surprise that she is willing to speak of it. Henry James's brother, William, was a prominent psychologist who was particularly active in psychical research in the 1890s. William researched a noted Boston Spiritualist medium, Mrs Piper, over many years, and Henry had agreed to deliver a report on his findings about her to a meeting of the society in October 1890. Henry was at this point far more sceptical than his brother, and found the meeting highly amusing.

66 *the Indian room*: although Oriental-style furnishings were common at this time, James is also invoking an association of the Indian subcontinent with mystical Eastern wisdom. In the late 1880s, Madame Blavatsky's Theosophical Society was at the height of its influence in London; Blavatsky claimed to gain occult knowledge and guidance from immortal Mahatmas hidden in the inaccessible fastness of Tibet.

71 *I was filled . . . sensation*: the New York edition changes this passage to: 'I was affected altogether in the sense of pleasure. I desired a renewal of my luck.' This amplifies the crude and egotistical nature of the narrator's reactions.

72 *There is . . . nervous*: the New York edition renders this: 'There is no doubt I was much uplifted', another coarsening of the response. James makes substantial changes to this whole paragraph: he excises the metaphor of the fountain and its 'unspeakable vibrations', and the reference to Sir Edmund is changed to the mocking 'our hoverer'.

76 *he killed himself*: suicide remained illegal in England until 1961 and was a source of religious dread and family shame throughout the Victorian era. As late as 1824, suicides were buried in unmarked graves at crossroads, with a stake through the heart to prevent souls from wandering. Victorian medical opinion tried to establish theories of temporary moral insanity, but it remained a morally horrifying event. In Thomas Hardy's *Jude the Obscure* (1896) the child suicide prompts anxious reflections on 'the coming universal wish not to live'. An epidemic of suicides is another sign of moral panic in Machen's *The Great God Pan*.

77 *with exquisite resentment*: Mrs Marden reacts strongly to the idea of her experience being reduced to one of thousands of case histories collected by the Society for Psychical Research. But perhaps this is what has happened: the framing of the story and the name changes suggest that James might be parodying the form of the psychical research document.

78 *a case of retributive justice*: the New York edition makes important additions to this passage, amplifying its Gothic resonances: 'It was a case of retributive justice, of the visiting on the children of the sins of the mothers, since not of the fathers.' This rewrites the biblical passage, from Exodus 20: 5, 'for I the Lord am a jealous God, visiting the iniquity of the fathers upon the children unto the third and fourth generation of them that hate me'. James substantially revises the following sentences to emphasize this (de-)generational anxiety: 'This wretched mother was to pay, in suffering, for the suffering she had inflicted, and as the disposition to trifle with an honest man's just expectations might crop up again, to my detriment, in the child, the latter young person was to be studied and watched, so that *she* might be able to suffer should she do an equal wrong. She might emulate her parent by some play of characteristic perversity not less than she resembled her in charm; and if that impulse should be determined in her, if she should be caught, that is to say, in some breach of faith or some heartless act, her eyes would on the spot, by an insidious logic, be opened suddenly and unpitiedly to the "perfect presence", which she would then have to work as she could into her conception of a young lady's universe.'

RUDYARD KIPLING *The Mark of the Beast*

First serialized in the *Pioneer*, 12 and 14 July 1890, and reprinted in the *Pioneer Mail and Weekly Indian News*, 16 July 1890. Kipling's early Indian tales frequently concern uncanny events, sometimes mocking Eastern superstition and credulity, but more often using the language of the Gothic and the supernatural to explore the peculiarities of the colonial encounter.

84 *Strickland*: Strickland appears in a number of early Kipling stories, including 'The Return of Imray', which centres on the haunting of a bungalow by a murdered colonial administrator. Strickland appears again

as the secret service agent who trains and handles Kim in the novel *Kim* (1901).

84 *Dumoise*: in the penultimate story of *Plain Tales from the Hills* (1890), 'By Word of Mouth', the death of Dumoise is foretold by an apparition of his dead wife.

Catch'em-Alive-O's: probably a pejorative term for border guards: it was used in England in the 1850s to refer to nonconformist preachers and ministers.

85 *Burma*: the British had occupied Rangoon in 1824, annexing further territory to form Burma in 1862. Kipling is referring to the unification of Upper and Lower Burma into one colony under British rule in 1886.

Fuzzies ... outside Suakim: after the occupation of Egypt by British forces in 1882, there was an attempt to contain revolutionary Islamic forces in southern Egypt and Sudan. This revolution was joined by the Beja tribesmen of the Red Sea area, who were known to British forces as 'Fuzzy-wuzzies'. Fearsome fighters, they defeated an expeditionary force under Colonel Valentine Baker before defeat at Suakim in January 1884.

Hanuman: one of the key gods in the Hindu pantheon, whose life and times is detailed in the *Ramayama*. A trickster figure, this monkey god is usually depicted with a mace to display his strength, and stories tell of his shape-changing powers. Devoted to the god Rama, who gives him perpetual youth, he is also associated with scholarship and knowledge of scripture.

Mark of the B—beasht: in the Revelation of St John the Divine, chapter 13 describes the emergence of two allegorical beasts in the last days before Judgement. The second beast 'causeth all, both small and great, rich and poor, free and bond, to receive a mark on their right hand, or in their foreheads; And that no man might buy or sell, save he that had the mark, or the name of the beast, or the number of his name' (13: 16–17). The mark of the Beast is therefore one of the brands of the Antichrist.

86 *'a leper as white as snow'*: in Numbers 12: 9–10 of the Bible: 'And the anger of the Lord was kindled against them; and he departed. And the cloud departed from off the tabernacle; and, behold, Miriam became leprous, white as snow.' Leviticus also details the extensive rules to be observed against 'unclean' lepers. The disease remained an emblem of physical and moral degeneracy, often linked to sexually transmitted diseases like syphilis. In Victorian times, expansion of the colonial frontier renewed contact with leprosy, which caused anxiety since its mode of transmission was still obscure. This is why touching is so charged throughout this story (how do you torture someone you can't touch?). Kipling was writing at the time when the National Leprosy Fund was formed, and Henry Press Wright had just published *Leprosy: An Imperial Danger* (1889).

91 *Hydrophobia*: literally the 'fear of water', this is rabies. Hydrophobia was understood to have a long incubation period, which is in part why it

cannot fully explain Fleete's sudden illness. Yet Fleete does follow all but the last stage of hydrophobia, as described in the 1910 edition of *Encyclopedia Britannica*: a melancholic stage; excitement in which 'the countenance exhibits anxiety and terror'; severe thirst and uncontrollable violence. After three to five days of 'suffering of the most terrible description', death is inevitable.

men in Pinafore, . . . cat: reference to Gilbert and Sullivan's operetta, *HMS Pinafore* (1878):

ALL. Goodness me—Why, what was that?
DICK. Silent be, it was the cat! [as in the whip, the cat o'nine tails]

B. M. CROKER *The Dâk Bungalow at Dakor*

96 *Dâk . . . at Dakor*: the system of mail delivery and passenger transport that works by relays of horses or oxen stationed along the route. Dâk bungalows were the rudimentary hostels where travellers could stay overnight.

Sir A. Lyall: citation from Sir Alfred Lyall, 'The Hindu Ascetic', from *Verses Written in India* (1889). Lyall (1835–1911) was an important poet of the Anglo-Indian experience as well as a leading colonial administrator. His poetry ventriloquizes a number of Indian speakers, as in the quoted verse.

tonga: a two-wheeled cart pulled by ox, often used on hill-roads. This and all subsequent glosses of terms derive from the famous *Hobson-Jobson: A Glossary of Colloquial Anglo-Indian Words and Phrases*, which first appeared in 1886.

97 *place called Chanda*: these details seem to place the story in the Central Provinces of British India; Jabalpur was an important city and railway hub, 600 miles north of Bombay.

dacoits: armed robbers.

98 *peon Abdul*: a footman or messenger.

chuprassie: wearer of a badge of office, usually an attendant in an important position in a large household.

99 *khansamah*: 'master of the household gear': head servant.

plenty bobbery: noise or disturbance.

102 *arrière pensée*: literally 'behind thought', in colloquial French it means 'ulterior motive'.

topee: a hat. This instantly denotes a European, as they were commonly referred to in India as 'topeewala' (one who wears a hat).

ARTHUR CONAN DOYLE *Lot No. 249* and *The Case of Lady Sannox*

'Lady Sannox' first appeared in the *Idler*, 4 (1893), and 'Lot No. 249' in *Harper's Monthly Magazine*, 85 (September 1894). Conan Doyle had been commissioned by the editor of the *Idler*, Jerome K. Jerome, to produce a series of stories, provisionally entitled 'In a Doctor's Waiting Room'. Jerome found the stories rather too 'strong' for his public, and published only three of the eight. They appeared in book form in 1894 under the title, *Round the Red Lamp: Being Facts and Fancies of Medical Life* (the red lamp being the sign of a general practitioner in England at the time). In a short preface, Conan Doyle defended the tales, stating 'A tale which may startle the reader out of his usual grooves of thought, and shock him into seriousness, plays the part of the alterative [sic] and tonic in medicine, bitter to the taste, but bracing in its result' (p. vi).

111 *second cataract*: the second cataract of the Nile marks the limits of the navigable river, and the start, to many Victorians, of 'darkest Africa'.

114 *Horus and Isis and Osiris*: in Egyptian myth, Isis searches for the body of her dead brother, Osiris. She finds it and reassembles it, making her the goddess of the dead and of funerary rites. Isis impregnates herself from Osiris's body, giving birth to Horus, who becomes the main link between men and the gods.

119 *a course of electricity*: the use of electricity through direct current or by devices like 'electropathic' belts was an extremely popular treatment to revive flagging energy in the 1880s and 1890s.

141 *south of Marylebone Road ... Oxford Street*: this identifies the area of Harley Street, still associated with private and exclusive medical clinics and consultancies.

144 *Almohades*: a Spanish corruption of the Arabic Al-Muwahhidu. This was an Islamic sect founded in the twelfth century by Mahommed Ibn Tumart, premissed on strict religious observance. An empire founded in his name stretched from Morocco to Egypt. Doyle might be invoking the memory of the movement's jihad, or Holy War, against Christian Europe.

145 *bistouries*: surgeon's scalpels, from the French originally meaning dagger.

GRANT ALLEN *Pallinghurst Barrow*

First published in the *Illustrated London News*, Christmas Number, 28 November 1892, and reprinted in Allen's collection of stories, *Ivan Greet's Masterpiece*, in 1893. The interest in prehistoric barrows was the subject of much debate amidst anthropologists and folklorists, because they were presumed to be surviving evidence of the racial precursors of the English/Aryan invaders. This tale is spun around Allen's own non-fiction essay on the subject, 'The Ogbury Barrows', which he published in *Cornhill Magazine* in November 1885.

151 *Krakatoa sunsets*: the Krakatoa volcano, located in the straits between Java and Sumatra, violently erupted on 26 August 1883. The explosion

was heard 3,000 miles away and over 36,000 people were killed in the subsequent tidal waves. The ash thrown into the atmosphere transformed sunsets around the world for many months.

155 *the distinguished electrician*: this characterization suggests that Allen has the physicist and electrical theorist Oliver Lodge in mind. Lodge was at the cutting edge of electrical theory in the 1880s and 1890s relating to ether, lightning, wireless, and high frequency energy transfers. He was also a leading member of the Society for Psychical Research, and later became one of the most famous public advocates of Spiritualism and the survival of bodily death.

156 *Baal's night ... St Michael's*: Baal was a god worshipped by Semitic peoples as early as the fourteenth century BC. Associated with fertility and seasonal change, rituals included human sacrifice. In the Old Testament, Baal is associated with Beelzebub, one of the fallen angels. St Michael's Eve (28 September) is indeed a Christian imposition on prior religious traditions. For the Celts, Michaelmas was also Lughnassadh, celebrating the birth of Lugh. A harvest day, it was connected with breadmaking, horse-racing, and marriage. Most relevantly for this tale, rituals of ancestor worship included a circuit around the burial ground, a ritual surviving into the early nineteenth century (as recorded in Anne Ross, *Folklore of the Scottish Islands*).

157 *hostess of Mahatmas*: Mrs Bruce, in other words, is a Theosophist. The founder of the Theosophy Society, Madame Blavatsky, had just died in 1891. She claimed to receive occult wisdom from the immortal Mahatmas in Tibet. Her synthesis of Eastern and Western religion, advanced theoretical physics and comparative philology, meant her work read just as Mrs Bruce sounds in this speech.

Novalis was right: Novalis was the pen-name of Baron Friedrich von Hardenberg (1772–1801), a leading writer of the German Romantics. Much of his later work was inspired by grief over the death of his betrothed, a 14-year-old girl. A typical aphorism: 'Where children are, there is the Golden Age.' In the scientific context of the 1890s, children were considered to be closer, in evolutionary terms, to primitive states, which perhaps explains why Joyce is the catalyst for Reeve's experience in this story. Allen was interested in educational development theory, and had written for the *Journal of Education* in the 1880s.

palaces of popular legend: this is a reference to MacRitchie's *The Testament of Tradition*, which argued that stories of elves and fairies are actually traces of the races native to England prior to their extermination by Aryan invaders.

158 *Childe Roland ... human sacrifice*: Childe Rowland is one of the oldest of English folk-tales, and Allen had undoubtedly read the analysis of its origins by Joseph Jacobs in an essay in *Folk-Lore*, 2: 2 (1891). Jacobs suggests that the story of Rowland rescuing his sister from the fairy king is based on bride-capture by warring races in prehistoric England, just on

the cusp between the end of paganism and the arrival of Christianity. Childe Rowland provides much of the subsequent detail of this story, including the need to travel 'widdershins' to gain access to the barrow.

159 *The Mirror of Trismegistus*: a plausible title for a mystic to write: it refers to the Hermetic tradition deriving from the work of Hermes Trismegistus, in which the world is seen as a mirror of heaven, and where divine pattern can be discerned through dedication to occult learning. Both alchemy and Theosophy placed themselves in the Hermetic tradition.

161 *Your fortune is forlorn*: this is actual folkloric material, directly lifted from the work of Joseph Jacobs. His *English Fairy Tales* appeared in 1890.

162 *dial of Ahaz*: this refers to the miracle in Isaiah 38: 8, where the Old Testament God reverses time—'Behold, I will cause the shadow on the steps, which is gone down on the dial of Ahaz with the sun, to return backwards ten steps.'

165 *Sesostris*: there are many surviving statues of one of the most powerful pharaohs, Sesostris III.

JEAN LORRAIN *Magic Lantern* and *The Spectral Hand*

'Magic Lantern' was first published in *L'Echo de Paris*, 14 December 1891, and 'The Spectral Hand' in Lorrain's collection of Gothic and super-natural tales, *Un Demoniaque* in 1895. 'Magic Lantern' was not, as Richard Ellmann's biography of Wilde claims, dedicated to Oscar Wilde, although Lorrain had first met Wilde in November 1891. Lorrain was a journalist and leading figure of Parisian Decadent circles who wrote gossip, savage pieces that often got him into trouble. This gossipy world partly explains the dense range of references to contemporary figures and fashions in these two tales.

171 *Berlioz . . . 1803*: Hector Berlioz (1803–69) composed *The Damnation of Faust* in 1846.

Michelet: Jean Michelet (1798–1874) was held in high esteem by Decadents and occultists for his venomous turn against established religion, composing *La Sorcière* in 1862, which argued that witches were martyrs of a tyrannical Catholic church. Black Magic was in vogue in Paris in 1891, following Karl-Joris Huysmans's novel about this subculture, *La Bas*.

Monsieur Verne: Jules Verne (1828–1905) wrote proto-science fictions, 'rationalist' adventures that mocked the superstitious and fantastic language of the Gothic.

Der Freischutz: *Der Freischütz* (*The Freeshooter*) was an opera by Carl Maria von Weber, first performed in 1821. The plot concerns a Faustian pact to win a shooting contest.

172 *Coppelius himself . . . wax doll*: the reference is to E. T. A. Hoffmann's tale, 'The Sandman', in which Coppelius constructs an artificial doll of

such perfection that it fools the hero. It is a key Gothic text, and the subject of Freud's famous essay 'The Uncanny' (1919).

Charcot . . . Salpêtrière: Jean-Martin Charcot (1825–93), professor of neurology at Paris and famed for his displays of female hysterics at his lectures at the Salpêtrière Hospital.

173 *the nuns of Loudun*: in 1634, a priest was burnt at the stake for allegedly bringing the devil into the Ursuline monastery of Loudun.

the convulsants of Saint-Médard: the alleged miracles associated with the grave of a priest in 1731 were the subject of internecine sectarian debate between Jansenists (who ascribed the events to God) and the Jesuits (who ascribed them to the Devil).

Tony Johannot stuff: Tony Johannot (1803–52), a book illustrator.

174 *Vaucanson*: Jacques de Vaucanson (1709–82) was celebrated as the constructor of mechanical automata.

175 *Jules Lemaître*: (1853–1914), a journalist and dramatist renowned for his damning reports of contemporary French society; in many ways, Lorrain's model for his own career.

176 *Balzac's Contes drolatiques*: Balzac's scurrilous *Droll Tales* were published in two volumes from 1832.

177 *Symbolic extravagance*: these details show the Comtesse the height of fashion. James MacNeill Whistler (1834–1903), painter and wit, was at the height of his fame; her clothes follow Edward Burne-Jones designs, a painter at the centre of the Arts and Crafts revival in England; lacquered chairs and Japanese frogs show the influence of Japonisme, the fashion for Japanese design that dominated Paris between 1867 and 1900.

Montesquiou . . . hydrangeas: the Comte de Montesquiou was Lorrain's idolized model for the aristocratic dandy. Lorrain, not of the nobility, was frequently mocked for his attempts to mimic this aristocratic style (and Montesquiou himself snubbed Lorrain).

178 *tulips . . . tablecloth*: Lizzie Deas in *Flower Favourites* (1898) records: 'The signification of the tulip is, above all, erotic. In India and Persia from very early times this grandiose flower has been employed to figure consuming love.'

Walter Crane: (1845–1915) Walter Crane was another leading aesthete, founder of the Arts and Crafts Exhibition Society in 1888. He illustrated *Household Stories from the Collection of the Brothers Grimm* in 1882.

Brueghel and Hokusai: Brueghel the Younger (1564–1637), painter, famed for his depictions of hundreds of depraved figures; Hokusai (1760–1849), Japanese painter and engraver, much coveted in Parisian collections of Japonisme.

Maeterlinck and the Goncourts: Maeterlinck (1862–1949), the founder of Symbolist theatre in the 1890s in reaction to Naturalism; the Goncourts,

the brothers Edmund (1822–96) and Jules (1830–70), writers and
aesthetes, were famed for their *Journal*, which was a running commentary on French literary life in scabrous terms. Lorrain was an intimate of
Edmund.

178 *Ibsen and Outamaro*: Ibsen (1828–1906), the Norwegian dramatist caus-
ing scandal in England and France for much of the 1890s with his late
Naturalist plays; Outamaro (1753–1806), another extremely collectable
Japanese painter.

ARTHUR MACHEN *The Great God Pan*

The Great God Pan appeared in John Lane's notorious Keynotes series for The
Bodley Head, which helped define English Decadence in the early 1890s. John
Lane launched The New Woman; his press also published *The Yellow Book*,
with its distinctive Aubrey Beardsley designs. After Oscar Wilde's arrest in
1895, the Vigo Street office of Bodley Head was stoned. This hysteria perhaps
explains Machen's anxiety to distance his work from English Decadence of
which, he said in the 1916 Preface to a reprint of *Pan*, 'I was not even a small
part.' Nevertheless, this text has since become perhaps the quintessential
example of the Gothic tale in the 1890s.

183 *Pan*: Pan, half-goat, half-man, is the Greek god of Arcadia, of shepherds
and their flocks, of nature as a whole (hence pantheism). He is said to
haunt caves, mountains, and lonely places, and if disturbed can produce
sudden irrational fear. He is also a god of soldiering, who can produce
fear in the enemy. Both of these senses produce the word 'panic'. Ovid's
Metamorphosis adds another myth, of Pan's pursuit of the nymph Syrinx,
who, trapped by the river, is transformed into reeds. Pan's sigh through
the reeds creates (Pan) pipes. The Greek Pan was transposed to the
Roman god Faunus, a deity who can reveal the future through dreams or
through supernatural voices in certain sacred groves. Faunus, Horace
reports, was also 'lover of the fleeing nymphs'. Pan had an extensive
presence in Victorian literature, which revived a particular classical narrative from Plutarch. In 'Oracles in Decline', Plutarch told the story of
Epitherses who on a boat near Paxi heard a disembodied voice command
the helmsman 'When you reach Palodes announce that Great Pan is
dead'. This was done, and 'a great cry of lamentation and surprise arose,
not of one voice but of many'. Early Christian commentary suggested
that this event took place at the time of Christ, and that the event marked
the driving out of demons and that the death of Pan marks the passage
from a pagan to a Christian world. In Elizabeth Barrett Browning's
poem, 'The Dead Pan' (1844), Plutarch's story is used to insist that a
properly Christian literature should abandon Greek mythology by insist-
ing at the end of each of its thirty-nine stanzas, 'Great Pan is dead'. The
Decadent fascination with counter-reaction and transgression therefore
made Pan an alluring figure. Machen might have been thinking of Robert
Louis Stevenson's essay, 'Pan's Pipes', or Algernon Swinburne's poem,

'A Nympholept', where Pan is the emblem of the delicious combination of ecstasy and terror.

184 *chases in Arras ... career*: the citation is from George Herbert's 'Dotage', from *The Temple* (1633), whose opening stanza is:

> False glozing, pleasures, casks of happinesse,
> Foolish night-fires, womens and childrens wishes,
> Chases in Arras, guilded emptinesse,
> Shadows well mounted, dreams in a career,
> Embroider'd lyes, nothing between two dishes,
> > These are the pleasures here.

Raymond is expressing a classic neo-Platonist view of reality, in which the revelation of a higher, hidden spiritual world is the goal of study. He is therefore an occultist rather than a materialist scientist. Neo-Platonism connects to the death of Pan theme: it is frequently identified as the last pagan school of philosophy.

Digby's Theory: perhaps an echo of Sir Kenelm Digby, the seventeenth-century medic and alchemist. He wrote on the interconnection of the body and soul, and claimed so many miraculous cures and healing powers that his contemporaries dismissed him as a mountebank.

Browne Faber's discoveries: this might also deliberately echo Charles Brown-Sequard (1817–94), a brain neurologist who was involved in contemporary disputes about the nature of localization of function in the brain.

186 *Oswald Crollius*: Oswald Crollius (1560–1604) was an Elizabethan neo-Platonist and alchemist, who explored the 'doctrine of signatures'—that every living thing had a signature of their divine plan.

196 *Et Diabolus Incarnatus Est. Et Homo Factus Est.*: 'And the devil was made incarnate. And was made man.' This is a blasphemous rewriting of the Nicene Creed, the early Christian Church statement of belief that stated 'Et incarnatus est de Spiritu Sancto ex Maria Virgine, et homo factus est' ('By the power of the Holy Spirit he became incarnate from the Virgin Mary, and was made man').

212 *Silet per diem ... maritimam*: this is a citation from Gaius Julius Solinus (a third-century AD geographer): 'The whole place is silent throughout the day, nor is its remoteness without horror; it glows with nocturnal fires, the chorus of the Aegipans rings through everywhere: both the sounds of the pipes and the clanging of the cymbals are heard along the seashore.' It describes a Bacchic orgy on the seashore beside Mount Atlas, a place haunted (as Pliny the Elder wrote in his *Natural History*) 'with the wanton lascivious Aegipans and Satyres whereof it is full'.

214 *for the act*: for Victorian attitudes to suicide, see note to p. 76 above.

216 *Whitechapel ... West*: a reference to the unsolved murders in Whitechapel, ascribed to 'Jack the Ripper', and which terrorized London

in the autumn of 1888. The slums of the East End, teeming with immigrant Jews, were in some ways almost expected to produce such murderous ferocity. Panic about contagions of all kinds moving from the East End to the West End of London were common tropes in *fin-de-siècle* fiction.

217 *in the Row*: Rotten Row, Hyde Park, was the place where wealthy Victorians promenaded.

222 *Piccadilly . . . Soho*: although within minutes of each other in central London, these were absolutely at opposite ends of the social scale in Victorian England. Piccadilly was the centre of wealthy society; Soho, an area of slums with a foreign population, was often associated with criminality and licentiousness. In the *Strange Case of Dr Jekyll and Mr Hyde*, a major influence on Machen, Soho is the area where Hyde chooses his lodgings.

227 *Latin . . . in great haste*: compare the opening comments of Richard von Krafft-Ebing's notorious medical compendium, *Psychopathia Sexualis, with especial reference to Antipathic Sexual Instinct: A Medico-Forensic Study* (1886): 'A scientific title has been chosen, and technical terms are used throughout the book in order to exclude the lay reader. For the same reason certain portions are written in Latin.'

M. P. SHIEL *Vaila*

Like Machen's *The Great God Pan*, Shiel's story appeared as part of the Keynotes series published by The Bodley Head. *Shapes in the Fire* was made up of six shapes or stories, divided into two equal parts, separated by an 'Interlude', a dialogue in which Shiel expounds his view that properly refined literature should 'paint a picture, not for the mind's eye, but for the *inner* mind's eye of fantasy' and aspire to the condition of music. This followed the famous injunction of the essayist Walter Pater, one of the central influences on Decadent prose. Shiel certainly aimed for an elaborately ornamental prose, but 'Vaila' proved too ornate even for Shiel. He rewrote the tale as 'The House of Sounds' for *The Pale Ape and Other Pulses* (1911). Except for one passage, I have used the unhinged first version.

234 *E caddi . . . piglia*: 'And I fell like one seized with sleep.' This epigraph comes from Dante's *Inferno*, canto iii, l. 136. This locates the reader immediately in Hell. The Canto concludes: 'When he had ended, the gloomy pain shook so violently that the remembrance of my terror bathes me again with sweat. The tearful ground gave forth wind and a red blaze flashed which overcame all my senses, and I fell like one seized with sleep.'

phthisis: principally used to refer to tuberculosis in the nineteenth century, it was also used more widely for any wasting disease.

feuille: shortened from *feuilleton*. This was light, sensational literature, printed across the bottom of the pages in French newspapers. It was held in contempt as a low cultural form.

235 *Oxyecoia*: hearing disorder, with extreme sensitivity to sounds at very low frequency.

pinna: Latin for wing: the external part of the ear.

236 *worm-wood and terebinth*: the quintessential drink for Parisian Decadents was absinthe, alcohol brewed from wormwood, powerful enough to induce hallucinations. The English Decadent poet, Ernest Dowson, wrote 'Absinthia Taetra' in ambiguous celebration of its powers. It was banned from sale in Paris in 1915.

237 *Zetland*: old term for the Shetland Islands, the archipelago north of the Scottish mainland. The older name invokes the era when Norway occupied the islands they called Hjetland.

phrenologists . . . brain: phrenology was the science of 'cerebral anatomy', by which character traits were allegedly readable from the shape of the skull. It was associated first with Franz Joseph Gall (1758–1828), who divided the brain into 27 faculties, of which the seventeenth was the sense of sound and musical talent. It became popular in England when Gall's rival Johann Spurzheim travelled to England in 1815. Phrenology had its heyday in England in the 1840s, when having your 'bumps' read was a popular pastime and only intermittently considered a serious science.

Sardanapalus . . . Nimrod: the last king of the Assyrian race, myths stated that Sardanapalus dedicated his life to sensuous pleasures, and burnt his palace and himself when finally besieged. An image of imperial decadence, he was a popular subject for nineteenth-century artists: Byron wrote a tragedy on the topic; his court was painted by Eugene Delacroix.

238 *Chronicle . . . follows*: in the original story, the entry that follows is written in a parody of Old English, which is very trying to read. When Shiel revised the story as 'The House of Sounds' he updated the language of this citation and I have used that version here.

241 *Cimmerian*: Cimmeria is another Northern race being invoked by Shiel— a mysterious, barbarous race that Homer suggested came from a land of fog and darkness.

243 *Hecuba . . . before me*: the opening of Euripides' play *Hecuba* is spoken by Polydorus, ghost of Hecuba's murdered son: 'Out of the dark door of the pit of death I come, the shadow land where no god walks.'

244 *Khoreb*: alternative spelling for Mount Horeb, where Moses camped with the Israelites for a year during the Exodus, according to the Old Testament; a place of extremity and tested faith.

249 *Paracusis Willisii*: an abnormal condition of hearing, in which the patient can hear speech more clearly against a noisy background.

254 *ouragan*: French for hurricane.

lyssa: raging madness – hence, Lyssa, the goddess of madness.

Deinotheria: literally, 'terrible beast', these extinct animals were the ancestors of the modern elephant.

256 *Quevedo's Tacaño . . . God*: Francisco de Quevedo y Villegas (1580–1645), Spanish poet whose work was censured by the Inquisition; Tycho Brahe (1546–1601), Danish astronomer and alchemist; George Hakewill (1578–1649) Archdeacon of Surrey, who published *An Apologie or Declaration of the Power and Providence of God in the Government of the World* in 1627.

Haller . . . dream: Albrecht von Haller (1708–77) was a Swiss astronomer and physiologist. In his last years, he treated his illness with opium and lectured and published on its effects in 1776. He is assumed to have died from the treatment.

From the Dhammapada . . . faith: *Dhammapada* is the Buddhist text, *The Way of the Doctrine*; Theodor Zwinger published *Theatrum Vitae Humanae* in 1571; Francis Bacon (Baron Verulam), published his *Historia Vitae et Mortis* in 1622.

She is not dead . . . sleepeth: Luke 8: 52, referring to the miracle of the resurrection of Jairus' daughter by Jesus.

258 *ataxie locomotrice*: the unsteady gait resulting from the degeneration of sensory nerves in the legs. It was often associated with syphilis.

259 *lamentation . . . in Ramah*: in the Old Testament, Jeremiah 31: 15, 'Thus saith The Lord; A voice was heard in Ramah, lamentation, and bitter weeping; Rachel weeping for her children, refused to be comforted for her children, because they were not.'

bouleversement: overturning or upheaval.

260 *dies iræ*: literally, 'day of wrath', it also invokes the Last Judgement.

261 *râles of death*: death rattle.

262 *Ahasuerus*: the Wandering Jew. This is the myth of the Jew who mocked Jesus for carrying the cross too slowly, and was cursed to roam the earth undyingly until the Second Coming of Christ. It is an anti-Semitic story that only begins to circulate in seventeenth-century Europe. Ahasuerus was another popular mythic figure for the arts in the nineteenth century: Eugène Sue's *The Wandering Jew* (1844–5) was followed by Gustave Doré's woodcuts, 'The Legend of the Wandering Jew' (1856).

265 *aurora borealis*: or, the Northern Lights, visible only from northern latitudes. The subject of much folklore, the constantly changing patterns of light are in fact the result of the interaction of solar particles with the Earth's magnetic force.

Rephidim: in the old Testament, Exodus 17 relates how the Israelites camp at Rephidim and still have no water after their flight from Egypt. Moses strikes the rock at Horeb, and water flows, thus ending the drought.

GEORGE ELIOT	Daniel Deronda
	The Lifted Veil and Brother Jacob
	Middlemarch
	The Mill on the Floss
	Silas Marner
SUSAN FERRIER	Marriage
ELIZABETH GASKELL	Cranford
	The Life of Charlotte Brontë
	Mary Barton
	North and South
	Wives and Daughters
GEORGE GISSING	New Grub Street
	The Odd Woman
THOMAS HARDY	Far from the Madding Crowd
	Jude the Obscure
	The Mayor of Casterbridge
	The Return of the Native
	Tess of the d'Urbervilles
	The Woodlanders
WILLIAM HAZLITT	Selected Writings
JAMES HOGG	The Private Memoirs and Confessions of a Justified Sinner
JOHN KEATS	The Major Works
	Selected Letters
CHARLES MATURIN	Melmoth the Wanderer
WALTER SCOTT	The Antiquary
	Ivanhoe
	Rob Roy
MARY SHELLEY	Frankenstein
	The Last Man

ANTHONY TROLLOPE

An Autobiography

The American Senator

Barchester Towers

Can You Forgive Her?

The Claverings

Cousin Henry

Doctor Thorne

The Duke's Children

The Eustace Diamonds

Framley Parsonage

He Knew He Was Right

Lady Anna

The Last Chronicle of Barset

Orley Farm

Phineas Finn

Phineas Redux

The Prime Minister

Rachel Ray

The Small House at Allington

The Warden

The Way We Live Now

The Oxford World's Classics Website

www.worldsclassics.co.uk

- Information about new titles
- Explore the full range of Oxford World's Classics
- Links to other literary sites and the main OUP webpage
- Imaginative competitions, with bookish prizes
- Peruse the Oxford World's Classics Magazine
- Articles by editors
- Extracts from Introductions
- A forum for discussion and feedback on the series
- Special information for teachers and lecturers

www.worldsclassics.co.uk

American Literature

British and Irish Literature

Children's Literature

Classics and Ancient Literature

Colonial Literature

Eastern Literature

European Literature

History

Medieval Literature

Oxford English Drama

Poetry

Philosophy

Politics

Religion

The Oxford Shakespeare

A complete list of Oxford Paperbacks, including Oxford World's Classics, Oxford Shakespeare, Oxford Drama, and Oxford Paperback Reference, is available in the UK from the Academic Division Publicity Department, Oxford University Press, Great Clarendon Street, Oxford OX2 6DP.

In the USA, complete lists are available from the Paperbacks Marketing Manager, Oxford University Press, 198 Madison Avenue, New York, NY 10016.

Oxford Paperbacks are available from all good bookshops. In case of difficulty, customers in the UK can order direct from Oxford University Press Bookshop, Freepost, 116 High Street, Oxford OX1 4BR, enclosing full payment. Please add 10 per cent of published price for postage and packing.